Valerie - Colin

Best wishes

Alan.

*signature*

May 2009

# I never met Ernest Hemingway

**by
Alan Shelley**

iUniverse, Inc.
New York   Bloomington

# I Never Met Ernest Hemingway

Copyright © 2009 by Alan Shelley

All rights reserved. No part of this book may be used or reproduced by any means, graphic, electronic, or mechanical, including photocopying, recording, taping or by any information storage retrieval system without the written permission of the publisher except in the case of brief quotations embodied in critical articles and reviews.

This is a work of fiction. All of the characters, names, incidents, organizations, and dialogue in this novel are either the products of the author's imagination or are used fictitiously.

iUniverse books may be ordered through booksellers or by contacting:

iUniverse
1663 Liberty Drive
Bloomington, IN 47403
www.iuniverse.com
1-800-Authors (1-800-288-4677)

Because of the dynamic nature of the Internet, any Web addresses or links contained in this book may have changed since publication and may no longer be valid. The views expressed in this work are solely those of the author and do not necessarily reflect the views of the publisher, and the publisher hereby disclaims any responsibility for them.

ISBN: 978-1-4401-2232-3 (pbk)
ISBN: 978-1-4401-2233-0 (cloth)
ISBN: 978-1-4401-2234-7 (ebk)

Printed in the United States of America

iUniverse rev. date: 2/27/2009

For Joey — again

# Preface

None of you will know of Percy Glossop, but what you are about to be presented with is a full and sometimes truthful chronicle of his life. Despite the title, this work is not concerned with American writers of any kind, whether hard-bitten or romantic, but what is given is an account of the loves and the wars, the ups and the downs, of a European man of the twentieth century with all his strengths and weaknesses, his prejudices and tolerances. The good, the bad — not too much of this — and the ugly.

There are few wildly dramatic events; the passions are relatively subdued but let us hope that the people he meets on the way, and where they meet, provides some relatively exciting or, at worst, even interesting moments.

Our hero has mixed fortunes with the ladies in his life but some are given an opportunity to speak for themselves during this history — as well as those where their parts are as minor, and as brief, as the words allocated to them between the Chapters.

# Chapter One

## Gloucester

*Lardy Cake*

*Ingredients. 2 oz lard; 2 oz currants; 12 oz white bread dough, risen; 2 oz caster sugar; pinch of nutmeg; drizzle of honey.*

*Method. Roll out the dough to an oblong. Spread on lard and sprinkle with sugar, nutmeg and currants. Roll up like a Swiss roll and place in a greased shallow baking tin. Cover and leave to rise for about 15 minutes. Brush lightly with honey and bake in an oven at 375F for 35 to 40 minutes. Serve hot with butter.*

## Alice

My path through life, and that of Ernest Hemingway, never crossed. I must have been one of the few English-speakers who happened to be in Paris at the time of the Lost Generation who never met the famous writer, affectionately known as 'Papa'. I sometimes amuse myself by wondering if everyone who alleges they met him is telling the truth, then how did he find time to do any writing? The Lost Generation: either he or Gertrude Stein is credited with the phrase that in this instance refers to a handful of literary notables living in that city in the 1920s.

*Alan Shelley*

I was in Paris at the same time because of my mother. When I was born she was very young and, as I was later to understand, inclined towards a cheerful promiscuity. After I was born, this continued for a while. She just enjoyed it, she said. My grandparents, only one set for me as you will discover, disapproved of their daughter's proclivities but accepted the situation for two reasons. Firstly, she was a whiz with the pastry and secondly, I was a captivating child. At least so I believe — and this is my story.

My second day in this world coincided with her seventeenth birthday. She told me my father was a Welsh rugby player; I believe he was a prop forward. She called me Percy. Now, you can hardly expect Papa to think it fit to meet a Percy. All right, we know about Percy Bysshe and I read lots of the adventure stories of Percy F Westerman when I was a boy, but I suspect that *To a Skylark* and tales of derring-do were not exactly to his taste.

But, to return to my mother's saving grace. She was a marvellous pastry cook. Her mother and father were bakers and Whitwells bread was famous throughout Gloucester but the icing on the gingerbread, so to speak, was my mother's confections. Her lardy cakes were the toast of the land. Rumour had it that Buckingham Palace had a standing order, through a third-party of course; Whitwells was not, 'By Royal Appointment'. The shop was Whitwells but they were Glossop, and so was I. Makes it worse. Papa and me, Percy Glossop, sharing a rum St. James at Les Deux Magots; I don't think so.

Even if we had, what would we have talked about? There is no evidence that he had the same relationship with cakes and biscuits as Marcel Proust and although I am far from being a teetotaller, he would no doubt have scorned the warm mild beer I used to drink at the Lower George. In addition, I was, unlike the aggressive Mr H, not too fond of boxing. No sparring with the rich and the famous for me; but I did in the future have some contact with a relatively celebrated British pugilist and also, on one occasion, I cooked for Georges Carpentier who was the Light Heavyweight champion of the world in the early 1920s.

Papa joined me in Paris — well not exactly joined; as I have explained we just happened to be in the same town at the same time. He had retreated from the USA to Canada and then to France because of prohibition. The British would never have stood for that troublesome item of legislation, although my father and his fellow countrymen were somewhat restricted on Sundays.

But I digress. I am about to recount the life and times of Percy Glossop — pastry cook extraordinaire, teller of tales and a citizen of the Europe of the twentieth century — and not that of a writer I only marginally admire and whose ownership of a Nobel Prize I question. Nevertheless, before I begin my story I must first tell you of the origins of Whitwells the Bakers where my journey began.

The genius behind Whitwells was a lady by the name of Alice Smith. She died in 1883, sixteen years before I was born, so of course I never met this remarkable woman, but my grandfather had a deep affection for her and the following description and events are as related by him to me, decorated with a little of my talent for words which, I trust, is already becoming apparent.

Alice was born about fifteen years after the Battle of Waterloo, the youngest of a large family. An uncle was killed when serving the Iron Duke who was famously scathing about his soldiers: 'I don't know what effect these men will have upon the enemy, but by God, they frighten me.' I presume Uncle Fred might have been one of those when his niece's redoubtable character is considered.

Her father was a stockman at a farm on the outskirts of the Forest of Dean in the county of Gloucestershire. This area of about forty square miles between the River Severn and the River Wye has a long history. It was occupied by the Romans in 50 AD and for centuries was used as a Royal hunting ground, but the 1800s saw the development of industry, principally charcoal production, iron working and coal mining.

For the period, the large family lived in a relatively comfortable cottage, a perquisite of Mr Smith's employment. It was mostly watertight and blessed with an unusually large kitchen. It was there that Alice began her culinary journey and where she became rather more than the commonplace cook to be found in most kitchens of the labouring class. Firstly, she learnt the basics of survival. She could concoct a nourishing soup without meat, and when such was available, knew how to make the best use of any remaining bones. She discovered how to utilise what could be found in the countryside; the nettles, edible fungi and the bliss of the blackberry season. With these attributes she was replicating the myriad of working class women throughout the land who engaged all their ingenuity, and the skills passed down through time, to feed the large families that were a feature of the age. Marie Stopes, the birth control pioneer, was not to appear for some years.

However, in the case of Alice Smith, who was a full-time assistant to her mother in both house and cottage garden from the age of thirteen until she married, there was a precious extra. This first manifested itself in the baking of bread. With the same flour employed in other households, and with the same water and the same yeast, she performed miracles. Her father was the envy of the farmyard. His dinner-time sandwiches may have been short of nourishing content, usually a scrape of dripping or, on good days, a fragment of cheese, but the bread enclosing this meagre fare was not to be bettered at Blenheim Palace or Chatsworth House

No doubt self evident, but it is reputed that when asked about her special skills she would reply: 'It is all in the fingers.' She would then place the fingertips of one hand on to those of the other and point them to the heavens for a moment of prayer before changing their position to demonstrate a kneading technique. She was no doubt praying to St Lawrence, patron saint of all who toil in the kitchen. Lawrence of Rome is accorded this honour because of the gruesome circumstances of his demise; he was cooked to death on a gridiron.

Alice's fingers were short but exceptionally broad. She was not very tall but strong of wrist. Thomas kept well out of range if he thought his deeds might result in a box around the ears. Not that this was a frequent occurrence — he was a well-behaved child.

As I have said, her uncle Fred volunteered to be a soldier and so he most probably had a dose of the same spirit found in Alice, but after those two there seemed to have been little left to share amongst the remainder of the extensive family. Two of her siblings died before reaching the age of thirty. Two of the boys worked on the same farm as their father and hardly left the purlieu of the Forest of Dean during their lifetimes. The father himself exhibited the same state of calm, the same quietude, as the beasts he tended. Said little, and ruminated. His wife bore him eight children that lived. She could not read or write and after her husband died she ended her days in the kitchen of the cottage occupied by the family of her eldest daughter. During her last years her hands were never still. Except when asleep — and until the day she died — she sat in the same dark corner of that kitchen going through the motions of washing her hands, or items of clothing. From this background, whence came the spark that lit up Miss Alice Smith like a beacon? The family lived in the same fog of penury as most of their neighbours but Alice's light could not be dimmed. How does the seed of ambition propagate in such a barren soil? A subject I often ponder on.

Whatever, Alice clearly had that something extra in her makeup, even if her many swains did not altogether fully recognise it. She was an attractive and vigorous girl. Her tongue was sometimes sharp but it rested between full lips of a natural shade of rose-pink and those broad fingers of hers came in useful when dressing her thick yellow hair. Her suitors were fully conscious of these female attributes but there was the added attraction, the culinary prowess that was becoming talked about in the area. The shortness of her temper and an inclination to plumpness — and rather ungainly feet — meant she was an unlikely candidate to be one of Thomas Hardy's remarkable heroines but that did not deter those in that part of Gloucestershire who sought her hand. There was fierce competition to arrange a transfer of her skills from the Smith kitchen to their own — but she opted for Clarence Whitwell.

Clarence was a shopkeeper in the village of Newnham, less than a dozen miles away from the Smiths' cottage. He sold pork products; cuts of the pig, their trotters, chitterlings and tripe together with faggots, haslet and meat pies that were fashioned, in a tiny kitchen behind the shop, by a succession of poorly paid and slatternly female assistants. He would haggle over pennies but this did not help his innate business inadequacies. He failed to understand the first rule of commerce — buy low and sell high. No one explained this to him, certainly not the pig farmers who were his main source of supply. He seemed unable to calculate that if, when cut up by the butcher, or analysed by the accountant, he paid the equivalent of one shilling for a pork chop and sold it for eleven pence, he was, according to Wilkins Micawber, inexorably on the road to misery.

He was a pork butcher because his father had been one — with about the same amount of success. Where Alice was small and slightly rotund, Clarence was tall and one step away from being emaciated. Under a bright light, his long nose appeared to glow with a pale tint which gave the impression that at the point furthest from the nostrils there was a permanent suspicion of a film of mucus. Sometimes this appeared to be of a dry texture — and at other times, particularly when agitated, quite damp. He was, I determined, essentially a gentle man but his backbone was long rather than sturdy. No one would describe him as clever but in his role as a shopkeeper he had developed nice manners — natural ones. In general people liked him even if they did sometimes take advantage of his lack of business skills. The sparring with his customers over pennies was often the perfect smoke-screen towards obtaining a discount of a shilling on a leg of pork. This was about to change. When Alice appeared on the scene with her sharp decisive mind, Mr Micawber was sent away on his holidays.

She was nineteen and Clarence twenty-nine when she chose him as a husband. It was for her a step-up in the world. Instead of sharing a room that contained a narrow bed, used by three sisters, and a truckle version occupied by two of her brothers — a canvas screen was lowered at night — she now lay with Clarence in the large brass bedstead he had inherited from his mother in the quarters above the shop. He was set in his ways, hardly a young Lochinvar, but as the villagers remarked, he chased Alice until she caught him. It was not wholly avaricious. Clarence may not have exuded masculine charm but he was of a kindly disposition, there were those sweet manners, and he had clean fingernails — something not encountered too often amongst the other suitors.

For her it seemed a match preferable to the union she might have envisaged for herself with a local farm labourer — and destined to finish up like the old woman who lived in a shoe. And then, there was the kitchen. The one in the rooms over the shop was not as large as that of her parents, but it was only utilised for cooking. At the Smiths' cottage the parlour, the other ground floor room, was only opened up on high days and holidays but the kitchen, where Alice began acquiring her skills, was also used for a variety of other purposes. It was naturally the family dining room. For those children who did manage to go to school, it was here they pored over their primers. It also belonged to three cats, when at home, and the domestic canine pet of the day. In his armchair close to the range, Mr Smith smoked his pipe and when Grandma came to stay, which she did frequently, it became her sleeping chamber. In addition, and on alternate days each fortnight, the tin bath was brought in from the shed and this all-purpose

Alan Shelley

room became a bathhouse, female on Friday and male on Saturday. And now she was the mistress of her own culinary arena. Even Clarence rarely entered.

Alice refused to have anything to do with the ground floor one attached to the shop where Clarence continued, inefficiently, to supervise the incompetents who attempted to convert parts of the pig into items for sale. Clarence also maintained his inevitable path towards bankruptcy as Alice, alone upstairs and for her own delectation, widened her range to include currant buns, the Swiss roll, Bakewell tarts and, predictably, the lardy cake. The birth of Thomas, two years after the wedding, was followed two months later by what was probably inevitable, the conversion of Whitwells Pork Butchers into Whitwells Family Bakers.

I can imagine the discussion that might have taken place preceding this change — an event that had such a dramatic significance for me and my family.

"Clarence. I met that Harriet Truelove in the village today. If you see her bearing down on your shop tomorrow, you best retreat to the back shed. She's on the warpath. Says she found mouse droppings in one of your pies. Why she can't bake her own like everyone else, I'll never know. Must think she's better than us because her brother's a curate."

"Are you sure it was one of mine, dearest."

"Well, who else is in your business in this area Clarence? Perhaps if you had some competition you might brighten up your ideas. If someone dies from the bubonic plague brought on by your sausages they will hang you, or at least transport you for life, and then what would Thomas and I do. It can't go on like this. You don't even make a profit on the legs of pork that you sell. Certainly not enough to pay for the lawyer you will need when you are charged with wholesale food poisoning."

"Oh, come on my dear. You do exaggerate so."

"Perhaps, but I've thought of a solution. Why don't we go from butchery to bakery? I know it is unusual, everyone makes their own bread, but I have a feeling that in these changing times a shop that does the baking for you might do well — and people do like my cakes. After all, we're well into the nineteenth century — there's been a railway line to Bristol these last ten years. I'd love to go and see one of those engines. Perhaps we might travel on it one day."

"What has that got to do with my pies? She's a mean biddy, Mrs Truelove. She's just trying to get her money back, I'll be bound, but perhaps bread is less dangerous. But what would we call ourselves?"

"Whitwells the Baker. You'll only have to paint out Pork Butchers and there will be less chance of poisoning all our friends with my bread."

"All right, you know best dear."

Alice was in charge of baking, and price-fixing, and Clarence, still wearing his butcher's blue-striped apron, served the customers. The noxious lean-to at the back of the shop was renovated and a good oven installed. This was used for the baking of the bread. Cakes and any other fancy items were still manufactured in the upstairs kitchen where Alice spent most of her day as soon as they were able to take on one of her sisters to deal with bread alone. The transition from the pork chop to the small brown was slow to begin with but as the good people of the village came to taste the products of Alice's genius, the enterprise soon came into profit and so the situation might have remained, and there have been no move to the metropolis of Gloucester, if it had not been for a minor member of the local aristocracy.

Captain Sir Luke Makepeace Thatcher Bt. He had resigned his commission when his uncle died and left him Stockton Hall and its adjoining one thousand acres. In later years I never went to visit but according to all accounts the house was not much of a place. Walls of an unattractive yellow brick stained in part by the weather to a dull green where signs of mildew had set in. The narrow heavily mullioned windows were infrequent but the chimneys were tall, even if some of the pots were missing. There was one redeeming feature; roofs covered in a dark blue Welsh slate although they had at this time become unseated in many places and allowed free access to the rain. The house contained about thirty rooms, including a so-called ballroom that was rather low and not large enough for a full-scale country dance. The immediate grounds were uncared for — the lake needed draining, the trees were well due for some attention and the condition of the ha ha was, according to the patrons of the Crown and Dragon, laughable.

Fortunately the agricultural estate had been well cared for by the long-serving factor and this produced sufficient income for Sir Luke to surrender the Queen's shilling and spend some money on repairing his dilapidated new home. He was a man of few parts, but what he could lay claim to was the fame of his stomach. Army life had turned him not into an efficient fighting machine but into an uncomplicated and unashamed gourmand. He adored food and ate prodigiously.

I trust I have already drawn a portrait of Alice that shows her to be a feisty female — and an articulate one at that — and I therefore believe she will have given my grandfather a vivid description of Sir Luke, even if this has lost some of its flavour by the time it was filtered down to me. Nevertheless, I can well imagine what sort of a man he was. I met one or two of them in the twentieth century British Army. He would have been fat of face and body — the only redeeming feature being a luxuriant pale moustache of which he was inordinately proud and prone to stroke at regular intervals. His voice is high- pitched and the accent so exaggerated as to render him near unintelligible. The skin is unhealthy in appearance with a number of unsightly blemishes, particularly in the region of the nose. He is very partial to port and claret.

Although only in his early thirties, gout is already beginning to raise a swollen toe. He has become inordinately fond of Alice's version of the apple turnover but a greater passion develops when he discovered her lardy cakes.

I can envisage what came next.

"By George, Shelton, those lardy cakes from the village bakery are first-class. Go well with a cup of tea and, I wager, a glass of port of an evening. They melt in one's mouth."

"Yes, Sir Luke."

"What's the name of that shop?"

"Whitwells."

"Have I ever met this Whitwell?"

"No. It's a man and wife that run the business, but I understand she makes the cakes."

"Does she now. We'll be having women in the army next." This remark is followed by a torrent of high pitched laughter. The factor ignores these guffaws and does not join in. He is not married and his acquaintance with the female sex, either in a capacity as soldier or pastry cook, is limited.

"Never you mind. She shall give it up and come cook for me. That harridan we have presently will pack her bags and go back to the Hades from where she was spawned."

"But, Sir Luke. Why would Mrs Whitwell leave her shop?"

"Because I say so. Give her good wages. I want freshly baked lardy cakes for breakfast."

Shelton grunted and left the presence of his insensitive employer as he muttered under his breath that the days of *droit du seigneur* were over. He did not welcome this task but he was a courteous and considerate man and however inexperienced, he approached Alice — and Clarence — with some care. This was to no avail.

"Mr Shelton. Have I heard you correctly? Sir Luke insists I come to Stockton Hall and be his cook. Clarence, what do you say to that?"

"Somewhat surprising, my dear."

"Surprising. Such arrogance. This is the nineteenth century, not mediaeval times. He needs less food, not more. Perhaps I should accept and fill him so full of lardy cakes that he bursts. What a sight that would be. Corpulent corporal splattering his innards all over the place. Wonderful, I shall do it."

"Alice, are you serious?"

"Of course I'm not. Do I look as though I've gone mad? Just as we're doing so well, to give it all up."

"Mr Shelton. Please advise his Lordship that my wife is fully conscious of the honour he does her, but she prefers her own kitchen for the moment."

"And he can go to hell."

However, Alice was uneasy. She was of working-class stock. Her father still touched a forelock, as it were and the gentry stuck together. Stockton Hall farm adjoined the one where her father worked and where was the family's tied cottage. She was not going to exchange her current independence to work for that arrogant man; that 'sad sack of lard' as she called him, but he could be a dangerous enemy: 'Uppity trades-people who needed to be put in their place.' She thought for two days and then told Clarence that as they had become one of the most successful retail businesses in the village it was time they spread their wings and transferred their undoubted talents to the big city. Clarence could see the sense in this; out of sight, out of danger, as far as the ex-soldier was concerned. The shop was sold to a neighbour, a seed merchant looking for more space, and within two months Clarence had signed a lease on a dilapidated property in a central location in the cathedral city of Gloucester and paid, with the proceeds from the sale, for the improvements and renovations that converted those premises into the place it was at the time of my birth.

The shop on Westgate Street was a few doors away from a public house, the Lower George Inn, and I can describe the premises as they were in my day, little changed from the 1850s when Alice and Clarence moved in. The three storey facade of the pub had some character, dating back to the eighteenth century, and its name was prominently displayed in raised stone lettering. Our shop, although of similar height, presented a more modest appearance but was sturdily built in keeping with the architecture of other retail properties on Westgate Street. At the shop there were essentially two buildings; the front property had the shop and living accommodation on the two floors over while the building behind comprised the bakehouse at ground level and above that, of the same size, a storeroom where the flour was kept. This was loaded from an alley at the back of the property just wide enough to allow for the passage of carts. At the flour store was a fixed gantry and a piece of block and tackle apparatus to hoist sacks from the carts to the first-floor storeroom. This was warm in summer and winter, thanks to the bakehouse fires below, and provided the perfect trysting place for Violet.

Above the shop window was a sign of painted porcelain which, by my time, read: Whitwells Bakers and Confectioners Established 1855. There were two steps down into the shop, which was rather poorly lit, and yet it induced a pleasant atmosphere, a comforting ambience, from its very first day. The smell of freshly baked bread was the major attraction of course but the old-fashioned marble-tiled counter and glass fronted oak display cabinets made all who entered feel at home — and hopefully hungry. There were gas lights on two walls which, in winter, produced a warm yellow glow and a gentle hissing sound that, I like to think, mingled in a cheerful way with the chatter of the shop assistants and the customers seduced by the incomparable aroma of the Whitwells loaf. The counter was at right angles to the street from behind which Clarence and his female assistants served. They all wore white hats. The best description of that favoured by the proprietor was that it was shaped like a normal bowler but appeared to have turned white overnight. The shock of the move perhaps.

Is there any shop more likely to encourage a sense of well-being than that of a baker? We were dealing with the staff of life, but I always believed there was more to it than that. Ladies enjoy visiting the dress emporium, amateur home improvers the hardware store and for children, the sweet shop is their nirvana, but for all and sundry I would suggest a visit to the baker and confectioner is the greatest pleasure of all. But then I would think that way, would I not. I recall the advertisements for Bisto. Nothing to do with bread but happy faces are depicted taking in the warm aroma of the beef gravy beneath their noses and exclaiming: 'Ah, Bisto!' — as was replicated by the olfactory pleasures enjoyed by the Whitwell customers.

The yard behind the shop was an enclosed area containing the coal shed and an outside lavatory. This convenience was used by everyone, be they shop staff or inhabitants of the upstairs living accommodation. In my day it was connected to mains drainage and the bowl and cistern was the best that Thomas Crapper could supply. The only variation, although I believe not unique, was that the seat provided was a fixed, well polished piece of wood, with an appropriate hole. It stretched across the full width of the apartment. The squares of newspaper provided, many of them from the local *Citizen*, were stacked to the left and right of the sitter and often provided suitable reading material if occupation of this chamber was an extended one. I first encountered Albert Einstein's name in one of the more interesting of these scraps. Not that I ever understood what his theories were all about and so perhaps the end use of the piece of paper bringing his name to my attention was fully appropriate. It is all relative of course — but pray excuse my feeble humour.

Alice was supremely happy with the new locale and the business did well. The reputation of her baking soon became well-known. On another front, she was less successful and that was in the field of motherhood. Thomas was a robust little boy, a great favourite with staff and customers alike, but he was destined to be an only child. Over the next five years there were two miscarriages and three children born alive, but in each case they only survived a few hours. Clarence and she were greatly saddened, all of their friends and neighbours had large families, but they had to accept that for them, this was not to be. Alice's failure in this regard was compensated for by a move towards even more elaborate sweetmeats that brought in new customers from across the city. They discussed opening another shop but Alice decided that as she was central to their success she needed to concentrate her skills at one location, and this paid dividends.

Thomas does not figure in my story except to say that his absence saw my grandfather into the position he eventually achieved. It was Thomas's inactivity that was to determine the destiny of the Glossop family. For the Whitwells, it appeared that their only son was not going to step into their footsteps and although not exactly planning a succession, they were sufficiently far-sighted to realise that another man about the place was needed as it was becoming fairly clear that their son's interests lay well outside the realm of the baking tin and the flour sifter.

## Violet

My grandfather, George Glossop, had worked at the Lower George Inn since leaving school. He had begun running errands, stacking empty crates and emptying ashtrays but by the time he came to the notice of the Whitwells he was behind the bar strengthening his biceps as he pulled pints and changed barrels. He got on well with the local clientele. These included Clarence and Alice who frequented the Saloon Bar, partly as a neighbourly gesture and also because she was no stranger to the delights of a mixture of port wine and lemonade. Her husband generally preferred the Bass. It was George's ability to relate to customers that prompted them to offer him a position behind the counter in the bakery as a change to standing behind a bar.

He was an immediate success. He enjoyed the more civilised hours; he did not have to work evenings so he could, if he wished, repair to the Lower George as a patron rather than a barman. In the early years he was required, on alternate mornings of the six-day week, to help in the bakehouse, necessitating an early start — four a.m. This duty fell away after his first two years and by the time he was twenty he had become second-in-command to Clarence in the shop. The long figure of Mr Whitwell, in his white bowler hat, tended to adopt the position of a major-domo presiding over the cash register of this expanding and successful business which left George and the lady assistants to charm the customers and wrap-up the wares.

Alice had her own helpers and trainees in the bakehouse but while Clarence was only too happy to divest some of his responsibilities, his wife was still very much in charge at the production end. Her cakes and pastries became more and more ambitious — and more and more sought after. It was during this period, when George was establishing his value to the business and she was at the peak of her powers, that her variation of the famous recipe for Napoleon Hats was born. These delicacies became something of a sensation for Whitwells and the bakehouse had difficulty in keeping up with demand — a position that remained into my mother's time when these confections became even more exotic as she added a variety of delicate flavours to the almond paste.

After George was able to dispense with an alarm clock — no more bakehouse duties — his life settled into a fixed routine. The shop closed for a half-day on Thursday, when my grandfather played football in the Thursday league, but stayed open for an extra two hours on Saturdays for the benefit of the shopping public. He therefore had more opportunity to spend his evenings with those young ladies of Gloucester who would succumb to his charms and, as he charmed the customers at Whitwells, he did the same with Maud Aylstone.

Maud proved to be exactly the right partner for the budding entrepreneur. She was three years younger than George and after leaving school had worked at the Gloucester market for an uncle who was a fishmonger. She was therefore familiar with the retail trade but she was glad, after marriage, to finally erase the smell of fish from her person and take up a new role as wife and mother. In less than two years Phyllis was born followed at regular intervals by Winnie, Arnold and Lionel. Violet came after the two older girls but her appearance coincided with the death of Clarence. He was only sixty years of age. Alice was more affected by his relatively early death than she was prepared to admit, either to her friends or herself, and whether this had any impact, she was to follow Clarence only two years later.

The business had been left to Thomas but by this time George had already stepped into Clarence's shoes and was the *de facto* manager of the shop and this position became even more established when, only months after his mother's death, Thomas departed for South Africa. Those who knew him well thought this precipitate departure was entirely in character. His mother tried to point out his responsibilities to the business, his inheritance, but she failed. He was an only child with rather more of his father's genes than hers. Nevertheless, her will named him as the sole beneficiary. What else could she do? Perhaps she thought ownership might lead him to change his ways, but this was not to be. A week before he left for the goldfields of the Rand he told my grandparents he was leaving and would they please look after the shop while he was gone.

George Glossop did exactly that. He managed the business and out of the shop income he paid his own salary, the wages of the staff, the flour merchant's bills and the rent and the taxes; the surplus then accumulated in the shops' account at Barclays Bank. George was scrupulous in his accounting. He awarded himself modest salary increases as and when he thought suitable, but the bank balance grew even though Alice's extraordinary fingers were no longer in play. However, the bake ovens were getting old and the premises needed some renovation but my grandfather did not see how he could authorise the funds that belonged to Thomas to be used to satisfy these needs. Fortunately, the absentee owner must have finally realised that he had been less than business-like at the time of his departure and two years after the death of his mother he wrote from South Africa to my grandfather. He told him nothing of his own fortunes during the intervening years but, surprisingly for Thomas, stated in explicit terms that he did not intend to return to Britain and that the business and all its assets and any bank balances are now gifted to George Henry Glossop. He even provided an address where the solicitor appointed by the bank could obtain Thomas's signature to the various documents considered necessary to formalise the transfer.

George decided not to change the name to Glossops the Bakers and so Whitwells of Gloucester remained as of old, but with another Alice in the wings, my mother. She was the third of the five children and was born in 1882. All of the family worked in the shop, until they married or pursued other professions, but it was discovered at an early age that Violet Glossop had the same magic fingers as Alice Whitwell nee Smith. There was no question of an inheritance of cookery genes: they were in no way blood related but whether by some peculiar osmosis — something within the atmosphere and fabric of those premises in Westgate Street — Alice Whitwell was reborn in the shape of Violet Glossop. Perhaps Alice was more serious about her talents than Violet. The twentieth century version, in keeping with the age, was rather casual about these gifts. She had not given the subject a moments thought. She could concoct the perfect sweetmeat and she enjoyed doing it. She was soon the *éminence grise* of the bakehouse and Queen of the confectioners. Like her predecessor, her lardy cake was considered a gem. She varied from the standard in much the same way as Alice had done. They used an additional quantity of lard in preparing the dough: simple, but decisive. Upon such trifles does genius rest.

My mother was a captivating lady. Her parents were upper working-class, just outside the definition of the waged-poor, and now of the family of independent shopkeepers; Napoleon would have recognized them instantly. Violet had two older sisters and two younger brothers. In due course they were all happily married, as far as I know, and added to the population of Gloucester at regular intervals. One brother and one brother-in-law worked at the Gloucester docks, Arnold served an apprenticeship as an iron-moulder at Fielding and Platt and the oldest sister, when she left Whitwells, married a regular soldier who was killed during the first Battle of Ypres in 1914. None of them denied Violet's right to take over the family business. At the beginning of her life she manufactured the confectionery that was in demand throughout the city, progressing in her maturity to be the proprietor of this venerable baking enterprise and married, strangely enough, to a conservative teacher of French.

He was said to be an excellent teacher of this language, assisted no doubt by the fact that he was a Frenchman, born in Calais. However, between the days when my youthful mother began to perfect her talents and take up her position as the confectionary genius of Whitwells, there was the interlude of riotous love and sex. I can only relay this to the reader as a result of hearsay. I was there, but too young to be classified as a reliable witness. If she had offered herself so readily for some pecuniary return perhaps her eccentric behaviour could have been better understood but that was not the case. Until Francois showed her that long-term relationships were much more satisfying, both physically and spiritually, she believed in love and practised it. She was like an un-tamed animal. There was no wickedness involved. She saw nothing immoral in accepting the pleasure she got from these activities with the same gratitude a starving child would have at being given one or more of her hot cross buns. However, dear reader, it should be made clear that every encounter was the result of falling in love.

I have not read anywhere what Papa's attitude was to the popular songs of the first half of the 20th century — or does it matter — but we do have Noel Coward's opinion. He recognised the potency of what he called 'cheap music', but

*Alan Shelley*

I recall how compelling it was for me when many years later Frank Sinatra introduced us to: 'I fall in love too easily'.

> I fall in love too easily,
> I fall in love too fast.

This was Violet's problem. She fell in love too easily — and too often.

My father was a miner from the Rhondda Valley visiting Gloucester to play rugby. I can paint you a picture. A Saturday in February; the steady drops of rain that are falling look like pearls against the gas lights that have been lit for the last two hours. Whitwells close late on Saturday evenings. The streets are crowded and business is brisk. My collier father is attracted by the smell of new bread as he saunters with his team-mates towards the Lower George. I wonder why he choose that one when there were more than twenty public houses on Westgate Street open for custom? I am very glad he did. He buys a hot roll and meets a hot girl. She joins him later for a drink next-door. He loves her curly hair, now released from the mob-cap she wears in the shop, and she cannot take her eyes away from his broken nose. It had been a hard game. The second team of his club is due to play Gloucester's second side in two weeks time. He arranges a demotion for himself and finds second impressions are even more delightful than the first. They are both very young. Even at that time of the year the flour storeroom is warm and they love each other passionately. When the football season ended, he never returned.

Why not? Was he simply a philanderer or had there been a mining accident. These were frequent in South Wales. Two hundred and ninety miners died at one pit in 1894. My mother tried to make some enquiries, but without success. Later on I did some research and there had been a mining accident at the Llest Colliery in August 1899 with nineteen fatalities. She was not exactly sure where he worked; which pit. It was evidently not a topic of conversation in that nest over the bakehouse.

She was naturally upset at the non-appearance of my father: the child she was carrying seemed destined to only have one parent, but a year or so on another customer caught her eye, and so it went on until Francois came along. It was not initially the cakes or the curly hair that attracted him, or at least so he maintained, but her hats.

When I left Paris, and before setting up in London, I had some months in Gloucester with Violet and Francois. This was the first occasion I had spent any length of time with my mother since joining the Army in 1917. It was a peaceful episode in my life, before moving on to pastures new, and it was also pleasing to see that despite the economic ills of the country, Whitwells appeared to be prospering. They had opened another shop and Francois had left teaching to deal with the administration and finance of the expanded business, leaving mother free to concentrate on the production side. She also had help from Marianne and Herbert. Marie was the shop manager for the new venture and my brother ran the Westgate Street one.

During those months my mother and I became even greater friends. She was only seventeen years older than me, and as I was by then in my late twenties, the gap seemed even smaller. She often talked of her youth.

"Percy, I've been a bit of a failure as a mother to you. It was not fair to deprive you of a father in your infant years."

"Not altogether your fault, Mum."

"I was a bad girl, back then, was I not?"

"No comment. I was rather young at the time."

"I know, but I'd like to try and explain myself. I wasn't a tart, you know. I've always liked men, but I never went with one that I did not feel for. I suppose after falling for you, I should have given up the 'being-in-love' lark, but I couldn't seem to help it. What I do regret is that I know so little about your father. He was the first one, of course. I did try to find out but communications weren't so easy in those days. No telephones. I couldn't just leave the shop and go off to South Wales in search."

"What do you recall of him?"

As you can imagine, this was not the first time I had quizzed her about my father and as a result had built up my own picture, but I could not help revisiting the subject.

"Well, he was a big man."

"Yes, most prop forwards are."

"But gentle. And do you know Percy, although you could see he was a miner from his fingernails, he always smelled nice. His hair was thick and curly. Black, like the coal he dug. He sang to me. Very softly, but beautiful. And he was so neat and tidy. Perhaps that is why you're so fastidious? What do you call those funny trousers you are wearing?"

"Oxford bags."

Besides my mother's early love life I talked about the sadness I felt on leaving Paris and then we discussed, at rather greater length, her political views. She was an ardent socialist and at this particular time in Britain's history she was more vociferous than usual. She was particularly vehement about the plight of the miners. Later on we rather fell out during the General Strike.

## Francois

My grandparents tolerated Violet's behaviour until she married. Although her love affairs were exuberant and wholehearted, she was relatively discreet and careful not to sire any more progeny. The already successful business became even more profitable as my mother widened and extended her confectionary concoctions and sharing in the increasing affluence enabled her to satisfy the second enthusiasm of her life, hats — or should it be the third after cakes and sex. Her expenses were low; she still lived at home and for the moment I cost little, but there was one area where she became wildly extravagant — she was one of the favoured customers of the milliner trading as Westgate Modes.

Her love of hats had no part to play in that other passion — for men. These mysteries of lace, feathers and cloth were not purchased to attract the male, she simply adored wearing them. I have omitted to say that during the tenure of Clarence and Alice a large mirror had been fixed to the wall behind the counter of the shop upon which was painted the legend 'Whitwells. The Premier Bakers'. Over the years the lettering became rather crazed and the silvering of the mirror deteriorated but until it was replaced when she became the sole proprietor, it provided an adequate accessory for Violet to adjust her newest acquisition in the way of headgear before setting off to meet her latest beau, or to visit her siblings, or to call on Westgate Modes to view the newest stock.

On visits to this shop she often approached her favourite emporium by way of the College Green that adjoined Gloucester Cathedral. This magnificent building had been a place of Christian worship for more than a thousand years; all the citizens of Gloucester loved their cathedral, and its setting. It seemed to be the symbolic and practical heart of the city where the soaring tower is visible from miles around. I do not know whether Henry became a favourite name locally but in the year 1216 King Henry III had been crowned there, at the age of nine, and in the eighteenth century a Gloucester choirboy wrote a piece of music that was eventually used by the author of the words for the *Star Spangled Banner.*

On one such journey Violet was crossing the Green when a sudden gust of wind detached her current darling from her head — hat pin and all — and blew it into the face of a young man strolling in the opposite direction to the now bareheaded Violet. He was wearing a straw boater. She did not know whether to laugh or cry at the sight of her hat now adorning this man's head — the boater had come off second-best in the contest with the female bonnet. She then decided it was no laughing matter — the present object of her affections was probably damaged. For a moment the man could not understand what had happened. Had he been attacked by a strange bird? As he realised the truth of the matter he quickly recovered his composure and made an attempt to return the hat to Violet. However, in doing so he scratched his left hand rather severely with the hat pin and this made him clutch her latest extravagance to his chest as he went on to tell her to be more careful in the future.

When my mother recounted this incident to her parents and me she tried to recall the conversation that took place — and also attempted to imitate the accent of the man she referred to as: 'Someone who was rather rude, and a foreigner as well.'

"Look at my hand. *Mon dieu*. You see *Mademoiselle* it is bleeding — *tres mauvais.* You are a danger to everyone. I take stroll in this quiet *parque* and I am attacked. "

"Sorry, but I can't help it if there is a wind. I'm not a danger to anyone and I didn't attack you. What nonsense. I'll thank you to keep a civil tongue in your head young man. And try and speak proper English."

"There is nothing wrong with this my English. Can you speak French?"

"No."

"Well then, do not criticise your betters."

"Betters! You are very rude. You are not a gentleman. Good day."

"But wait a moment. Do not depart without your *chapeau* — your hat."

"You've probably ruined it. It was my favourite."

"Well take more care in future."

"You are impossible. Do not tell me what to do."

"I apologise, but I was never battered by a hat before. I can see it is your English secret weapon. No doubt explains why Napoleon lost at the Battle of Waterloo."

"What rubbish you talk. What do I have to do with Napoleon? Are you mad?"

"No *Mademoiselle,* but can I see you to your *résidence*?"

"Residence? Oh, where I live. All right, why not. It's not too far."

I was five years old at this time and so my first memories of Francois are relatively clear even if I have needed to recreate the dialogue exchanged at their first meeting with a certain amount of artistic licence. Very unusually the local grammar school had recruited him to spend two terms with them to add some polish to the teaching of French. The school in question was known by all and sundry as, 'Tommy Richs'. We did not see many of the boys in the shop — the school was on the other side of The Cross at Barton Street. There were about three hundred in the school when Francois arrived for his short stay that, thanks to my mother and her hats, became of a more permanent nature.

He spent the rest of his life curbing Violet's impetuous nature and, as far as I can tell, he was victorious in this campaign. He failed however to persuade her not to call him 'Frankie'. She loved to croon the popular song when he was most stern and it was months before he discovered that of the two lovers, Frankie was the girl and Johnny the boy. They complemented each other perfectly. I was a page at their wedding and for the first time in my life, and my mother's, we no longer awoke each morning to the smell of newly baked bread — we now had our own house. This was a modest terraced property of the kind known as a 'two up, two down'. It was close to the shop and we all loved it. Francois was offered a permanent appointment at the school and mother produced even more extravagant pastries under the admiring eyes of her parents who were delighted to see their wayward genius settled down. Within a little over two years of the marriage, I had a sister and a brother.

I trust the reader has by now acquired an adequate picture of Violet Chambord née Glossop to begin to understand and appreciate her character. Except for the volte-face into unqualified faithfulness to her new lover and husband, marriage only strengthened her vivacious nature and she still derived an intense pleasure from her contribution to the burgeoning prosperity of Whitwells. After school I would call at the shop and walk home with her pushing the pram with the two infants who had been her companions during her cake-making day. Perhaps flour and sugar and yeast are soporific as Marianne and Herbert caused little interruption to her labours. If anything, these babies seemed to attract even more customers when on display alongside the chocolate éclairs and orange sponges, but I must tell you more about my new stepfather. As my story will inform you, I went through my itinerant life with two crucial skills; the culinary arts bestowed upon me by my mother and an aptitude for, and a love of, the French language thanks to François.

He was Gallic in appearance, short and dark and lively of movement but his speech was careful and calculated. In his nature he could easily have been mistaken for the most conservative of Englishmen. His parents died when he was young and until appearing on the Gloucester scene he lived in Calais with his grandmother. She attended the wedding and although I met her frequently in the following years, until her death, I never saw her when she was not clad from neck to ankle in some black material. I think it was known as bombazine but when I was near it appeared to radiate a near lethal charge of static electricity. She was very demonstrative. When embraced by the strong arms of Madame Harriet Chambord, and cushioned deeply within her ample black-draped bosom, my feeble frame was shocked to its core. I am sure that the electricity travelled around the belt holding up my short trousers and finished at the snake buckle making my belly-button tingle.

If I was uneasy with *Grandmère,* I was enraptured by her grandson. Looking back I realise I had reached the age — I was six when they married — when I was beginning to need some masculine discipline and influence. Although my grandparents had a baker's dozen of grandchildren, I was with them every day and as they tended to favour my mother over their other children, they probably felt the same about me. For this reason I was spoilt and probably badly behaved. On the other hand, perhaps I was in some fashion neglected. They were all busy in the shop or the bakehouse for long hours, six days every week, and until I went to school there were few opportunities for mixing with other children.

The introduction of Francois converted this family of an unconventional mother and an illegitimate child into a conformist lower middle-class unit living in the Edwardian era when the British Empire was at its zenith and our navy ruled the seas. It is ironic that it was a Frenchman that brought about this transformation in our lives. He was, I suppose, what you would call 'steady'. Although in later life I could rarely be accorded that sobriquet, the stability provided in my early years must have made some contribution to my character. Perhaps my ability to avoid panic when faced with severe dangers, if in fact I have that virtue, was one result but also he was just as lovable as my mother and until I left home in my late teens, I luxuriated in the happy atmosphere their union created. My adult life was hardly conventional but my childhood was much the same as any of the other boys growing up in the city of Gloucester. We played cricket in the Gloucester Park, swam in the canal or played marbles in the local gutters.

I left behind some of these activities when I was admitted to Tommy Richs. My reading and writing skills, together with my half-competent French and the influence of Francois, who was now a permanent member of the scholastic establishment, persuaded the school to offer me a place and ignore my total ignorance, if not indifference, in all other subjects. I also seemed to have developed one other strength: I was becoming a bit of a sportsman, shades of Papa H, with a natural well developed eye/hand coordination that manifested itself most prominently on the cricket field. As a result I began my life-long love affair with the game.

Francois never fully understood the rules, what Frenchman would, but he often came with me to see Gloucestershire play at the Spa Ground. I saw many of the masters of the day and I must say that in my peripatetic future life it was one of the joys of England that I missed the most. In particular I recall Gilbert Jessop, who was the captain of Gloucestershire from 1900 to 1912. He was one of the fastest run scorers ever. I did not see him score his 234 at Bristol in 1905 against Somerset, but this was much the hot topic of conversation in the shop at the time — achieved in only two hours and ten minutes. The other hero was Charlie Parker. He began his career with the team in 1903 as a medium fast left-arm bowler but after the war he switched to left-arm spin and during the 1920s he invariably took over two hundred wickets each season.

Before moving to Tommy Richs I had observed from the primary school in Clare Street that the house at number 18 seemed to be inhabited by an extravagant number of young. By this time of course I had a brother and a sister, a small family by the norm of the day, but at that house I could never accurately assess how many there were. What did seem clear was that they were all girls. My most immediate contemporary was one called Flo, a very autocratic young lady, who wanted no truck with me. For a while I had the honour to be the ink monitor. This required me to fill all the ink wells on a Monday morning in both the boys' and the girls' classrooms. I then discovered that in this capacity I had to act as a postman delivering notes to some of the girls from members of my class declaring undying love. I decided to join in the fun and while pouring the ink, I delivered to Flo a piece of poetry I had written in her honour.

To Flo
I can row you up the river.
Wouldn't that be funny.
I can row you up the river.
If you'll be my honey.
I can row you down the river.
We'll be home for tea.
I can row you down the river.

And so happy be.

There was no response whatsoever and as I left the primary school my interest waned. Not a particularly auspicious start to a lifetime where an admiration of the fairer sex played a fairly major part. Had I inherited my mother's gastronomic skills but not her ability in the field of romance? You could also say that my first poetic attempt did not presage much promise towards a future literary career.

Tommy Richs was a posh school, to quote my grandparents, and although I left early, the chance to have that educational start to my life was crucial: another reason to be thankful for the advent of Francois. On the other hand, if I had not discarded my school blazer to help my mother at the bakery I would most likely have matriculated at eighteen and, being eligible to move on to university, would have led to being offered a commission when called up for army duty. However, the fates decreed that I should meet Colonel Kim in a more lowly capacity than might have been the case if I had been a common-or-garden platoon subaltern. And, based on the statistics, in that capacity I would have been unlikely to have survived to tell this tale.

My grandparents died during the early years of the war, Maud in 1914 and George a year later. Violet therefore found herself in sole command at Whitwells and in view of my inclination towards the kitchen, it seemed only reasonable that I should move from the classroom to the shop as soon as convenient within my scholastic programme. This was determined to be at the age of sixteen, shortly after George Glossop died. I did have some regrets, particularly as I was at that time on the fringe of selection for the first eleven, but the attraction of the flour and sugar, and the love and admiration I had for my mother, brought the balance down on the side of the cake and not cricket.

My days at Tommy Richs were mixed. The tutors of science and mathematics soon gave me up as a lost cause although I must have done sufficient work in those subjects to avoid being kicked out of school. Nonetheless, even today I am still unable to check whether the modest royalty payments I receive every quarter are correct and as for space travel, I am rather more interested in who might be captaining Gloucester next season.

Other than the cricket field — and despite my genes I found little attraction in football, be the ball round or oval — the most vivid memory I have of my school days is the time I spent in the classroom of the head of English, William Waverley Rogers MA. He did not come from north of the border and I never had the temerity to ask if his parents were fond of Sir Walter Scott but what I do know is that he was an inspirational teacher. I did not always find favour with him. The essay during my final year that sought to show the superiority of the verse of Verlaine over that of Keats was considered close to blasphemy but it was my description of a mildly passionate relationship between a local squire and a gypsy girl that incurred his most scathing comments. I admit I did tend towards hyperbole, particularly when faced with subjects like: 'What did you do during the holidays', but on the whole he mainly tolerated my minor idiosyncrasies

But it was not the written exercises I recall most vividly; it was the passion this man was able to impart of the joys of reading — at least to some of his pupils. Unlike most schoolboys of my age, Shakespeare was from the beginning a joy and not a chore. Perhaps because of my unconventional mother, I was somewhat uninhibited and I found myself on the stage in the school hall with parts as varied as Mrs Malaprop — this was of course an all-boys school — Puck in *A Midsummer Night's Dream* and Oscar Wilde's, Archibald Moncrieff. Despite these forays into dramatic art it was the novel that aroused my greatest interest. Before I went to Tommy Richs I devoured *Tom Sawyer* at more or less one sitting, rating it at the time far superior to my former favourite, *Treasure Island*, but it was Mr Rogers who showed me that beyond Dickens and Scott there were other masters. It was some years before I read *War and*

*Peace* but, perhaps precociously, I had before joining the Army been enraptured, thanks to Mr Rogers, by *Anna Karenina* and Theodore Dreiser's *Sister Carrie*.

If I admired Mr Rogers, I loved Miss Rosen. It is an indication of her ability as a teacher that she was allowed within the masculine precinct that was Tommy Richs, but my infatuation was not a result of having an independent mother running a successful business enterprise in a man's world; it was surely that Miss Rosen was in her early twenties, had round blue eyes and a prominent bosom. She was allowed through the school gates, three afternoons each week, to tutor the handful of students who had elected to learn the language of our foes. There must have been some debate in the school Council as to whether offering teaching in German was unpatriotic but I can imagine the Chairman, who was a retired general, lecturing his fellow members with phrases like, 'know thine enemy'. They would not of course have countenanced a national as they did with my stepfather but the charm of this particular lady would have helped to woo the conservative governing body — and her command of the language was rather good as well. I was a member of her class. I did not decide to study the German language so that when a soldier I would be able to swap pleasantries with the Bôche facing me across no-man's-land. My motives were much more pedestrian. By signing up for German, I was able to avoid two periods of physics and three of chemistry and as my command of French seemed to indicate an aptitude for foreign tongues, I was allowed into Miss Rosen's presence.

I was to discover that she was christened Elizabeth Mary but went by the name of Liza. She was not reticent when it came to explaining why she spoke the language so fluently. Her grandfather had been born in Hamburg. He was in the shipbuilding business and as a young man had found work in Glasgow, where he remained all his life, and where he found romance with a 'wee Scots lassie'. The frequency of the German spoken in that Scottish household was sufficient for Liza's father to be able to escape the smoke of Glasgow for the Cotswolds of England where he secured a position as a language teacher at Malvern College. Liza, so she told us, had ambitions to study to be a doctor but while negotiating entry into a medical school — not an easy task for a woman in 1915 — she was happy to have this part-time post — and became the object of my wildest desires.

The pattern my life was to take was determined, in a number of ways, by the ladies of my acquaintance and I shall always be grateful for Miss Liza Rosen as she provided me with my first lesson, however innocent, on the often rocky road of romance.

After my rebuttal by Flo of Clare Street, I had conducted my life in a female-free world, despite some of mother's younger assistants flirting with me in an off-hand and light-hearted fashion. I was therefore ripe and ready for Liza during my last year at school. I was not yet sixteen. She was in her early twenties and I had many rivals. Of a class that ranged from twelve to fifteen scholars, I numbered those claimants for her affection to be never less than ten. She did nothing to encourage us. Her clothes were modest, there was no make-up and no provocative movements. I had one advantage amongst the other competitors; I proved to be the star pupil and I suppose it is natural that teachers favour those who are the easiest to tutor.

And then, there were the cakes. I thought carefully about this. It was well known throughout the school — at least in my class — that my putative father was a master at Tommy Richs but my mother was a shopkeeper. I was occasionally referred to as the 'Baker boy' but could I turn this to my advantage? Instead of 'an apple for the teacher', what about a chocolate éclair? As German was only available three half-days a week they were concentrated sessions that necessitated a mid- afternoon break. During one of these I explained to her that my mother had been over-generous with the snack prepared for me and would Miss like one of Whitwells famous confectionery items. She politely accepted the offering and as I handed it over a blush spread across my cheeks, which persuaded me not to repeat this tactic.

Looking back, I try to analyse the form this infatuation took. If the Goddess of Love had mysteriously transported Liza to my bedroom — or the storeroom over the bakehouse — clad in a diaphanous negligee, what would I have done next? Probably stuttered a few words, even in German, and taken to my heels. If I had chanced to meet her one night in some dark alley, would I have thrown my arms around her dainty neck and passionately attached my lips to hers? Very unlikely. That is not to say that my emotions were false. Oh, the agony of those teenage urges. I suppose I loved her as the epitome of the ideal woman, not in my bed, but on a pedestal. I have often wondered if creatures like she are aware of the impact they have on the spotty, hormone-fuelled teenagers they stand in front of but in my case there was just one incident when it became something more than worship from afar.

My relationship with Francois was a good one. I admired the success he had made as my errant mother's husband and the way he had integrated himself into all things English. For one crazy moment I contemplated raising with him my interest — whatever that amounted to — in his fellow language teacher, with whom he was quite friendly, but quickly realised that would be a serious mistake. Two reasons. Firstly, I would be ragged mercilessly by him and my mother and secondly, what could he do about my unreasonable passion. So I kept quiet — but Francois did in fact have a part to play in this farcical love story; he and those chocolate éclairs.

Over supper one evening, a few days after the gift of cake at break- time, Francois told my mother that she had another fan amongst the teaching fraternity in the shapely form of the new German teacher. He did not of course use the word 'shapely'. Violet and her husband had some mild fun about young Percy trifling with her affections with gifts of sweetmeats, but I became even more flustered as I listened to the conversation this issue prompted.

"She is an interesting woman. Wants to be a doctor. Difficult. Tells me her mother and father are not very supportive in that direction."

"I can imagine. Back to the kitchen, little woman. How dare you seek to invade the masculine domain."

"I understand they're very conservative. I bet he's one of those teachers that have never changed his lessons in ten years and if his pupils don't like it, he resorts to the birch. I've told her all about you. She is full of admiration for what you have done as a woman — and after only one tasting, she is in love with your chocolate éclairs."

"A discerning girl, I can see that."

"I thought I might ask her round to meet you. She leaves early on Fridays, as I do as you know, so I thought we might meet at the shop for tea and an exploration of your wares beyond the incomparable éclairs."

"You're not getting sweet on this paragon are you, Francois Chambord?"

"Of course! She's been my mistress for the last two blissful months."

At this point my mother threw the tea cosy at Francois's head.

Whatever, it was determined that such an invitation should be issued. I panicked. Should I stay late at school? Find a cricket practice I had to attend? Go swimming? Such indecision. Should I absent myself or take the chance of sitting shoulder to shoulder with my heart's desire around the tea table? In the end of course, I could not stay away.

It was a lively affair. My mother took to her straight away and they were quickly on to the subject of male chauvinism. Violet explained how her predecessor, Alice Whitwell, had been the impetus behind setting up the business in the first place and how, incredibly, she seemed to have passed on her cooking skills even though there was no blood connection. I was more-or-less relaxed, not too embarrassed, until my mother decided to further this train of thought with the observation that Percy was also becoming a competent hand with the flour and water. This brought the involuntary colour of pink to my cheeks but Liza made no attempt to treat this as a subject of fun. She clearly thought that if a woman could be a doctor, why not a man in the kitchen. Fortunately my mother did not talk about prop forwards.

All very pleasant, and no real disasters on my front. I was able to answer when spoken to and I do not think the others were aware of the cursory glances directed at Liza's front but when she left, disaster struck. What was she doing? Perhaps in honour of her Gallic host she ignored my outstretched hand, outstretched to accompany the series of polite good-byes we were all engaged in, when she took my head into her delicate hands and kissed me on both cheeks. It would have been bad enough if I had blushed even more deeply than normal, or if tears had sprung to my eyes. I may have done both of these things but more dramatically, I fell over. I fell forward. Was it a momentary fainting fit? Whatever, my angel could not avoid collapsing over the just-quitted tea table that contained a plate of uneaten chocolate éclairs. As she rose, unhurt, the back of her delicate white blouse was stained with tea and cream and chocolate but I could not hear what was being said because of a loud ringing sound. While Francois was helping his colleague to her feet, my mother, without a moment's pause, had given me a powerful box of the ear as though I was a little boy found stealing her current buns. She had well-developed wrists from kneading the dough. My embarrassment was total. As I regained normality in the audio department, sufficient to make a whispered apology, I could think of nothing more to do than to quit the room without another word. My world had suddenly been turned upside down. What a naïve creature I was at sixteen.

In the future Francois and my mother treated the incident as a great joke. 'A kiss on the cheek was enough to take away this foolish boy's senses', but I was of course unconcerned what they thought. How was I to walk into Liza's class on the following Monday afternoon, but I did. She made no reference to the shameful episode although it did seem to me that for the remaining few lessons we did appear to be concentrating on German vocabulary in the gastronomic field. Francois and my mother may have thought about inviting her back for more tea and cakes but she did not remain in the school much longer — she was accepted to read medicine at a London teaching hospital.

I never discovered if Liza shared my passion for books. My mother did not. She may have consulted Mrs Beeton on occasions, even though most of her recipes were home-grown, but Dickens and Trollope were strangers to her. I could fantasise that my collier father read in bed, using his miner's lamp for illumination, but my limited acquaintance with prop forwards leads me to believe that such are not often of a literary or intellectual persuasion. In addition to the influence of Mr Rogers, Francois directed me towards Zola and Balzac — and Marcel Proust — although like many other men of culture he had not progressed beyond the first hundred pages. My life-long interest in the art of fiction is of course reflected in the bizarre title I have given to these memoirs, but at this juncture, the object of these ramblings is to ask the question as to why the First World War generated such a wealth of prose and poetry, compared with the follow-up affair that began on the 3rd of September 1939.

This apparent disparity on the literary front was paralleled by the different attitude there was in the hearts and minds of the British people in 1914 compared to 1939. Today's young, coming from the age of 'make love not war' must find it difficult to comprehend how we all felt when war was declared in 1914. I was only fourteen, going on fifteen, at the time but I was caught up in the extraordinary fervour of patriotism that spread like the most virulent of plagues. Because of course that is what it turned out to be; a modern black death. The miseries resulting from the second world conflict of the 20th century were intense, but the one in which I was first involved was so much more confined in terms of geography that the horrors seemed the greater. Perhaps this is why it spawned the more poignant literature. Not to disparage Norman Mailer or *Catch 22* but for me Graves and Eric Marie Remarque made me ache inside for the tragedy they described. Our Gloucestershire war poet was Ivor Gurney who was a boy chorister at the Cathedral and was at Arras about the same time I was.

Not that I was ever out of work, or involved in any sustained military action, but I like to believe that was not for want of courage. As it was to be for so many stages of my life, it was my fingers and my tongue that determined the path my career in His Majesty's armed forces was to take, not my ability with the rifle.

As I have said there was no apparent reason why the genius, if I might call it that, of Alice Smith should have been reborn in my mother but there was every reason why her aptitude in the realms of flour and sugar should have found a home in the next generation, namely me. Violet did not set out to pass on her talents to her children, and in the case of Marianne and Herbert this did not happen, but from an early age I had my hands in the mixing bowl and my face was often decorated with the flour that my energetic fingers had agitated into the immediate atmosphere. Mother was of course delighted in my interest but she made no conscious effort to enrol me as a pupil. I watched, I stirred, I tasted and I burnt my youthful fingers on the ovens and cookers in use, so that in time I became — a cook. I developed into one who could put together a number of raw ingredients and produce delectable dishes. Initially within the confines of Whitwells these were only of the flour-based variety but by the time I became a lowly member of the famous Gloucester Regiment, I was half way to becoming a competent, if limited, chef. When the Guildhall was used for special dinners, my mother was

*Alan Shelley*

often invited to prepare the deserts and when I became a full-time member of the Whitwell team, I began to accompany her. These excursions allowed me to develop my nascent talents and I was often given the responsibility for the fish course. My earliest version of the Sole Véronique was particularly praised. It was due to these early experiences, and my knowledge of the language of Moliere and Racine, that I was present at one of the most significant peace treaty gatherings in history, that at Paris in 1919.

In James Hilton's *Goodbye Mr Chips*, we are told how the hero causes some consternation when he includes, in a list of members of the school who had fallen in the First World War, the name of a former master at the school who was German. In our family there was no such conflict; my mother and stepfather were on the same side but I often wondered what would have happened if Francois had succeeded in his attempt to volunteer in 1914, as he so urgently desired. Would there have been a wish to serve under Foch rather than Haig? This was never put to the test. He was thirty two when the war broke out and at that age he could easily have sat on the side-lines for the time being but no, he reported to the Gloucestershire Regiment's Depot as soon as war was declared. He was, by that time, a naturalised Briton but he fell at the first hurdle. His poor eyesight would probably have kept him out of the trenches, but his initial medical examination found him to be suffering with an asthma condition and so he was sent back to his classroom to join Mr Chips as they both mourned their ex-pupils, destined to be slaughtered on the Western front or at the Gallipoli peninsula. When, three years later, I was called to attend at the same depot, no medical defects were found. I was headed to that mess of a war.

*If I thought finding a medical faculty to take me was difficult, it was as nothing compared to the prejudice, and even downright hostility, I faced when inside that bastion of male superiority. I may have unintentionally set some young hearts beating when a schoolteacher, but those arrogant snobs at the Middlesex paid no attention whatsoever to any female charms I might possess. They were so convinced that you can only make a doctor out of something that is endowed with a penis they ignored me, or scorned me. I often thought it would have been better, more natural, if one or more of them had tried to make love to me, but they did not. The tutors were polite, if distant, but my fellow students paid more attention to the cadavers we dissected than to me. Of course it was made worse when it became known that my grandfather had been German. If they thought about me at all, one half labelled me as an enemy spy and the other as a Jew.*

*I often thought of quitting and returning to Gloucester to delight that Percy Glossop and his friends, but having fought my way in, I was dammed if I was going to give up. I kept in touch with Francois and he encouraged me in this. He was even more of a foreigner in a foreign land than I was but he has settled well into this strange mixture that is Great Britain. Of course, the misogynist attitude I faced was mostly to do with class. Not only was I unfit for the medical profession but my grandfather had worked in a shipbuilding yard, and in Glasgow at that.*

*It got easier. At my first hospital appointment after qualifying I began to be appreciated for my skills, never mind gender. And so I progress. Perhaps I should not complain. By now more women are being trained as doctors and my generation did not hit the near impregnable wall of prejudice faced by our illustrious predecessors. There were a few notable doctors of my grandmother's generation who were able to find training, but were denied licences to practice thereafter. Elizabeth Garrett Anderson was the first in Britain to have her name*

*Alan Shelley*

*entered on a medical register but before that she had to fight to secure instruction in a variety of institutions.*

*Francois wrote and related his son's experience of a military hospital. Shot in the arm, I was told. He was a funny mixture that boy but I think he will have some success with women during his time on this earth.*

**Liza Rosen June 1918**

# Chapter Two

# War

*Brotsuppe*

*Ingredients: One quart of meat or vegetable stock. Quarter of a pound of brown or white bread. Salt and pepper. Nutmeg. Two eggs.*

*Method: Put the stock to boil. Break the bread into small pieces, including crusts, and put into a saucepan. Pour the boiling stock over the bread. Add salt, pepper, a little nutmeg and simmer all gently for fifteen minutes. Beat the eggs well in a large bowl. Gradually pour the soup, which must be below boiling point, over the eggs, stirring vigorously all the time.*

# Arras

Within the armed forces there is one particular tradition that is invariably invoked at recruiting offices; the authorities first ask of your occupation before joining up. With this information, deep-sea fishermen and steeplejacks are posted to the tunnelling section of the Royal Engineers, together with airline pilots; surveyors are spurned by the Royal Artillery and sent to the Labour or Army Pay Corp while arctic explorers are invariably fitted out for the deserts of Arabia. This did not happen to me. My culinary skills, such as they were, had been noted and so by the autumn of 1917 I found myself part of the establishment that ran the officers' mess at the Divisional Headquarters located close to Arras in Northern France. We were about ten miles from what was then the front line.

I had not enjoyed basic training with the Gloucesters and, as it turned out, I never served with the regiment. During my short military career I was seconded, for pay and rations as it is described, to a Divisional Headquarters from where a Major General and his staff determined the fate of around twenty thousand troops. As a result, I was never to experience the *esprit de corps* that was such an essential ingredient towards accepting life in the trenches, although I did wear my regimental cap with some pride. We were the only British regiment that had cap badges at the front and the back, thanks to an illustrious campaign in Egypt many years ago.

Some of my readers will have their own experiences of the apparent utter futility of basic training at the outset of an army career — and I assume this applies to other branches of our armed forces and those all over the world. I appreciate that we needed to understand the importance of discipline — it might save our lives in the future — and in many cases the recruits had to improve their physical fitness, but were the asinine rules and even more asinine Non-Commissioned Officers really necessary? These morons had a hold over us that was total and complete. Outside of the army we had the luxury of a freedom of choice, we could decide our own fates, but now these were in the hands of a coterie of sadists who would probably find it hard to make a living outside of the barrack square. At least, that is my view. Hours spent shining boots and applying blanco to webbing: whitewashing the stones around the guard room or the company office: petty punishments — and the class system — at its worst. I was told later of an incident that occurred during one of the Somme offensives: a true story and a prime example. A Company Commander at a rear depot overheard an ordinary soldier addressing a Lance Corporal by his Christian name and for this monstrous offence the NCO was demoted and the 'familiar' soldier subjected to Field Punishment. They probably lived next door to each other in Civvy Street, drank in the same pub — even married to each others sisters. And this contravention of 'Good order and military discipline' was played out against one of the most heinous examples of warfare in the history of mankind.

For me, basic training was made more tolerable because included in my intake was Robert Hatch, my contemporary at Tommy Richs and the wicketkeeper for the Second Eleven. He had been something of a rebel at school and both he and the teachers were pleased with his departure at the age of sixteen. We managed to arrange adjoining beds in the training barracks and found comfort that when complaining about the treatment meted out by the training sergeants and corporals — and all the other injustices — we did so with some background in common. In addition, his sister Brenda was rather fond of me — or so I was lead to believe.

He was not discharged until the spring of 1919 but when on leave, a month after the armistice was signed, he made a bee-line for the Lower George hoping he might find me there. He did. Physically he was unscathed but the former rebellious spirit was clearly subdued. What had survived was his affability, his easy-going nature. His hair was rather longer than normal for the time, despite the army's regime of 'short back and sides', but it was kept in place — as was mine — by a discreet application of household lard. We were about the same height but he was slimmer than me — had a waist like a girl, I thought.

Bob tried to describe the horror of the trenches. By the time he first experienced them they had become rather more sophisticated — if that is the right word. At least, compared to earlier years, many of them were relatively sheltered and the number of days the infantryman spent at the front at any one time was better regulated. However, his battalion had been pushed back as far as Albert during the German advance in the spring and early summer of 1918 and he had been involved in some of the bloodiest battles of the war.

*Alan Shelley*

"You know Perc, you were a lucky bugger being at Headquarters. How did you swing that one?"

"Well, you see Bob, I'm not just battle fodder like you. I'm a skilled artist."

"Bollocks. But good luck to you mate. You would not have wanted to be with my lot. I saw three platoon Lieutenants killed in my short service, together with dozens of soldiers who had become like brothers to me. Let me tell you of just one incident. I remember, it was a Sunday. We had withdrawn but found ourselves in a rather superior set of trenches. Thank God by that time we were not in a 'charging the enemy' mode. 'Up boys and at 'em. Barbed wire, smoke and gas.' There were three of us on the fire step. I couldn't see any Hun but just as we were about to be relieved, those on either side of me were killed. I couldn't believe it. Snipers. They were deadly. Chris must have been hit in the face by three bullets in quick succession. One eyeball was hanging over his cheek, but his nose and mouth were obliterated. If I'd not known who was next to me, I would not have recognised him. The other bloke must have turned around at the crucial moment. Several shots in his neck. Head nearly severed from his body. I fell off the step, swearing, crying and afraid. How had I escaped?"

"How awful! Does it keep coming back?"

"Yes and no. There were so many incidents, they get blurred together. I am still scratching myself. The lice. You couldn't get rid of them. They lived in the seams of our uniforms and however we deloused ourselves, they never perished. They were breeding as we were dying. We got used to the rats, but not the mud and the wet. Some of the boys found the mud more trying than the bullets, but for all of us, the shelling was the ultimate horror. After a while the sniper and the machine gun are not the real enemy. It is the shelling. Mostly the Hun fired over our heads to destroy ammunition dumps and the like in our rear but even then, the continuous noise sent us all mad. But when they targeted the trenches, usually before an attack, the results were horrifying. I can hardly describe it.

The incessant bangs and reverberations and the ice-cold fear that the next one is going to land in your trench and blow you to kingdom come. Sends a shiver down my spine as I speak about it, even now. Will I ever get it out of my brain? Bullets we could ignore but those bloody shells couldn't be avoided. More than once I spent hours sifting through the mud trying to find sufficient body parts to assemble enough for some kind of burial."

"Was it worth it?"

"Corse it weren't! Have another pint."

Bob Hatch tried to explain how incidents like that and the constant fear of your own imminent death, together with the day-to-day hardships, did seem to engender the most remarkable comradeship amongst those who shared these hazards. I told him of my limited exposure to some real action but not having experienced the same togetherness that he had, I found it somewhat difficult to comprehend. It amazed me that there were so few deserters. Was it enough that these trench-dwellers — and the others — were all in the same boat, so they put up with it?

Whatever kept them going? The losses were horrendous. The delegates who assembled in Paris in 1919 to agree a peace treaty had the following statistics as a baseline, as it were. During the period from August 1914 to 11th of November 1918, the casualties on our side were British and French dead totalling over two million and five million wounded out of a total mobilisation of around thirteen million. On the other side, the figures for Germany and Austria-Hungary were three million of the dead and eight million wounded. The Russian and Turkish deaths added a further two million. But never mind the big picture, all I wish to describe is my own small cameo on this stage of horror. Within this catastrophic performance of indiscriminate killing I had very few lines to say and the briefest of appearances but, even though I was not a front-line soldier, I saw sufficient from the wings to vow that if war reappeared in my lifetime, I would not be auditioning for a part.

*Alan Shelley*

Nearly as amazing as how this carnage spawned such camaraderie was the humour that emerged. Perhaps it is just a British thing. When in Paris I did not meet enough French veterans to know if they had their own version of this phenomenon, but presumably the Germans did not. There was a famous cartoon in the Bruce Bairnsfather's *Old Bill* series where Old Bill, a pipe smoking Tommy with a walrus moustache, is in a trench with a mass of ruined buildings in the background. Bill says to his companion: 'Looks as though the mice have been at that lot', whereupon there was an official response from the German headquarters saying it was not the mice that caused the damage but their shells.

Bob told me of the standard field postcard that was issued to the other ranks to help them in writing home to their families. There was a list of bland comments like: 'I received your letter of …'.or 'I have not had a letter since…' and you simple crossed out what did not apply. Bob got hold of a spoof one where amongst the options were:

I am in the Pink of condition
> night dress

I Love you more than ever
> less than ever.
> not at all.

I myself had seen issues of the *Wipers Times* which was one of the most well-known of the trench magazines that were published by soldiers on active duty. The paper consisted of poetry, in-jokes and lampoons and there were often mock property advertisements such as:

'Building land for sale — Hill 60' or:

'The Salient Estate. Underground residences ready for habitation.'

Reflecting the men's concern with the supply of alcohol, the newspaper ran a serial entitled *Narpoo Rum* which featured Herlock Shomes who was on the track of the rum thieves. I wondered if the Bôche had a similar rascal stealing the schnapps.

*I Never Met Ernest Hemingway*

After basic training I was swiftly moved to the Divisional Headquarters that was to be the locale for my short and undistinguished military career. It was not purpose-built for our use and as I became more knowledgeable about things French, I realised it was a somewhat shabby chateaux, unashamedly of the second division, where most of the *grand salons* had been partitioned into rooms used by the officers and clerks planning our next debacle. The officers' mess, other ranks' dining room and the kitchen were in an adjoining stable block.

My bayonet was kept sheathed most of the time, but that did not prevent me being apprehensive; we were, after all, fairly close to the front line. As you will have already gathered, I have a sensitive nature and the thought of a ruthless Hun pointing his unsheathed weapon at my stomach made me shiver and shake just like the aspic I was preparing for my version of the Melton Mowbray pork pie. My comrades did not help. Most of them had been in the army for much longer than me and one or two had actually been involved in some real action. With some glee they fanned the fears I tried to keep hidden so that I often found myself starting up in my sleep mouthing: 'I surrender. I surrender.' However, before I heard a shot fired in anger, or at least one near enough to cause me any bodily harm, I was concerned with a surrender of a different kind, and in a different bed.

I shared a room at the mess with Chalky White. He was batman to Brigadier Jenkins who was seconded to the divisional planning team from the Royal Artillery to advise, appropriately enough, on artillery tactics. The Brigadier was addicted to coffee and so Chalky needed to be close on hand to satisfy this and was therefore allocated a room close to the kitchen, from whence the coffee came, and I bunked in with him. Handy for me as well even though in addition to kitchen detail I sometimes waited at table and served behind the bar.

As I have alluded to, most of the other ranks at Division were an unlikable mob but with Chalky we soon became good friends, which was fortunate since we lived in close proximity to each other. I hazard that our room had been a potato store. There was a small window, six feet above floor level, which fortunately did not allow sufficient daylight to reveal the rough state of the concrete walls and floor although Chalky had acquired a scrap of carpet to place his feet upon when getting out of bed.

"I see by your cap badge you're from the so called Glorious Gloucesters. Must say you don't look very glorious."

"And you, I suppose, are of the Royal Regiment of Batmen."

"Cheeky bugger. Your bed space is over there. Keep it tidy, and no farting."

"You can talk. You wait until you try my cabbage soup."

"Not likely."

"Anyway, where you from?"

"East Ham mate. Good footer team."

"I thought that was West Ham. I prefer cricket. How long you bin in?"

"Since the end of 1916. Flat feet, so got job as batman, but don't know whose worse, my Brigadier or the Bôche. See, at it again. Shouting for his coffee. When I get back to bleeding Blighty I shall never make another cup of coffee as long as I live."

Everyone at headquarters worked long hours. The next offensive was very important at this stage in the war and the brass wished to get it right, not something they were very used to. Nevertheless, in the interest of good morale, all of the staff in the mess were excused work for half a day every seven-day week and on my first one of these I was taken on an excursion by Lance Corporal Bernard Stanley (Chalky) White. The object of our little outing was for his room mate to be deprived of his virginity.

When Chalky had discerned my innocence in this department — was it so obvious — he did not tease me; he simply took me by the hand and delivered me into those of

Clarice. It was not exactly a brothel. In the nearby village the only café still operating, Très Roget, had some ramshackle rooms at the back where Clarice and her younger sister entertained those of the British soldiery whom they found acceptable, and who could afford the modest rates they charged. Chalky led me to believe that he was a particular favourite, but then these ladies probably had their preferred clients when the front line moved and the German army had been in occupation.

I had only been in France for ten days, and this was the first time I had been to the village. It was not a pretty sight. The damage to be seen had been inflicted successively by our forces, and then the Germans, depending on whoever was 'king of the castle' at the time of this sad portion of French soil. There was still some minor evidence that the streets had once been paved and level but they were now so rutted and pitted that the pools of water they hosted needed to be avoided at all costs. If not, the unwary would have found themselves up to their waist in a cold brown liquid which, when disturbed, gave off a more noxious stench than the pungent one emitted in their stagnant state. It was winter, and it was dark, but the pale moon was just sufficient to recreate the ruined buildings as a line of abstract monsters bearing down on us with sightless eyes, represented by the vacant windows, and a jagged Mohican style hairline by the haphazardly destroyed upper floors. This image, which the insignificant moon just managed to light up, did not presage a romantic evening and so I suggested to Chalky that we return to our cubby-hole; but he persuaded me of the delights in store, and on we went.

Our first port of call was the café itself. There was a small scattering of soldiers — none I recognised — wrapped in their greatcoats and intent on consuming the maximum quantity of the only alcohol on offer, a red wine as coarse as sandpaper. There were a sufficient number of customers to generate a certain amount of body heat, thank goodness, because the Très Roget did not appear to have any alternative source of power to raise the temperature; although they did manage to boil some of the noxious brew for those who preferred their poison to be above room heat.

I was as inexperienced in the consumption of liquor as I was in affairs of the heart, or the loins. The somewhat insipid mild ale served at the Lower George could not have prepared me for what was now on offer, plus the fact that I was cold and apprehensive. I therefore consumed that dreadful vinous liquid at twice the rate of Chalky with the result that as we moved to the rear of the establishment, I needed him as a crutch to make the journey. He spoke little French but I understood both sides of the conversation that followed.

"Here we are again. Full of fun. Brought you some fags. I'm off to see your sister, my little rosebud, but here is a special one for you."

"Come in you bastards. *Mon dieu*. They get younger. Looks like a schoolboy. Skinny too. I thought we might be getting a night off. Those in the bar are all drunk, and so is this one by the look of it, but I suppose if he can't stand-up, he can lie down."

"Look after him. He's new. Be gentle. He's got the price in his pocket."

"Bugger off you cocky devil. Leave him to me. He got any money?"

"Have fun Percy. See you in a bit. But don't be too quick."

"I've told you, scram. Looks ill. Better hurry up."

The only claim to fame of one of the boys at school, he was not a member of the cricket team, was a small collection of picture postcards that he had found amongst the possessions of his father, who had been a merchant seaman. One of them was of a black woman, known as the Hottentot Venus, who had the most enormous buttocks. I am not suggesting Clarice's measured up to that phenomenon, but she was certainly larger, in proportion, below the waist than above. This was not immediately pronounced as the room was dimly lit and my hostess was fully clothed. As I handed over the prescribed entrance fee, based on Chalky's instructions, she gave me a kiss on the cheek and then commented again on my obvious adolescence and puny frame.

She was not aware of my mastery of the French language but on this occasion such ability was of little use as her scathing remarks did nothing to bolster my waning confidence, even as the state of inebriation moved up from my weakened legs to my fevered brow. Muttering further derogatory observations about soldiers in general, she undressed and the Venus promontory was revealed in its full glory. For a moment she reminded me of one of those dolls that roll back upright when pushed over. I had not had an unfettered view of Miss Rosen's breasts, but she was, I am certain, a clear winner as to shape and size compared those of Clarice. The French lady's were not pendulous, you might even say pert, but from thereon, looking downwards, the frame became wider and wider. Her belly did droop but not sufficient to hide the pitch black shock of hair between her legs. I use the word shock in two senses; abundance and surprise. Are all women so adorned?

She could not help notice the keen interest I was displaying as this body was unfolded to my gaze but the interest, for the moment, was only in the eyes; it was not replicated lower down. She smiled at me, kissed me again on the cheek — lips were evidently verboten — and began to take off my clothes.

Even now I am hardly prepared to reveal in detail what happened next. I gave Chalky a vivid account of my resounding victory but in truth it was a sorry affair that I have attempted to expunge from my memory. In view of my inexperience, Clarice determined that I should be positioned closest to the ceiling, but I fell off. She was so round. It was like trying to stay relatively horizontal on a huge medicine ball. When we changed positions I could not breathe. She was very heavy and she appeared to delight in projecting her body force in the same direction as gravity, to enhance my discomfort. Then I was sick into the bucket she kept under the bed. This receptacle appeared to contain evidence of a former user, which did not add to my composure. I suppose, as a result of

*Alan Shelley*

some adroit manoeuvrings by the lady, I did lose my innocence in that awful room, but what I am sure of, it was hardly a night of careless rapture.

Chalky managed to support me back to the mess sufficiently well to avoid those pits of water in the village street. Some now had a coating of ice. The wine did not improve my view of the landscape but for a moment my brain cleared and I saw this devastated village for what it was; a piece of France, fought over by opposing forces for little gain, that had been the homes, the birthplace, the heritage of ordinary French workers; farmers, tailors, butchers — even bakers like me. These ruminations sobered me up for a moment and I instinctively realised I was growing up fast, but Chalky brought me back to earth as he talked about a return visit arranged for the next week. Thankfully, the Germans intervened.

On the 16th of November 1917, the seventy-six year-old Georges Clemenceau was appointed the Prime Minister of France — for the second time — and four days later the campaign to take Cambrai began. Most of the Headquarter officers I fed and waited on were planning this offensive which was going to be the 'Grand Victory'. For the first time ever the main thrust against the enemy was to be by tanks, over three hundred of them, supported by a thousand guns and three hundred aircraft. Even so, the city was never taken and by the 3rd of December all gains made by the allies had been recovered by the Germans. On a six mile front, a quarter of a million of us faced an equal number of the Hun and at the end of the campaign there were, on our side, over forty thousand British and Canadian soldiers dead.

At Headquarters we had been warned that our services might be needed at the front line but there was still some surprise that rather than an orderly movement to join our fighting brethren as they advanced against the Bôche, we found the German infantry moving on us as they counter-attacked. We were therefore drafted into active service to help oppose this attack — rather earlier than expected — and before dawn we were mustered outside the Chateau offices that housed the planning team. Planning was now of little moment as this odd assortment of cooks, clerks, batmen and signallers were taken into action led by the supposed intelligentsia amongst the officer corps. Was I exhilarated, or just plain frightened? To be honest with myself I really think it was a mixture of both although I was soon to have the question decisively answered.

Sergeant Taffy Roberts, seconded from the Welsh Fusiliers and chief clerk of the HQ office staff, was in charge of the platoon I found myself a member of. I had only been in France for a few weeks and I hardly knew well any of my fellow combatants, or our leader. In civvy street Sergeant Roberts had been a clerk with the Great Western Railways and I thought it showed. He was obsessively neat and tidy. Even at this hastily convened assembly his boots shone in the early morning light like buns covered in a rich dark chocolate icing — and he appeared to have found time to shave his pale cheeks. He stood no more than five feet two inches and could not have weighed too much more than the .303 Lee Enfield rifle he carried. We were all similarly armed although most of us had in the past only pulled a trigger when on the range during training. Despite his lack of inches — and pounds — he was clearly a good leader because when this motley crew was ordered to move down the road towards the advancing enemy, he seemed to have installed some spirit into me and the others and we marched briskly on, altogether — and initially in step

We had been listening to shellfire for some days not knowing whether it was friend or foe but twenty minutes after leaving camp a shell, that I assumed was one of theirs, landed in the field next to the road we traversed and although no one was hurt we were immediately streaked in a cold khaki coloured mud that had been dispersed by the explosion. It matched our uniforms perfectly. It was cold, it was November, and there had been a recent fall of snow, now partially melted.

*Alan Shelley*

As the ringing in our ears eased, machine-gun fire was heard and we were ordered off the road. Taffy led us over the ditch into the crater made by the shell and we lined up on the edge of this scar on the landscape and peered eastwards. Someone had ordered up smoke, from which side I had no idea, but it was believed that the advancing Germans would be using gas and our intrepid sergeant quickly ordered masks to be donned.

Even we unskilled backroom stragglers were aware of the horrors of gas attacks — and when at Etaples I saw sufficient examples of the devastating wounds resulting there from to justify our apprehension. The French introduced a fairly innocuous tear-gas grenade at the start of the war but it made a more potent appearance in Ypres in 1915 when French troops saw a grey-green cloud approaching their positions. This was chlorine gas. It was only fatal if the attacked were exposed to high concentrations, but its irritant effect could be very painful. We had been taught during basic training that if there was any danger of chlorine gas about, and we had no masks, cloth soaked in our own urine and held over the mouth was an effective counter measure. When so informed, I vowed to make sure I always had access to a mask

The mad scientists inevitably came up with a more effective killing agent. At school I was not fond of science, an antipathy that was only reinforced on the Western front and particularly after my hospital experience. Phosgene came next; more deadly, but by that time the improved gas masks provided an effective counter. The most notorious was Mustard gas, first used by the Germans at the third Battle of Ypres in July 1917. Chalky had been there. He told us, in graphic detail, how it had been fired at our positions in artillery shells filled with an oily liquid that resembled thick yellow pus, to use Chalky's words, which settled on the ground and remained deadly for days, if not weeks. If you got too close it could result in the most excruciating of pains. Chalky told of blistered skins and sore eyes but later I was to discover that it could cause internal bleeding and strip away the mucus membrane of the bronchial tubes. As I was to observe at Etaples, if it was a really bad attack, the victims needed to be strapped to their beds for the four or five weeks it took them to die.

With my mask firmly in place I squinted through the haze in front of me but as I leaned forward to get a better view I became conscious that we were being fired upon. I jerked my head down below the rim of our hideout with such vigour that my helmet fell backwards and clattered against the rifle of my neighbour. Taffy swore — at least I think they were blasphemies — in Welsh and then, reverting to my tongue, he told me in no uncertain terms to: 'get a hold of myself.' The smoke cleared so we could now observe the enemy had gone to ground about three hundred yards from us. Unfortunately they had a machine-gun — an item not included in our armoury.

What was my state of mind at that moment? I was scared. I was shaking all over. It was not just a tremble; more like the dance associated with St Vitus. No wonder I had lost my helmet. It was clear we were all going to be killed, very soon. I think it was this fearful thought, and that something in my nature that means I have never been one to sit and wait for events to happen, that when our sergeant called for volunteers to try and get behind the German machine gun, I was away.

Try to picture the scene. It is cold. A light rain is falling. The sky is a dark grey and here am I, a young man of township upbringing and habits. The nearest I usually got to the countryside was the cricket arena and as to any experience crawling across a muddy field imitating a snake with the minimum part of my body exposed above the ground, forget it. Our traverse, there were four of us altogether, was made while Taffy and his motley crew directed their rifle fire at the German position as rapidly as possible. Amazingly we reached, without detection, a small crop of fairly dense bushes on a line with the machine-gun post. At this point we realised, from viewing the terrain on the other side of our refuge, further progress was going to be more difficult than our journey to date but when I explored the landscape more closely there did seem to be a sort of field drain — or what was left of it — that might provide some secrecy along the line between us and the gun emplacement. At this point the arrogance of youth took over as I signalled to my companions to lay low and indicated, by detaching from my belt the one grenade I had, that I intended to use the drain to get within throwing distance. Although I had been given limited training in the tossing of hand grenades, my returns from third man were reckoned to be rocket-like. I therefore thought that I ought to be able to get within throwing range, rather than lobbing distance, without too much trouble. How wrong can you be?

The drain petered out long before I had hoped but having gone that far I had to do something. I pulled out the pin, counted to five and stood up. It needed to be an accurate throw, middle stump at the very least. I drew back my arm, thought of the Gloucester parks in the summer sunshine, and as the grenade left my hand my right foot slipped down the side of that accursed drain so that my long throw deposited the grenade in a line of 45° from me and well behind the target. I followed my right leg into the mud beneath the field's surface, cursing and fuming, just as my ears were assailed by a loud explosion. From somewhere a British gunner had miscalculated the range resulting in a chance bull's-eye on the machine-gun stronghold my grenade was intended for. I looked over the rim of the drain, wiped the mud from my wet eyes, and shouted: 'Howzat'.

Obviously Taffy was on the ball and I could see him and the others moving rapidly towards the shattered German position. I then realised that there was a pain in my left elbow. My position at deep mid-wicket had clearly been observed by at least one German rifleman who had hit my non-throwing arm just after release. I could now see the blood. It seemed that as I had begun to fall, I had thrown my left arm skywards in an abortive attempt to retain my balance. I did not of course succeed but the German sniper was able to pinpoint my left elbow with an accurate bullet — and the wound was now issuing forth a copious stream of blood.

My companions on this futile mission were now by my side.

"Bugger me Perc. You ain't going to be pulling many pints with that arm — but serves you right, you crazy bastard."
Little did they know of the accuracy of that last statement — although I might question the use of the word, 'crazy'?

"Looks like the bullet went straight through. Quick, let's get your tunic off, we must stem the blood."

I think our lovely Welsh sergeant appeared about then. I was feeling faint. One of his motley crew had worked as an assistant to the doctor attached to the mess and so he was called into action. Because we were not a regular fighting unit we were not accompanied by the usual medical back-up team, but thanks to the fact that the German counter-attack was fizzling out, and our lot were told to hold their position, I was moved back to an aid station in a remarkably short space of time. That was the good news. The ill-tidings were introduced when one of the medical orderlies told me, with some gravity in his voice, that my injury was rather more serious than a flesh wound. Until then I had hardly had time to consider what I had done, and the possible consequences of my action, but now I became really apprehensive. Was an amputation in prospect? Gangrene — or was I just going to die? Perhaps I do tend towards over-dramatisation sometimes, but consider. The pain is getting much worse; I feel I have a high fever, I am scared and I am cold — and I certainly have a very well developed imagination. I try to focus this in another direction.

Jacko, the medical assistant, also worked for the Chaplain attached to the mess and so, to think through the pain, let me tell you about that particular man of God.

I had grown up in the shadow of one of the Anglican religion's most famous landmarks, Gloucester Cathedral, but within the account I have given to date there has been no reference to the place of organised religion within the lives of the Smith and Whitwell families, or that of the Glossops. Clarence's parents were sporadic in their church attendance but when he married Alice, the ceremony took place in the Parish Church of St Peter at Newnham on Severn. Alice may have thought that Mrs Truelove had delusions of grandeur because her brother was a curate but in point of fact most of the inhabitants of that small county town considered themselves members of the Church of England, including Sir Luke Thatcher who was afforded pride of place in the family pew. When they moved to the city, Alice, in a quest to make a completely clean break, began to attend the closest Methodist Church to the shop and in his youth Thomas was a regular at the Sunday school. Very appropriate as the founder of the Sunday School movement, Robert Raikes the Younger, was a Gloucester man. Alice often wondered whether the trips they arranged to Weston-super-Mare, that Thomas enjoyed so much, had begun his wanderlust.

My grandparents were married at the St Mary de Lode Church in Gloucester, where they were, more often than not, in the congregation at Christmas and Easter. They lived their lives according to Christian precepts but a formal Christianity was not part of their everyday routine and their children were raised in the same *laissez-faire* atmosphere. Some deal must have been struck to enable me to be baptised in the church where my grandparents were joined together in holy matrimony but I spent most of my youth surrounded by exemplars of the Catholic faith. This of course stemmed from Francois. My mother never converted, but she and her Frenchman were married at the local Catholic church, St Peters, and she had no strong feelings about Marianne and Herbert being brought up within their father's faith — but it was too late for me. Presumably Francois accepted this — much to the chagrin of Father Donaghue, who often visited the Gloucester Chambords

My agnosticism, whether created by circumstances or from my genes — the chapel-going Welshman and my free-thinking mother — meant that I could scrutinise the Chaplaincy within the army with what I liked to think was a detached, but open-minded view. During basic training I attended the compulsory church parades — everyone did except for a handful of Jewish recruits — but in France, Captain the Rev Thomas Grantley was a member of the mess and he took a keen interest in all of the raggle-taggle bunch of strays that constituted the rank and file of this Reserve unit. I liked him. Whenever I was acting as wine waiter, and he accepted a third glass, he would reproach me with a smile on his face and call me: 'an imp of Satan'. Without his white collar he would still be recognized as a man of the cloth; his rubicund cheeks were the most notable give-away. I always thought he had the appearance of a man of Trollope rather than Dickens, but do not let me deceive; he knew what the wider flock in the trenches — or following the tanks as they tried to move towards Cambrai — were facing and during his visits to the front I am sure he brought as much comfort as words can possibly supply. I enjoyed him and I admired him. At drinks before dinner he cradled his glass of gin between what was left of his left arm and his chest so as to leave his right hand free for a cigarette — or a spirited wave: 'how'd you do'. He had left the absent arm at a casualty field base during one of the Battles of the Somme.

    I went to see him one day just before the Cambrai offensive began. He was liberal in the time he gave to other ranks and encouraged anyone with problems to seek him out. Mine was not complicated. I had no previous battle experience that might have spawned the symptoms of shell shock. I had no wife or sweetheart who had written to say they had found another and I was not in a funk about the possibility of going into action. Not then anyway. What I was deeply concerned about however was something I felt I could not discuss with anyone else — or perhaps even admit to myself? In a nutshell; I was ashamed that even at this early juncture in my military career I felt guilty that, for the present, I slept each night between crisp white sheets while nearly all of the other members of my regiment were spending two weeks out of every six with a mud pillow and a greatcoat as a blanket. The nearest they got to the colour white was when the snow fell.

I overstate the case of course. My sheets were more grey than white and were only laundered occasionally but you can appreciate why I could not discuss with this with my colleagues working in the mess, or other members of the reserve battalion. However, when I raised this with Captain Grantley he understood my dilemma immediately. You, my patient reader, will have dismissed all of this to be of no matter. Count your lucky stars, I hear you saying, but whatever, I had this niggle and although I never lost it, the Chaplain helped considerably.

"God works his will in mysterious ways and if you are destined for a non- combatant role, he approves."

"I'm sorry Sir, but is that not rather a platitude? Does he also approve of this useless slaughter?"

"Glossop, if I could give you an acceptable answer to that question I wouldn't be here in France. I would be supervising the See of Canterbury or delivering my Easter message at St Peter's in Rome. What I do know is that faith does help and it can help you reconcile yourself into accepting who you are — and where you are. We all have our place you know."

"But what is mine, Sir? What real contribution am I making?"

"I suggest you wait and see. You are very young. Who knows what your position will be in the pageantry of future humankind. Certainly your culinary skills are going to be a worthwhile contributor, never mind where your life leads you. Take what it offers, and live it to the full."

For the rest of my life I remembered him. Perhaps it was just a commonsense, home-spun philosophy, but how right he was. I have taken what was on offer and believe I have lived it to the full.

But back to France, and my medical odyssey. By the time I joined the ranks of the wounded, medical services for battle casualties had become more and more efficient, despite the ever increasing patient list. The British Army had entered the war in 1914 with the knowledge that treating the wounded during the Boer war had been less than proficient; more soldiers died from typhoid than combat wounds. In normal circumstances we would have had a Regimental Medical Officer at the front line with us, but as we were not part of a regular military unit, the aid post provided was not really up to standard. It was therefore decided to send me back to the nearest Casualty Clearing Station as soon as possible. The makeshift aid post had cleaned the wound and cut away that part of my flesh that was already nearly detached from its neighbour. It was a gaping injury that would need some more technical surgery than they could provide, but they had effectively stemmed the bleeding. They had also raised my body temperature with extra blankets and lots of hot, strong and sweet tea. The ditch that had become my temporary abode after my infamous action was well below freezing point and very damp. I was also given a tetanus injection.

At the Clearing Station they confirmed that during its passage into my elbow the bullet had taken away a lump of my flesh and a fair chunk of bone. The medical opinion was that I was lucky the bullet had not stayed embedded in my arm, and that once properly cleaned and dressed there was no cause for concern. However, that initial view proved to be over-optimistic and within twenty four hours the flesh around the elbow joint changed in colour from a quiescent pink to a violent green. Perhaps the first clean-up had been less than efficient and septicaemia had begun its deadly work. It was because of this I was transferred to Etaples and quickly found myself in one of the minor operating theatres where the diseased flesh, and some bone, was removed before I was encased in a plaster soaked bandage.

I was never told how close I came to losing my arm but it was several years before I discovered for certain that as a result of the Battle for Cambrai, I had one arm shorter than the other. I had suspected this fact for some time but it was not until I had moved up in the world and was to be measured for my first tailored suit that this was confirmed. Before then, the left sleeve of my jacket or shirt seemed to obscure my wrist watch when I wanted to steal a surreptitious glance during a long church service, or a boring concert, and so I had taken to wearing it at my right hand. Additionally, I found it more difficult during my sporadic cricket career to keep my left elbow down the pitch and as a result I found myself, more often than not, demoted from number nine to number eleven.

## Etaples

If I felt some guilt about wearing an apron in the officer's mess and not ammunition pouches in the trenches, I experienced even more qualms when I compared my injury with the other wounded I found at Etaples. Before the war this small fishing port, about a dozen miles from Boulogne, had been home to a population of around five thousand. By 1917 it was a vast military camp and hospital that at some stages housed nearly one hundred times that number. When I had arrived in France, only a few weeks ago, I had been sent direct to Divisional Headquarters but many of the new recruits, or those returning from leave or going on leave, were funnelled through this extraordinary establishment. I met very few of these; my companions were the wounded who were there to be treated, or to spend time recovering from their wounds, or were en-route to the UK for further attention. The Etaples I experienced was virtually a hospital city. The Royal Army Medical Corps were of course very much in evidence but there were hundreds of support staff from the ranks of the Queen Alexandria's Imperial Military Nursing Service, the Voluntary Aid Detachment (VAD's), other nursing units and hundreds of minions, mostly locals, who cleaned, cooked and laundered for the thousands of the sick.

*I Never Met Ernest Hemingway*

It was a mammoth enterprise. Imagine the logistics involved in caring for the multitude of broken bodies that flowed from the fighting lines in a torrent like the Severn at the time of the full bore. There needed to be highly qualified surgeons dealing with traumas rarely encountered other than in wartime, and this was one of the most punitive of wars mankind had ever experienced. New ways of inflicting injuries were being introduced and as the death toll rose, the surgeons had to keep pace with the armament inventors to try and rescue those not already dead. At the other end of the scale was the person who, before burial, washed the remains of the men who had not survived. In addition to doctors, nursing staff and pharmacists there were cooks and there were clerks; there were cleaners, who tried to keep infection at bay, and there were carpenters who repaired the temporary hospital buildings we occupied. I assume there were also gravediggers.

I will never forget Etaples. I was not there long but, as I think back, it epitomised for me, most poignantly, the utter futility of all wars, all armed conflicts. I saw some minor action in Spain. One of our chaps avoided the blade of a Nationalist bayonet and then incapacitated his foe with a blow to the head from his rifle butt. As the battle moved on, our ambulance units raised up the fallen man and administered first aid. Futile. Knock them down, and then pick them up. I appreciate Etaples was not like that. This was a massive establishment set up to cure our own troops, although there were a few German patients, so that at least some of them could go back and batter some more Boche about the head. Too simplistic? Perhaps, but if we were not trying to kill the Germans, and they us, there would not be a need for a hospital where hundreds of surgeons strove to keep men alive; where hundreds of nurses tended our wounds and where thousands upon thousands simply died. I can hear your response to my ramblings. We have to defend our country against the enemy but is that what we were really doing on French soil. I thought about the tragedy of the village where Clarice plied her trade and of me shouting

*Alan Shelley*

'Howzat' in joy because a dozen men of that German machine-gun section had been blown to pieces. It made no sense to me, anymore than it did to Peter Southern.

By this stage of the war the hospital was, in the circumstances, very well organised. Good order generally prevailed but I think someone overlooked me. The reason I had been sent to Etaples was genuine enough. Some medico had thought the early deterioration in the flesh around my wound might lead to an amputation but it was due to the rapid and superior treatment I received at that seaside city that prevented this. But I was still there. Perhaps someone thought there might be a relapse and I needed to be kept under observation but when nothing happened, after I had been there two weeks, I really thought I had been forgotten. Alternatively, perhaps the authorities knew best and I am downplaying the extent of my injury, but even so I could hardly believe my good fortune to be away from that horrible Mess Sergeant for as long as I did. At the same time there was another positive from my somewhat extended visit to Etaples in that it gave me the opportunity to observe for myself, in specific individuals, examples of the horrors resulting from this meaningless conflict — as I saw it.

During my first few days there I quickly became acquainted with my two bed neighbours. On the port side was Clive Bettany and on the starboard, Peter Southern. There was no discourse with the former. The section of the hospital that dealt with injuries caused by gas attacks was overcrowded and so a place had been found for Bettany next to me. He could see me and I could see him, in fact I never saw his eyes closed, but the blisters around the mouth made speech impossible. He was soon to die. I say he could not talk, but he could register audibly the pain he suffered. Not very audible; a low constant and insistent whine like the sound emitted from a very small kettle as it comes to the boil. When I awoke on the third morning of my hospital stay, the kettle had boiled dry and the bed he had occupied was empty; stripped down waiting for the next occupant.

The constant noise that he made kept me awake for the first twenty four hours, but after that, I am ashamed to say, I slept through his strangulated cries of pain. He had been at the Western Front since 1915. He was a corporal in the Sherwood Foresters and had survived the battles of the Somme and the third Ypres. I say survive, which I suppose is correct, but he was no stranger to the hospital at Etaples. After Passchendaele he had spent several weeks there while the surgeons removed some dozens of fragments of shrapnel from his back and buttocks — including one serious piece of metal lodged within a quarter of an inch of his spinal cord. But for that quarter of an inch he would have been paralysed — and there must have been some doubt that, with such a damaged spine, he would have survived the evacuation from the battlefield. Anyway, Etaples patched him up and sent him back to fight but this time he seemed to have drawn the Ace of Spades.

His platoon had been part of the 51st Highland Division that, after fierce fighting, had taken Flesquières on the way to the important objective of the heights of the Bourlon Ridge. The Ridge was never taken. There had been a sporadic campaign of gas attacks by the Germans during this offensive and for reasons I was never to discover, Clive Bettany had been at the epicentre of one of those attacks and as a consequence he now lay in the next bed to mine. I was to remember Flesquières the following year when in March 1918 the Germans saturated that area with mustard gas — not as part of an attack but as a preliminary to an offensive. They planned that this silent weapon would lead to a withdrawal of our forces without having to fire a single bullet.

The First World War had many terrible tales to tell but for me, and probably most other servicemen, the use of gas was the most horrible. I was to live to see pictures of the use of flame-throwers but in my war, gas was viewed as the most diabolical of all weapons. Silent, and if you did not have your gas mask on, deadly.

It was difficult to determine what visage Clive had enjoyed before the injuries inflicted by this awful scourge. As I have said, his never-closing eyes were visible but the nose and mouth was so deformed with blisters and sores they resembled a badly burned omelette. His left cheek was unscathed and showed several days growth of whiskers but on the right side the flesh was burnt away and the surface concave. The flesh that remained was stained to a colour midway between grass green and bright yellow. There was no visible evidence that he had a right ear. The head was the only part of the body visible for inspection. His torso, his arms and his legs were swathed in bandages that were changed, behind a screen, twice a day. That screen was the indicator that this was taking place, but even if I had my eyes closed I was made aware of the fact by a perceptible increase in that pitiable whine. The extra agony he endured while the dressings were changed injected into this unfortunate man sufficient lung-power to increase that sound of pain by a decibel or two.

It is not possible to know the hurt he suffered. I had experience of the sharp pain arising from burning my fingers on a baking oven — or from a splash of hot fat while frying sausages — but this man had severe burns to more than 90% of his body. There was no relief. He was given morphine but this only cut the anguish for a short time. His dressings were changed because that was the accepted procedure, and perhaps this gave some short-term respite, but I wondered if this was for the best from the patient's point of view. There did not seem to me to be any reason to worry about infection setting in. Death had priority.

I knew of him for only three days and so why do I spend relatively more words describing him and his sorry state than I have in drawing for the reader a picture of Sergeant Taffy Williams or Jacko, the platoon medical attendant? How could I do otherwise? Bettany epitomised the awful individual outcome of this tragedy. Statistics tell us that there were over forty thousand causalities on each side during the battle to take Cambrai, but can anyone visualise what forty thousand dead and wounded men look like? For me, the real face of that number was represented by the man who lay in the bed next to mine.

My other neighbour came from a middle-class family. They owned a factory in Birmingham that before the war manufactured screws and nails but now bullets and shell casings. As I subsequently discovered, he was a contemporary of Siegfried Sassoon at Clare College and by the end of 1917 it was clear that they had other things in common besides an *alma mater*. After university, so he told me, he joined the family firm and at the start of the war, when he was twenty seven, he was excused from active duty because the authorities believed the important role he had in the supply of armaments was more valuable than being at the front line, firing his own products at the enemy. If I thought I had a problem reconciling my role as a minor chef with my companions in the trenches, spare a thought for this man. Not only was he safe and sound in Birmingham, adding value to the family firm, but the handsome profits earned were at the expense of the sorrow experienced by millions of German mothers whose sons were dispatched from this life by a bullet, or a shell, that had begun its existence in the workshops and forges of W. Southern and Sons (Birmingham) Ltd. When I became acquainted with the play, I could see some parallels in Shaw's *Major Barbara* and Peter's position.

Peter Southern was a sensitive man, and there was only one solution to this dilemma. He obeyed his father for over two years but eventually, in 1916, he joined the Warwickshire Regiment. In view of the conflict in his breast he felt that as he had sat on the fence since 1914, he should now place himself as close as possible to experience the ammunition manufactured in a factory like his in Hanover or Hamburg. He therefore refused to accept the commission he was offered even though as a subaltern he was just as likely to feel the effect of a German bullet as an ordinary soldier. Nevertheless, by the time I met him he did carry three stripes on the sleeve of his tunic, although only one set; there was only one sleeve. He had lost most of his left arm at the Battle of the Somme although to be accurate, it was there that the wound was inflicted, the amputation took place at the Etaples base. He had refused repatriation and so had been found a position as a senior member of a signals unit attached, before the push towards Cambrai, to one of the Reserve divisions.

During the counter attack that provided the scenario for my first and only taste of combat, Southern had been with his unit of signallers when most of his crew had been killed by two shells that had exploded, one immediately after the other, in close proximity to their location. The only damage suffered by the one-armed Sergeant was a shell fragment that had pierced his cranium and was still there, in close proximity to his brain. He was back at Etaples for medical experts to decide whether this intrusion into his skull should be removed and if so, whether the operation could take place in France or he be shipped home. No decision had yet been made. Should they see if this man could continue to live with this piece of metal in his head or should they risk the possibility of bringing his life to a premature end by undertaking the dangerous operation to remove this fragment?

When the patient was away being examined once again by the surgical team, his personal history, and medical record, was recounted to me by Ida Scrutton, the Queen Alexandria's nurse in charge of the ward. Although she was at least ten years older than me I liked to think we became good friends, even if I did tease her a little. Her family ran a small private hotel in Brighton where she had helped on the catering side. Initially I felt her interest in me went only as deep as the number of confectionery recipes she could steal, but that proved to be an unfair assumption on my part. We had the kitchen in common but I think she must have been taken by my boyish charm. I still only needed to shave every other day, and the damage to my arm had not affected my adolescent rosy cheeks. Perhaps it was maternal? In point of fact I think she was equally nice to all the patients but I am allowed to believe that I was a favourite if I like. Using an expression I picked up some years later, our Florence Nightingale was no oil painting, but for most of the men she was first of all of the female sex, and secondly, a caring and efficient nurse.

On reflection, as I got stronger I was not really very nice to her. She was always so busy, and I should have been more solicitous. I was at my worst when she was changing the dressing on my elbow and could not just walk away and ignore my prattle.

"Well, nurse, do you have lots of boyfriends back home?"

"That's no affair of yours, young Glossop. You mind your tongue."

"I saw you without your hat yesterday. You've got lovely hair. Can I stroke it?"

"Cheek. I'll have to see if I can't get the doctor to give you something to calm you down."

"Oh come on. Just a little stroke."

"Time you were back in the trenches, you young blighter, and if I have any more sauce you'll be back to the front before you can say Jack Robinson."

"Ah, but I'm not a trench man. I'm too valuable. They need me to look after the brass — but going back to your boyfriends. If one of them throws you up, I've got a solution. You make a gingerbread-man — I'll give you the recipe — stick pins in it and then eat it. How about that."

"You're mad. I'll get Dr Murchison in to see you and get you sent to the loony bin — or shot at dawn. And keep still."

"Ouch, that hurt. You did it on purpose."

"Well, behave yourself."

"Okay. Tell me a bit more about the family hotel. What's the favourite dish on your menu, other than me that is?"

"I'll ignore that. We're very traditional but our rabbit pie is considered to be pretty good."

Alan Shelley

"I've come up with a twist on the usual Peach Melba. I'll write it out for you."

"Thanks. Nice to see you've calmed down."

"Not really. I'm still consumed with passion for you Nurse Scrutton. One little kiss."

"Away with you. I'll be glad to see the back of you. Go to sleep."

"With you?"

"Bah."

Talk about unsung heroes, or heroines in this case. Ida had two VADs and some orderlies to cover two wards with what must have been more than one hundred patients — and often more when in an emergency stretchers were placed on the floor between the beds. She must have seen such an overabundance of horror. I wonder how she remained so calm. She did say she found the gas-burn cases the worst. They needed so much attention and whatever the nursing staff did gave little comfort. Of course there were other terrible injuries but in our ward we did not see the main surgical cases, they were in a separate wing.

But back to Peter Southern. If my other neighbour was virtually mute, this one was eccentrically voluble. Ida explained that although the doctors could not accurately explain the scientific origin of his behaviour, all realised that the metal embedded in his head was dormant for some time and then triggered a reaction that resulted in Peter becoming a raving maniac. In his quiet period his humour was that of a gentle poet, and at the other end of the scale, he became a monster. It was as though that tiny piece of iron could, when it fancied, create a Frankenstein.

During his calm moments he talked, not about specific incidents in his army experience, but of the utter disgust he felt for the leaders of the supposedly civilised world that had allowed this conflict to begin, and to continue. He fully supported the stand of his Cambridge contemporary who had become one of the most famous pacifists of the time.

## I Never Met Ernest Hemingway

This was the first time I had met a man of his intellectual ability. Francois was well educated but Peter Southern was from a class that was new to me. My assessment, from within the narrow range of my experience, was that he represented the best of the English middle-class; enjoying a close relationship with his factory workers and eschewing the extremes of the iniquitous class system that was such a feature of British society. We had a love of literature in common even though the breadth of my reading was minute compared with his. He had read English at Cambridge. Where Mr Rogers had directed my footsteps along the well trodden path of the European and burgeoning American modern classics of fiction, my Etaples mentor widened the scope to include the real classics; Milton, who had escaped me until then, and some poets rather more modern than my schoolboy Wordsworth. When, years later, I was a resident of Paris I bought Peter a copy of Joyce's *Ulysses* from the Shakespeare & Co bookshop as recognition of the guidance, and friendship, he so generously gave to that callow, half-educated youth. I am indebted to the fates that gave me the opportunity of his acquaintance, however short it was, and however horrifying it was to see him in his Mr Hyde personality.

When the piece of shell touched a different nerve, or surface, or nodule of the brain, he would begin by snarling like a wolf and then moving, within minutes, to a scream that sounded like a gigantic piece of chalk being dragged vigorously over a sheet of glass or a school blackboard. One of the doctors had a pet Scotch terrier. When Peter was in full cry the poor animal would become demented and run around in circles trying to swallow its own tail. After this happened the first time, the owner kept the animal confined to his quarters until the fate of the screamer had been determined.

When this change from peace and tranquillity to manic-man first took place, no one in the ward was prepared. Thereafter, at the first hint that the metal trigger had been pulled, Ida, or one of the other staff members, moved into action swiftly. The

*Alan Shelley*

only procedure that was effective required the poor man to be restrained by a series of four leather straps, housed under his bed, that held him rigid while some form of gag was applied to lessen the horrifying sounds that burst from his mouth He suffered this awful transition for more than a week until the Chief Medical Officer decided that the danger of moving the patient back to the UK was too great and they would have to remove the metal, as best they could, in the limited operating theatres at the Etaples base.

Much to my amazement, and I believe that of everyone else involved, he survived. He was never brought back into his former ward but I did, a little while later, meet him during a concert that had been organised by, and for, the walking wounded. Although the metal fragment had been removed without any after-effects, he had been discharged from the army, which was all for the best, as it is doubtful, considering his state of mind, if he would have agreed to serve again, whatever the circumstances. Would such a refusal have led to a court martial or would he have been moved out of the public eye by a transfer to such a hospital as Craiglockhart, as was the case with Sassoon?

I do not know why Sergeant Southern chose me as a sounding board, but he did. Now that he had become an ardent pacifist he was more than mildly agitated on the subject of British soldiers who had been shot for desertion or cowardice. The possibility that one of his bullets had brought their lives to an end became a nightmare. He could no longer accept the slaughter he had witnessed — anymore than Sassoon and many other veterans. The poet's anti-war letter to his Commanding Officer entitled: 'A Soldier's Declaration' was sent to the press and debated in Parliament. However, because of who he was there was no court martial. He was declared unfit for service, due to shell shock, and not shot at dawn as some of those who invaded Peter's conscience.

# Colonel Kim

By the end of January I was back at the officers' mess. The doctors were satisfied that the wound to my left elbow was fully healed and as a result of a regular exercise routine the joint was working well; although I could not quite achieve an angle of 180°. I did so by the summer. And what a summer it turned out to be. I saw no more action but there was plenty of it about. By March, Russia was out of the war and with the force that was released from the Eastern front, the Germans were able to launch a massive attack in France and Belgium. This began on the 21st of March with the objective of taking Paris and reaching the Channel ports. They never made it, but by the middle of the year the front-line in some parts had been moved westwards more than thirty miles. The powers-that-be were clearly worried and I discovered in Paris that a number of the Allied leaders sitting around the table admitted they had been involved in planning campaigns for 1919.

    I kept a copy of Sir Douglas Haig's Special Order of the Day, dated the 11th of April.

> To all ranks of the British Army in France and Flanders.

Three weeks ago to-day, the enemy began his horrific attacks against us on a fifty-mile front. His objects are to separate us from the French, to take the Channel ports and destroy the British Army.

In spite of throwing already 106 Divisions into the battle and enduring the most reckless sacrifice of human life, he has as yet made little progress towards his goals.

We owe this to the determined fighting and self-sacrifice of our troops. Words fail me to express the admiration which I feel for the splendid resistance offered by all ranks of our Army under the most trying circumstances.

Many amongst us now are tired. To those I would say that Victory will belong to the side which holds out the longest.

Alan Shelley

The French Army is moving rapidly and in great force to our support.
There is no course open to us but to fight it out. Every position must be held to the last man: there must be no retirement. With our backs to the wall and believing in the justice of our cause each of us must fight on to the end. The safety of our homes and the Freedom of mankind alike depend upon the conduct of each one of us at this critical moment.

I later read that Vera Brittain thought this stirring message gave courage to many. Perhaps it did for those at the front but for me, I just thought about Peter Southern. He would have gained little comfort from it.

However, I am not in the business of writing a diatribe on war, or even a history of the conflict I was so marginally involved with; my need now is to introduce to you a man who was the first major signpost standing at the crossroads of my path through life. If I had not met Colonel Frederick James Kimball MC, would I have spent the remainder of my life baking cakes and other goodies for the fine people of Gloucester — and retiring, in due course, to Cheltenham Spa with a grandchild on each knee? This did not happen.

I never addressed him as such, but in my thoughts, and in this writing, I refer to him as Colonel Kim. It seemed natural to do so. He had spent most of his army service seeking intelligence for his official masters; not exactly a spy in the Kipling mode, but I always found there was an element of mystery about him. He was certainly different and he made a big difference to me; I was about to be translated from that prosaic officers' mess outside Arras to the splendours of Paris.

Colonel Kim, at six feet or so, was two inches taller than me and where I might just about qualify for the middleweight boxing division, he was at least cruiser-weight. As the fashion of the time dictated, the hair on his upper lip was profuse, if a little grey, but as to the pate, none at all. He joked that the African sun had burned it away but in truth he had begun to lose it during his twenties. His eyes were small, but they seemed to me to always be on duty. He did not miss much. His smile turned a somewhat plain visage into a pleasant one. That smile was usually in place, but the manoeuvres of some of his erstwhile colleagues in Paris brought about flashes of temper, although these were generally exhibited in private. He did not gladly tolerate fools or people who stood on their dignity — and there was a lot of that to be found around the conference tables in 1919 — but because he had a better brain than most of those he dealt with, he was normally diplomatic and calm.

It is not perhaps for me to say, but I believe that where the Allies made the right decisions about Africa, his hand in the matter was very evident. Although he was unhappy that the peace treaty ending the Boer war had not dealt with a future black franchise, I believe he was sympathetic to the South African cause — he certainly admired Jan Smuts — and felt they needed to be properly rewarded for their help in defeating the Hun. On the other hand, just as he had deplored Kitchener's actions against Boer civilians, he was horrified when the news was received of the massacre at Amritsar.

My experience of members of His Majesty's military forces was limited. The NCOs in basic training were there to do a particular job — to teach a disparate bunch of civilians the difference between the independence of their past and the absolute discipline of the future. Few skills were required for this task, certainly none of an intellectual nature — which could also be said for the group of mess servants I joined. This leaves the officers. I was never to serve under the archetypal brave subaltern, many of whom had a short life-span in this war, so I cannot comment on them. The officers I did have contact with were mostly more senior, members of the Staff who were planning operations, gathering intelligence or ensuring the efficient supply of army stores to the fighting troops. A fair proportion of these officers were regular soldiers who had made their way steadily through the officer ranks to Major and above without too much effort. Subject to an absence of serious aberrations — seducing the Colonel's wife, or his daughter, might be typical ones — they progressed inexorably, through the passage of time. This could be a slow process during peacetime — but more rapid now — until the red braid was acquired. There were one or two who had risen from the ranks but in the main they were instantly recognisable, by ear if not by eye, as members of the Edwardian upper-class. They came from families who dined together, spent weekends at the great country houses where they shot the partridge and hunted the fox together — and married their own kind. That was the way it had always been and initially I assumed Colonel Kim was from the same stable; but he was not.

He was born in London and served in the Boer War as a Second Lieutenant. Thereafter, and very unusually, he remained in Africa, or was concerned with Africa, in a variety of capacities before being transferred to the Western Front in 1916 with the rank of Captain. By the end of the war he was a forty four year-old Colonel.

The Kimball family had done business with India for generations but Frederick's father also became involved in trading with Africa, buying cocoa, palm oil and coffee in exchange for manufactured goods such as textiles and bicycles. Colonel Kim was a third son but even so it was a surprise to the family when, at the age of twelve, he tentatively suggested to his father that when he grew up he would like to be a soldier. Perhaps he had been inspired by the story coming back from Khartoum about the death of General Gordon but whatever, Kimball senior was not a man to sit on his hands. As soon as he was convinced that his son had serious intentions — or as serious as they could possibly be at that age — he made inquiries and as a result the boy was sent to Wellington School where nearly all of the pupil's ambitions matched his.

The transfer from Wellington to the Royal Military College at Sandhurst seemed automatic and seamless — to use his own words — and he then joined the Gloucestershire Regiment.

His first contact with the Dark Continent was when he served with them during the Boer War and then from the time the peace treaty was signed at Pretoria in 1902, until he arrived in France, Africa was his bailiwick.

After the Boer War, he served in the West African Frontier Force in Nigeria under Lord Lugard. Like so many countries of the Empire, Nigeria was founded on trade, as Colonel Kim was to discover. He related to me the story of how traders had been vitally important in the formation of the West African Frontier Force — and of the frontiers of Nigeria; the bringing together of a diverse fusion of people to form a new country in Africa that was named by Lugard's wife as Nigeria. The country and the West African Frontier Force — and Lugard himself — revolved around an extraordinary individual, one George Goldie Taubman: he soon dropped the Germanic Taubman and is known to history as George Goldie.

His family lived on the Isle of Man and had made a fortune from smuggling. George was the fourth son who went into the army, the Royal Engineers, but after two years gave up his commission and then lived for the next year or so in the deserts of the Sudan with a beautiful Egyptian woman. He tired of this but he was about to embark on another African adventure that had all sorts of consequences. He went to the River Niger.

His family bought a near-bankrupt firm that dealt with palm oil. George was put in charge and by 1879 he had amalgamated the family firm with others in the same trade under the banner of the National Africa Company. One of these companies was Miller Brothers of Glasgow with whom Colonel Kim's father co-operated for many years, to their mutual benefit. From this amalgamation emerged the Niger Company, later, the Royal Niger Company, that ruled most of Nigeria, as it was to become, on behalf of the Crown under a Royal Charter. In 1894, Goldie, now Sir George, took on Lugard — who had already made a name to himself as a soldier in Uganda — to expand, if possible, the Niger Company's trading areas. Before the end of the century the British Government had bought out the interests of the Royal Niger Company, and this led to the establishment of the West African Frontier Force and Lugard taking over from Goldie.

Frederick Dealtry Lugard, later Lord Lugard of Abinger, was to become the High Commissioner for the Protectorate of Northern Nigeria and in this role, by 1901, he governed an area of three hundred thousand square miles of Africa with a population of around twenty four million. This was controlled by a civilian staff of one hundred, backed by the West African Frontier Force that had between two and three thousand black soldiers and two hundred officers. Colonel Kim was one of those

When he left Nigeria at the end of 1907 he was delighted to be approached by the Colonial Office with a proposition. He was, at that stage, not enough of a political animal to know whether our future confrontation with Germany was foretold in Whitehall, but some wise men proved to be prescient when they decided to advance their intelligence of the African empire of that country. Colonel Kim did not speak German but he had been in Africa since the Boer War and his records would show that his father had an associate in Hamburg, who traded with Germanic Africa.

He was given a crash course in the language while Whitehall negotiated with Berlin that an invitation be issued for him to meet with their military men on African soil and exchange views on: 'The Training of Native Troops', or something along those lines. As a result, and except for a period as a junior lecturer at the Royal Military College, he was stationed in London and visiting Africa until he went back to Regimental duties in Nairobi in 1913.

The countries of the German African Empire, like those of Britain and France, were of recent origin — at least politically. They had been formed and acquired during the 'scramble for Africa' that had occurred around the 1880s and 1890s and as such were undeveloped, unsophisticated and largely unknown. European leaders may have seen them as adding prestige to their countries but on the ground what was of importance was trade — the export of raw materials and the import of goods manufactured in Manchester or Hanover or Marseilles. Colonel Kim found therefore that the expatriate trader was often more informed about what was happening in their countries than the government official, or his military counterpart, and as a result he used his father's contacts to some effect.

When as a major attached to GSO (I) at the 12th Division in France, he was able to bolster his antagonism — and that of some of his colleagues — against our German foe as a result of what he had seen of their conduct in their Colonies, particularly in South West Africa. After a rebellion by local people, the Germans had hunted them down like game, or assigned them to labour camps; an action that amounted to a death sentence. Seventy five per cent of the Nama and Herero tribes were killed, or had died in those camps, by the time he first visited the country. The scale of barbarism was of a lesser degree in Togo and the Cameroons, but in both territories local people were in many cases treated like animals. Flogging men to death was commonplace and there was even a report that in the Cameroons the military leader of an expedition shot all the men and women in a village and then the fifty four surviving children were put into baskets and drowned like kittens. And this was by a German officer who had been dispatched to negotiate a treaty.

When war broke out in 1914, the then Governor of Togo proposed to his counterparts in the adjoining countries, the British Gold Coast and French Dahomey, that Togo should be declared neutral territory so that the natives would not see the white man fighting each other. That would never do. Our supremacy depended on the assumption that we could not be harmed by the bullets the Germans had used to kill tens of thousands of Africans over recent decades. The Governor's suggestion was ignored with the result that the first shots in the

*Alan Shelley*

First World War were fired during the Anglo-French invasion of Togo — and the surrender on the 26th of August 1914 was recorded as the Allies first victory.

Colonel Kim was received with courtesy when ever he visited the centres of the German African Empire but, as he said, their methods of control and government appalled him. The British were not always benign but what he had seen of Lugard's methods left him in no doubt which form of rule was the more digestible. Nevertheless, the Colonial Office had been fore-sighted and when these colonies were discussed in the Paris of 1919, he was certainly better informed on the subject than our French colleagues.

He was undoubtedly the expert on German East Africa. Just before war broke out he was in Nairobi where he had been posted to strengthen the intelligence liaison between London and our minute forces in Kenya. As soon as war was declared, and with Whitehall's permission, he was seconded to the King's African Rifles. The euphoria of confidence at the beginning of hostilities with Germany, the 'all over by Christmas' syndrome, was matched in Nairobi and he joined in, relishing the prospect of some active service before it was all over; wielding the sword again rather than the pen. However, hopes of an immediate call to arms were quickly dashed when our Governor said we should not be concerned with the war, it was a European affair.

This of course proved to be a naive statement — World War One was not described as 'World' without reason. The fight with Germany and their allies spread across the globe but, to excuse the Kenyan Governor, he was well aware that we had too few troops to contemplate a serious campaign against the forces over the border in German East Africa. Initially the Germans made a similar decision but von Lettow-Vorbeck, the officer commanding the German army, thought otherwise and he was still leading us a merry dance when Colonel Kim left for the Western front in the summer of 1916 — and he continued to do so until the end of the war.

*I Never Met Ernest Hemingway*

I have gone to some lengths to describe his career to date because it did critically influence his role in Paris — and, tangentially, what happened to me, but to return to Arras. I had already finished making the puddings that would be eaten to celebrate the end of the war — and our Lord's birthday — when Colonel Kim appeared again in the mess having, so I was told, just returned from London. The next day he called me into his room.

"Well Glossop, thank God it's over. How's your elbow? I've never been able to decide whether you got shot while being brave or just plain stupid."

"Neither have I, Sir."

"No doubt the gossip has done the rounds and you will have heard that I have just returned from London."

"There has been some mention."

"Well, this is the your ears only for the moment, but I have been asked to be in the British team that is going to try and draw up the terms of the final treaty with the Hun — and who gets what all over the world, particularly in Africa, where my expertise lies. What would you think of coming with me, in some role or other? To help with the language and look after me generally? You seem to be a bright sort of chap and I'm told your French is a lot better than mine — and I do like those biscuits you make."

"But I'm going back to bake those biscuits in Gloucester — for my Mum."

"Well, think about it."

I did, for two minutes.

"Are you suggesting a job as a batman?"

"Yes, if you want to call it that. I think I can arrange a posting."

I thought for another two minutes while the soon-to-be delegate filled his pipe.

"Sir. I haven't been in the Army long, but my hankering to get as far away from the khaki, begging your pardon Sir, is just

*Alan Shelley*

as great as with the old sweats. But if I might be so bold, I'd love to take the job as a civilian, if you can swing it?"
He blew smoke in my face and replied:

"Okay, Glossop. I'll take you on as a personal aide. Won't be much pay but I suppose we'll both get free board and lodgings."

Looking back, it all seemed incredible. I was just twenty years of age and except for my army sojourn in France — and visits to Calais with François — I had hardly ever left the city of Gloucester, but Colonel Kim had his own way of doing things. Surely his eye had not lighted on me because of a concern for his stomach? Even at the end of that awful war the Paris cuisine satisfied those needs and no doubt the delegation would have a legion of translators — female at that and much prettier than me — even if my French was probably better than theirs. Did he really know why he wanted me around? Was it just instinct, or was he more foresighted than that? Needless to say, I did make some contribution to the work he did at the conference, in a number of ways, but for my part I could only bless Dame Fortune for the opportunity — and how it was to lead to my Paris adventures.

After leaving Paris, I kept in touch with this man who had such an influence on my life and at first we did meet just occasionally; for instance, he came to our wedding. Even so I was somewhat surprised when he wrote in 1932 with an interesting piece of news; he had recently married. I recalled his romantic history. There had been a local girl who had been killed in a riding accident while he was in South Africa during the Boer War but after that his peripatetic existence in Africa had rather limited the opportunities for female intercourse. I recall when we were in Paris that he was hoping to marry the widow of one of his colleagues who had been killed in 1917 in the push towards Cambrai. He had been the best man at their wedding but was never destined to return to a church with her in a capacity as groom; she died in January 1920, a casualty of the Spanish flu epidemic that swept throughout the world.

It was devastating — more American soldiers died from that disease than were killed in action. Colonel Kim was distraught and saw her death as an indication that he was destined to be a lifelong bachelor. I was so pleased he had finally found love. Her name was Helen.

When we first reached Paris, Colonel Kim told me it was my appearance at the Armistice concert that had finally determined him to offer me the job. He said it was not my talent as a mimic or a comic he was attracted to but the material I had used. He did not explain this but perhaps he saw a similarity with his own sense of humour, and of the absurd. For me of course it was a foretaste of my life to come; the written word and, to some extent, the stage?

The concert episode came about like this. Before Christmas 1918 it had been decided at the mess that at the dinner arranged to celebrate the armistice, both officers and other ranks would combine to present some form of entertainment after the food had been consumed, including my early Christmas puddings. One of the strange customs in the army is that the other ranks are served their Christmas lunch by the officers and NCOs but on this occasion in our mess it was decided that although we did all the cooking, the festive meal would be shared by all. I found myself sitting next to the senior medical man on site and I have to say I found him very boring. He needed some medical attention of his own. I could not believe that braying every two minutes like a mule in agony was natural. He must have had a polyp, or something nasty growing in his voice box.

Fortunately I escaped, as soon as I had tasted and admired my pudding, to become a member of the group of players — and a very odd group indeed. Peterson played *Lily Laguna* on the spoons; Captain Anderson gave us *The Charge of the Light Brigade* while, most extraordinarily, the Mess Sergeant found some women's clothing from somewhere and sang, *My tiny hand is frozen* in an unconvincing falsetto voice. I had been persuaded to do an imitation. I did seem to have a natural

*Alan Shelley*

talent for mimicry and would often entertain my fellow kitchen hands with representations of those members of the brass with the most distinctive accents. I was particularly accurate when copying the Welsh. Whether this was because of my genes, or because the Gloucester accent closely resembles the speech of the Principality, who knows, but I thought it might be amusing if I gave the audience the pleasure of the company of our own Commander-in-Chief, and one of the finest orators of the day, David Lloyd George. I was soon able to view him up close in Paris and when I did I thought my interpretation was not half bad.

I must, at this juncture, confess that my tasks within the mess were fairly light. Beyond the green baize door we were, in my opinion, overstaffed; an experience I was never to encounter again in any kitchen where I laboured. However, as a result I did have a fair amount of free time and certainly enough to be able to compose my Prime Minister's speech with some care. I have kept a copy.

The Major Quartermaster had a tailcoat — members of the Quartermaster stores can usually lay their hands on anything — and this, with a cushion under a white shirt, was as far as my costume went except for a liberal amount of false hair on the upper lip. Not awfully convincing, but I rather thought my words were a trifle more authentic.

My gallant soldiers and countrymen. I salute you.

You are an inspiration to all in the free world.

As the popular song goes: 'There's a long, long trail a winding…'

Well, it has been a long trail for us the victors, but we have prevailed.

We shall always prevail.

'O death where is thy sting? Oh grave, where is thy victory?' (Corinthians 1.55)

There have been too many graves, my brothers, but our cause has never been less than just and noble.

The Lord is on our side.
'He will swallow up death in victory; and the Lord God will wipe away tears from off all faces.' (Isaiah 25.8)
We have shed our tears. We have our victory.
The British soldier is the finest in the world.
Your valour will be rewarded.
I thank you from the bottom of my heart.
The valleys will echo with your praises.
We rejoice in our allies. The glorious citizens of France.

Pregnant pause to allow the audience to express an opinion.

The brave and courageous Americans.

Longer pause with some encouragement towards a scattering of jeers.

Gentlemen. I give you the toast. 'Peace in our time.'
And I shall of course look for your votes in due course. Goodnight and God bless.

I had thought of finishing off with a few verses of *Land of our Fathers* but was not sufficiently confident in my musical ability. I do however wish to acknowledge the help received from my friend the Chaplain in composing these words.
And now, it was off to 'Gay Paree'.

*Alan Shelley*

*I was lucky to be live in Brighton. I think people from seaside towns are happier than most. The sea air perhaps?*

*My two brothers had no choice. When they became eighteen they were required to join His Majesty's forces. Both went into the Navy — and survived. Brian was at sea, but Leslie never left Portsmouth. He was commissioned on entry and spent the war dealing with naval supplies. Brian's experience made up for his brother's lack of action. Jutland — but he came through unscathed. Over six thousand of his colleagues did not.*

*I did have a choice. I could have remained helping Mum and Dad with the hotel, but like many other young women at the time, I was anxious to help if I could. Initially the Red Cross trained me as an ambulance driver but with this under my belt I was able to negotiate a transfer to the Queen Alexandria's Imperial Military Nursing Service who provided nurse training. Raymond, my young man — we are not officially engaged — was wounded at the third Battle of Ypres. I say, wounded, I should be more medically professional. His right knee was shattered and there is, I'm told, a real risk of osteo-myelitis.*

*This made me even more anxious to be at the medical front line. Etaples was certainly that. During training I had seen some overcrowded hospitals but this was nearly beyond description. The whole set-up was an enormous military town, where soldiers were siphoned 'up to' and 'back from' the front line and the enormous hospital was part of that metropolis.*

*The burn victims caused me the most distress. Somehow, bullets and shells seemed to be legitimate weapons of war, but not gas. Most of the patients in the hospital had wounds inflicted by that hardware but if the gas victims were in the minority, we in the wards found them the most difficult to deal with. Many of them were going to die in a few days, or weeks. All we could do was to change their dressings as tenderly as we could but however careful, this operation was invariably accompanied by cries of anguish.*

*We had German patients as well, but I never served in that section.*

*There were some men being treated by the psychiatric team; men who could not stand the horrors any longer. They were grouped together under the cover-all heading of 'shell-shocked'. When he first arrived, the young man with ambitions to be a chef was nearly in need of psychiatric help. He put on a brave face but I could see he was terrified inside that if he lost his left arm his cooking days would probably be over. Fortunately, the surgeons were able to patch up his elbow; nearly back to good as new which, as you can imagine, cheered him up no end.*

*We were always busy. Sometimes, I was on my feet for one hundred hours a week but when there was a lull, young Glossop and I swapped recipes. He was really only into cakes and pastries but if he ever achieves his ambition, I'm sure he will thank me for the culinary tips I handed on. I think he was a bit sweet on me, but they all were. And not just me. After the horrors they had been through they appreciated any feminine presence. Seemed to me some of them were even prepared to 'bill and coo' at the Matron!*

*The budding chef was fortunate to have Sergeant Southern — I think that was his name — as a bed neighbour. Seemed his family business made armaments. When he had recovered from that head wound — a miracle Captain Blanche said: 'one of the most difficult pieces of surgery I have ever been involved in' was his remark — the sergeant, who had seen rather more service than most, could no longer reconcile himself to killing other men using his company's products. As a result he became a somewhat vociferous pacifist. Luckily he had been medically discharged but the authorities seemed to get him back to Birmingham, asap. I cannot believe he went back into the family firm — probably joined up with that Bertrand Russell and his lot.*

*Unlike most of the people back home, I saw at first hand the results of this war, the ravages on human flesh and*

Alan Shelley

*spirit, but what could we do? We were in it for reasons my brothers and I supported, even if we sometimes forgot what they were. And so we carried on and did our best. Having said that, I must confess that when I fell on my bed, too tired to undress, after twelve hours of 'doing my bit', I did sometimes send forth a few lady-like curses at those who had started it all. Thank goodness I am going on leave next week.*

      Ida Scrutton August 1918

# Chapter Three

## Paris

*Langue de Chat*

*Work together, in a bowl, nine ounces of fine sugar and half a pint of fresh cream. Add nine ounces of sieved flour, one tablespoon of vanilla flavoured fine sugar, and, when the mixture is quite smooth, five stiffly beaten egg whites.*

*Rub a metal baking sheet with pure wax or line with heavy waxed paper and, using a forcing-bag with a round nozzle, pipe the mixture to make little strips about one inch apart, so that they will not run into one another during baking.*

*Bake in a hot oven for about eight minutes.*

## 1919

The British Empire delegation took over five hotels near the Arc de Triomphe, the largest of which, and the centre of activity for us, was the Hôtel Majestic on Avenue Kléber. Colonel Kim had a modest room there — and for me, one of even more modest proportions that I shared with Trevor Perkins, a kitchen hand from Nottingham. The British party were so concerned with the French spying on their delegation they used Scotland Yard personnel to empty waste-paper baskets and cleared the Majestic of French underlings, up to and including the chefs, replacing them with staff plundered from hotels in England, mainly the Midlands. I thought this a great shame. I had to undertake some kitchen duties and was looking forward to observing cooking in the tradition of Escoffier but as a result, it was Brown Windsor soup and roast beef and Yorkshire pudding instead of Chicken á la Matignon and Coq au Vin. In any case, it was a pointless exercise; most of the office work was carried out at the Hôtel Astoria where the French staff was still in situ and available to read our secret papers, if they should happen to come across them.

Perkins was not a lively companion. While I thought I had died and gone to heaven, he found no attraction in Paris whatsoever. He could not speak the language and made little effort to meet any of the 'frogs' as he called them. In his opinion, which he voiced interminably, it was their incompetence that had led to the death of so many of our Tommys. They could not be trusted and stank of garlic. He had no knowledge of the French contribution in the war and he failed to listen when I talked about how many of them had been killed. He had never served in the armed forces — some medical reason that he did not elaborate on. I some times wished it was tertiary syphilis. He smoked incessantly, which seemed to exaggerate the whine that formed the major constituent of his speech patterns. He was barely literate, never read anything, but had firm opinions on every subject under the sun. A fully paid-up member of the flat Earth Society. If I had not found him so objectionable, I might have discovered some humour in his tactless ignorance.

"We should have left them to it."

"Who?"

"The Frogs. I prefer the Germans."

"Well, you're off your rocker. I'm not going to accept that all of those men were killed totally without cause. There were mistakes, I'm sure, and we didn't do too well at Polygon Wood. I was there — but we had obligations. Something you wouldn't understand."

Polygon Wood. A little exaggeration on my part.

*I Never Met Ernest Hemingway*

"Oh yes. Well, my obligations, as you call them, are to myself and I want to be back at the Victoria, drinking at the Flying Horse and down Meadow Lane of a Sat'day. This place is crap."

"I refuse to respond. You are lucky enough to be in one of the most beautiful cities in the world. You're surrounded by culture, if you know what that is, and you whine on about football."

"Shurrup, you poncy twat."

You can appreciate my reluctance to form a life-long friendship with this pathetic creature, or to record any more of our illuminating dialogues. Although we never actually came to blows, I was tempted to pee into one of the half empty bottles of beer that littered his bed space. He did not wash too often and the aroma of his socks will stay with me for ever. I did not help the situation of course. I was of the same humble background as he and liked my pint at the Lower George, but his arrant stupidity brought out the worst in me. In his company I refined my accent and talked about the treasures of the Louvre and the joys of the French cuisine, particularly the *grenouilles*. If he had known that this delicacy comprised the leg of the frog, he would have exploded. It would have been like pouring petrol on a bonfire.

I had the pleasure of his company for two months before I was able to negotiate a single billet, which was fortunate in view of Simóne.

Even though my accommodation there was miniscule — if it had formerly been a maids' quarter, she was a very small maid — I had never seen anything as majestic as the Hôtel Majestic. I was told that before the war it was the favourite resting place of rich Brazilian ladies visiting Paris to view, and buy, the latest fashions. This, for me, rendered the place even more exotic. Paris had been so much closer to the front line than London, but the ability of the 'City of Light' to continue to sparkle, despite the ravages of war, was fully reflected in that hotel. Not that I was familiar with the equivalent in London.

*Alan Shelley*

The hotels of Gloucester, such as they were, could not have prepared me for this. I really felt that I had come up in the world, which of course I had even if I was required to pay for my drinks, which was not the case for those members of the delegation that came from the Dominions and India. This annoyed some of the British, but it did not worry me. I was sufficiently intoxicated by simply being in Paris and, in any case, had little money to pay for alcohol of any kind.

There was a medical centre within the hotel — with a doctor and three nurses who I have to say were somewhat younger and prettier than Ida from Etaples. We had access to a billiard room in the basement. Not that I played; I hated that static ball — I preferred it coming at me as in tennis or cricket. Never took to golf either. What I did enjoy was the ornate ballroom that was used for the theatrical productions that we put on ourselves and, as you can imagine, I was an active member of that thespian group. I never repeated my imitation of the Prime Minister. Hardly appropriate; he was too prominently present and he was our boss. There were also the most splendid dances; sometimes three a week, Tuesdays, Thursdays and Saturdays. I was in my element. Colonel Kim told me there was some criticism about these dances; frivolity at a time when we were discussing the future of Europe, and indeed the whole world, but he did make the point that our affairs were much less extravagant than those at the Congress of Vienna.

My mother loved dancing. As a young girl she frequented one of the dancing schools in the city situated on the first floor over a shop, or shops. One of the most popular was called, if my memory serves me right, 'Brown's Academy'. She practised on me when I was tall enough and then I followed in her footsteps and went fairly regularly to one upstairs room or another. In my day the one in favour was Ma Kings.

It took some time for my role in relation to Colonel Kim to establish itself. I am sure that in the early days he was still wondered how wise was the instinct that had led to choosing me, but it turned out well I think, for both of us. A number of the British delegation were serving officers, like Colonel Kim, and they generally wore uniforms that were laundered, and buttons that were polished, by the batmen they had brought with them. I did the same but where the others shoe-shiners did little else after their officers left in the morning, a routine was soon established whereby I carried my master's briefcase and sat with the secretaries during some of his meetings.

Meetings! Paris 1919 was awash with meetings. Perhaps the most formidable set of meetings the world has ever known. There were virtually no other official activities, only meetings. They could be between just two people within the same national delegation, or between two people from different countries. Sometimes only the leaders of the four main powers got together, USA, France, Britain and Italy, with their own private secretaries — and in fact much of the substance of the Treaty of Versailles was hammered out at these small gatherings, unlike the grand-standing that tended to take place when hundreds were assembled. At the final signing at Versailles each of the big powers was allocated sixty tickets. What a horde. Colonel Kim most often met with his opposite number amongst the French who was another African expert. I always had difficulty remembering his name. It was so long-winded I took to calling him Capitaine Philippe — CP for short.

There were official meetings with a formal agenda and impromptu ones, an important example being those in the heavily guarded suite of rooms occupied by Colonel Edward House, the power behind the throne of President Wilson. He was a little frail man from Texas who, as I was told, wielded enormous political power, which he loved. He was a fixer who manipulated people with a quiet tongue and a formidable intellect. Rarely on view, but Sylvia had access to his rooms at the Crillon and she was a great admirer. She was also seduced by my éclairs. I say seduced; not exactly but I will elucidate in due course.

There were plenty of people around to have meetings with; thirty countries were represented at the conference and as you can imagine there were lots of hangers-on. The British delegation alone numbered four hundred and the French and the American probably many more. To these could be added such diverse people as Lawrence of Arabia, the Polish pianist Paderewski — I'd never heard of him — and, so I was to learn many years later, a man working in the kitchen at the Ritz by the name of Ho Chi Minh.

Colonel Kim's brief was to help make recommendations to the big powers about what was to become of the German Empire in Africa. For him this principally meant the fate of what had been known as German East and South West Africa. The future of the latter colony was relatively straightforward, at least in Paris, when it was mandated to South Africa and to be controlled by them until they became a pariah nation after the next world war when the situation did become more complicated. For me, I concentrated my studies on the East, and although Colonel Kim probably knew more about this area than anyone at the conference, he had served there, I was able to make a small contribution.

He knew the German mind, and how they ran their empire, and this was shown to be so true in Paris. This special insight was in addition to the in-built conceptions of empire that many of we British have, but for the Americans, they did not really understand empires at all. The Spanish were the great experts at the time of Christopher Columbus, and for a century or two after that. Then came us and the French. We had been rubbing shoulders with each other all over the world, particularly in Africa, as we sought to conquer those open spaces by use of the sword or the Bible or the flashy trinket. The Italians were relative amateurs at the game and the Congo was not a fiefdom of any country; it was the personal property of the king of the Belgians. In this snapshot of empire authorities, Sylvia was even less educated than her masters.

Like Colonel House, she too was from Texas and I must say that at the beginning of our friendship I had some difficulty in understanding what she was saying. I had always assumed that the way she pronounced, 'you all' was the word for a carpenter's tool, or a species of sailing vessel, but nonetheless, to slip into an Americanism, I thought she was cute. With Francois and my mother it was a hat. With my American friend it was her left shoe.

I would probably not have noticed her; the street was very busy and it was raining. At first sight all she represented to me was a voluminous, very wide and very long, raincoat of a startling light green colour, above which she wore a sou'wester of a similar shade but with a yellow band at the rim. She would not have looked out of place on the foredeck of a whaler. She was hurrying along the Avenue Marceau when someone in the crowd, must have been a Frenchman, bundled her into the gutter where she trapped the heel of her modest shoe in the grille of a drain. As a result, she lost her balance and I caught her before she joined the wet detritus in the street proper. Quite a big girl, plus the capacious piece of rainwear, and I needed to summon up my sinews — as Papa H might have written — to prevent both of us crashing to the ground.

I can hear my exasperated reader wondering whether any of the ladies in Percy Glossop's life are not associated with meetings that depended on mildly violent accidents; my mother and her hat, Liza and the cream tea and Ida, thanks to that sniper outside Cambrai. And now this one. Well, I retort, you wait till we reach Simóne; a chance no-action meeting of the most quiescent type, but one that was to have long lasting consequences.

The principal in my encounter with the raincoat thanked me, in English, or a variety of it, and then instructed me to: 'Have a nice day'. She then proceeded on her way. Two weeks later she turned up at the Hôtel Astoria in company with President Wilson's adviser on, I think it was Macedonia, who had come to meet the equivalent British expert. I did not recognise her. She was wearing a rather severe blue jacket and skirt where the hem of the latter garment extended to several inches below the knee. There was a gleaming cream blouse and a sort of pillbox hat. Dressed like that how could I recall her but she remembered me and when her superior had found his opposite number asked if I would like to have a cup of 'cawfee'. Least she can do, she says. 'You sure saved my dignity that day. Thought I was destined to finish up in the gutter on my fat arse.' She was a forthright female.

In a year or two I was to become aware of Gertrude Stein and Alice Toklas but as Sylvia Faulkner sat drinking coffee, I was more than unacquainted with ladies of a certain sexual orientation. Truth is in fact, I was totally ignorant, but this gap in my education was soon to be remedied.

At our second chance meeting I asked if she would like to come to one of the Hôtel Majestic's famous dances. We were encouraged to fraternise with our allies, particularly those who spoke English, and she accepted drawling that 'darn her but it would be the greatest of pleasures'. Out of that rainwear and her business suit, she looked very pretty as she entered wearing a sort of chintzy dress and high heels so the usual roués on the dance floor rather envied me. We had a splendid evening. There seemed to be some whisky on offer, and she drank her fill. You can envisage what happened next. I walked her to her hotel determined to steal a passionate kiss — to be followed by a little cuddle as we said goodnight — but all I got was a sharp rap about the head and an invitation to lunch next Sunday to meet: 'Her very best friend in all the world, Margaret du Broer, who hailed from Boston.' She never again mentioned my fumbles of that night but we became close friends and met on a number of occasions before she finally left Paris.

Sylvia was very patriotic — most Americans are — and she unashamedly hero-worshipped President Wilson. For her, he could do no wrong. The United States of America was going to save Europe and show us all how to avoid the mistakes of the past. His 'Fourteen Points' were the Holy Grail to Sylvia but, as I have said before, her country was not too experienced on the subject of empires; and neither was she. The result of this was that although she avoided talking to me about what she believed was her country's stand on the controversial issues of the day, issues such as reparations and the future border between France and Germany that plagued the conference from the start, when it came to Africa she could be unknowingly indiscreet.

It was not a bribe, but as I was called upon to do some shifts in the Majestic's kitchen, I was occasionally able to indulge in a little surreptitious cake-baking. She loved my cream doughnuts.

"Percy my dear, those bonbons you left on Tuesday were delicious."

"For you, the light of my life, nothing is too much trouble. You must try one of my lardy cakes."

"Good lord, no! They sound very fattening. Marge would hate me to get any heavier. What have you been doing today?"

"My Colonel had a one-to-one with CP, and I sat in. CP's French is rather excitable and rapid at times, and my boss needs me to explain some of the nuances. CP doesn't mind. Hardly seems to realise I'm there. I think he's a bit deaf and takes no notice when I whisper into Colonel Kim's shell-like"

"Shell like? Are we onto crabs?"

"No. Slang for ear."

"Goodness, you Limeys. You're so quaint. What was the subject at your very important meeting?"

"No details, my little spy, but you won't be surprised to hear it was East Africa at the top of the agenda."

We talked on about some gripe she had with one of Colonel House's staff, and I told her about our last week's concert where I had given a comedy turn based on a pastiche of *Hamlet,* concentrating on 'To be or not to be'.

"East Africa. I heard Colonel House on this. Something about — must be made a trustee territory. You should not have a link from north to south on the east coast. Talked about a man called Rhodes and a crazy notion about the Cape to Cairo. Do you know what that is all about?"

I explained about the arch empire-builder Cecil Rhodes. Rather laid it on for her benefit to make him into a caricature of those 'Men of Empire' the Yanks hate.

"How strong do you think the Colonel and the President are on this?"

"Well, I can't say, but Colonel House sounded quite vehement."

I passed this on to Colonel Kim. It was hardly news to him, but he said it was very useful to have confirmed what they suspected to be the American's attitude on this subject. He recommended I should carry on with the doughnuts.

Sylvia's next unknowing imprudence was rather more significant. I have not told you that she was a clerk-cum-typist within the American team advising on the Balkans. She sometimes boasted that one of her ancestors was a gypsy and so she was admirably suited for such a role. I did not say so, but I suspect that her masters were more concerned about the speed of her typing and her ability to keep her mouth shut, than the presence of any Slavic blood coursing through her veins. She never said a word to me about the vexed question of the future for the Balkans, and I could believe that her fingers were nimble and speedy but, as I have already mentioned, she was not always so circumspect on matters dealing with Africa. I sometimes wondered if she knew where the Dark Continent was. She probably thought it floated somewhere off to the right of Australia, but perhaps I am being unfair just because I caught a severe chill, thanks to her.

It was April in Paris — when the blossoms flourish and love is in the air. Not so in 1919. It snowed. Sylvia had appeared on the first Sunday of the month and insisted that I take her for a walk in the Bois de Boulogne. She was clad in her ample rainwear and was in a very bad temper. I suspected a tiff with Marge but my whaler-sea captain did not say so. What she did tell me was that one of the middle cadre of staff in the American camp was insufferable, pompous, narrow-minded and a woman hater. In addition, she said, he had bad breath.

I listened to all of this as we walked — or should I say galloped along; she had a determined stride when angry. She was obviously better attuned than I to matters meteorological as she was well-equipped for when the snow came. I was wearing a sports jacket, a soft shirt, a long scarf and a straw boater. I got very wet, and cold, and as a result spent two days in bed. There were two consequences resulting from this excursion. Firstly, I was visited twice a day in my sick quarters by Doreen, the prettiest of the three nurses, and secondly, I had something to report to Colonel Kim.

The object of Sylvia's ire was one Sean Kennedy. It seemed his great-grandfather had emigrated to the USA during the Irish potato famine and since then the British were *persona non grata* in the Kennedy family — in spades. It was said that successions of Kennedys always had a picture of the then British monarch pasted on the kitchen door and that after saying grace everyone at the table threw a dart at this image before tucking into their boiled beef and cabbage. This Kennedy was a minion within the American section dealing with Africa, but Colonel Kim had never heard of him. However, this Paddy and Sylvia were lodged in the same hotel and I think I heard, *soto voce,* that some comments had been made about 'dirty dykes'.

"I think the bastard had been demoted, or had some pay stopped, because of the language he used around the office, but that was no excuse to vent his anger on me. The misogynist swine."

"Sounds like a nasty piece of work."

"He is. Marge loathes him. He kept ranting and raving that he works harder than anyone in his office and this is how he has been treated. By the way, I failed to mention that he likes the sound of his own voice. Typical Irish — gift of the gab. Crack, he calls it. I'm glad there aren't too many of them in Texas."

"Well, doesn't sound as though he would be much good as a cowboy."

Sylvia glared at me. Was that a slur on the Lone Star state, she wondered, but went on.

"He was bursting. Reckoned they'd been working twelve hours a day on a plan to 'stick it up the Limeys' as he described it. The Belgians were involved. And the Portuguese, I think he said. We were going to side with them to make sure the Brits did not get all of German East Africa. There was even some talk about an approach to Smuts."

"They talk about perfidious Albion. Sounds now like perfidious Uncle Sam."

"What are you talking about? Who is this guy Albion?"

"Nothing. What else did this noxious fellow say?"

"Something about the Belgian case being justified and that your lot were imperialist dogs who treated black men like animals."

"I don't suppose you talked about slaves in your south and 'Damn Yankees'."

By this time, the snow was thickening and I was wet through. We retraced our steps and Sylvia simmered down. Before I was confined to my room I passed the gist of our conversation on to Colonel Kim.

He later told me what the background to this was, and the outcome, which was partly influenced by the information I had passed on.

No one in the British or French camps knew the USA was considering a divergence from them on Africa, and I understand Lloyd George and Clemenceau were briefed of the stand Wilson might take — the first hint of which had come from Sylvia. I do not know how this was dealt with in the most inner of inner sanctums, but Colonel Kim thought the American President had so many other priorities where he wanted support from his European colleagues that in the end we and France generally had our way over Africa. No doubt during that inner sanctum meeting the French Prime Minister enjoyed his favourite biscuits at the tea break. I had suggested to Colonel Kim that I should bake some *langue de chat* for the leader, but he thought that would be rather inappropriate. The Frenchman's delicacies should be prepared by a Frenchman.

Clearly Colonel Kim was aware of the reference to Smuts. Early in the discussion on German East Africa, Jan Smuts had suggested, but not vigorously, that perhaps Portugal should be given some of the ex-German possession at the northern end of Mozambique in exchange for a piece at the south to be transferred to South Africa so as to give it a latitudinal border rather than a longitudinal one. This was never pursued but virtually all of the final decisions on Africa were those that had already been agreed beforehand by Britain and France. The latter got Togo and most of the Cameroons. Ignoring the Smut stratagem, Portugal thought they should get some of the territory north of Mozambique, particularly as they suspected that when the map was re-drawn a bit of their Angola would go to Belgium to give the Belgian Congo access to the Atlantic. This proved to be the case, much to the annoyance of Portugal. The Belgians were also very dissatisfied with the final outcome; like Colonel Kim they had been involved in the war against the Germans in East Africa and thought they should be rewarded for that, but in the end all they got were mandates over Rwanda and Burundi — and what a poisoned chalice that turned out to be. The most important mandate, as I have already explained, was that of South Africa over South West Africa

I very nearly did not make it to Versailles for the final ceremony. There was, for a lowly minion like me, no reserved place in the Hall of Mirrors where the signing was to take place but I did expect to be one of the many who stood on the fringes. Funnily enough I had already become relatively

*Alan Shelley*

familiar with the Palace of Versailles because of the peaches. This magnificent complex, perhaps the greatest monument ever to absolute monarchy, had been built by Louis XIV, the Sun King; I read somewhere that at the height of the building work, thirty six thousand men were employed on the site. The gardens matched and complemented the Palace and included extensive glasshouses that grew the most extraordinary variety of fruit and flowers, as I was to discover.

A celebratory dinner was planned for the British Empire delegation to mark the signing — the end of all their efforts. I had persuaded the Head Chef — he came from Sheffield and had in the past graced the kitchens of Chatsworth House — that my Peach Melba should be included as one of the deserts on offer. This took me to Versailles where I met the senior gardener in charge of the fruit growing section of the acres of glasshouse at the Palace. He was a curmudgeonly fellow. I tried to explain my quest for the best available peaches but he became very heated when I explained to him, in my very best French of course, that I was a chef.
I translate our conversation.

"It is simply not possible for an Englishman to be a chef. Someone is trying to pull the wools over our eyes."

"Well, as the saying goes, the proof of the pudding is in the eating."

"Oh, I see now. You can only cook the pudding and presumably only rice pudding — without the nutmeg."

"Look, you arrogant frog"
Actually I was more polite than that but these unspoken words were on the tip of my tongue.

"I can cook anything you can and it will taste just as good without using your fancy names."

"But these names go back for centuries. *Tripe à la mode* was first presented in 1751."

"Yes, and they say it was the Chinese who discovered roast pork when the pigsty caught fire."

"Chinese, what have they got to do with this? What are you cooking for your people tonight?"

"My version of Chicken Marengo."

"*Mon dieu*. Sacrilege."

This of course was not altogether the truth. We were just as likely to have bangers and mash for dinner that night at the Majestic.

My antagonist deigned to introduce me to Irene, his oldest daughter. She, unusually for the time, worked with him. If my fingers were light, hers were green. Her father was a taciturn man but he did repeat, at regular intervals, phrases that extolled his offspring's' virtues. The translation from the French loses some of its piquancy, but my best translation is as follows:

"My Irene can sprout cabbages on a dead donkey's rump."

"She could teach those Hollanders how to make proper tulips."

The peaches were delicious. They had a lighter than usual yellow hue with a golden fuzz that seemed to glisten when struck by the light magnified by the clear, clean glass of the greenhouse. Irene's complexion was similar, but without the fuzz.

After this excursion, you can imagine how keen I was to return to Versailles for the signing. Who knows, I might bump into Irene and also I wanted to sample my supreme desert at the dinner to follow. We were promised an extra course to our normal fare at the Majestic — and there was to be champagne. However, three days before the historic gathering I received a telegram from my mother to say that Francois, as a result of his asthma, appeared to have developed a serious infection of the chest and pneumonia was feared. I went immediately to Colonel Kim and he, in his decisive way, called in one of the senior army clerks on duty to arrange a seat on the next train to Dover. The French railways were not yet running a full service and the earliest time I could leave was the following afternoon but just before I left the hotel for the *Gare St-Lazare*, another telegram arrived telling me that the crisis was over; it was a false alarm and Francois was back from the Gloucester Infirmary and up and about.

I should explain the feelings I have for my family. I trust I have already indicated that I greatly admired my mother; her attitude when she was young towards the conventionalities of life has no doubt influenced the eventual trajectory of my rather odd existence, but more than admiration, I had a deep love for her. I saw Francois as a mirror image. He had been a valuable father-figure when I was young and I had him to thank for the gift of the French language. When I left for the Western Front my siblings were both still at school and I was never home long enough after that to get to know them intimately; which raises the fundamental question that with the feelings I had for my mother, and Francois, why was I not at home long enough to get to know them better?

I am not sure I can satisfactorily answer that question. I enjoyed my irregular visits to Gloucester but circumstances seemed to arise that found my head, more often than not, resting on the pillow of a bed away from my hometown. If I had really wanted to spend the rest of my days in the West Country of England, I could have done so. A livelihood was always available and after the war there was no shortage of female company but, as you will discover, I was first seduced by Paris and thereafter it seemed natural to become a Londoner. I know my mother was disappointed, but I was often in my home-town for the elver season. Very important.

These are the eel family that are to be found in estuaries, particularly that of the River Severn. During the ebb tide they move out of the current towards the bank so as not to be washed out to sea and that is when they are caught. If ever you are fortunate enough to come into possession of a pound of these delicacies, try them; one of the supreme delights of the British cuisine.

When it became clear to all concerned that I was not in the near future likely to return to Whitwells the Bakers, my mother and Francois decided that I should be made an allowance out of the profits of the business to recognise my membership of the family — and perhaps to tempt me to give up my wayward life and return to them. I could see Francois's hand in this. What was determined was that after a proper stipend had been paid to my mother and Francois, and the other two children when they became full-time workers, I was to be given a ten per cent share of the profits. This was to be paid annually in arrears to an account Francois opened for me at the local Barclays Bank.

I had never had such an account before. When I worked in the bakery mother gave me pocket money, I was of course still living at home, and when I went into the Army I lived on the King's shilling and in the King's accommodation — and ate his food. Much the same in 1919. I was fed and housed at the Majestic and was paid, arranged by Colonel Kim, the equivalent pay as would have been drawn by an army Corporal. I spent little of this.

The generous allowance, courtesy of Whitwells, was duly deposited. Sometimes my pot of gold was full, sometimes empty, but there is no doubt that these funds, for some years to come, gave me a freedom that without such largesse I might have lived as a beachcomber, a bum or a hobo singing: 'Buddy, can you spare a dime.' I am sure Francois understood this. It was a risk they took. A share of the profits might keep open the option of an early homecoming but then again, it gave the errant boy the chance to find a life away from Gloucester and the bakery.

When I received that second telegram to say that Francois was out of danger, the relief was powerful indeed. I wanted to be with my mother, but her message had been so positive about Francois's full recovery that I concluded I would, after all, be able to go to Versailles.

I have already tried to analyse for you, and for myself, my attitude towards organised religion but it is at times like these that doubts and prevarications melt away. I needed to take some action. I wanted to give thanks for Francois's recovery and so, being the sort of person I am, I took myself off to the very heart of the Church in France, the Cathédrale de Notre-Dame de Paris, where I went to pray. I could hardly have chosen a more impressive venue for this, my first formal recourse to the Christian Church. I was aware of Victor Hugo's hunchback but up to now I had not visited this masterpiece of gothic architecture around which the history of Paris has revolved for centuries. You might say that this young and ignorant agnostic never did things by halves; if I was to approach God for the first time, what a platform. I cannot say whether the time I spent on my knees before God gave me any real sense of comfort. I think it did and I could not be other than impressed with this example of one of his houses. Francois was well, that was the crucial matter, but in addition, the Cathédrale de Notre-Dame de Paris, the church of Our Lady, was about to become the site of another crossroad in my life; a meeting with a lady named Simóne.

As I rose to leave the sparsely occupied church I could not help but observe a young girl in a pew at the rear of the nave with tears streaming down her face. She was not on her knees but sat with her body hunched towards the altar and with those tears falling on the velvet cushion at her feet. She made no noise, but her cheeks were awash with sorrow. She looked to be about my age, or thereabouts. She had a blue piece of tattered cloth covering her hair and wore a white nondescript frock that did not look as if it had seen soap and water for some time.

I was reluctant to disturb her. She looked so pathetic but I walked on, hoping that God would come to her aid. One of the features of this Cathedral is that the floor plane is at one with the adjoining street — unusually there are no steps up or down. When I reached the street — it was a gloriously fine day

— I instinctively looked back into the darkness of the Church to offset the glare of the sun; I was standing at the same level as that holy interior and the heavy doors were wide open. The distraught girl had quit her pew and was walking towards me. She was still sobbing but as she left the building the reverence it had inspired evaporated and her grief became loud and heart-wrenching. I walked towards her and gave her my relatively clean handkerchief. She looked stunned. She did not seem to comprehend what I was offering her. By a gentle touch of the elbow I directed her towards a nearby bench and sat down by her side. This action seemed to add power to the ducts behind her eyes and the tears splashed copiously onto my white linen trousers.

Neither man, nor women, can cry forever. Eventually the flow eased and I smiled at her. Without too much by way of conversation I moved her from the bench to an immediately adjoining cafe table where there were two chairs. I ordered lemonade and, after some hesitation, she drank it down with gusto. We sat there quietly for some time and then, as she regained some composure, she told me why she was in the church and why she was so distressed.

"You speak French, *Monsieur*?"

"I do."

"You are very kind."

"I am so glad to see you have stopped crying. What is the matter that you are so sad?"

"I am Simóne Boutet. I work for Lagon, who make candles. I have never known my father. My mother died two weeks ago. That makes me sad, of course, but today I come to church to pray to Our Lady that I find somewhere to live."

"I am so sorry about your mother. I was at the Notre Dame to give thanks for the recovery of my stepfather. He is French. It is from him I learn the language. But how is it you have lost your mother and your home?"

"*Monsieur.* She was concierge at a block of apartments near Square St Lambert. I lived with her in the concierge rooms. Now they have found a new one and I must leave by tomorrow. I have no money. My last pay from Lagon went to pay a debt of my mothers. I shall be on a bench in the Bois de Boulogne tomorrow."

Was this just a sob story? A pale and tearful face attempting to beg for money, based on a tale of woe? It sounded authentic enough, and the tears were certainly real, and as I looked at her again I was forced to believe what she had told me.

As she related this sad story, her eyes widened and I realised that without the tears they were shiny and blue. I thought about someone else who had never met a father but who now lived in a state of utter luxury compared to this creature. I asked if she knew where the Hôtel Majestic was. She nodded her head. I told her to go back and gather up her possessions — I assumed they were few — and I would meet her at the kitchen entrance to the hotel in two hours time.

All of the British delegates had their own identity cards. They had to be shown, without fail, when entering the hotel. Security was tight, but as our occupation of these splendid premises was coming to an end, a little laxity had been in evidence. In any case, I had discovered recently that kitchen workers — even if only part-time like me — could move fairly freely through the servant's entrance. Perkins did not avail himself of this; he rarely left the hotel. I trusted that an easy access would be the case today.

I was there at the appointed time. She was not. Twenty minutes later she appeared carrying two bundles and out of breath. It was a long walk, she said. She had asked no questions of me. I do not think at that point she was even aware of my nationality. Before we went inside I explained my plan; she could stay in my room tonight and tomorrow I would give her some francs so she could rent a room of her own. We reached my quarters on the top floor, with no alarms being raised, where she sank down on my bed and immediately fell asleep. I went down to my dinner and then brought up for her some bread and cheese. She was still asleep and I did not waken her. I made the best of it on the narrow and threadbare strip of carpet by the window — which was fully open. It was a warm night.

We made a similarly discreet exit early the following morning, with one minor hiccup. One of the secretaries saw us as we moved between the fourth and the third floors, but she only winked. I think she was rather sweet on me — but obviously not the jealous type. Simóne left me with some strangulated words of thanks and with her bundles that now contained a small number of franc coins.

The day following, the 28th of June, was appointed for the signing ceremony. It was significantly the anniversary of the assassination of the archduke that had started all of this. It was to take place in the splendid Hall of Mirrors at the Palace and Colonel Kim was privileged to be present; but for me, I joined the throng congregating on the outskirts of this significant moment. Even on the fringes I revelled in the atmosphere and then later I was able to view part of the ceremony for myself through the eyes, and art, of Sir William Orpen, the British delegation's artist in residence, thanks to his painting: *The Signing of the Peace in the Hall of Mirrors, Versailles*. The artist shows an image of the high windows behind the ceremony distorted by the famous mirrors. It is a dazzling backdrop for his depiction of this important event. Most effective. The principal players can be clearly recognized: Wilson looks rather satisfied with himself, but not Clemenceau. Was his moustache so really large and droopy? It gives him a dismal countenance but Orpen has captured in Lloyd George that quizzical look in the eyes as though he is about to tell a joke — or kiss a girl.

I drank a great deal of champagne that evening and Simóne disappeared from my consciousness, particularly as on the following day we had our final Hôtel Majestic dance. It was a gala affair with balloons and things and an attempt was made to persuade those attending to come in fancy dress. Mine was not very inventive; a white apron and a chef's hat but Sylvia and Margaret, whom I had invited, had found from somewhere short dresses that were decorated with flounces and tassels and displayed expansive areas of *décolletage*. They were very eye-catching but they still had to explain to all and sundry who flocked to their side, and these were many, that they were supposed to be Wild West chorus girls. We all had a wonderful time although I was not too happy that the two girls brought along another man.

The ratio of men to women was seriously out of kilter and we did not need him to make it worse. On the other hand, he was an interesting fellow. He came from Boston, and his family and Margaret's were known to each other. As I understood, Hubert Richardson Junior was a Boston blueblood but the bohemian in the family and unlikely, in the immediate future, to be joining his father and brother's in the investment banking world. Through these family connections he had been able to arrange some form of attachment to the American delegation as artist in residence — the equivalent of Sir William Orpen with us — but, from what I could make out, without the talent. He was a very tall loose-limbed creature who danced like a drunken praying mantis and who sported a French beret and smock as his contribution to the fancy dress. He was certainly an oddball, to use another Americanism.

After she had left I kept in touch with Sylvia by letter until the 1930s when our correspondence seemed to fizzle out. Margaret was still around and they had set up in the business of selling made-to-measure ladies underwear. I could not make up my mind whether this was a suitable profession for them although, after further consideration, I came to the conclusion that it probably was.

Colonel Kim and I were scheduled to spend some more months in Paris. There were a lot of loose ends. About the end of July I was enjoying a glass of Bordeaux in the servants mess when Charlie Rice came and told me I had a visitor in the main foyer. It was of course Simóne. She was rather more smartly dressed and was wearing a narrow smile. I took her out to the front of the hotel where she pressed into my hand the money I had lent her. She said that fortuitously she had been promoted at the candle factory and the extra pay had enabled her to make this refund. She still looked very thin. I asked if she had eaten that day. She said no, whereupon I bought for her a substantial dinner of carbonade of beef and potatoes at the modest Mon Plasir close by. I saw quite a lot of her thereafter.

## Simóne

As soon as the treaty was signed, the overseas leaders and senior officials promptly departed Paris but the rump of the British delegation included Colonel Kim and me. There were many details to agree — particularly between ourselves and the French on the precise borders of some of the African countries. The Cameroons was a tricky issue. In due course it was divided by a League of Nations mandate into the West, and much smaller half, being ours and the Eastern bit French, and re-named Cameroun. This left the headquarters of the British Cameroons at Buea which boasted a German *schloss* that would not have looked out of place on the slopes of the Hartz Mountains in Lower Saxony.

In later years I met an English girl who had worked in Buea in an office at the Secretariat — in the Secret Branch — that had a door which was half glazed and on which was written: 'Adjutant und Melde.' The building had obviously been used in the past by the German administration. She told me that Buea was considered to be a 'suicide station' because of the mist that came down from the mountain around 2 p.m almost every day until night-fall, and this could make everyone very depressed. Evidently, during the German occupation the adjutant was told that in addition to his tour of duty he would have to serve some further months at the station. As a result he went mad, shot his immediate superior and then went up to the Schloss to similarly deal with the Gauleiter. He killed another five or six people before turning the gun on himself and they were all buried together in the graveyard behind the house where this girl lived. She used to joke that she worked with him all day, and slept with him at night.

Our stay at the magnificent Hôtel Majestic needed to be brought to an end but fortunately, as my superior and CP began to look at the Cameroon detail, the Frenchman solved the problem of where we might move to. His brother owned a small block of apartments near to the *Gare Montparnasse* and a two bedroom unit there was available to rent. Colonel Kim's allowance just about covered this and I was offered the small second bedroom at no charge so, once again, I was living and enjoying Paris, rent-free. Was I not the most fortunate of men?

After a short and limited acquaintance, I was totally enraptured with the city. During my first six months there had not been the opportunity to visit and fall under the spell of its wonders, but away from the British enclave that was the Hôtel Majestic, I began to feel like a genuine visitor seeing it properly for the first time. Colonel Kim kept me busy with one thing or another. I still helped when there were language difficulties between the still excitable CP and my more phlegmatic superior but there were no attractions tempting me to stay confined to that tiny room and so, when work was over for the day, I became an evening wanderer. A wanderer who supped and ate in bistros and bars from Monmarte to Montparnasse, along the Left Bank and in the shadow of the Notre Dame and the Eiffel Tower. I was an innocent abroad — and I wallowed in it.

Hemingway also drank and ate his way around Paris. He insistently detailed the names of the establishments. It was as though a litany of the smart watering holes that he and his crowd frequented was *de rigueur* to prove that they were truly part of the Lost Generation. They did not seem very lost to me. Certainly their knowledge of the geography of central

Paris was very impressive. In just two pages of his semi-autobiographical work, *A Movable Feast*, mention is made of the Nègre de Tolouse, The Select, the Rotonde and the Dôme. He was similarly detailed as to what he drank and whom he met. He always met someone he knew and if not, many of the proprietors of these establishments were acquainted and addressed him by name, even if his last visit had been a year ago. When on the odd occasion he found himself to be on his own he could always attract a *poule,* who would then become a part of the narrative.

But I knew no one, and no one knew me. I did not care. I was in love and you cannot be lonely in that state — at least not at the beginning of the affair. There was me — and there was Paris. I will not bore you once again with another detour into the realm of popular music but I am sure that as I tramped the city I whistled all of the songs extolling her virtues. Of course these referred to Paris in its former glory but, as I was succumbing to her charms, there had been four years of war. It was shabby, food was short, and one could forgive if in some parts it gave off the sense of an unfinished act of mourning. Too many wives and mothers had lost their men. There were a lot of fatherless children. Clemenceau's campaign at the Peace Conference for reparations by Germany and his insistence over the future Rhineland frontier were understandable in view of the losses his country had suffered. The cafes and bars I discovered were mostly operated by women and it could sometimes seem as though Paris was mainly populated by them — and me.

Wherever I roamed I tended to have a last drink close to home at a small and not very smart establishment at the back of the station. It was called the Trois Perroquets but the proprietor, a Madame Ricard, was never able to explain the origin of this rather bizarre name or how she had becomes so fat? Where had she found the food during four years of war? She had lived in Paris all her life and when the war was mentioned it was necessary to make it clear that you were referring to 1914 and not 1871. It was many months before I saw her feet. She sat behind and at the end of the zinc covered bar on a high stool with a back rest of dubious strength that seemed to have been a later addition. She was invariably dressed in black — reminded me of the *Grandmère* from Calais. She drank a rough white wine from Provence all through the opening hours and never fell from her stool, at least not to my knowledge. She was an extremely odd combination of the affable, even flirtatious, and the dour. Perhaps it depended on the weather — or the phases of the moon? She began to notice me as a regular late-night drinker, calling me her '*étique* Englishman', and when in a good mood she would attempt to kiss me as I paid for my saucers. She never succeeded; her bulk made such a gymnastic manoeuvre a near impossibility.

Besides the bar and a few very unsafe stools there was an eating area divided from the drinkers by a grey and dirty curtain with a frill across the bottom of bright red fleur de leys. The Trois Perroquets catered for a maximum of twenty five diners. There were four tables with a reinforcement of chairs stacked in the passageway leading to the kitchen. These were rarely called up. The atmosphere in the bar, mainly due to the impressive presence of Madame Ricard, was pleasing, at least to me, but the eating area was gloomy and the food execrable. There, I have said it. We are in a Paris bistro and the food is awful. I could hardly believe it. In those early days I ate there twice. What was happening in the kitchen, I do not know, but after my second experience had left me unfit to work the next day, on further visits I contented myself with a coffee and a *fine*.

Julietta, a niece of Madame Ricard, or was it a great niece, was the only permanent waitress but there was another female family member somewhere in the district who appeared if the dining clientele exceeded ten. I was told the kitchen was controlled by Julietta's uncle, or so-called uncle. I rarely met him but encouraged by the aunt, Julietta and I enjoyed a friendly flirtatious relationship which was not, on my part, going to progress beyond that. She was what Miss Rosen would have called a 'bonnie lassie'. She had jet black hair and a narrow waist but I was rather put off by the fact that in a particular light I could discern traces of a moustache on her upper lip.

But, I hear you cry, what happened to Simóne? I must admit I had hardly thought of her. I was busy tying up loose ends with Colonel Kim and fanning the flames of my passion for her home city. During our last meeting at the Mon Plasir she told me, while rapidly disposing of the beef and potatoes I had purchased, where she had rented a room but the exact address had not entered my memory. However, I did recall in general terms the district where she was living and when in that area during my quartering of the city, I wondered if our paths might cross.

One Sunday, just as the sun was about to disappear, they did; there she was walking in front of me. I made no attempt to catch her up. It was early December. The day had been clear but it was very cold and from what I could see the coat she was wearing was thin, more like the sort of overall shop assistants use. Her hair was covered with the same blue scarf and at her feet the shoes did not appear to be very substantial but the most vivid image I had was of the droop of her shoulders. She was walking slowly, her shoes hardly leaving the pavement. She looked even smaller and thinner than when I last saw her. A sad sight I thought. At the next junction I turned right.

I was enjoying discovering all the positive elements of the city and so did I really want to become more acquainted with the reverse side — which at that time was represented by the Simóne I had just seen. I was well aware of the opposite face of the Paris that so attracted me. It was there for all to see, unavoidable. There were beggars on the streets, there were a lot of prostitutes about, not that I was in a position to say whether there were more than usual, and many sad and poor-looking women eking out a living cleaning the streets or attempting to sell a wide variety of items from their sale's pitches in the gutter. Buildings were grubby, there had been little maintenance during the last four years, but there were more personal signs of neglect. The generality of the populace were poorly dressed and the evidence of poverty hard to ignore. As I have said, women were in the majority, but when men were to be found many of them displayed the wounds of war — emaciation, missing limbs, scarred faces and sightless eyes.

The joy I found in the city could not assuage the anger and sorrow I felt for these poor wretches. I could see the physical deprivations but who could know their mental anguish. Other than second-hand from Bob Patch, and my observations whilst in the hospital at Etaples, my experience of the war was so limited that I could only half imagine what many of these men had been through. There was one particular group that congregated at the main entrance to the *Gare Montparnasse.* One man, who had lost both legs, propelled himself along on a low wheeled trolley of the sort children might construct from odds and ends. His usual companions were a man with an arm lost from the shoulder down and another who still had an elbow. They acted together as a group of beggars, and I'm sure they shared the collection equally, and yet I always had the feeling that they were not met together on the station steps specifically to beg; they were companions in adversity as they had been in the trenches.

However, some of that female majority were still to be seen on the Rue de Rivoli and other fashionable streets displaying evidence, in their elegance, of the renowned Paris chic. Their gowns and hats and shoes were probably not new but, although I could be critical of the contrast between them and the sad people I have just described, I applauded their effort in putting on a brave face. If Paris was to return to its former glory these ladies were doing their best to hasten the day. The popular cafes were busy, the Opéra was open, as were many of the theatres, and the Luxembourg Gardens were being restored to their pre-war grandeur. I liked to think that I was on the verge of having one foot in this rejuvenated society so what did I want with a forlorn candle maker.

Why, therefore, did my peregrinations seem to take me more often than not towards the district where she lived? Did I feel responsible for her? Was I being quixotic? What could the attraction possibly be? Or did it matter? We cannot always find a rational explanation for impulses of this kind. I saw her twice more before I placed myself face-to-face. On each of these two furtive sightings she seemed no happier, or more attractive. I say face-to-face. I approached her from behind and tapped her on the shoulder. She started, as though she had been shot in the back, and turned around to confront her assailant. What I recalled later was that surprisingly she recognised me instantly and produced that thin smile of hers. I doubt if my recognition would have been so immediate if she had surprised me. She timidly extended her hand and I took it into mine. Neither of us spoke for a moment or two. We just looked at each other. I broke the silence.

"Simóne. How nice to see you again. Are you faring well? How is the work?"

"Monsieur. Yes. I still make the candles."

"Remember, my name is Percy. You are still very thin. Do you eat regularly? Are you in the same room? Shall we go and drink some coffee?"

She nodded, her hand was still held by mine. I tightened my grip and we walked along, hand in hand, like sweethearts. I had not envisaged a next step when I had tapped her on the shoulder. A blind impulse, with no thought for the consequences, but I was being dragged further and further into a situation where Simóne was destined to become central to the next phase of my life. Over coffee she began to tell me what had happened to her since we had met in front of the Notre Dame.

"I know your mother is dead. I'm very sorry, but do you have any other family? Brothers and sisters? Aunts and uncles, cousins?"

*Alan Shelley*

"I told you false about my mother. It was my aunt who was the concierge and died. She was my mother's older sister. My mother was killed in the war."

At this point tears began to gather in her eyes so I did not explore further the reasons why she had lied when we met at the Notre Dame. I ordered some cake to go with the coffee.

"I am now well settled in my room, thanks to you. My wages get better. I have bought some new shoes."

"Do you have a boyfriend?"

She blushed and answered my question by a lowering of her eyes and a barely perceptible shrug of the shoulders.

I told her how I was enjoying Paris and how glad it made me to see it recovering some of its former splendour, day by day. This seemed to pass over her, not something she had thought important — or even agreed with. The shoulders were again hoisted a little. I suppose our situations were different. In fact, there was no supposing about it. I was engaged in work I enjoyed and the city was a new experience to me. She was involved in tedious manual labour, and although she may now be in a better condition than when I first met her, she was clearly not exactly enjoying a comfortable lifestyle. As I have already observed, she was very thin and her skin looked unhealthy. The blue scarf she covered her head with was dirty, as I saw was the hair itself when she removed that headgear. I thought of my mother's hats — and her rosy complexion. The contrast was heart-rending.

I walked her back to the room and we shook hands. As I said goodbye I mumbled that I would call and see her again soon. I did not keep that promise, partly because I was still unsure whether I really wanted to get to know her better — and because I was diverted by Madame Ricard.

During one of my visits for a coffee and a liqueur, I had eaten elsewhere of course, I told her that my important job with His Britannic Majesty's Government was about to come to an end and that I was expecting to hear soon what medal or honour was to be awarded for my valuable services. She ignored this

*I Never Met Ernest Hemingway*

but asked if I was going back to my mother and the baking of patisseries. Over many evenings I had told her of my talents as a chef and about Gloucester and the fine establishment my family owned within the shadow of a cathedral that was superior to the Notre Dame. Without waiting for a reply she suggested I forego the paradise of Gloucester and stay in Paris and work for her.

"Monsieur Percy. I do not believe an Englishman can be a cook."

I recalled the irascible gardener at Versailles.

"It is not possible, but your French is good and you have the very nice smiling face. If, as I"m sure is the case, you can only cook the fish and the chips, you can work behind the bar with me. We need some younger blood. You and Julietta might be able to attract some better customers than the riffraff we have now. And there's a spare room on the top floor where you can live, but behave yourself."

I was taken aback. Why, after such a minimal acquaintance, was this formidable woman offering me a job and somewhere to live? I do have a 'nice smiling face', but I was an Englishman and I have sufficient experience to know that the two races, despite the Entente Cordiale, do not always get on well together. I had seen plenty of examples of this during the Peace talks but, why make a puzzle out of it? If Madame Ricard had taken a fancy to me, *Ça va?* On the other hand, I thought, was this dingy cafe to be the birthplace of my private-sector culinary career? Was the kitchen capable of any form of rebirth and if so, was I sufficiently skilled to act as its midwife? If I was going to stay in Paris I needed to find somewhere to live and once on the premises I could surely depose the uncle — and it would be very agreeable working alongside Julietta. I did not at that moment think I made a comparison with Simóne, but subconsciously I may well have done so. The moustache suddenly became less prominent.

"So, I will be given a chance to show you I can cook, and like a Frenchman. But what about the uncle?"

"Oh yes. You can learn from him, not so."
That will be the day I thought, but I learned over the counter and kissed the fat lady's hand and said:

"I accept, Madame. The best decision you have made for many a long day, for sure."

To celebrate this momentous occasion she did not remove the special armagnac from its hiding place beneath the bar, but she did pour out another small cognac.

Colonel Kim was due to leave before Christmas. He thought a return to regimental duties was in prospect and so I told him of the position I had secured. He knew of my wish to stay in Paris but was doubtful that working at the Trois Perroquets would be the answer. He asked me to keep in touch and write to him care of his bank, Cox and Kings, Pall Mall, and if ever I decided to rejoin the colours he would try his best to find me a position working for him. I was very fond of this splendid gentleman but back into the army was not what Percy Glossop had in mind as a future.

The uncle proved more of a stumbling block than I had expected. Madame Ricard, for some strange reason, called him El Greco although she kept to the bar and never entered the kitchen. Julietta had tried to describe him, but she failed to provide an adequate picture. He was an ogre. To begin with he was several inches taller than me, and twice as heavy. He was very hairy, at least above the waist; in the kitchen he rarely wore a shirt or vest. He did not say much but when he did open his mouth the guttural speech was loaded with obscenities. He had as a kitchen assistant a North African called Moses, but I never heard him referred to as anything other than 'you, Mohammed'. The odious uncle spent most of the day flicking at his underling with a wet cloth. Better results might have been achieved if the chef de cuisine had spent more time learning to cook and less chastising this poor fellow. I had a real task on my hands and quickly decided that a direct confrontational approach would not work. When in doubt, bypass the enemy and attack via the boss-man, or in this case, the boss-lady.

I first needed to discover the reason why Madame Ricard was so indifferent to the catering side of her business. The bar did reasonably well. The passing trade amongst passengers using the station was brisk and there were a goodly bunch of regulars. The Trois Perroquets opened early and closed late. She seemed content to sit on her stool for long hours exchanging gossip with those regulars she liked and being friendly to some of the other drinkers. My conclusion, not too difficult was it; she liked the status quo and was basically idle. Julietta and Moses and the ever-changing bar hand re-stocked from the storeroom at the back, washed the glasses, emptied the ashtrays and swept the floor before the opening hour but the Madame who handled the cash register just smiled, and chatted at her whim, but did nothing else. It was indolence personified.

Based on this assessment I perceived a strategy that would leave her as the queen bee, but in charge of a more profitable business and therefore more inclined to view the second stage of my attack, on the kitchen, with more favour than I might find now. The façade of the Trois Perroquets had not, in my estimation, been redecorated since the Franco-Prussian war. The sign above the dirty window was so disfigured that the casual drinker would have been unable to tell his wife the name of the café he had used for just one drink before catching the train that returned him to her loving arms. There was another and more important defect to this enterprise. It must have been the only bar or cafe or bistro or *estaminet* in the whole of Paris, perhaps the whole of la belle France, that did not provide, in the summer months, tables on the pavement outside such establishments.

I gradually raised these defects with her. I first told her I believed she was too busy, she needed to relax a little more, and so I would work in the bar full-time to give her more opportunity for chat with the customers — something more important than the quality of the drinks themselves. She liked that. I then said that to cover my costs we needed to attract a new clientele and so I got round to persuading her to invest in some paint, a sign writer and some extra tables and chairs for alfresco drinkers. There was an initial reluctance, the state of inertia was very strong and she was careful with money, but eventually my sweet tongue brought her to agree. The results were virtually instantaneous. By April, the Trois Perroquets was exhibiting a new face and as the weather was unseasonably warm — no snow in the spring of 1920 — the outside tables were soon in use. As the ring of the cash register became more frequent, so my status grew.

The next step was more difficult. I decided on a dramatic approach rather than any subtle manoeuvre. Julietta had hated the uncle well before I came on the scene and as she began to regard me with more and more favour, I fed the fires of her dislike for that hairy monster and persuaded her to join in my plan for his precipitate departure. She would tell Madame that he had twice tried to get her into the storeroom alone with him and she could not stand it any longer and was going to the gendarmes to report an attempted rape. The story was told and Madame Ricard erupted. She even left her stool. We heard the clatter of pans in the kitchen. I rather hoped she was using a frying pan but whatever, I could hear that her voice was drowning out any protestations from him. I moved to the alley alongside the cafe and saw him leave, pulling on a shirt, as he protected himself from the missiles issuing through the kitchen door. Game, set and a match.

With no chef, the kitchen was closed and a sign attached to the dingy curtain announcing, with regret, that the service of meals was temporarily suspended. The next step was to persuade the proprietor that I should be the replacement chef.

"Madame. You cannot be a Paris bistro and not offer meals. Your regular customers will soon look elsewhere."

## I Never Met Ernest Hemingway

There were no regular diners of course but she did not realise this. She had never comprehended how revolting the cuisine had been.

"I shall take over the cooking but first you need to spend some money, just a little, to smarten up the kitchen."

I did not tell her that the major expenditure would be used for cleaning and redecorating and for the place to be fully disinfected — the cockroaches must be served with notice to quit. There was in fact nothing wrong with the stove or the ice room although some of the pans and other utensils were beyond recovery.

"The bar is now doing well. Worth spending a few francs behind the scenes."

My menus were modest. I was well aware that this was to be the scene of my apprenticeship and so, for a time, the cuisine at the Trois Perroquets was never too extravagant. Most diners were content with a variety of soups, Coq au Vin or Beefsteak with pommes frits and so this is what I provided. The desserts were not a problem, particularly as I added crêpes to complement the Breton cider available in the bar; Montparnasse had always been a Breton area. But, more importantly, I needed to learn. I had to acquire the important skills of what ingredients to buy, and from where; how to cook at top speed when the restaurant was full; how to keep food hot; how to estimate quantities and how to get the pricing right. I was an eager pupil even if I was my own tutor. It was a wonderful opportunity to acquire the basic knowledge needed to run a kitchen; I was so fortunate to be provided with such a training ground where I was not chided about my mistakes, which were many to start with. When demand was brisk Julietta helped very willingly and I could see that when she came back from the *boulangerie* with an armful of baguettes she was looking in the future to see me being encased in those arms. We were however too busy for her plans to reach fruition, just yet, and I could not erase Simóne from my mind and the un-kept promise to see her again.

*Alan Shelley*

What was wrong with me? I do not believe I am by nature naturally perverse but why did an image of that forlorn creature keep reasserting itself when I had the cheerful Julietta only too happy to smother me with love and comfort? I decided that the only way to deal with this matter was to see Simóne again and, if necessary, get to understand her better so as to be able to exorcise this mad absurdity once and for all. There had been few diners on that particular Sunday and on the Sabbath there were only a limited number of railway travellers who might frequent the bar. Julietta had gone to see her sister and Madame was in her usual place perched on the stool so I left the café and knocked on the door to Simóne's room.

This brought forth a strangled exclamation from within and after a delay of a minute or two the door was opened by about three inches. Simóne recognised me and the opening was widened, a little. She did not invite me in. I asked if she would like to go for a walk. She nodded and ten minutes later we were sitting side-by-side on a bench in the nearest park. I quizzed her much as I had done at our last meeting. Was she well? How was the job? I received the same monosyllabic replies. Then there was silence between us. Just as my exasperation at this pointless encounter was getting beyond simmering point, she turned towards me on the bench, grasped both of my hands in hers, and kissed me with an intense passion such as I had never experienced before. Her tongue darted in and out of my mouth and as she pressed her thin frame to my chest I felt myself becoming aroused. She detached her lips from mine and pulled me to my feet. She then kissed me again forcing her body alongside mine to its full length. I was embarrassed that in such close proximity she could not avoid feeling my erection at the level of her stomach. She was not very tall.

Even when she had detached her lips from mine there was no conversation. She tugged my hand with surprising strength and began to pull me along the path in the direction of her room. I still said nothing. She was breathing heavily; it was clearly audible. We stumbled up the stairs. She found the key and had pulled her dress over her head before the door was closed behind us. Her arms encircled my neck and I could feel the nails digging into my scalp. Her eyes were blazing and there was a thin dribble of spittle descending her chin. She paused in her man-handling of me long enough to remove her shabby underclothing and stockings. Her breasts were as flat as the saucers we used at the Trois Perroquets but her nipples were prominent and cherry red. She went down on her knees and scrabbled at my trouser belt, as if in a frenzy. She tried to pull my trousers down before the buckle was undone at which stage I decided I should take some part in this action. Until now it had been a solo performance and I needed to convert this unexpected and extraordinary turn of events into a duet. I lifted her to her feet. I kissed her gently as I completed the lowering of my trousers. They sat around my shoes. There was a tremor moving up and down her body, but I held her shoulders and guided her towards the bed. As I removed my clothing she seemed to calm down a little but as I recalled afterwards, I could not rid myself of the feeling that she was in total control of the act of love that ensued. She was directing the ceremony, calling the tune. I was the instrument, she the player.

    I did not stay with her very long. She said little and made no attempt to persuade me to remain. Nor did she suggest we meet again. I tried to comprehend what had happened. I could not help saying to myself is she real or is she a ghost — a spirit? Is she a waif or is she a monster? How could such a tiny frame conjure up so strong a passion? Had I been bewitched? As you can imagine, I quickly realised that I needed to see her again as soon as possible to try and find an answer to this conundrum.

    I was not sure what hours she worked but in any case it was unlikely that our free times coincided. I therefore needed to exercise patience and so on the next Sunday, carrying a bag containing a bottle of burgundy and some bread and cheese, I knocked on her door. She appeared immediately. She looked different. There was a wide smile on her face, her eyes were bright and it appeared she had washed her hair. It was shiny and seemed thicker and healthier than before. She squeezed my hand, and positively chortled when I showed her the wine and the food I had brought. She found two glasses, in fact one was a jam jar, but needed to go downstairs to the concierge to borrow a corkscrew. I opened the bottle and we drank all of the contents while she chatted about her neighbours, her fellow workers, how she adored red wine and that she had bought a new dress. Would I like to see it?

The contrast was remarkable. She said more in the first two minutes of this visit than she had uttered during all of our previous meetings. It was as if I was a long-term boyfriend making his usual Sunday afternoon call on the object of his affections. All of a sudden she was ordinary. She was a young girl, full of life, optimistic and even vivacious. Was this the real Simóne? Had that single experience of frantic lovemaking hatched a butterfly from the morose and sad chrysalis I had met in the past?

She said she preferred red wine but it seemed that her experience of drinking it was limited. When the bottle was empty she sat on my lap for a moment, then lay on the bed and fell fast asleep. This, I recalled, is what happened at the Hôtel Majestic. I sat and looked at her. Compared to the previous occasion she looked content and happy. Was this all due to me? Perhaps, but I suspected there was some other trigger at work in this unusual creature. I remained watching her until the sun had set and then went home. I was no nearer solving the mystery that was Simóne.

I needed a second opinion. I told Julietta everything about Simóne — well not exactly everything. I recounted how I had met her in mourning at the Notre Dame and how she puzzled me. I was by now, or so I thought, sufficiently experienced with the female psyche that from the way my story was framed, Julietta did not see Simóne as a rival. I tried to explain that

*I Never Met Ernest Hemingway*

I could not understand the swings from extreme misery to unfettered joy. It was complicated. I could not mention the falling asleep in my room, or hers, but I told how perplexed I was. I presented her to Julietta as a sad lady, and it could be that it was as simple as that. She was a cheerless young women with little in her life to be happy about and perhaps happenings in her past that rendered her depressed and forlorn. Understandably Julietta could offer no explanation; they had never met. I therefore determined to remedy this omission.

I met Simóne at her room the next weekend and suggested she should come and visit the Trois Perroquets where I worked and meet the French lady who had been so kind as to offer me a job and a roof over my head. Julietta knew of my intentions, Madame Ricard did not. I introduced Simóne to her as a friend whom I had met while serving His Majesty's Government and was it not a pity that Wilson's League of Nations was only stuttering into existence. Madame appeared to have no idea what I was talking about but amazingly was soon captivated by this apparently insignificant young lady I had brought into her presence. Madame was some times very affable, and some times not, but Simóne, without saying too much, seemed to cast a spell over this formidable woman to such an extent that an outsider would have thought them to be lifelong friends — or a grandmother with her favourite granddaughter. Julietta could not comprehend this any more than I could. My fellow worker was drawn to Simóne, there was a natural friendliness in the way they talked to each other, but she too was amazed that the Madame had befriended this urchin so instantaneously — and with such warmth. Julietta proposed she should walk with us as I returned Simóne to her room. Simóne raised no objections. Indeed, she seemed to encourage it, and so I left her at the door being no further forward in my quest to understand. Julietta was no help. As we walked back to the Trois Perroquets she talked about what a nice girl Simóne was — and that was that. I was no further forward.

I think Julietta and I kissed outside the cafe before we parted but I was still too intrigued by the affect Simóne had on everyone to register the fact. There had to be an explanation. Where or what was the key to this women? I was becoming obsessed. Until now the people who had crossed my path had been straightforward. My grandparents were hard-working and honest; my mother lovable and fun; my early roommate at the Hôtel Majestic was a moron and Colonel Kim upright and honourable. Etaples Ida was kind and generous, Sylvia naive and hearty and Miss Rosen, simply beautiful. But what was Simóne?

A few days after the successful visit to my place of work I was on my way to see her when to my surprise she appeared walking towards me. Our eyes met, I stopped, and she walked right past as if in a trance. She never said a word, and neither did I. I turned on the spot to see her retreating figure. She seemed to be walking more quickly than when I had seen her approaching me. You could ask why I did not call out, but I was so amazed at her conduct; I was speechless. There was no doubt in my mind, she had seen me. What was happening?

I should perhaps have followed her but without quite knowing what I was doing I carried on towards her room and sat on the stairs outside the door and pondered. Had I said anything to offend her? Was she jealous of Julietta? But if so, why had Simóne been so friendly at our last meeting? I did not have to wait long. I heard her light tread on the stairs. She looked thoroughly depressed; I think there was even a scowl on her face but before I could rise to my feet she fell across me and began to kiss me with the same wild abandon as before. When we reached the bed she became even more frenzied as she fell on me again, pinning me down to that horsehair mattress where she brought us both to a more or less instant orgasm. I could not explain where the strength came from. These intensities of lust seemed to give her the muscles of a heavyweight boxer. She did not mention ignoring me in the street only thirty minutes before and somehow she had bundled me out of her presence before I could ask her about the incident. As I sat on the stairs putting on my shoes and socks I realised that the ambiguity of this strange woman was no nearer a solution.

As I walked home I realised that any enquiry into the enigma that was Simóne needed to concentrate on one specific mystery; how was she able to influence people's opinion of her? If you had met her on the street, or standing next to you in a shop, there would have been no second glance. There was nothing arresting, or unusual, in the appearance of this slip of a girl and yet she appeared, quite unconsciously, to be able to make everyone she met like her. From what I have already described it is clear that she had already begun to exercise this power in my case, but how had she been able to work the same spell on Madame Ricard? The proprietor of the Trois Perroquets was a very formidable lady, she sometimes frightened me, but Simóne had the Madame eating out of her hand after the shortest of acquaintances — and very few words. Simóne's ability to entrance people was not achieved with the tongue, she said very little, but there had to be something in her aura that did the trick. What other explanation is there? Julietta was another of her captives. They were so different and Simóne had made no attempt to be overtly friendly and yet, to hear Julietta talk about her afterwards, you would imagine they had lived together for years without a single cross word. And these were not the only examples, as I was to discover later.

I was very busy learning how to run a kitchen and as a result I managed, for a time, to remove the problem of Simóne to an inner recess of my mind. It was clear to all that the Trois Perroquets had been given a new lease of life. As summer approached and the weather became warmer I persuaded Madame to add two more tables for outside use and two more for the bar area. Julietta brought along a friend of hers, Liselle, who found favour with our formidable proprietor and so was added to the small establishment. Liselle had an abundant head of striking red hair. She reminded me of the paintings of Toulouse-Lautrec and was soon a great hit with the customers. We began to offer a restricted menu, soup and omelettes, to those who sat at the tables away from the dining salon. In that area a *menu ā fix* was available at lunch and dinner of the same soup followed, as I had already determined, by a choice of a chicken or a beef dish. For dessert our clientele was spoilt for choice from the traditional crème brûlée to a variety of tarts and the popular crêpe although I had not yet had the temerity to produce a lardy cake. Moses, away from the wet- cloth weapon of his former boss, was proving to be an excellent assistant. He was quick and seemed to have an intuitive grasp of what I wanted to happen next. Sometimes it was quite uncanny. If I decide in my mind that the omelette today was to include tomatoes, Moses was cutting up the same before I had said a word.

The Trois Perroquets prospered but this was not the same elsewhere in Europe. Much of the continent soon began to experience the economic consequences of the war, particularly Germany where there was no effective central government to deal with the extreme crisis facing that country. In France, large areas were still devastated as a result of the conflict and everywhere, to a greater or lesser degree, most of the people faced a severe shortage of food, lack of fuel, inflation and the deadly influenza. The next instalment in the Simóne story was to take place outside of Paris and so I was able to view for myself evidence of this poverty from the windows of the train that took us to the coast.

Although Madame Ricard had never left Paris, she did condescend to close the café for the first two weeks of August so the more adventurous members of staff, if they could afford to, might go to the seaside or visit friends or relatives who lived outside the city's boundaries. When I became aware of this I resolved that I would use one of these weeks to take

Simóne away on holiday to see if time spent together, away from that room of hers that I was now beginning to see as something like the den of the devil, would reveal what made her act in the way she did.

She displayed some mild enthusiasm when I made the proposal and seemed to have no difficulty in obtaining a leave of absence from the candle maker. We left the *Gare St-Lazare* by the earliest train to le Tréport where I secured a room for us in a modest hotel three streets back from the plage. I signed the hotel register as Mr and Mrs James Smith. On two afternoons of that week we made love, but not every night. Whether it was the sea air, or the wine consumed with our suppers, but on three, or was it four occasions, she was asleep before I had finished cleaning my teeth. I enjoyed the lovemaking although Simóne's attitude towards this was just as confused as her swings between gloom and gaiety. I have already described the ardour she displayed during our earlier encounters but more than once during that holiday she rebuffed my advances with a determination that verged on the venomous. On those occasions she gave the distinct impression that she found sexual intercourse repulsive — my arm around her shoulders would make her shiver as though she had just emerged from an ice-cold bath. However, it was not amour I looked for, or necessarily wanted. What I sought was an understanding and I think this was achieved, in part. We swam in the sea. At least I did, Simóne was too timid. We walked along the promenade. We built sandcastles and went on donkey rides. And we talked.

The difficulty, dear reader, was that although some of Simóne's past became revealed, I could never be certain she was telling the truth. More than once she contradicted a fact that had been given the day before and by the time we returned to Paris the jigsaw picture I had hoped to put together still had a number of pieces missing — but let me describe to you what was in place.

*Alan Shelley*

First I must tell you that before the holiday I had received some help in putting together this analysis, partial as it might be, from Francois. He was still in touch with Miss Rosen, the object of my childhood infatuation. Not only had she qualified as a doctor with flying colours, she was now training to be a specialist in psychiatry at St Mary's Hospital in London — and was married to one of those doctors who had initially given her a such a hard time because of her gender. I always knew she was a winner. I wrote quite frankly to Francois about Simóne and he passed my letter on to Liza who was quick to provide me with a professional opinion that was very helpful. From the information she had available she thought Simóne might be suffering from manic depression and when she listed the indicators, I could see how many were exhibited by Simóne. The contrast between depression and mania was stark. In the former state, symptoms included feelings of unhappiness that do not go away, bursting into tears for no reason, avoiding contact with people and an aversion towards sex. When in the mania mode they become happy and excited, optimistic and manifest a greatly expanded sex drive. Liza said that this awful condition often ran in families but it could also come about if the sufferer had been subjected to some particularly stressful experiences in the past, and when Simóne told me of her childhood, it was clearly events from there that appeared to be the principal culprit.

The story she told me was this. She had been born in a village some miles to the west of Reims, the only child of a young mother. Her father was a farm labourer and it is likely that she had been conceived out of wedlock. They were poor, but the mother was by disposition a cheerful soul and Simóne's early childhood had been relatively happy. Her father, as far as I could assess, had been a gentle man but somewhat dim-witted. He had received very little schooling and probably his lack of intellectual strength was the result of inbreeding. It was a small close-knit community. However, this did not prevent his recruitment into the army within days of war being declared and Simóne and her mother's penury became more dire as they needed to exist on what the soldier could remit to them from his meagre pay. In addition to poverty they were in some physical danger, being close to the front line, but their hamlet was not overrun by the Germans and during the last three years of the war, Simóne's father served in a Division that was based only a few miles from his home village.

These facts were made clear by Simóne, over time. What happened next was more obscure. What certainly occurred was that her mother was brutally assaulted, raped more than once and then strangled by one of the assailants who was more drunk than the other attackers. Simóne had not actually seen what happened but had heard her mother's cries, and the men's sounds of satisfaction, from her hiding place in the loft over the barn where the deed was perpetrated. There were however two other factors that I believed had pushed Simóne over the edge into the mixed-up creature she now was. Firstly, these rapists were not Germans. This group of men were not the Bôche that killed babies and slaughtered the innocent; they were French soldiers, unhinged no doubt by the horrors of the three years of warfare they had suffered, but more significantly being out of their senses with the rum stolen from a supply depot partially destroyed by a German shell. The final horrifying detail was that Simóne's father was one of this party. He had, in all innocence, led the soldiers to where he worked in peace-time. He wanted to see his wife and daughter and offer his colleague some fresh milk, or eggs, but he was too drunk himself to gather any such provisions, or prevent the disaster that ensued.

What could I say after she had told me this horrifying story? She was too stressed to explain what happened next and I did not press. I assumed she had moved to Paris to be cared for by her aunt, the concierge, and I further conjectured that when she said she had never known her father she had simply erased his existence from her mind. Perhaps he had been killed — in the war — alongside so many of his fellow countrymen. I was never able to discover if this was so. However, the problem I had was that I was falling in love with the sunny half of this split personality and this was so strong, so certain, I could for the moment ignore the dark side of her nature. 'What is this thing called love.' We had few interests in common and she was only semi-literate. She was not pretty, and only occasionally vivacious, but I was drawn to her as if by magnetism. I was her handful of iron filings. When at her brightest she made me happy, both in and out of bed, and I was beginning to find I needed to be with her at all times.

We returned from our holiday, me a little more enlightened but she continued to display the same inconsistency of personality that had been present from the first. She sat next to me on the train but would not enter into any conversation and seemed to find my presence objectionable. There was no holding of hands and she kept the side of her body out of contact with mine. I should of course have been more forceful but, once again, she seemed able to drain the spirit out of me but when I left her at the 'devils den' she came alive for a moment and, as we said goodbye, thanked me for the holiday with some signs of pleasure and stroked my hair.

I told her I would be with her on the following Sunday but on impulse decided to surprise her, and so went during the quiet period between lunch and dinner a day earlier, the Saturday. I assumed she would not be at work but what I had not foreseen was that she was not alone. Ah, I hear you say, she has another lover, but that was not the case. At my knock the door was opened, vigorously, by a young woman, but older than Simóne. All she said was, 'Yes' and then Simóne's face appeared over her shoulder. Her expression was blank, as though she was viewing a stranger, but by that familiar shoulder gesture she indicated that I should come in.

She made no attempt to introduce me to the visitor. After a moment of awkward silence the stranger said she was Simóne's cousin and I explained who I was and what I was doing in Paris. After that nothing more was said, and as it appeared clear that Simóne did not welcome my presence, I left. I was angry, but was this feeling of sufficient intensity to rescue me from the inexplicable love in my heart? Was it strong enough to continue to accept such humiliations from the one I am supposed to be in love with, or will more of this behaviour extinguish what I feel?

The following day, in the afternoon, the cousin appeared at the Trois Perroquets asking for me. I suggested we should sit at one of our pavement tables and drink some coffee, which we did. After she had told me her name was Marguerite, and had complimented me on my grasp of the French language, the next piece of information she volunteered was most unexpected.

"*Monsieur*. Simóne tells me you have been very good to her and that she is in love with you."

I have tried to faithfully describe my relationship with this girl and I trust that you are as surprised by this statement as I was. The word 'love' had never been uttered by either party, and certainly not by her.

"Marguerite, may I address you as such. She has never said this to me. Sometimes I think she is totally indifferent to my very existence. Your cousin is a strange girl but I suppose what happened to her mother during the war would be sufficient to render anyone strange."

"Oh, *Mon dieu*. What story did she tell you? The one where she killed her father with a pitchfork?"

"Goodness, no. About the attack on her mother."

"Simóne was born in Paris and has rarely left the city. My mother disowned her sister before the war. She was a dissolute woman who went with many men. She never knew which one was Simóne's father. She disappeared in 1916 and we looked after Simóne. She was a difficult young woman, perhaps with good cause in view of her mother — and an unknown father. She did not like school and when she left made no attempt to find work. My mother did not know what to do for the best. Simóne acted as an assistant concierge for a year or two, if she could be persuaded to leave her bedroom, but then there was a big row and she simply left. We heard later she found work as a servant with a retired officer of the French army. I think she might also have been his mistress. We never had any contact until a few weeks ago when she came to tell me she now lives alone — and all about you."

I was speechless. Marguerite went on.

"I do not know why she is so strange. She herself thinks it is because her father was of the aristocracy, a Marquis at least, but so mad he had to be restrained in an asylum. From the expression on your face that is another of those stories new to you."

I spluttered an affirmative.

"I have of course been concerned about her. I believe she suffers from the medical condition known as 'manic depression'. I feel so sorry for her but thinking back to our first meeting, what was she doing at the Notre Dame?"

"Oh, she told me that she often went there to pray — and to cry when most distressed."

"How sad. But back to what you said. She has never said she might love me but I have found I can't help myself from falling in love with her. What am I to do?"

"My mother and I have asked the same question. Before she ran away we tried to get medical help. One of the tenants in the apartment block is a doctor and although not a psychiatrist he talked about schizophrenia — or as you say, manic depression. He saw her once or twice but did not seem to be able to help controlling those impulses she has, or the lies. She has such a vivid imagination, although when you meet her you wonder where she gets it from. She does not look like a person who would tell the stories she does, but then I suppose that's how she convinces people. We were often quite frightened by her changes of mood. Frequently they were of a silent nature. She would not speak to us for days and barely left her bed — and then she would rant and rave and accuse us of all sorts of horrible things. Keeping her prisoner; hiding her father from her. We did our best to find her when she ran away but Paris is a big city and everyone was distracted by the war."

I put my head in my hands and looked at this rational young woman. What a contrast to Simóne. I fetched some more coffee.

"I must tell you Marguerite that I think there has been an improvement since we first met. Just a little more confidence, and she cries less often. Sometimes I cannot seem to connect to her at all but recently, when we have been together, she has generally been more relaxed. On the other hand I must tell you frankly I worry for the future and that makes me nervous about allowing the love I think I have to flourish — to fully express itself. I have never told her about this but I feel I cannot desert her. Is this the classic love dilemma? I cannot live with her — and I cannot live without her."

As the story of Percy Glossop that I am recounting to you is essentially of the romantic genre, you will not be too surprised that at that moment Simóne appeared. She sat down and smiled at both of us. I had never seen her dressed so well. A patterned blouse, a long black skirt and a red beret but more importantly, the wide smile on her face and the sparkle in her eyes made her beautiful to behold. At least to me. I stretched out my hand and she grasped it in both of hers.

"I have been so horrid to you, *Mon Chéri*. I have told Marguerite all about you. She told me she was coming. She is my messenger. She comes to express the love I have for you that, because I am such a bad girl, I have been unable to make in my own words. Please, you must forgive me. Truly, I cannot help myself. All those stories. All those lies. Where do they come from? Drunken soldiers. Pitchforks. My mind is full of those pictures but they're all false. I know I am doing it but I seem to lose control of myself. You must think I am mad, or going mad. Perhaps I am. Or am I just wicked? Please, I cannot help it. I shall die if I lose you. You are making me better. I can be better. I love you. There I've said it. Can you love me?"

I sat transfixed. It did not look like the Simóne I knew, nor did it sound like her. She carried on in this vein, at breakneck speed, until a characteristic feature did appear. Her eyes filled with tears. I looked across at Marguerite. Her eyes were also wet and, frankly, so were mine. Simóne was still holding my hand. I raised hers to my lips and kissed them.

*When we got back to the States, Marge and I could not agree whether to live in Texas or New England. We compromised on New York.*

*We had both decided that Paris was gorgeous, but most of our fellow countrymen and women there were plain bums and so we were delighted to be home. Percy raved about the food but frankly I was glad to get back to the clam chowder and the T-bone. I never said it to Marge, but in my opinion those crabs were the best thing that ever came out of New England.*

*When I next heard from Percy he was still in Paris, shacked up with some French flower girl or other. I told him to come and live in the land of opportunity, a suggestion he did not respond to. Probably as well with the depression just around the corner. Marge and I do not do too badly. We set up as corsetieres. Seems there is always money around to ensure that 'my ladies figure' shows the right curves.*

*We never went back to Paris.*

Sylvia Faulkner May 1924

# Chapter Four

## Interlude

*Custard Josephine Baker*

*Beat three eggs with three tablespoons sugar. Mix two tablespoons flour in a little milk and add two cups more milk. Mix with sugar-and-egg mixture and strain. Add two teaspoons kirsch and three tablespoons liqueur Raspail. Add three bananas cut in thin slices and a few tiny pieces of the zest or rind of a lemon. Mix well, pour into a fireproof dish, and cook in a preheated 400° oven for twenty minutes. Serve cold.*

## Hemingway

Ernest Hemingway's fiction first came before the public with his collection, *Three Stories and Ten Poems,* published in 1923 by Robert McAlmon. Only three hundred copies were printed but I acquired one and this prompted me to begin a pastiche adopting his style. It was a poor imitation but over the years, as my skills improved and his output increased so as to provide more examples, my little story became the following. Still not very convincing I admit.

# The Cat in the Bar

The gas lights in the street had just been lit. It was difficult to see if it had stopped raining. The curtains were open but the windows were misted over. Spirals of moisture decorated the panes. He was not wearing a hat. The suit was old, but clean. He had unusually bushy eyebrows. Steve noticed him but continued to rest his elbows on the bar counter. It was above average height, as if designed to fit the barman's frame.

"Can I get a drink." he said.

Steve half nodded and without hesitation drew a pint of mild ale and placed it before the stranger. The only other person in the room was an old woman. She sat in the shadows, fast asleep. She snored at a low pitch that was not unpleasant to hear. The hair was thin and more yellow than white.

"She all right?"

Steve grunted.

"Should I buy her a drink?"

The words seemed to echo around the empty room. She stirred.

"Shouldn't think so."

Two young men entered. Both were unshaven but the incipient whiskers did not camouflage the pallid skin. The rain was heavier. The shoulders of the identical plaid jackets they wore were wet and with the warmth of the bar, the wool of the coats gave off a gentle exhaust of steam. They ignored the stranger and Steve pulled two pints and slid them across the damp bar top in their general direction. He said nothing.

"Where're we going to night?"

"Dunno."

"Let's try The Feathers."

The smaller of the two returned his jar of beer to the counter with a clatter. The old woman woke and stood up. She moved alongside the stranger, who smiled at her. She was indeed very ancient, but her eyes had a shine of metallic blue.

"That Charlie Chaplin was in here."

*Alan Shelley*

"Oh yes. When was that?"
"He was."
"Very well, but when? He lives in America."
"Must have been after the war."
The two young men were listening.
"What war would that be then?"
"The Great War, you young bastards. What do you think?"
"Was he a regular?"
"How should I know. Only seen him the once."
"Did he make you laugh?"
The old woman did not understand the question. She moved back to her corner and closed her eyes. Steve lit a second gaslight over the bar.
"Just like the Blackpool illuminations." one young man commented. He attempted a laugh.
No one reacted.
"Where are we off then?"
"I'm thinking."
Steve said they should stay where they were and have another pint. Neither said a word but pushed the tankards a few inches closer to the beer pump. The old lady suddenly rose to her feet and moved over to the stranger with no hat.
"Where you come from, me duck?"
"Oh, here and there."
"Why don't you wear an 'at?"
"I left it on the train."
"Oh, I not ever been on a train. Is it a thrill?"
"Yes ma'am, it is."
"Ma'am! I'm called Mother Thomas. My hubby, God rest his soul, came from Cardiff."
"Nice place, Cardiff."
"Never been. What's your name?"
The stranger looked at a sign prominently displayed behind the bar.
"Worthington. Ernest Worthington."

"Well Ernie, what about that drink you promised me. When you first come in."

No one had noticed the cat. It was under the table furthest from the front door. The old lady quitting her seat had aroused the feline who decided to inspect the clientele. It ignored Steve. His scent was familiar. The cat's targets were extended to include two young women who had entered and stationed themselves at the end of the bar furthest away from the men who well into their second pint. Mary Gordon stroked the cat but by the time she had ordered a lemonade shandy, it had disappeared.

"I wish I had a cat." she offered to Steve.

"You can have that one, if you can find the bloody thing. No use to me."

The stranger looked at the two girls. Both had short skirts but Mary Gordon was wearing a white beret. The hair of her friend was piled on the top of the head. She wore spectacles that magnified her eyes. Like fried eggs, Steve thought.

"Nice place this. Well lit."

They ignored him.

"You regulars?"

"What ya mean?"

"Do you often drink in here — and would you really like a cat? Very independent creatures, you know."

"Well, I like cats and cats like me."

"That's all right then."

The two young men moved towards the girls, who ignored them but giggled.

"Let's go to The Feathers."

'Sure. A bit quiet in here, ain't it."

The girls left. They did not say goodbye. The stranger did. As the old woman continued to snore she moved in her sleep and slid further down the bench she occupied under the gas lamp that was not yet lit. The cat re-appeared and sat washing its face on the seat next to the women. Cats always know the best places. They are survivors. Steve appeared to sigh as he wiped down the bar with a torn and dirty cloth that advertised Bass beer. It was still raining.

Much later I showed this piece of frippery to my own agent. Her comment was a pithy one: 'The great man has nothing to fear from you, Mr Glossop'. Possibly so, but it amused me. I wonder if Alice Toklas would have joined in the joke. From what I was told, she and Gertrude Stein did make fun of Hemingway. They thought his best writing was going to be when he wrote the story of his life — and how perceptive they were. His finest fictions are about himself — whether as a drinker, fighter or fisherman. It was said that he was teaching a young man to box and during the tuition the pupil knocked out the master. I told this story to Georges Carpentier when he dined at the Trois Perroquets shortly after he had lost his title to Battling Siki. There may be some odd names for restaurants around the world, but these boxers also come up with some extraordinary sobriquets.

I also did not think my little story was likely to knock out the master.

## I Never Met Ernest Hemingway

*He came into the bookshop several times. I remember him because he was an Englishman, who was a chef in Paris. Strange. He spoke very good French. He normally turned up late in the afternoon, presumably a slack time in his kitchen, and seemed more interested in talking than looking at the books, although he did borrow some fairly often. He prided himself on his literary interests, but had an irrational dislike of Ernest, even though they had never met. He was very persuasive about* Ulysses. *He insisted on two copies, one for a distinguished British poet, but he omitted to say which one. I recall he was accompanied on one occasion by a young French woman. Rather odd creature, I thought. He talked about an American friend who had obtained some success in the Paris art world, but if he had, his fame had passed me by. He invited me to dine at the restaurant where he cooked — near to the* Gare Montparnasse. *I avoided this.*

Sylvia Beach July 1924

# Chapter Five

# Paris

*Bavarian Cream Perfect Love*

*Mix 2 cups sugar and 8 yolks of eggs until lemon-coloured. Slowly add 2 cups hot milk in which six cloves have been heated. Put in a saucepan over the lowest heat. With a wooden spoon stir continuously in the same direction until the spoon remains thickly covered. Do not allow to boil. Remove from heat and pour over half tablespoon powdered gelatine that has been soaked for five minutes in quarter cup of cold water. Stir in the same direction until the gelatine is completely dissolved, then strain and stir from time to time in the same direction until cool. When cold, mix with 3 cups whipped cream, to which the grated zest of two lemons has been added. Pour into a lightly oiled mould and place in refrigerator for four hours. Remove from mould to serving dish. The cream may be flavoured with a fruit purée. Two and a half cups purée and one tablespoon lemon juice are mixed with half cup icing sugar.*

## Hubert

What is Paris famous for? Firstly, just for being Paris, one of the most beautiful cities in the world, but what virtue would you choose next? The cuisine, the fashion, the can-can? Perhaps, but when I lived there it was still the centre of the world for the visual arts, products of the paint brush, the sculptor's chisel and even the photographer's lens — the American Man Ray considered Paris to be his true home. For me, culture had tended to involve the written word, but I was now called upon to use my eyes in a different way as a result of a chance meeting with the very tall Hubert Richardson Junior, the American Sylvia and her friend had brought to that farewell dance at the Hôtel Majestic.

He was quite a distinctive figure and so when he walked into the Trois Perroquets one evening with two girls, I remembered him even though we had only met once before. I have known a few Americans in my life and so, with hindsight, I can best describe him to you as an earlier version of Jimmy Stewart, without the good looks but with the same laconic laid-back attitude towards life — although he was to display more serious traits later as he began to make a name for himself in artistic circles. He was now even thinner than I remembered. His clothes were dishevelled; a creased suit that might once have been white, a garish bow tie sited off-centre within a bedraggled shirt collar and a battered trilby hat. His thin fair hair hung like a curtain in front of his eyes. No wonder he did not know who I was; his sight must have been seriously impaired by that fringe. When I greeted him with some warmth he must have thought I was interested in one of his lady friends but by then I only had eyes for Simóne. I asked him if he had heard from the delightful Sylvia Faulkner, but I am not sure he knew what I was talking about.

Even so he was a friendly soul, like Americans so often are, and as he began to frequent the Trois Perroquets we came to know one another better; and then one day he asked if I would like to come and look at some of his paintings. What a surprise. This large, easy-going and languid individual painted, in miniature, street scenes of Paris in the most meticulous detail. He told me he had not sold anything yet, but was hopeful. The remittance he received from Boston must have been substantial; his studio was close to the Boulevard Saint Michel and was extremely spacious, including a servant's quarter that housed an ancient French housekeeper who seemed to go with the property. His French was not very good but she seemed to know what he wanted. She was an indifferent laundress but the premises were kept clean and she was adept at producing the right drink at the right time of day. I never saw her the worse for wear, but I suspect she shared in the tenant's wine-stock, as did I. She had a grandson living with her.

I met with Simóne whenever possible but, without discussing it, we subconsciously decided that she would remain in her room while I continued to occupy the garret at the Trois Perroquets. This could be seen as an unsatisfactory and unengaged arrangement for two people who had now expressed their love for each other, but what was the practical alternative? I did not want to move into her room; to me it epitomised the dark side of her nature and it did not seem appropriate that I should bring her into the family of the Trois Perroquets, particularly as my accommodation was so small. Madame Ricard may well have welcomed Simóne moving in with me; she approved of her and would no doubt have seen such action as proof that I was at last losing my British phlegm and finally acquiring some French verve. On the other hand, I was still not sure that Simóne's state of mind would welcome such a move. Should I disturb the status quo? We had reached a satisfactory and stable position in our relationship and I was content for our love-making to take place in her bed, rather than mine. She no longer turned me away and sometimes reacted with the fierce ardour of our first couplings, but mostly our love-making became conventional, expressing the natural love that most young lovers have for each other. But were we that?

I did of course question the long-term future in this: I could not remain as a gentleman-caller forever. Hubert provided a solution. His detached and uncomplicated nature was in total contrast to that of Simóne — at least when she was tense and slipping into a spell on the dark side of her personality — but perhaps because he was so easy-going her moods seemed to pass him by and indeed he became quite fond of her. And she of him. As he and I became more friendly he suggested that as my reputation as a chef grew, at least locally, I needed to improve my image and why not move to a smarter address, his, where he would introduce me to his small circle of friends and I could move up in the world. And bring Simóne with me.

I was not sure how moving to a fashionable address was going to better my status as a Parisian cook because, of course, I had no such status. I was preparing simple dishes in a modest establishment within nose-wrinkling distance of the smoke emanating from the steam engines passing into, and out of, the *Gare Montparnasse*, so what reputation could I have possibly acquired? In her fashion, Madame Ricard expressed neither concern nor pleasure at the prospect of her chef no longer living on the premises as long as he continued to perform his duties as before, but what mostly concerned me was what would Simóne's reaction be. Hubert's apartment was on two floors. His studio and living quarters took up one of these and on the other was the housekeeper, Hortense Jacquet, and two rooms currently used to house the rubbish Hubert had accumulated during his stay in Paris. Not that there was a great deal of this. He had been in the city for less than two years and most of his acquisitions were hardly worth saving. Both of these rooms had views over the roof-tops of Paris, it was the top floor of the block, and Hubert offered them to me. The rent was well within my resources.

"Percy, my friend, I can easily clear those two rooms and then they're yours. Simóne can move in with you so you can make a proper job of making a dishonest woman of her."

Hubert's humour was occasionally rather heavy-handed. It is sometimes the way with Americans.

"I would appreciate the company but, my budding Escoffier, there is a condition. It is an onerous one — possibly one that is incapable of being accomplished."

"You want me to teach you to speak like a Parisian?"

"Well, no. Not quite that difficult. What I want you to do is to tame Madame Hortense. I love the apartment, but she frightens me. You know what a gorgon she is. When she brings in my breakfast I shiver in my dressing gown as I wait to be told what blasphemy against French manners I have now committed. She shouts at me. I do not know how to deal with her. When not shouting, she babbles on so quickly I hardly recognize a word she says."

I had only met this apparent dragon on three occasions. To me she appeared to be a typical French woman of her age, and profession, and I suspected that part of Hubert's bewilderment stemmed from his upbringing. No one in his family raised their voices and their servants no doubt glided through the house with a soft-shoe shuffle and addressed my new friend as 'Massa Hubert'.

"Hubert, a most generous offer, but how will you gauge that I have successfully paid the rent? Would an exchange of francs not be more suitable?"

"You can charm all and any Frenchwoman. Simóne is a simple example, but look how you have Madame Ricard under your thumb and if Simóne was to throw you over and run off with a Foreign Legionnaire, Julietta would be in your bed before you could change the sheets. No. I have no doubt you can rid me of this pestilent priestess. Gosh, I don't mean that. She runs the place well and I suspect she is just as much a permanent fixture as the plumbing. Just get her to stop shouting at me. Act as a barrier between us."

I agreed, although I did insist that in addition to the onerous task I had been given I would, because of my generous nature, add a modest monthly payment in specie.

Each of the two rooms were twice the size of my accommodation and Simóne's put together. One could be a bedroom and the other used as our sitting room where the dragon could provide meals, on request, when we were not dining with Hubert or eating free of charge at the Trois Perroquets. And there was the view. If I was in love with Paris at street level, I was utterly captivated by the roofs of the city. They were of slate and they were of tile. There were cupolas and skylights: mansard roofs and dormer windows: lead and copper: roof terraces for sunbathing and the hanging out the washing: pigeons and seagulls: flat roofs, conical roofs and spires; herb gardens and tropical palms and, in the heat of summer, the concierges escape from their hot and humid boltholes to sit on the roof and knit, like the ladies attending *Madame Guillotine*. Nursemaids could be seen making sure their charges did not fall over the edge. There were old married couples holding hands, and young lovers locked in close embrace who sought privacy above their habitats. I was enraptured. I had found my 'stately pleasure-domes'. And we could see the Seine.

Simóne was less enthusiastic. I think she was genuinely glad to quit her cheerless room, and she was excited at the prospect of our living together, but her nature would not allow these pleasures to be unalloyed. I could perhaps appreciate this. Although very different circumstances, the last time she had shared any living space on a daily basis with anyone else was when part of the household of the French soldier. She never revealed his identity but referred to him as General Georges. Over time she told me more about this period of her life than any other. She never talked about her mother but on the subject of *Mon General* she became relatively loquacious.

"He was very old. Been in the Army for twenty years or more. He was already a general at the start of the war. His wife let it be known that he was not a very good soldier — but his sister was married to a cousin of Marshal Foch, so they tolerated him."

Is it not always the case, I thought.

"They would not trust him in the front line — found him some job at a barracks in the south until 1916, when he was retired. His wife refused to go south with him. She stayed in Paris."

I could picture the situation; clearly a devoted couple.

"He was harmless. Pompous, but really a doddering old fool, but she, she was a formidable monster. If she had been the soldier, the Field Marshal's baton would have been in her hand well before the first Battle of the Somme. She always said she was of the Bourbon family and so looked down her nose at everyone, including her husband. I was the lowest of the low. At everybody's beck and call, but treated most horribly by that awful woman. I'm not sure why. I did what I was told, but she was really vindictive towards me."

I wondered if she saw that something special in Simóne that could not be understood and for that reason she was so cruel.

"She made a point of seeking me out wherever I was working in the house specifically to accuse me, amongst other things, of visiting her husband's bed. As this charge was made, day after day, she would spit in my face, or smack my cheek, and then shriek with laughter and make fun of me saying that even that old man would not sleep with such a pitiful creature as me."

As I was to discover, Simóne was not without pride, and this behaviour must have been difficult to bear. Why did she not leave and go back to her aunt — and I never really discovered why she had left in the first place — but Simóne, being the creature she is, stayed and plotted her revenge on that frightful family. It took some time, but as Choderlos de Laclos wrote: 'revenge is a dish best served cold'.

"I had to escape from this humiliation but before going I decided to get some retribution for their cruelty. I began to make the General notice me. Although something of a roué in his early years, it had been some time since any female had taken any notice of him and he was flattered by my attention.

Eventually, he instructed me to visit him in his private quarters. I had a plan. I went to his room but persuaded him that I was too young and he needed someone with more experience. He accepted this advice, whereupon I became his procurer and night after night smuggled into the house a succession of prostitutes, of the worst sort. The planned result was achieved and I only left the house when his wife discovered that her husband had contracted a serious dose of syphilis."

After that, the money Simóne had saved from the meagre wages earned at the soldier's household soon ran out and she was indeed about to become homeless when we met at the Notre Dame. Her action against the General — and particularly his wife — had been carefully planned but I was convinced that the love that had grown between us did not result from any calculated effort on her part. Nonetheless, she still hesitated for a moment at the thought of our living together; but this changed. After we had been ensconced in Hubert's rooms for a month or two I could see the improvement in her personality. Her black moments became fewer and fewer; she grew to be happier, and so did I. And then our landlord became a saviour for a second time by suggesting that Simóne should quit the candle-making business — and become a full-time model, for him.

Before I begin to chart Hubert's career — with his new model and his new inspiration — I must tell you something about the art scene in Paris in the early 1920s. This is not an introductory lecture for a 'History of Art' course but a few details from my own experience. During my stay I did have some contact with Alice Toklas, the lardy cake recipe was involved, but at this stage I confine my remarks to her companion, Gertrude Stein. She was a wealthy American writer who spent most of her life in France — and at the time I speak of, in Paris. Her salon on the Left Bank at 27 Rue de Fleurus was decorated by the paintings she and her brother had bought before the war. It was an amazing collection; Cézanne, Gauguin, Delacroix, Matisse, Renoir, Toulouse-Lautrec and Picasso. This was

*Alan Shelley*

broken up when her brother moved to Italy, but after the war she continued to support Picasso, in particular, and other avant-garde painters such as Juan Gris and Georges Braque. She was their patron, and their friend. They visited her at the salon but so did figures of equal standing from the literary world: Hemingway, Ezra Pound, Thornton Wilder, Scott Fitzgerald and Sherwood Anderson. I was never invited, although if I had been I might have needed to find another title for this epic of mine.

Hubert was not even on the outer fringes of this world but he was in Paris with some form of artistic identity — at least according to information provided by Sylvia. He had turned up in the city early in 1919 and found a position for himself with the American delegation at the Peace talks. Just as that awful General had a remote connection with Marshall Foch, and as the popular saying goes: 'Lloyd George knew my father', well, Colonel House knew Hubert's father.

I must halt the flow for a moment. If the Welsh Prime Minister knew my father, it was more than I did!

Hubert was able to convince someone on House's staff that his artistic hobby, as a painter, should be utilised by the Yanks and he be appointed 'artist in residence'. No one took this very seriously. It cost them very little but I never saw any evidence that his residency ever resulted in pictures of any kind. What could be said however was that he had 'a jolly time'. But, back to now. Hubert did not have the talent, or the energy, to enter the Stein circle — or even a very minor version of it — but he was such a relaxed and contented soul this did not concern him. He simply enjoyed what he did. When I was ensconced only a flight of stairs away from his studio my own extravagant ambitions persuaded me to try and change all that. I told him it was a mortal sin not to use whatever talent he had been born with to the maximum limit; a few square inches of canvas depicting the Sacré-Coeur, which took two months to produce, was just not good enough. He was prostituting his talents. He should look at the Impressionists, Cubism and

Fauvism. Go and view the works of Duchamp and Mondrian, as well as Braque and Picasso. He ignored my advice. It is doubtful if he knew of any of these masters, but he smiled at me while displaying his ignorance.

However, my entreaties brought about the first change. He decided that painting people might become a pleasing alternative to buildings and, however modest his talents, he must have seen some elusive virtue in Simóne that persuaded him to suggest she should be his model for this experiment. Perhaps he saw the same quality that explained my love for her. She had not exactly blossomed since our first meeting but she was not quite so thin and her complexion had somewhat improved. She still had the appearance of a stray waif, or a frightened fawn, but there was certainly a greater confidence and she was much more articulate, particularly with Madame Hortense. Nevertheless, she was not an obvious example of an artist's model — I could not believe Picasso would have been interested either for that purpose or as a bed-companion, but am I the best judge? She had bewitched me and she seemed to have enchanted Hubert as well.

Simóne accepted the position and instead of miniature portraits of shops on the Champs-Élysées, or a distorted study of The Opéra, Hubert now produced similar sized pictures of Simóne in various settings and wearing dresses of chintz or organza — and invariably a straw hat. The similarity was striking but in point of fact he had never even heard of Fragonard. With the approval of Madame Ricard, I had hung some of Hubert's paintings of Paris attractions on the walls of the bar and the restaurant and let it be known to our clientele that these masterpieces were for sale. One of our regulars, after taking one more drink than usual, was persuaded to give up a few francs for a distant view of the Eiffel Tower, but otherwise, our new wall decorations went unnoticed. However, when at infrequent intervals the pictures that featured my lover made an appearance, things changed. The buyers seemed to have been attracted to Simóne, even if only in the medium of oil paint, in the same way that she had, in all innocence, won over Hubert and me. The sale prices were still very low, but the artist was delighted. He gave all the credit to Simóne — which was perhaps only fitting.

I think she was also pleased over this success but, as usual, it was difficult to tell. What it did achieve however was that she had now become rather keener to follow the informal programme of cultural improvement that I had instigated. I was not about to become a Svengali, or even a Professor Higgins, but the intellectual chasm between us was so great it seemed to me to be worthwhile attempting to build some sort of bridge, however flimsy, for her to use to come across to my side. I am not sure that I had any success in this cultural bridge building, but with the visual arts, there was no reason why her eyes should not be the equal of mine, if not the superior — as proved to be the case. With Hubert we began to visit art galleries and salons that sold paintings. Hubert and I never once agreed on the merits of a particular work. Simóne sometimes sided with me, and sometimes with him, but more often than not her view coincided with that of the gallery curator or the dealer.

However strange her behaviour could sometimes be, I was to experience further examples of the innate intuition with which she was blessed. I prided myself that I was a good judge of people but Simóne saw deep into folk — saw traits that the more intelligent Percy failed to notice. In particular this came to the fore in the affair of Henri Pascal and Poppy Sackville. She was one of the two American girls who had been with Hubert when he first appeared at the Trois Perroquets. The other was Abigail Trabant — but before I take up their role in my story I need to tell you of Hubert's earlier history and how he came to be in Paris. He was reluctant to relate this to me but as we became closer, he did. It was the familiar story; rich boy falls in love with a girl from the wrong side of the tracks and the family acts, but in this case, the action that was taken made my stomach crawl.

"Hubert. I think Abigail's fondness for you has reached a more serious stage. I like her. Not that I've met many, but she is certainly the nicest Yankee lass I have ever known. I was fond of Sylvia but Abigail is pretty, she is smart and her ankles are divine, so why do you allow her attentions to go unnoticed."

Hubert spluttered.

"She's the one for you my friend."

"Mind your own business, you limey cook."

"Limey, I am happy with, but 'cook'. I am, I would like you to know, the chef de cuisine. Long John Silver was a cook but I'm another creature altogether. But you are trying to divert me. Seriously, why not Abigail?"

"Can I tell you, Percy, I've noticed a very bad trait in you. You can be very charming sometimes, but you are a bit of a nosy parker. People might see you as a man filled with curiosity but I wonder if you're not really a voyeur. The way you probe into people, and then go on and on about them. For instance, I feel as though I know your old soldier boss, Colonel Kim, as well as I know my own mother."

"I just like folk. I like you. That's why I'm telling you to do something about Abigail."

"It's too soon for me to fall in love again."

"Why?"

"I can hardly bring myself to explain. It was so horrid."

"I'm a good listener, Hubert. And it might do you good to talk about it."

He screwed up his face and sucked the end of his paint brush.

"Percy, my family can trace their ancestors back to the Pilgrim Fathers. Not only do we dine with the Cabots and the Winthrops, we exchange Christmas cards with the Rockefellers and the Vanderbilts. Our fortune is based on the family bank established by my grandfather around 1840 and ever since then nearly all of the male members have been, or are, involved with that wretched place. Uncle Cuthbert went

*Alan Shelley*

to Mexico and married some black-eyed beauty so he was cut off and never heard of again. His brother did not disgrace the family because he rarely got off his yacht but my father, and my brothers, carry on making money and wearing the starched collars."

"I was not interested in going to Mexico — and I get seasick very easily — so there seemed little alternative when I left Harvard, even though I did suggest I might be permitted to move to New York and set up an artistic wing of the family. Not a hope. My father is very persuasive. All charm and smiles, but ruthless. The iron fist in the velvet glove."

"My idea of moving away from commerce to art was not based on a yen for the visual side — it was music and not painting that first captured my interest then. I am a natural pianist; could not read music but just seemed to have a talent and because of that I greatly enjoy jazz. Not that Boston was exactly famous for such but there were one or two places — hardly nightclubs — where some local people played Dixieland and the like, with the occasional visiting group."

"Yes, not much of that sort of thing in Gloucester either."

"I was a regular. When not called upon to squire some rich and vacant Boston dame to a dance, or be her partner at tennis, I went to one of those clubs and it was there that I met Janine. She was even keener on the music than I was and sometimes sang with one of the local bands. Her father had been a circus hand but was now a stevedore at the docks and her mother worked in a shop that sold cookies. Janine also worked in a shop. They had settled in Boston around 1914 but prior to that she had traversed the whole of the Eastern United States with the circus. She was a small girl but had a big voice. She sang like Ma Rainey."

"I think my mate Bob Patch had some of her records — and Bessie Smith."

"I heard her sing and fell in love, although it was not the music that struck the chord, it was love at first sight. Initially she thought I was ridiculous. Although she was not a regular performer, I acted like the traditional stage-door-Johnny. I sent her flowers. I made sure I was there whenever she was scheduled to sing. I sat at her feet, as it were, and eventually she agreed to have supper with me one night when she had been in particularly good voice. And then she fell in love with me. She refused my gifts but Miss Janine Lacroix took me. I was ecstatic. I spent hours comparing her with all the other girls I knew. They were empty headed, selfish, haughty and vapid. She was funny, had more common sense than I found anywhere on the Harvard campus, and she was pretty. A natural blonde with green eyes and the grace of a ballet dancer — but of course, she was not of our sort."

"I can see that."

"It was not long before my father discovered how I was spending my leisure hours. He called me into his study, told me how when he was twenty he had a crush on a vaudeville girl but soon got over that and, thank goodness, married the pearl who was my mother. Forget about her, he said. At that stage I did not react. I shook his hand and he gave me a glass of his special scotch. After two months I was back in that study. I had by then asked Janine to marry me and she had accepted. There was no scotch this time. No reminiscences about his youth. My father said he would not allow this to happen and then reminded me that I was committed to spend the next five days at Bar Harbour for a family wedding and after that we would discuss this matter further."

"Hubert, he does not sound like a very nice man."

"He is not. I was away five days. I never discovered how it was arranged but as I pieced the story together later, Janine was arrested at one of the clubs where she sang and charged with immoral behaviour. She was initially kept in the holding cell at the police precinct with all the other women prisoners but the next day she was moved and kept in solitary confinement. Two days after being so incarcerated she was found dead. She had, so they said, made a rope out of her silk petticoat and hanged herself. I wonder how much that cost to arrange."

"That's unbelievable."

"The family tried to suggest that this incident proved what a piece of low-life she was. You can guess my reaction to that. I threw an inkwell at my father's head and attempted to crown my older brother with one of the study chairs, but it was too heavy. I have not seen my father since then but I am told that the scar on his forehead glows when my name is mentioned. I caught the first train I could to New York but the family lawyer soon tracked me down. I signed the document. They could not change my grandmother's trust, which gives me a good slice of capital when I reach twenty-five, but the stipend from the family seemed to reflect my father's guilt as the allowance proved to be a generous one — but if ever I returned to Boston, it would lapse. The last thing I would ever want to do was to return to the Beantown — and so I chose Paris."

I said nothing. I could see the strain in his face.

Over the next few months, and however painful it was, he told me more about Janine and this only reinforced the repulsion I felt for the way she had been treated — the way she had been removed from the scene in the name of American high society — and this only made me contrast his world with the society from whence I had emerged. I compared George Glossop to those arrogant Bostonians. Was there nothing more that Hubert could have done? He had never met Janine's parents but decided it would only make it worse if he called on them now, after the tragedy. He was, indirectly, the cause of their daughter's death and nothing could change that. He thought of going to the police and the newspapers but the former were clearly complicit in this outrage and even if the editors were prepared to oppose the Boston Brahmins, he could not prove any wrongdoing and Janine's family would not want any further publicity.

I told him I could not accept this. There must have been something he might have done other than scarring his father for life but as I could see how upsetting this was, I did not pursue the matter further. Although Sylvia had introduced him to me as Hubert Richardson Junior, the 'Junior' had disappeared long ago. As can be understood, he did not want to be referred to as the junior of his father, a man he now vehemently hated. I think he had contemplated changing his name by deed poll, and then thought better of it. Such an action would have been irrelevant to what had happened but if he had chosen a new name I thought that when he was still painting Simóne in frocks, Gainsborough would have suited well.

Reverting to the love-sick Abigail, although love-sick is my description rather than a reflection of reality. The lady in question was too tough to sit around exhibiting a broken heart but I should first tell you about these two damsels — not that they were in distress, I might add. They were not from Boston. I rather think that if they had been Hubert would never have befriended them and on that subject I believe he no longer eats baked beans, a prejudice I fully endorse. The girls had some connection with a man who had been at Harvard with him — a Texan I believe — but they hailed from Brooklyn where they went to school together, and stayed friends thereafter. Both families were middle-class; Poppy's father worked in the family leather business and Abigail's was a journalist. The girls reached their twentieth birthdays in the year 1920 and decided that if they were to achieve their ambitions before the next one came round they needed to use up all their savings and sail for Paris, immediately. The fact that their ability with the French language had hardly progressed from what they were taught at school did not deter them. While part of the artistic life of Paris, Poppy was going to become a female Henry James — or at least a latter-day Edith Wharton — and her friend was going to paint. John Singer Sargent was not mentioned. Their talents in both of these areas may have been limited but they were eager, they were young, and they were good company.

*Alan Shelley*

Why is it that all Americans look so healthy? It cannot be the climate; Montana and New Mexico differ considerably. Must be the diet — all those steaks — or is it genetic, so many differing ancestors all mixed up to produce the strongest brew? And their teeth. It seems akin to a religion that from an early age parents concentrate on correcting any faults in their young so that as adults they can produce the smile that sparkles. Also, they always look so clean. Is it the plumbing? Your response to this is to argue that there are plenty of the Uncle Sam brigade with pasty skins, nicotine stained teeth and narrow eyes, but most of those I have met are more like my description than not. Particularly the female version. Lots of energy, naturally curly hair and long tanned legs.

Abigail and Poppy were perfect examples of my definition. Both had dark complexions and used the same pink colour to highlight their full lips. They equally talked a lot, especially Poppy. As a result of the introduction to Hubert, they became the first members of his salon — before Simóne and I arrived on the scene. I liked both of them. Their confidence and optimistic no-nonsense approach to life appealed to me and they were certainly more intelligent than Sylvia, their corsetiere compatriot. Simóne's attitude towards them was more complicated. She found them brash to begin with, but as the phenomenon struck again, they were soon enraptured with her and so became great friends and fully-paid up members, with Madame Hortense, in the all-men-are-beasts club that the young ladies set up.

The two youngest members had managed to inveigle a small allowance from their fathers, just about enough to keep them in modest circumstances in Paris where the cost of living was relatively low, but to add to this Poppy had found some part-time work at the American Embassy while waiting for the muse to strike and as for Abigail, the kindly Hubert allocated a corner of his studio for her to set up her easel. His talent, as I have already revealed, was limited but I thought in the case of Abigail that the sooner she found a rich husband, the better.

Not that that was why she was romantically inclined towards Hubert. As I was by then something of an expert in this field, I was convinced that on her part it was the real thing and that is why I was acting on her behalf with our landlord.

But, alas, to no avail as I could see he had other things on is mind than the sweet Abigail. Since Simóne had become a part of the painting establishment he had changed. Was it her again? Who knows, but he had certainly become more ambitious. He was no longer prepared to be another unknown and ungifted amateur artist using Paris as an excuse to waste money on oil paints and canvas; he needed to produce some worthwhile paintings that connoisseurs would appreciate and want in their collections. He aspired for his work to be found hanging on the walls of 27 Rue de Fleurus rather than being ignored by the diners and drinkers at the Trois Perroquets. I thought this was totally unrealistic — pie in the sky — and I told him so, but Simóne encouraged him in this mission and it was she that was instrumental in setting his feet on the ladder towards some of the wider recognition he longed for. In her own quiet, but intensive way, she persuaded Hubert to give up his minimalist style and paint big pictures of her — but in the nude.

What was my reaction to this? The strange workings of Simóne's mind were still something of an enigma to me but I could not oppose this brave move because I had already seen too many examples of the gift she had for making decisions that turned out well. Perhaps it was only since she had met me that sagacity began to feature in her makeup. I have already used the metaphor of the magnet and the iron filings. Did she need me, her scrap of metal, to become more steady — and more wise? On the other hand, when Hubert had got over the surprise at her suggestion — and started to warm to the idea — I became somewhat sceptical and began to wonder if an unclothed Simóne was going to provide the inspiration for this studio's great paintings? I did not think she would have found favour with Rubens, or with Pierre Auguste Renoir.

*Alan Shelley*

# The Boutet Nudes

Simóne was not as emaciated as when we had first met, Madam Hortense was mainly to thank for that, but she had very few curves and her skin was often somewhat pallid. The nipples provided some colour, and she had grown her hair so that it lay in waves across her shoulders, but was that enough? Perhaps; it would depend on how she might inspire the new Hubert. Would she emerge on his canvases to resemble the women in *The Demoiselles d" Avignon*? Initially both Abigail, for she joined in, and Hubert painted what they saw — what was superficially on view — and the results were uninspiring. I did not take any of his early efforts to the walls of the Trois Perroquets but gradually there was a change. He became very disheartened, and neither my cooking nor Abigail's attentions could help, but that magnet perched on a stool, or draped over the chaise longue, gradually began to exert an influence as the paintings became less realistic, more symbolic — and different. Even I could see that some new energy was being discharged along those paint brushes, Hubert's that is; it never happened to Abigail. It is difficult to explain. He was not following a trend. He was not copying others. It was still the work of Hubert Richardson but I can only suggest that the strange lady who shared my bed had transformed the artist within that lanky frame — moved him on to another plane. These new studies of Simóne were too large to hang at the Trois Perroquets but even if Hubert was unsure, I was convinced that somewhere in Paris was a dealer who would welcome the opportunity to represent this latter-day Lazarus — and there was.

Not only had Hubert moved into a totally different field, he was now moving at a much greater pace — in fact it might be described as feverish. A clothed Abigail became an additional subject, but it was the 'Boutet Nudes', the accolade they were eventually given, that occupied most of his working day. Not that he became obsessive. I was rather tied to my chef's apron strings, but Hubert would often announce at breakfast that he proposed an excursion that day and even if I had to decline, he invariably had both Simóne and Abigail as his companions, and sometimes Poppy. The favourite was a trip on the famous Bateaux-Mouches on the Seine and we all thoroughly enjoyed viewing the bridges and landmarks of the city from this vantage point. At this time my relationship with Simóne was a happy and settled one and my admiration for her only grew after observing the impact she had on my mother and François when they came to Paris. I mention the visit of the Gloucester bakers because they too thought the evening we all spent cruising the Seine to be the high point of their holiday.

If the city is to be seen in its finest glory from the river, our little coterie decided the early evening cruises were to be preferred. It is often said that without the Seine there would be no Paris, and certainly if there was no river it would not be the supreme city that it is. It was the men who operated the river trade that came, during the Middle Ages, to be the leading citizens of the town. Not for nothing does the badge of Paris portray a boat. The Bateaux-Mouches are a familiar sight but what is not so familiar is the origin of the name given to these vessels. Are they named for their designer, Jean-Sebastian Mouche — who may or may not have existed — or were they christened after a quay in Lyon called 'quai de la Mouche'? Still others believe that they were named after a small spy boat. Although the French word 'mouche' generally refers to the insect 'fly', the word was used, in old slang, to mean a spy. Whatever, we all enjoyed them.

My mother and Francois had already been with us for ten days. Their business was doing well, my ten per cent dividend was evidence of that, and they had been able to arrange this holiday, the first for some years, because of the quality of the under-management they had. Marie and Bert were being looked after by Uncle Arnold who was the works manager at a small engineering company in the city, and something of a rugby player, so I was told. He and his wife Ivy were great favourites of Violet.

My mother was nearly forty but even so, and much to the amusement of Francois, she could not help flirting with Hubert. He was quite embarrassed at first, poor fellow, but he came to enjoy it — which is more that can be said for Abigail. What was even more bizarre than to see Hubert simpering at my mother's coquetry was to observe the clash that took place between Francois and Madame Hortense. While she tolerated me, adored Simóne and still mildly bullied Hubert, she put on her pointed hat and mounted her broomstick when my stepfather appeared. I think she reminded him of his grandmother from the time when he was in short trousers because our formidable housekeeper similarly treated him as a schoolboy who had spilt ink on the shirt she had to wash. Eventually he joked about it, and I think for her she welcomed having a real Frenchman around to practise on, but Simóne and I thought it was hilarious.

The party in the salon were into the second bottle of champagne when my mother and I decided to watch the sun go down from the front of the Bateaux.

"When you first wrote to us about Simóne, we were very worried. You do tend to choose the wrong girl."
I knew she was going to raise, once again, that foolish passion for Miss Rosen.

"And by the way, Liza has nearly finished her training as a consultant psychiatrist. Hasn't she done well. But, back to Simóne. Francois is already a bit in love with her. How does she do it? She is hardly a classical beauty but Percy, we're both impressed with you. She is just right. She might be able to keep your feet planted on the ground — if such a thing is possible."

"I am so glad you like her. She has had a tough life and you know of the ups and downs there have been between us. She seems very settled at the moment but I do sometimes worry if it will be long-lasting. Did you meet Madame Hortense's grandson? Simóne rarely has any contact with him but when she does he seems to bring out the worst in her — and then she takes it out on me. Should we marry?"

"A big question, my boy. Are you going to stay in Paris? If you moved back home, would she be happy? Her English is almost non-existent. Luckily Francois prodded me to pick up some of his lingo. If you want my advice, wait a bit longer. I can see there is a lot of love there but that's not always sufficient. I should know, with my experience. Who would have thought I would be happily married to a boring but lovely French teacher — and don't you tell him I said that or I'll box your ears."

Perhaps, like Madame Hortense, my mother still sees me as a naughty schoolboy.

"She's so winsome. That's the right description, and everyone seems to like her so."

At that moment the object of our conversation left the others and joined us. As she came along the deck, wearing an outfit I had not seen before and a hat that would have had done credit to my mother's wildest eccentricities, my heart turned over. Surely we would be together for ever, our love would be everlasting.

The beauty I saw became reflected in Hubert's latest canvases and although I may have been a prejudiced critic, I still thought they had a wider future than leaning against the walls of the artist's studio — other than the one I particularly liked that was in temporary residence above our bed. I have shown you already that when roused, or faced with a challenge, I take action. The machine-gun position outside Arras; the chance to go to Paris; taking over the Trois Perroquets; when in doubt, take the bit between the teeth, move forward and, if possible, aim high. My aim at Arras was not too good but for Hubert I contemplated the most famous picture dealer in Paris, Ambroise Vollard. At a time when most dealers and critics ignored or castigated the modernists, he bought their work and his gallery on the rue Lafitte had become the rendezvous for the avant-garde. He was a shrewd businessman who bought

*Alan Shelley*

cheap and sold dear to adventurous collectors, including the Steins. I was told that he was a difficult man but he so inspired some of his artist friends that they did studies of him; Picasso, a Cubist work, Bonnard a picture of him as a genial host while Renoir painted a toreador.

However, I got cold feet and decided he would not be my first point of call. I did not have that much temerity.

Hubert had been told that his fellow American, Gertrude Stein, had bought a motorcar so he decided to do the same — and chose the same model — but there was something of a problem; he was a terrible, if not lethal, driver. Fortunately, from the age of seventeen Poppy had driven the van used to deliver the product of the family factory to wholesalers and she proved to be an efficient chauffeuse as I traversed the city forcing my way into art dealers, of a more modest category than M. Vollard, with one or two of Hubert's nudes clutched to my chest. We should have saved the petrol. As I was to find when I began my writing career, rejection of the unknown is second nature to these people. They seem to revel in it.

Still, as I have come to expect in my life, a remarkable coincidence occurred. Remember Capitaine Philippe — CP? My contact with him during the Peace negotiations had been limited. I usually sat behind Colonel Kim when they faced each other across a table but I came face-to-face with our adversary, if I can term him as such, in the foyer of the Hôtel Majestic. I was making a sentimental return, something I did occasionally, just to remind myself of how lucky I was to be young, handsome, in love and living in Paris. CP was meeting a friend. He did not recall who I was but when he did he said he was surprised to see me still in Paris and then asked me to have a drink with him and his friend in the old familiar bar.

I had always seen the Hôtel Majestic as a lucky place for me, and so it proved again. I told my host and his friend, after the second glass of Chablis, what I was doing; my restaurant life; my girl; my landlord; his paintings and the frustration at getting anyone interested in them. The friend then told me that his brother worked for a small art gallery lost in the backstreets west of the Place de la Bastille and would Hubert like to display some of his paintings there? From what I could gather they were happy to have anything to put on their walls as an alternative to the works of the amateur weekend painter — interminable copies of the Mona Lisa, muddy watercolour representations of the Eiffel Tower and portraits of family members wearing berets and doing something peculiar with a string of onions.

The address carefully noted, Hubert and Polly and I, and the Ford, were there the next morning but by the time we eventually found the street where our art gallery target was located, I had already written off this excursion as another waste of time. CP's friend may have been well-intentioned, but I wondered if he had recently visited his brother at his place of employment?

It was predominantly a commercial area. There were small factories manufacturing items as diverse as cart wheels to roof tiles. We could smell the abattoir and I am sure Poppy must have felt at home with the many shops selling saddles, bridles and other items originating from the leather industry. Prominent amongst the properties we passed was a depot for Hansom cabs and from the attached stables there was an ammoniacal smell robustly vying with that from the slaughterhouse. Dozens of narrow fronted cafes served the working population. The charcuterie and boulangerie establishments appeared to have no produce on display, even though the narrow broken pavements were busy with pedestrians striding purposefully forward, this way and that. After leaving the Place de la Bastille we passed two substantial churches so at least the souls of the local population were well catered for but as a centre for the artistic *avant garde,* I rather doubted. You can imagine therefore that when we finally reached our destination I was not exactly filled with confidence, even though I must admit my spirits rose a little when I saw there were three other

*Alan Shelley*

establishments devoted to the art world on the same street, even if they all looked as dilapidated as each other.

At number 37, 'Martineau Fine Arts. Established 1901' was painted on the window. The letters that made up this inscription were so worn, and the window so dirty, it was difficult to know whether this flourishing business had been set up in 1901 or 1861. This insignia reminded me of the crazed mirror at the shop in Westgate Street where my mother admired her latest millinery purchase but unfortunately the interior of the gallery reflected the sad façade and not the warm and welcoming ambience of the bakery. We were received by an untidy individual who seemed to be in charge — indeed, he was the only person on view. He cursorily inspected the paintings we had brought and then said he would be delighted to show them for sale. I suggested an asking price, a negotiation Hubert had no part in: he could not speak. He was so delighted. He thought he had broken through and finally joined the Paris art elite.

His optimism proved to be more accurate than my despair. Parisian traders and buyers in the art market evidently spread their nets far and wide because the following month a message came from the Martineau establishment asking if we could provide more of the same; someone had bought both of the paintings we had left in that back-street at prices not too far away from the listed ones. My friend and landlord became incoherent at receiving this news but I wanted to know who the purchaser was and were these representations of Simóne going to a good home? Was the new owner an oddball who liked to have on his walls pictures of naked ladies, however bizarre, or was he a perceptive trader who believed, unlike most others in the Paris art world, that there was a niche for Hubert's work if marketed to the right collector? Martineaus had strict instructions not to reveal the name of the purchaser. I could not understand this. Why the secrecy? Was he, or she, a superior dealer who did not want to admit they deigned to frequent galleries such as Martineaus — or was this how the game was played in the trading of art works? All the gallery could tell me was the apartment block to where the pictures had been delivered.

Detective Percy Glossop was on the case but I was stymied at the first move. The address given turned out to be one of the largest residential blocks in Paris but in which of the many apartments lived our mystery man? Simóne, who else, came up with an idea — Madame Hortense should be recruited as my Doctor Watson. She did not exactly use that expression but her suggestion targeted the fact that the housekeeper was sure to be a prominent member of the concierge's mafia and the first enquiry should be made by her with her opposite number at the apartment block where our unknown benefactor resided. I am sure I would have come up with such a proposal in due course, but nevertheless I gave Simóne a hug.

Hortense became quite excited at the prospect of a role as a private investigator but she did suggest that if she provided any worthwhile information, she would be rendering an account. I agreed. The first report was disappointing. The apartment block in question was so large that there were three ground floor entrances and each had its own guardian. Hortense had paid her respects to all three keepers of the keys and had discovered that only one of them was in the habit of receiving parcels covered in sackcloth that were probably paintings, but of course she could not divulge the identity of the recipient. On the next visit Hortense carried in her capacious carpetbag a bottle of a rather splendid cognac, of the kind never to be seen at the Trois Perroquets, and returned with a name and an apartment number.

Paul Nerval lived alone. He appeared to be a wealthy man, was rarely seen before noon and hardly ever ate luncheon or dinner in his own apartment. He had a wide circle of eminent friends. Francine, the concierge, recognised some of them: she was, according to Hortense, an avid reader of the gossip columns in newspapers. He spent the whole of the month of August in Cannes, staying at The Carlton, to where his mail was forwarded and there was a manservant, whom Francine rather disparaged. He came, she reported, from Africa, or somewhere foreign. As far as she knew, M. Nerval was an art dealer and pictures were often delivered to that address. Sometimes, she complained, they were very large. The dealer tipped well but his purchases were often heavy and unwieldy and Francine was a martyr to the arthritis. She must have been glad not to be faced with examples of the sculptor's art. If the new owner of Hubert's paintings should come across a Rodin or two, our informant would have been in trouble.

I assumed Paul Nerval had not taken that awful journey to the Martineau Gallery himself but the pictures had been spotted by one of his many sub-agents who understood his tastes and with Hubert's work he had taken the risk and bought 'sight unseen'. At this stage the risk was a small one. Not a great deal of money was involved but the fact that the Martineau Gallery had asked for more seemed to indicate that Nerval had found a market for his speculative purchases. Unless, that is, Simóne's form now graced his own walls.

I was later to discover that Paul Nerval only had on his walls the pictures he chose to have. He was a man of impeccable taste with that little extra that can see merit in something new, something out of the ordinary, but more crucially, he knew everyone in Paris of any importance and could usually find a buyer for anything he had invested in. You will often have heard such a boast before. 'Everyone in Paris...' What does it really mean? How do you measure importance? What I wish to convey is that he was a member of a wide circle of wealthy people who had artistic tastes — and were potential purchasers. That may sound cynical but people like Paul Nerval did not simply profit from the situation; they influenced taste and many aspiring artists might have starved, or even worse — given up on their ambitions — but for the existence of these important middle-men; these cultural arbiters.

Hubert was only too pleased to pay the fee the Martineau gallery required but after that we both could see the merit in making personal contact with the purchaser. But, M. Nerval only mixed with the best of Paris society and however privileged was Hubert's background, I perceived that if we rang his doorbell, it might put him off the Boutet Nudes for ever. We needed our own middle-man.

While waiting to determine where such a person was to be found, Hubert continued painting. You might wonder why a need to contact Nerval was at all necessary. If he was truly interested in more of the same, why would he not come directly to the source, but it did not seem to work like that. If his scouts could not identify more paintings at the Martineaus, or other galleries, he would turn his attention to other artists. He must have known that by divulging his address we could, if we so desired, discover his name but had that really helped a great deal. In any case, what was Hubert and I trying to achieve? The artist had gained some recognition. He had sold two of his major paintings, now owned we presumed by a man or woman of sensitive taste, but for me I wanted Hubert to be as successful as an artist as I intended to be as a chef. And working for a more successful Hubert would please Simóne.

Who did any of us know; who could provide an entry ticket into this man's circle? In addition to CP, Colonel Kim had dealt with a number of senior French officials who worked at the Élysée Palace but I could see no avenue there. Could Poppy charm the American Ambassador to help? I thought not but at this point I stopped and said to myself, who do you think you are Glossop? You're still a boy with culinary ambitions and little else. But I had a card up my sleeve that I have not divulged until now.

The extraordinary relationship that had developed at Etaples with Peter Southern had resulted in a desultory correspondence between us. During the Peace negotiations I had the temerity to write to him, care of the family firm, telling of the minuscule contribution I was making towards the treaty that would ensure peace forever as some recompense for the recent slaughter. After some delay, he replied. He had sold his shares in W Southern and Sons (Birmingham) Ltd, was living in Cambridge and trying to write poetry. He soon succeeded in this and sent me a copy of his first published collection. He had kept well away from the war as a subject and concentrated on philosophical themes around man's loss of faith and the diabolical nature of the post-war world, particularly amongst the labouring classes. At least, that is what he told me they were about.

Just after Simóne and I moved to Hubert's apartment, his second set of poems was published and he sent me a copy of a laudatory review by Jean Cocteau. I think he only bothered to send this because it was, of course, written in French. I read it out to our little company but as you can imagine only Poppy was interested and indeed from then I think she paid me rather more respect, being a friend of a man who wrote poetry approved of by such an eminent French intellectual. At that time I considered asking Peter if he would like to have a holiday in Paris but then got taken up with the visit of my mother and Francois and thought no more about it. With the problem of finding some access to Paul Nerval, I resurrected the idea. Might Jean Cocteau prove to be the key we were looking for? I did not explain the ulterior motive, but Peter responded positively to my invitation; I think he had in mind visiting some of the very active French socialists there were on the Parisian scene at the time.

It was rather a bizarre mix. Poppy was somewhat star struck, Abigail thought him strange, Hubert was his usual affable self but Simóne was puzzled. She could not understand why if this sensitive man was so opposed to war and slaughter he had not expressed his views before experiencing the conflict. For her, the menace posed by the Germans needed to be opposed. She said as much to Peter within a short time of meeting him but because he had raised the same questions within himself many times, he could only tell her that her view was valid and he could not explain it. This response touched Simóne and thereafter they became great friends.

I showed Peter my Paris. I shod him in the shoes I had worn during my first discovery and he responded as I instinctively knew he would. My line of enquiry when first tramping the city had been biased towards the food on offer but Peter, particularly in his new guise as a man of letters, was interested in visiting locations relevant to Voltaire, Balzac, Victor Hugo, Proust and others. He was not aware of the American writers who were part of Gertrude Stein's circle but he did spend some time at the famous bookshop, Shakespeare and Co. On a later visit to the shop I bought two copies of the *Ulysses* that Sylvia Beach had published and sent one to Peter. Being the sort of man he was, his thank you letter expanded into a two-page critique of Joyce's masterpiece that, I must confess, heightened the pleasure I got when I found chance to read the book for a second time. Like most people, I found the first encounter baffling, but Peter provided insights that were extremely valuable.

Now we were re-acquainted, I could see how inappropriate it would be to ask Peter to visit Jean Cocteau on our behalf. I never even raised the question but just enjoyed meeting him again. As a result I came to the conclusion that if it was considered necessary to pursue the advancement of Hubert's career through Nerval, the direct approach was inevitable.

I drafted a letter for Hubert to send. There was no response for some weeks but then, a little surprisingly, Hubert was invited to meet our middleman for an aperitif at the Crillon at around 6 p.m. the following Friday. I cannot now recall whether it was my idea, or his, that Simóne should gatecrash this rendezvous although later, as I considered more carefully, it was probably Simóne herself who suggested it. She dressed modestly but the hat was stunning and as they left I saw she had that glint in her eye. On their return they gave me, between them, a potted version of what had happened, although I could read from their faces that it had probably been a satisfactory meeting.

Initially they had both been dismayed by his hauteur towards them but, although this was not spelt out, I can well imagine that Simóne then switched on that special power of hers and the atmosphere changed.

"Monsieur Nerval, I am most grateful for this invitation and for your interest in my work. As you will observe I have taken the liberty of bringing with me the subject of my recent paintings. She has been my inspiration and her name is Simóne Boutet."

Nerval seemed somewhat annoyed at Hubert's temerity but his innate good manners required him to recognise the female intruder.

"As you well know, I am an American. I come from Boston and I believe my father gives investment advice to a number of wealthy Parisians and others whom you probably know. The Duchess of Clermont-Tonnerre in particular, as well as the Steins, both brother and sister."

Hubert and I had concocted this falderal. We both decided it was unlikely these falsehoods would ever be revealed as Nerval would not discuss the personal finances of a member of his charmed circle. Whatever, when this information was imparted, his manner relaxed a little.

"Let me tell you something about Simóne. Without her, the two paintings you have bought would never have come into existence."

Before he could go any further, Simóne interjected.

"*Monsieur*. Mr Richardson is too modest. His talent was deep inside him and it was due to come out in the fullness of time, and I happened to be there to see that happen."

Hubert glowed at this, even if not altogether the truth.

"As you can see, I hardly have the conventional female form to be a model. According to my boyfriend, people like Renoir would not find me suitable, but Hubert seems to have seen something that has inspired his new style of painting. My boyfriend is an Englishman, now living in Paris, and is a cook at a small and modest restaurant near to the *Gare Montparnasse*. Before I became a model I worked for a candle maker. I was brought up by my aunt — a concierge.

My mother deserted me when I was very young and I have never met my father."

None of this had been rehearsed. Hubert looked astonished at Simóne. Was such a revelation to this man of the upper class a good move? As for Nerval, he was listening intently.

"I am not a well-educated person. I left school very early. My boyfriend is trying to improve me, but I know nothing about art. And yet Mr Richardson's paintings are affecting the heart. It is not just paint on canvas. It is a picture of the agonies of the human condition."

Where does she get it from? How does she do it? Nerval was as transfixed as we all are when Simóne turns on that supernatural dynamo she cradles behind that flat chest of hers. He called upon the waiter to pour her another glass of champagne and stared into her eyes where there was a hint of a tear. Hubert was ignored. He said afterwards he felt like the beggar at the feast.

As the gist of this meeting was related to me Hubert said that as they parted company, a limp handshake for him and the most elegant of bows and a kiss on the hand for Simóne, Nerval asked that further studies of this lady be shown to him before anyone else. He believed he could guarantee at least three more buyers; or perhaps a more satisfactory result, if there was sufficient product, would be for Simóne's new fan to arrange that one of his friends should stage a small exhibition of Hubert's works. I am sure that at this point Simóne smiled at him.

There was a successful exhibition, and Hubert's name began to circulate amongst the artistic world, but his future in that world took a surprising new direction: but then again, perhaps not so surprising. Love walked in. In fact, it had been around in Hubert's apartment for some time — as a lodger you might say — but whether the achievement of his artistic success was the reason for what happened next, or whether it was that unknown force that I believe is a permanent constituent of the Parisian atmosphere, he finally noticed

Abigail. She had adored him from when first appearing on the scene and, unlike Hubert, she made no secret of her sentiments. It would seem that however perceptive Hubert was of her feelings he could not put down his paint brush long enough to acknowledge them — and, even more crucially, to realise that he felt the same, but now the paintbrush remained in the jam jar and Abigail moved into his arms. It was touching. We were all delighted, particularly Simóne, who was a great believer in the concept of true love. Poppy was similarly glad for her friend because she had recently been infected with the same disease, as will be revealed.

Abigail's parents had been very lenient when their young daughter announced she was moving to Paris to paint but when she told them that the currently famous Hubert Richardson, a fellow American, had asked her to marry him, tolerance went out of the window and a steely resolve came in. Not that they objected to the groom-to-be. They were sufficiently confident that their daughter would have corralled the right man but what they were insistent upon was that the marriage should take place in the 'good old US of A'. This fact caused some consternation for a day or two but as I thought Hubert's paintbrush had been mothballed because of Abigail, I could now see that it might be some time before it was put to use again. Hubert had had his flourish, his day in the limelight. It might come again, but he was not a man consumed by art — a good thing I thought. Man does not live by paint alone.

The parents prevailed. The family lawyer, sworn to secrecy, purchased an apartment for the young couple in Greenwich Village and the seal was set. It was all very fortuitous. Simóne and I had a new home in prospect so Hubert was able to give up the apartment without misgivings, except for regrets at leaving Hortense. My rent was fully paid-up because by now the dragon and the hesitant American were at ease with each other. She still shouted at him sometimes but thanks to my insidious intervention, not very often. In fact, the two of them were often to be found in her sitting room exchanging reminiscences about her detective work over a cup of hot chocolate.

There was a splendid party the night before they sailed. Even Paul Nerval came, as did of course the other member of our little band, our intrepid chauffeuse, Poppy. She brought to the send-off the man she had fallen in love with, one Henri Pascal. Hortense's grandson was also there. Nerval had insisted on providing the champagne, Louis Roederer's Cristal no less, and in copious quantities. A memorable time was had by all except that Simone had, for the first time in a while, a brief episode of unease. Not exactly a black mood but she was clearly troubled and as I was to discover, Poppy's man friend and that grandson were the cause.

Henri Pascal had only recently discarded his uniform. His war record was impressive. Despite the rapid promotions resulting from the appalling casualties the French army had suffered, he was still very young to have been discharged with the rank of Commandant. He had completed a law degree before being called up and was now working at the Department of Justice in a relatively minor capacity. There was the distinct impression that he resented the change from his army rank to his present position but the latter was not taxing and as he had a private income he managed to overcome that antipathy and take full advantage of the good times on offer in gay Paree. He and Poppy had met at the perfume counter of the Galeries Lafayette department store when he asked her advice on a bottle of scent he was buying for his aunt's birthday. He was slightly taller than Poppy but his military bearing added stature and his neat moustache and liquid brown eyes added glamour. At least to Poppy. They had been inseparable for two months at the time of Hubert and Abigail's farewell party.

I thought he was a splendid fellow. He was modest about his soldiering achievements, interested in matters of cuisine and clearly very fond of our friend. He came alone and dined twice at the Trois Perroquets and I thoroughly enjoyed his tales about the petty bureaucracy to be found in the Justice

Ministry. I suppose it is like the civil service the world over, not that I had any experience, but Henri told me of instances where a staff member would complain that someone junior to him had a larger carpet in his office than his own. Most everyone fawned on the official next up in line as all and sundry fought for promotion. He complained, or made fun of, the boring and repetitive work; of the pointless recording of unnecessary information; of the suspicion of a spy network under cover within the ministry to see if anybody was stealing secrets. What secrets, Henri intoned. The fact that there was a proposal to change the law on dog licences or a move afoot to introduce a different coloured wig for junior counsels. He made me laugh and complimented me on the cooking.

With Poppy, Simóne had met him a number of times. He put on his most charming manner for her but she did not like him from the start. I could not understand this. Since we had been together she had grown in confidence and invariably we found our tastes in people complemented each other — but not with this man. Simóne could not explain her reservations, but she had them. Only I knew of this. Poppy only had eyes for the ex-soldier and he believed he could charm all women, and that Simóne would be no exception.

Poppy told us he lived in the 7th Arrondissements with his aunt. She was a wealthy lady of aristocratic pretensions who was not fond of Americans, or of most other nationalities, and indeed she hardly admitted any liking for any of her own countrymen and women. Poppy had never met her, but as their relationship strengthened, Henri said farewell to the aunt and as soon as the liner had left Cherbourg, took Abigail's place in the small apartment the two girls had shared. More or less immediately after the departure he gained an important promotion at the Ministry but unfortunately this entailed a considerable amount of travelling to visit Magistrates and their courts throughout France with the result that he was away for most of the week, and even occasional weekends. Nevertheless, Poppy was blissfully happy and in this contented state found her writing more fluent and was pleased with her latest work. She had even extended her interests to poetry and at the farewell party read a short poem. It was not very good.

The situation involving Simóne and the grandson of Hortense was of a more serious nature than her involvement with Poppy's new lover. The grandson, his name was Peter Lons, was a porter at the *Gare Montparnasse.* He was a dull-witted fellow who seemed content to live with his grandmother; we never learnt what happened to his parents. Although we lived in the same property, Simóne and I rarely saw this young man but whenever I did, I always found him to be morose and unfriendly as though he blamed the world for his lowly position in life. His grandmother complained that he was a bad timekeeper and was always getting into trouble with his employer because of this; and in the future he was to cause a great deal of trouble for me.

## The Trois Perroquets

While Hubert was moving forward with his career, two things occurred that proved to be the next and crucial steps on my own ladder towards culinary fame and fortune — although in truth both were relatively limited — even if it began in sadness.

One busy Friday evening Madame Ricard did fall from her stool. The regulars were astonished but unfortunately this soon gave way to sorrow. When those closest to her tried to replace her on the perch she had occupied for so long, they could not. She had suffered a heart attack and must have died as she fell to the floor. She was seventy two. I was shocked and saddened: we had never been close friends but I admired the strain of Gallic tenacity she had. Her moods were variable but she treated me like a favourite grandson. She made fun of my nationality and mocked my cooking skills but it was because of an odd regard for me that I became part of the Trois Perroquets. I cried at the funeral.

Her will was quite detailed and I wondered when she had found the opportunity to consult a lawyer. She never seemed to leave the premises but then perhaps her wishes had been expressed while at her usual place as the Notaire sipped a glass of wine — hopefully not the acidic stuff she drank. I had never met any of her family, except for Julietta, but evidently Madame Ricard had kept track of all of them with the result that her estate was divided equally between two nieces, one of whom was Julietta's mother, after about twenty minor bequests to more distant relatives. Julietta received several items of old-fashioned jewellery that she was unlikely to ever wear and probably had little monetary value.

What the will did not cover was who should now run the Trois Perroquets and take over the stool at the bar? Neither of the legatees had ever been near the place and in any case, when details of the estate emerged, the cash deposits at the bank greatly exceeded the value of the restaurant property and so, soon after the funeral, Julietta carried a message asking if I would like to buy the property which I had been managing in the interim?

I had enjoyed the recently completed *Forsyte Saga* but was I now to become, 'A Man of Property'? Of course not. My family were still tenants of their shops and very few working-class, or even middle-class, folk owned their own houses at this time. The occupants of the archetypal Acacia Avenue villa, who had a live-in maid, were not property owners; they paid a rent of around £125 per annum and were fully contented with that. Equally, Madame Ricard's relations did not want to become involved in real estate, either as landladies or restaurateurs — but I could not solve this problem. My ten per cent fund provided the little luxuries of life for Simóne and me over what I earned as a chef, but there was no possible way it could be finessed into producing a real capital sum.

My readers may have foreseen what happens next. Hubert buys the property, I take over running the place and then pay him a fair rent out of the takings.

All of this was taking place in the background during the time Hubert was finding success with the Boutet Nudes, but just before he and Abigail made the decision to return to the USA, there was another development on the Trois Perroquets front, although in fact it was not at the front, but rather in the rear. Behind the bar was a warehouse, used as storage space by a furniture dealer, which had became surplus to their requirements and so, at my request, Hubert included that building in his Parisian property empire and his capital was then used to cover the conversion costs — for which I paid more rent. His Trois Perroquets expenditure made only a small dent in the funds in his grandmother's trust that he now had access to.

I can hear you say — in real life such does not happen, but I can assure you this is exactly what did occur. Look at it from Hubert's point of view. He had enjoyed having Simóne and me in the apartment and I liked to think I was partially instrumental in opening his eyes to the charms of Abigail. Fair enough, but what had really changed matters for him, at least as an artist, was the introduction of Simóne into his artistic life. It was she who had encouraged him to move from the chocolate-box pictures of buildings to portraits of her. It was she who had been the model for the larger nudes. It was she who had inspired the style that had attracted Paul Nerval, amongst others, and established Hubert as an artist out of the ordinary — and of course it was she who had won over Nerval in the first place. It could therefore be said that his largesse was a reward to Simóne, rather than to me, but whoever has the credit, I grasped the opportunity with both flour-smeared hands and began my crusade to see if I could acquire anything like the reputation Hubert had, but in my own field. In all honesty, I never quite succeeded in this. His work had become almost unique but as we all know there are lots of very good chefs in Paris. Whether the little fame I did achieve was due to the bizarre attraction of eating food cooked by an Englishman, or whether my genes can take all of the credit, I do not know, but as I will reveal, I did make some impact.

    I have never really explained in detail the layout of the Trois Perroquets, or the district where it was located. It was a mixed neighbourhood; mostly residential but there were a number of artist studios in the area. None of the same prominence as those close to where Hubert had lived and painted, but the workrooms of Chagall and Modigliani were nearby and added some artistic flavour to the district. Across the road from the Trois Perroquets was a particularly dingy bar which most of the railway workers used and where, it would appear, the proprietor welcomed the stream of prostitutes that used it as a resting place. I cannot think they picked up any customers there, unless some engine driver was having difficulties at home and he had just received his pay. A few yards further along was the Hôtel Paradiso which these ladies used when their clients were flush. It had no connection with Georges Feydeau. It was more likely to be the setting for the worst of human tragedies — love for sale in shabby surroundings. There was little of the light-heartedness of farce on those premises: the rapid exits and entrances were only to admit new clients rather than cuckolds and mistresses.

    It was not exactly a brothel. There were plenty of these in Paris and while I lived in the city I was told that many of them had been upgraded from the sordid enterprises of the past to more luxury establishments that were particularly busy on Saturdays and Sundays where supposedly respectable businessmen and students were entertained at low fixed prices. Madame Ricard had made sure that ladies of the street were not welcomed at the Trois Perroquets. In some of the literature of the time attempts were made to suggest that they were interesting creatures that added glamour to the bars and cafes of the city, but Madame Ricard had a very different view. If one came into her bar, either alone or with company, they were simply ignored and orders for drinks not accepted. When I was in charge I saw no reason to change this state of affairs.

The Trois Perroquets was at the corner of an alley-way, just wide enough for a cart to reach the warehouse and other premises at the rear. The bar stretched across the front of the property with the entrance in the façade furthest from the corner. The bar area gave into a corridor, opposite the front door, which provided access to the dining room and kitchen and a store behind that. The kitchen had a door into the alley through which the uncle had made his exit when being removed by Madame Ricard. The furniture dealer's premises at the rear was about the same number of square metres as that occupied by the Trois Perroquets so, with the addition of this extra space, the existing operation could be doubled in size.

I did not need a Le Corbusier, or any other architect, to advise on how to plan the Trois Perroquets of the future. No architects, but there needed to be an artistic input, particularly if I was to succeed in making the dining room rather special. Pictures on the walls was the answer and so, with some help from Simóne and Polly, I revisited the Martineau gallery and their two neighbours and bought, within the budget, what took our fancy — or to be more accurate, what Simóne's eye recommended and Polly endorsed. The other input was a commercial one and here my upbringing was the crucial factor. The Trois Perroquets was a corner property. What about a corner shop? A small patisserie would fill the bill with all of the product on sale being cooked in the new kitchen. We would not be baking bread — there were plenty of *boulangeries* in the area — but I was determined to introduce to the Paris market Gloucester's famous lardy cakes as well as the more conventional confectionaries. For the actual construction work, Julietta was most helpful in finding a reliable local builder.

The existing dining room was added to the bar area to give more room for subsidiary dining and the kitchen, store and part of the new premises were transformed into a grand dining room that, because of the difference in levels with the rear property, I was able to arrange with a crescent of banquettes at the rear raised above the remainder of the salon. The balance of the property became a greatly improved kitchen and when Hubert gave up the apartment at the Boulevard Saint Michel, Simóne and I moved into the first and second floors of the improved Trois Perroquets. This gave us even more space than we had enjoyed with Hubert and there would be ample accommodation to provide a nursery, a necessity that came to be a little over twelve months after the new Trois Perroquets began trading.

When Simóne told me she was pregnant, I immediately asked her to marry me. To this proposal she made no reply but I could see the idea, in some way, troubled her. As her history demonstrates, she was far from being conventional. We had now lived together, mostly in the happiest of circumstances, for nearly three years. Although an Englishman, I was establishing myself in her home city and was not a philanderer; I was seriously in love with her, so why the hesitation? I would have thought that Simóne would have welcomed the security marriage would offer. She was an emotional person to be sure, generally expressed in a lovable ordinary manner, but her overriding characteristic was her intuitive ability to see beyond the obvious — beneath the surface. What was she thinking? It is doubtful if her mother had been married. Outside of Abigail, she had no married friends and she had learned recently that the husband of her cousin Marguerite had deserted her. Although we had lived happily together and she had made a notable contribution to my life — and that of Hubert — she probably still saw herself as unworthy, or nervous, of joining the ranks of other women in moving from love and the wooing to the sacrament of marriage. On the surface this might seem illogical but Simóne did not always act rationally. She was far from being a fool and she must have known that for most women at this time, marriage was the career of choice. Women worked of course but by the 1920s hard physical labour was mainly the man's province. There had been some changes since Catherine worked under ground and pushed carts loaded with coal in Zola's *Germinal.* Simóne asked for time to think about it. I was rather hurt at this reaction but understanding her as I did, I agreed and for the time being it seemed to me that the joy of our relationship grew stronger.

Since Hubert's departure Simóne had been without a full-time job and so I wondered if the prospect of becoming a mother would solve this problem — but I rather doubted it. I could imagine she would take on the role with care and good sense but she was not, at least in my opinion, what would be termed naturally maternalistic. She had this strange energy within her slender frame but I did not see it being applied, full-heartedly, to the birthing and rearing of children. Of course, I could well be mistaken. Perhaps this event would remove her from the clutches of those demons that still troubled her, even if they had been quiescent for some time. There was no suggestion that the birth be prevented but on the question of marriage, the decision was delayed. I did not press the matter but I could see Simóne was still trying to come to terms with the idea. I know she discussed this with Poppy. The two had become close, particularly since the departure of Abigail and Hubert, but her attitude towards Henri Pascal was still an uncertain one. He and Poppy seemed well suited, but Simóne, so she told me, still felt uneasy about the man.

She suffered little by way of sickness in the first months of her pregnancy, which I was very pleased about. I read somewhere that when Hemingway's first child was announced he told Gertrude Stein that he was too young to be a father. I did not feel that way. I was delighted and in addition, while he was trying to find his feet as a writer, I felt that I was well on the way to achieving the first of my big ambitions — running my own restaurant.

The new Trois Perroquets kept me very busy. I had thought whether the name should be changed but considered it would be disrespectful to Madame Ricard who had been so kind to that gauche Englishman who had the temerity to describe himself as a cook. So it was still the Trois Perroquets and Moses agreed with this. He was all that was left of the former kitchen staff. I have already described how he became valuable using some form of intuitive skill or oriental wisdom to fit in to what should have been an alien environment to him. He had become my Chef de Partié in charge of vegetables in the old kitchen but now those three mangy parrots were to be re-hatched as an elegant swan, he quickly moved into a new role altogether. This was something we had discussed in the past that our new facilities could now bring to pass, namely we would begin to introduce, slowly at first, a number of North African dishes as an addition to the classical French cooking that I intended to offer. I hesitated to try the same experiment with British fare. I did attempt to find a wider audience for the lardy cake, but the inclusion of boiled beef and carrots into my menu was not likely to endear the Trois Perroquets to the new and more affluent clientele I was seeking. On the other hand, an occasional offering of a lamb stew, slowly cooked in a traditional tagine and served with couscous, became quite popular. Moses masterminded all aspects of this *Spécialité de la Maison,* sourcing all the ingredients and importing the cooking utensils from his native land.

Julietta no longer pined for me. In fact she let it be known, using both Hubert and Simóne as messengers, that she sought someone rather more handsome than that Englishman — however nice he might be — and she soon found what she was looking for. He worked at the fruit market and they had been married for about a year before the grand opening of the new Trois Perroquets. When her great-aunt had died, Julietta had taken over the running of the bar and her husband had left his work to come and help her. I was not certain that he was more handsome than me but there is no accounting for

*I Never Met Ernest Hemingway*

taste and he was a willing young man. He had a ready smile, a confident manner and a quick turn of phrase. I will not tell you of the nickname he gave to me. His name was Claude.

With the new enterprise I needed to consider how it would be staffed, in addition to Moses, Julietta and Claude, and once again Simóne had her part to play in this. At her suggestion I approached Poppy. She seemed to have abandoned her writing ambitions — to concentrate on being in love — but at the same time her part-time position at the American embassy had come to an end; so, if this Englishman was going to have a Moroccan in the kitchen, why not this pretty American girl as the Maître d" Hôtel?  She was delighted with this idea, particularly as Henri was still travelling a great deal, and she became a great success. She knew little about food but she was efficient and charmed everyone. Thank goodness her French had improved since she first came to Paris. It is often said that the bedroom is the best language school of all.

Simóne found her own niche. She did not actually sit on Madame Ricard's stool, it had in any case been discarded, but most evenings she helped in the bar and became a great favourite with the regulars. Wonder of wonders, she developed a sense of humour. Her rapport with the customers did not include the badinage of the late lamented Madame but Simóne seemed, in a quiet way, to hold her own in the rough and tumble of the conversation that echoed around her. Hortense's grandson, Peter Lons, became a regular customer, dropping in on his way home from work. This had begun before Madame Ricard's death but after that he continued to patronise the remodelled premises. Simóne still not like him but they were polite to each other.

It took some time before the number of drinkers and diners grew. The pastry and cakes proved to be popular so the shop was soon making a worthwhile contribution to the total turnover but if I was going to generate enough income to pay the extended staff numbers — and the rent to Hubert — we needed to sell more meals. There had been a gradual increase in the trade at midday as local workers approved of what I was offering — at keen prices — but it was the aficionados of fine dining that I needed to entice. I widened the evening menus, I improved the wine list, I advertised, I arranged speciality evenings but I did not set out to emulate the famous cafes at the Boulevard Montparnasse. I was never going to compete with La Coupole, one of the largest brasseries in Paris; a cavernous space decorated with murals and attracting a wide variety of Parisian diners. The others on the Boulevard were also well beyond my reach — Le Dôme, La Rotonde or Le Select. The latter establishment stayed open all night and, as I was told, served Welsh rarebit.

Perhaps I should offer the same delicacy in view of my ancestry but I was not in a fashionable area, and in any case, I was not interested in attracting the Americans of the Lost Generation, many of whom were the impecunious clients of these cafes. According to Hemingway, when you have no money the best place to go was the Luxembourg Gardens because there you are out of sight, and away from the aroma, of the myriad of Paris cafes and shops offering food. My ambition was to attract the Parisians who appreciated my cuisine, at my prices, and were also pleased to try something new. Moses and I were proud of our Moroccan Chekchuka.

Nevertheless, progress was slow until, at Simóne's suggestion, I contacted Paul Nerval. If we had thought making an approach to this man on the subject of Hubert's paintings was scary, it was as nothing compared to an attempt to persuade him to desert Maxims or the Ritz and come and dine in the shadow of a railway station. On the other hand, I had nothing to lose. I wrote to him. I did think of planning a themed evening where the menu would include a Picasso risotto and a Matisse chocolate soufflé and would he do me the honour of accepting an invitation to the event. I soon discarded this but I did ask him to dine, for a specific evening, without the flimflam. He replied, eventually, to say he was busy that day but he had some friends visiting from Lyon and he would be gracing the Trois Perroquets with his presence on the 14th of the following month — and would require a table for ten, if that was convenient.

He and his two most important guests arrived in a Hispano-Suiza driven by the African manservant. The remainder came in taxis. I was glad the driver was able to take the car away during the meal; in our district I hesitated to think what might have happened to the vehicle if it had been left unattended. Simóne moved from the bar to the dining room and she and Poppy wore their smartest frocks. Moses and I decided to be brave and include two Moroccan dishes as alternatives on the menu. Most of his guests tried them and there were no complaints, nor for the Crepe Suzette I prepared at the table using the very best cognac I could find as well as the traditional Grand Marnier. As they left M Nerval congratulated us all and promised to recommend to his circle that this new restaurant near to the *Gare Montparnasse* was quite, 'up and coming'. His recommendation did not solve my worries overnight, there were still too many empty tables in the evening, but I felt the tide was turning.

And it was. By the point two months before the baby was due, business improved daily and I began to discard my worries about the success of the Trois Perroquets and concern myself with Simone and our daughter. I was convinced that with Violet as a grandmother and Simóne as the mother, this embryo could only be of the female sex. Elizabeth I thought.

After the visit by Paul Nerval and his friends, some of my competitors in the neighbourhood — and further afield — woke up to what was happening at the Trois Perroquets. Until now this young English upstart had been ignored or, if anyone had heard of me, scorned, but now the green-eyed monster began to appear. Let me put this into perspective. The great Escoffier was thirty two when he opened his first restaurant in Cannes but was only nineteen when he began to work at the Le Petit Moulin Rouge in Paris. I was twenty five and an Englishman, but there was my blood. My mother was born with a natural ability to make out-of-the-ordinary cakes and pastries. I had inherited that skill but I believe the accident that brought me to Paris added another dimension. By the twentieth century it was generally accepted, even by the British, that the cooking in France was superior to that practised anywhere else in the world, but in Paris, this was doubly so. The only English dish that Escoffier's eminent predecessor, Antoine Carême, was prepared to include in his menus was our turtle soup. And he should know his onions; he was chef to the Tsar of Russia, Talleyrand and the Baron Rothschild.

In Escoffier's invaluable text of over eight hundred pages, *A Guide to Modern Cookery,* he has great fun with the recipe for this soup.

For soup, take a turtle weighing from 120 to180 lb., and let it be very fleshy and full of life.
To slaughter it, lay its back on a table, with its head hanging over the side. By means of a double butcher's hook, one spike of which is thrust into the turtle's lower jaw while the other suspends an adequately heavy weight, make the animal hold its head back; then with all possible dispatch, sever the head from the body.
Now immediately hang the body over a receptacle, that the blood may be collected, and leave it thus for 1 ½ or 2 hours. Then follows the dismemberment: etc etc.

It goes on like this for two pages.

My copy of Escoffier's masterpiece was found for me by Sylvia Beach and was, I can assure you, put to good use.

By the time I was cooking at the new Trois Perroquets I had imbibed some of the inherent French culinary ability but, in addition to the contribution of Moses, I believe there was an added facet with me. I was more or less starting from scratch. I had no preconceived habits, good or bad, handed down by mother or grandmother who believed their cooking methods were the best. Even with pastry, my mother had left me to my own devices and so it was with all the other dishes. I loved cooking but taught myself from a standing start which I considered added another dimension to my skills. I believe that the menus at the Trois Perroquets were less ostentatious than at other restaurants — less rich and heavy — but just as carefully prepared as the dishes offered by my competitors.

The one of these who caused me the most irritation was Maurice Ringgold, who owned and cooked at the Brasserie Pep located just off the Avenue du Maine. During the time I was still working for Colonel Kim, and discovering the pleasures of the city, I ate at the Brasserie Pep on one occasion. The food was certainly superior to anything that could have been obtained at that time from Madame Ricard's kitchen but however good the cuisine, the service was slow and the atmosphere in the dining room unfriendly. When I came to know Ringgold better, I could understand why.

He was a big man and a fat man. This may well be an advantage in creating the image of the traditional French chef but I believe the expansive waistline shielded a dyspeptic stomach that added fire to an already bad tempered disposition. I can well imagine the members of his kitchen staff were not in awe of him because of his culinary skills; they were simply frightened of him because of his bulk and his ill temper and this was translated into his dining room.

When he dined at the Trois Perroquets he did not book a table but simply walked in one night and in his arrogant manner announced who he was and that he had come to see what this Englishman was capable of. There was a Moroccan dish on the menu that evening, and he partook. I joined him at the table while he drank his coffee. He made no comment on what he had eaten but asked about the cooking of the North African item. I told him about Moses and how he was a valuable member of my team — if not now second in command.

A few days later Moses told me that a messenger had arrived from the Brasserie Pep asking for him to call and see Chef Ringgold who was prepared to allow him to work in a proper French kitchen and the pay would be better than that offered by the upstart Englishman. Moses had already replied, thanking him for the kind offer, but he had no intention of leaving such a fine gentleman as Mr Glossop.

Andre Michelin was already producing a simplified guide for drivers to help them find decent lodgings and meals, but it was not until after I had left Paris that the custom of awarding stars came into being. However, some inspectors were employed to assess entries in the guide and I had my first visit just after the encounter with Ringgold. We were not told in advance that the inspector was coming but this particular man had visited our bar before dining and Simóne seemed to have discerned his identity, or perhaps he was loose-tongued. He informed her that he had dined the previous evening at the Brasserie Pep and the proprietor had been telling all who would listen that they should avoid the Trois Perroquets at all costs as they were serving disgusting foreign food that was a disgrace to the French tradition. After sampling what was on offer, my visitor left in possession of a different opinion, but I still wondered what to do about the malicious Ringgold. He was prepared to steal Moses from me to add his dishes to their menu and when his offer is refused, begins to slander me. Nevertheless, after careful deliberation I decided to do nothing because, as they say, imitation is the sincerest form of flattery. My rival retired soon afterwards. Doctor's orders, I was told. His prodigious belly was straining his heart.

No doubt other nearby restaurateurs rather raised their eyebrows at an English competitor in their midst but by the time I was fully operational, Paris was well on the way to recovering its former glory and as a result there were plenty of customers for all. During this time the receipts earned by the Folies Bergère were second only to those of the Opéra and the cinemas were even more popular. Business was booming and there were enough diners to go round if your operation was well-run and by 1925 I believe that could be said of the Trois Perroquets.

After the expanded Trois Perroquets had been in operation for a few months, and the wrinkles associated with a fresh venture ironed out, I decided that, like some of the more popular restaurants in Paris, we would close on one night of the week and I chose Monday. This gave me the opportunity to look at my other main interest away from the kitchen — the literary world — and as a result I became a regular visitor at the Shakespeare and Co bookshop. I was not too ambitious. Miss Beech was helpful in suggesting what was new, in English and French literature, and I thought about beginning a writing career with a detective story; not perhaps of the Conan Doyle type but something more substantial such as *The Moonstone.* I soon put this notion to one side and turned my attention to short stories based on the life of an intellectual abroad. They were prosaic in the extreme.

One day at the bookshop I observed, Sylvia Beech in lively conversation, in English, with a small woman in a battered hat perched above an animated and expressive face. She was not handsome. If I had thought when first meeting Julietta that she had a suggestion of hair on the top lip, this lady's hirsute traces were clearly visible, even in the restricted light of the bookshop. After she had left I was told she was Alice Toklas, companion to Gertrude Stein, for whom she typed and ran the establishment at 27 rue de Fleurus. For me she was most interesting because of her reputation as a cook. I talked to Miss Beech about her and asked if she thought Miss Toklas would be interested if I sent her a recipe of my own. The bookshop lady was amused by this but said she would be pleased to act as a go-between and if I would like to write this out, she would make sure it was passed on. It did not take me too long to decide which recipe to choose.

Alice Toklas was an American who had come to Paris in 1907 when she was thirty years of age and had lived in France ever since, even through the war years. It was therefore unlikely she would have tasted, or even heard of the lardy cake, and it was this recipe that I sent her with a fairly brief note that included references to her namesake, Alice Whitwell *nee* Smith, and my mother. I had a charming reply, even if it was typed and not hand written. When I left Paris this missive became mislaid so I cannot reproduce it for you but she said she was grateful for my interest and that she would attempt my recipe when she had time. I believe my recollection is correct when I tell you that she used the word 'curious' as an adjective in describing that splendour of the cuisine of Gloucester. I had no further contact but I must say I was somewhat disappointed to find no reference to me, or the lardy cake, in the *Alice B Toklas Cook Book* that was first published in 1954.

If I was pleased with Moses' progress in the kitchen, I was delighted with Poppy's performance. She presented to all of the customers of the restaurant the face of the rejuvenated Trois Perroquets and I received from many quarters compliments on her efficiency in this role. Henri's absences meant that she was happy to spend long hours with us and in addition, when not presiding over the serving of my more and more elaborate concoctions, her brain was alive with new ideas and suggestions. It was she who designed the menu cards and the uniforms now worn by all the staff. She had a magic touch with flower arrangements for each table but her particular pride was the ladies lavatory. Not that I visited this too often but our female diners appeared to appreciate the variety of Eau de Toilette she provided. I believe that in addition Poppy had found some interesting prints for the walls of this chamber; her argument was that why should the discreet nudes, on view in the gentlemen's conveniences, not be available to all. I could not argue against that but urged decorum, even though I was satisfied she would not go beyond the bounds of good taste.

Quite often Mondays proved to be the day of the busman's holiday when I liked to entertain friends to dinner and cook in the kitchen that was part of our living quarters. Simóne also enjoyed these little dinner parties. She was still inclined to shyness with people she did not know well but this was improving, particularly since working in the bar downstairs.

She would put on her newest dress, put up her hair and even apply a modest coating of cosmetics and a spray of scent. On the latter score, she had Polly as an adviser. This perfume consultant often came to these little occasions with Henri when Simóne and I could observe at close quarters how happy they were together. He still made fun of the Justice Department but was seriously pleased with the success his partner was having at the Trois Perroquets. When they looked at each other over my Beef Bourguignon the love between them was palpable but, unfortunately, it was not to last.

One morning Poppy appeared at the Trois Perroquets unusually early and with an unusually serious expression on her pretty face. She handed me a letter received that morning from Henri's aunt summoning my Maître d' Hôtel to call on her that day at four o'clock in the afternoon. Henri was away on one of his perennial provincial visits. Poppy wondered what was afoot and whether she should even deign to comply with this peremptory command until she had spoken with her lover. However, she was clearly intrigued. She had never met this imperious lady and, as far as she knew, there was now no contact between Henri and his aunt and so Poppy, with the inherent self-confidence of the Americans, had already determined to go. I offered to be at her side but at this suggestion she first smiled and then giggled. After that I was told, in a polite manner, to stick to my kitchen.

She was not smiling on her return. She was furious and nearly unintelligible. When calmed down, she told me what had happened. She was kept waiting fifteen minutes in the vestibule of the apartment on the Avenue Bosquet before being shown into the drawing-room by a liveried footman. The aunt was not present but came into the room soon afterwards with a small dog in her arms. Polly thought it was a pekinese. The footman took the dog and positioned it carefully on a velvet cushion that sat on a low mahogany stand that appeared to have been designed solely for that purpose. The uniformed fellow then withdrew and Francine Pascal, for so she was named, indicated by a movement of her finally coiffured head that Polly should be seated

Henri's aunt was a small woman, wearing an elaborate full-length gown. She had sharp features except for a rather flattened nose. Her hair was more white than grey and she appeared to be well over seventy years of age. With her perceptive nose, Poppy could discern an aroma surrounding this lady reminiscent of stagnant water — or perhaps it was some outlandish perfume too expensive to have come to Poppy's attention hitherto. It was certainly not of the kind she would have recommended at her first encounter with the nephew. She surveyed Poppy through a bejewelled lorgnette and began her address. The conversation that followed was recalled by Poppy as the following — her interlocutor speaking in accented English — but in a voice that was extremely harsh for such a tiny woman with aristocratic credentials.

"You are Sackville?"

"Yes, I am Polly Sackville."

"You are, I understand, from America, and only visiting."

"Yes and no. I am from New York, but I now live in Paris."

"Doing what, I pray."

"I am going to be a writer but at the moment I work at a restaurant."

"As a waitress?"

"Why these questions? What do you want of me?"

"I believe you are acquainted with my nephew, Commandant Henri Pascal?"

"Yes. We live together but he is no longer in the army. Why do you call him Commandant?"

"Don't be impertinent with me, young woman."

"Well, I would appreciate a suspension of this third degree."

"What are you talking about? What degree?"

"We live together and we are in love. He is the sweetest man I have ever known."

"So, you have known lots of men in the past, I suppose?"

"Mrs Pascal, that is none of your business. Does Henri know of this meeting?"

"No. I want to tell you about my late husband's family. Most of them were soldiers and all were of noble birth. Henri's great-grandfather, the Count Pierre Pascal, was killed at the Battle of Waterloo — he was a member of Bonaparte's war council — and his father, the General, was awarded the Croix de Guerre as a young officer in the Franco-Prussian war. But there will be no more wars, thanks to my good friend Georges Clemenceau, and I have therefore decided that my nephew will find success for the family in the law. I shall arrange for him to be appointed as a magistrate before the end of the year and then on to be a senior judge in the Courts of Assizes."

"I hope he does."

"Do not interrupt me. To achieve this he must have a proper wife; a French girl of noble birth. You must leave him — although I suppose after he is married there is no reason why he should not set you up in some rooms somewhere"

When Poppy reached this point in her account she picked up a carefully folded napkin from the dining table at which we sat, spat into it, and threw it vigorously across the room. 'Set me up', she expostulated. She began to breathe more easily and then continued to recall, to the best of her knowledge, the remainder of the conversation.

"You insult me, Madame. I have already told you we are in love. We shall marry."

"You will not. What you do not know is that I am already down to a shortlist of two. Sisters. Daughters of old friends of mine who live in the most delightful chateaux close to Troyes. Henri usually stops with them when he is visiting in that area. I believe I will allow him to choose which one. His office tells me that he is there at the moment."

"This is 1925. You cannot decide whom he will marry. I do not care if he marries me or not, but we are staying together. I can hardly take in what you have said to me. Henri will be furious that I had been treated in this way. You are living in the past. You remind me of an evil version of Lady Bracknell."

"Lady Bracknell? I have never met her."

At this point, the furious aunt rang a small hand bell that summoned the footman to show Poppy off the premises.

After listening to this I was not sure whether we were dealing with a comedy or a tragedy. Was it Wilde or Ibsen. Unfortunately, the Norwegian won. Henri returned two days later. He told Poppy that although angry at what had happened, he was not surprised. He had not seen his aunt for some time but he knew of her intentions. Nevertheless, he would never give up Poppy at her say so, and what is more, he was not even sure he wanted to be a judge. He was not quite so emphatic when Poppy asked about the daughters at Troyes. Why had he never mentioned them? He replied that on his travels he stayed with a lot of people and those at Troyes were nothing special.

That night I told Simóne the whole story. She listened quietly without any interruption until I had finished. At that time she made no comment but two days later, after a long talk with Poppy, she told me what she thought was going to be the outcome of this affair. The doubts she had from the first about Henri were now crystallised. She described him as a mixture of arrogance and weakness. With only the first of these defects, Poppy's future could well be a secure and happy one. She was a brave girl and could combat a conceited nature with her own brand of self-confidence, strengthened by love, but she could do nothing about weakness, and this was the deciding factor. In the end it was rather more than weakness. It was, in my opinion, the worst form of cowardice. He had been a brave soldier but for his treatment of Poppy he should have been shot as a deserter from the trenches.

Poppy was convinced that Henri would not succumb to any family pressure, and he assured her of this, so their life together continued as before. He went off on his trips on behalf of the Department of Justice and Poppy continued to charm the enthusiasts for my cuisine but, two months later, he simply did not return to the apartment where Poppy had been so happy. She went to the Avenue Bosquet but was refused entry. She looked for the postman every morning, but there was no letter from Henri. As can be imagined, she was distraught. She had never known which office at the Department of Justice he worked, but she pestered everyone there who would speak to her until she found someone who told her that he thought Henri Pascal had been posted out of Paris. Troyes was mentioned.

Simóne and I tried our best to console her. I think Simóne was rather more successful than me in this regard. I never quite knew what went on between them but it was Simóne who shortly afterwards brought me an invitation to visit Poppy's apartment to assist in the burning of all of the possessions Henri had left behind that were capable of incineration. Those not of an incendiary nature went straight into the rubbish shute. For the time being Poppy made no plans; she stayed in the apartment where she had lived with Abigail, and then Henri, but eventually decided to leave Paris, which she did at about the same time as I did.

Simóne told me, as we were undressing for bed, that it had been confirmed that night, at least to her, that Hortense's grandson, Peter Lons, was an anarchist. I was astonished. What was anarchy to her? I myself knew little about French politics, and even less on the subject of anarchism, but even so it was impossible to live in Paris and not feel that somewhere within the country, someone was planning a revolution. After all, they had some tradition in this activity. It seemed to me that French soil was more fertile for dissenters than within Britain where the London working man was more concerned with the success of the Arsenal football club than any violent political protest. What I did know was that in 1921 the communists and anarchists in France had split from the main left-wing union to form their own movement, but whether Lons belonged to either body I never discovered. I suspected that he was simply

*Alan Shelley*

a discontented troublemaker but Simóne so disliked this man that she took his talk at face value, and believed him to be a threat.

This was the gist of our bedroom conversation that night.

"A few weeks ago I overheard him, and those two other dirty men he drinks with, talking about how awful it is to live in the France of today and they should move to Russia where everyone is equal. I said to myself, the sooner the better, but they went on about how they were going to change things. No one in the bar took too much notice but it hurt me to hear a relation of Hortense talking like that. She was so good to me when you and I first lived together. She is like the mother I never had."

"Do not let it worry you, my dear. There is a lot of that sort of talk going the rounds and that's all it is — just talk."

"You might say that but tonight I heard something more serious. I have found that even in your noisy bar my hearing is very sharp and I am pretty certain they were discussing a plan to leave a bomb in a Government building. To begin their revolution."

"Idle nonsense. Come to bed."

"No. I think they were serious. I could not ascertain what building but thought afterwards about the *Gare*. They all work there. It is always busy, full of people. A big bomb would kill hundreds. I must stop it."

"Simóne, my love. What do you know about bombs? Where are those people going to get a bomb from? What can you do? Forget it."

"I won't. I shall go to see Hortense tomorrow morning."

As I have already shown, Simóne can be very stubborn and very decisive when she wants to. I made no attempt to prevent the planned visit to Hortense but when Simóne returned I was sorry I had not been more firm. She told me that when she had reached the apartment the good lady had been absent, shopping no doubt, but Lons was there and Simóne, being the brave little thing she is, had faced him with what she suspected and warned him that she would report this unless he promised to give up the idea of a bomb. She did not tell me what had been his response but he could no doubt see how serious she was. I became nervous about this turn of events but the dining-room was fully booked for both lunch and dinner on that day and I needed to concentrate on a new dish I was offering. *Timbale de Ris de Veau* requires a lot of care and attention.

The following day Moses and I were discussing a new idea he had for introducing North African sweetmeats to our dessert menu when Julietta burst in. She was upset to the verge of hysteria so that for a moment I could not understand what she was saying, but as I gathered it concerned Simóne, I rushed into the bar. She was not there but I heard an altercation outside the Trois Perroquets and my heart sank as I saw what was happening twenty metres down the side alley. Simóne and Lons were locked together. It was not an affectionate embrace. He had his hands around her throat and was shaking her tiny frame as though it was a rag doll. There was now no noise. He went about his work in silent concentration and Simóne's throat was so constricted by her assailant's hands she could not utter a sound. As I dashed towards them he threw her against a wall with such force that the silence was broken by the thud of her body against the brickwork, followed by a high-pitched screech from her as she slumped to the floor. I ignored Lons and sank to her side. Blood was dripping from her mouth and the high pitched shriek had become a low moan as she clasped her hands over her extended belly. The smock she wore in the bar was torn down the front and hung loosely from her shoulders. I could see she had wet herself.

From the time I appeared in the street, to the moment I cradled her in my arms, took around ten seconds but so much had happened in that brief instance. She looked at me. She was weeping and the tears were mingling with the blood. Her body was in spasm, and as she continued to clutch her stomach, the weeping and moaning became an excruciating and heartbreaking cry of pain. All this time I was expecting Lons to continue the assault with me as his target but as I turned away for a moment from Simóne, I saw Moses and Julietta standing behind me with Lons on the floor at their feet. Julietta screamed as Moses knelt down beside me and said he thought the man was dead. Moses and I carried Simóne inside and then carefully upstairs to our bedroom while medical help was being summoned. The local doctor had been engaged in his morning clinic and was on the scene within less than ten minutes. He did not hesitate. Simóne must be taken to hospital as soon as possible; she did not appear to be injured but he feared for the baby.

As for Lons, the story as pieced together later was that he had entered the bar, just before noon, very angry and aggressive towards Simóne. We were told afterwards that he had been drinking since early morning and could hardly stand. There were only two other customers in the bar at that time but Simóne had managed to usher her enemy outside and they had moved into the alley. Clearly he had been building himself up for this confrontation since Simóne's visit but quite what he expected from this was hard to tell. Perhaps he thought that by intimidating her she would not report what she knew of his activities, and those of his cohorts. As they had left the bar Simóne had taken with her the knife used to slice lemons. She would not have left the safety of the Trois Perroquets, and Julietta, if she had thought this man would really physically attack her and yet some instinct had prompted her to be as prepared as possible for such an eventuality. With his hands at her neck she had plunged the knife into his heart. As I knew, she was, when necessary, possessed of surprising strength and this was so on this occasion. The blade was not much more than twenty centimetres in length but she had pierced the serge jacket he was wearing and most of the knife was deeply embedded into his body. He was dead by the time Moses and Julietta had arrived on the scene.

Simóne was in hospital for four days. She was discharged on the day that would have seen the end of the twenty fourth week of her pregnancy. Our daughter had been delivered dead.

The doctor told us that Simóne had suffered no physical harm and talked about both of us being young enough to have many more babies in the future. I could not question his superficial diagnosis but he could not know the impact this tragedy would have on Simóne's fragile mentality. This was not helped by the questioning of the police. She admitted there had been no friendliness between her and Lons when they had lived in the same apartment building, and she may even have slyly hinted at some attempt he made to persuade her into his bedroom, but the assault had taken place because she had moved him from the bar — and he was drunk. There were no references to bombs and anarchists and, after two visits, the gendarmes left us alone.

Was his death, and the loss of the baby, a stupid accident that should not have happened? As I later discovered, the anarchist movement was active in France in the nineteenth century but after the war, and the Russian Revolution, many so-called anarchists joined the Communist Party. Whether any of this had any relevance to the miserable wretch who had killed my daughter is questionable. My acquaintance with him, in his capacity as the grandson of Hortense or as a drinker at my bar, was very limited but I cannot believe he was serious about any political movement. He had always struck me as an ill-tempered working man with a chip on his shoulder and not someone who was prepared to try and improve his lot in life. Was it possible that Simóne attracted him? Was that why he frequented my establishment? He certainly had nothing of Hortense's character in him. Explaining to her what had happened was very difficult. She grieved of course, both for him and our daughter, but she quickly understood and shrugged her shoulders as the French do. She dismissed as nonsense any suggestion that her grandson was political. He could not even spell the word, she said. She was a splendid lady.

Simóne tried very hard to immerse herself in the activities of the Trois Perroquets but it was clear to me that her heart was not in it. She laughed and joked with the customers and staff but I never saw that special smile of hers. As she regained her full fitness, sex between us became more and more passionate but this was driven, on her side, not by more love for me, nor a sense of desperation to become pregnant again as soon as possible. It seemed it was wholly fired by her dark side. It was as if because she had been involved in such an act of violence she needed, in the confines of our bedroom, to continue to act aggressively to try and expunge from her mind what had happened in that alley — and the consequences of that awful moment. When she was at her calmest, and in my arms, she would weep quietly for an hour at a time, wetting the sheets with her tears and constantly repeating to me in a low voice: 'I'm sorry. I'm sorry'.

I did not know how to comfort her. I suggested a holiday but she refused. I might have sought help from Hortense if the circumstances had been different, but I did write to Liza and asked her advice. Without meeting Simóne she could hardly give a fair diagnosis but she did write that the reaction fitted in with what she would expect from a manic depressive faced with the loss of a child. She then volunteered to come to Paris and see if a face-to-face consultation would help. I thought about this for a while. Liza did not speak French so any discussion between patient and specialist would have to be done through me and this might make it more difficult for the consultant. And was there a possibility that such an intervention would make Simóne worse and drive her more deeply into despair? On the other hand I needed to take some action and so decided, eventually, to ask Liza to come with my mother and Francois. However, before I could extend this invitation, Simóne disappeared.

It was as simple as that. She had left the bar one morning, gone upstairs and packed some of her clothes and exited the premises without anyone noticing. When I went to our bedroom before lunch to change my shirt I could see evidence of her hurried departure. The wardrobe was open, as were several of the drawers of the chest where she kept underwear and stockings. All I could think to do was to run down stairs and into the street shouting her name. When it was clear she was nowhere in the area, I ran to Marguerite. She had no news. Poppy was at home that day. I went there and she joined me in the search. We went to Hortense. Nothing. Poppy restrained me when I wanted to go to the police and visit all of the hospitals in Paris, but the next day I did report her as missing. She had vanished. I employed a private enquiry agent, but as there were no leads I could give them, they soon abandoned the quest.

I never knew how he discovered that Simóne had disappeared, but I had the kindest of letters from Paul Nerval expressing his sorrow and asking if there was anything he could do. I went to see him. We were not exactly friends but he dined at the Trois Perroquets occasionally and of course he had also been one of those people Simóne had captivated. He was distressed at what had happened. I told him I had engaged a private investigator, but nothing had resulted from this. He said he would try whatever avenues he could think of but he moved in circles that would be unlikely to come across Simóne in their normal walks of life.

Liza said such irrational behaviour was in keeping with her character as I had described it to her, but that was little comfort. Surely my love was so strong it would bring her back. The magnet and the iron filings. On other occasions, I felt angry with her. At times she had been difficult to live with but I had always accepted her dark moods as being out of her control. So, for what reason had she to put me to this distress? It was her precipitate action that has led to the loss of the baby. I was the one left on my own for no reason of my making — but then

*Alan Shelley*

a picture came into my mind of the Simóne I first met. Was she again living in dire poverty, homeless and unhappy? I could not continue my anger for long but I needed to do something. After six months with no sign or sight of her I decided that the only escape for me was to quit the city I loved so much, and where I had experienced so much love. The Trois Perroquets had by now acquired some goodwill value. Polly had already returned to New York and so, with Hubert's approval, I sold the business, deposited the proceeds within my ten per cent fund at Barclays Bank and returned home to my mother. Hubert retained ownership of the property for some years; proved to be a good investment, he told me later.

When I finally left Paris I found I could not take with me the Boutet Nude that had hung above our bed ever since Hubert had gifted it to us. In itself the picture was just too painful. I did not want to look at it any more. It recalled so vividly the time we had spent together as part of Hubert's establishment; those happy times. I would never forget Simóne but I needed the real thing and not this stylised representation of her. I did not abandon the picture. I discovered that by that time it had become a valuable asset and so it was sold. I contemplated remitting the proceeds to Hubert but then Simóne spoke to me, within my head, and I gave the money to Marguerite to use as she wished. I rather hoped that one of those uses might be to succour Simóne should she ever re-emerge. While saying this to myself, I made a resolution. I would return to Paris every year and visit the Cathédrale de Notre-Dame de Paris on the 21st of June, the date of our first meeting. Regretfully, I rarely did.

*Hubert has begun to paint again. I have not — I'm about to become a mother, an occupation I relish. We both miss Paris but it is nice to be back close to the family and New York is buzzing. We hear from Percy on a regular basis. He does love words; long rambling letters that invariably include a new recipe. Why? He knows I don't cook, and secretly I prefer the hamburger to the* Coq au Vin.

*As I think back, Percy is not the only strange man I've met in the last few years; Hubert for example. I sat in the corner of his studio for months and he hardly noticed me; and then suddenly his eyes opened and we're married. Simóne saw the situation from the first day but then she's brighter than she seems. A slip of a girl but her instincts are rarely wrong. I think the reason Hubert found his niche as a painter was because of her. She seems to be able to inspire by just being there. Does not say much, but she's one powerful dame, let me tell you.*

*There is still a lot of criticism here about what was referred to as Wilson's shenanigans in Paris. They said he should have taken some Republicans with him. We never did join the League of Nations. People started to say: 'Took too long and got it wrong.' What one of my wiser friends said was that although the President did his best, we did not know whether the League was to represent a benevolent man of God or a baton-wielding policeman? The punitive sanctions against Germany did not work, certainly over disarming. Some years later there was a joke doing the rounds that a worker in Berlin was smuggling parts out of a factory making prams. He had a new baby, but when he tried to put the smuggled items together they became a machine gun.*

*Hubert had a stressful day yesterday. He finally went to see Janine's parents. I don't think the visit helped anyone, but he felt he should try. Of course, he refuses to see his family. I don't want to meet them anyway.*

*Alan Shelley*

*And then today we heard from Percy that Simóne has had a miscarriage. Hubert wants us to sail for Paris at once, but quickly realised how impractical that would be at the moment. He has telegraphed for more details.*
Abigail Richardson May 1925

# Chapter Six

# Interlude

*Gloucester Elvers*

*450g (1lb) Whole Elvers. 8 Rashers Bacon, rinds removed. 2 tbsp Lard. 3 Large Eggs, beaten. Salt and Pepper, to taste. Thoroughly clean the elvers. Rinse in large bowls of cold water to which a handful of cooking salt has been added. This should be repeated three or four times to ensure cleanliness. Drain and dry. Melt the lard in a frying pan, add the bacon and fry until crisp. Remove the bacon with a slotted spoon, to leave the fat in the frying pan. Arrange the bacon on a serving dish, keep warm. Add the elvers to the frying pan and stir, cooking until they turn white. Add the beaten egg, season and cook briefly, stirring constantly, until the egg has just set. Pour onto the serving dish. Serve immediately.*

# Herbert Montcalm

When I left Paris I made tracks for Gloucester and stayed with my mother and Francois; they had now moved to a more commodious house at Longlevens. I was devastated at leaving Paris and heartbroken because of Simóne. However much I thought I understood this complicated and astonishing person, I was not able to understand why she had left. Her words, 'I'm sorry. I'm sorry', haunted me. Why had I not been able to comfort her more? Why did she see leaving me as the only solution? Un-answerable questions.

I stayed in Gloucester for three months. Helped in the bakery and watched cricket. I was not back home in time to see Jack Hobbs equal WG Grace's record of one hundred and twenty five centuries. This was at Taunton in August but I was at the Oval the following August when we beat the Australians in the Fifth Test by two hundred and eighty nine runs. It was a triumph for Herbert Sutcliffe; seventy six in the first innings and one hundred and sixty one in the second, but it was Wilfred Rhodes who won the match for us. From *The Times*:

England's last nine wickets fell at rather frequent intervals and when the Australians went in to make 415, they were put out for 125.
The explanation is simple. We had Rhodes on our side. Larwood, Tate, Geary and Mr Stevens all bowled well. Larwood, in particular, rendered invaluable service by getting rid of Mr Woodfull and Mr Macartney. But these bowlers might possibly have been worn down. From the moment that Rhodes went on the match was over.

After Paris I found I could not stay in Gloucester long term. I greatly enjoyed being back with my family and seeing at first hand how Whitwells was thriving but I felt stifled, like a cheese soufflé that could not rise for being cooked in the wrong sized dish. Perhaps I did not try too hard having already decided that my aspirations, my interests, could not be satisfied in this provincial town. For the rest of my life writing became my principal occupation, and that can be exercised anywhere, but my spirit moved me inexorably towards London. I had to some extent found myself in Paris by accident but my move to our capital was a deliberate choice, even if my mother saw it as a totally irrational act. I rented a small flat in Paddington, found some temporary work at the Great Western Hotel, and began to write. The first story about my chef who dabbles in detection, one Herbert Montcalm, was never published but I thought it was quite creditable for a first effort. What do you think?

## The Tablecloth Mystery

Someone was stealing the restaurant linen. Not just the occasional napkin but the latest inventory revealed that three tablecloths had gone astray. This was more irritating than disastrous; I consider my staff are well treated and paid more than the industry norm, so who would steal from me? I was sufficiently incensed about this that on Monday evening, as soon as the last *plat principal* had been cooked, I departed, telling Georges that I was going to have an early night. I drove round the block and parked out of sight but where I could see the kitchen exit. I lit a Montechristo and listened on the car radio to the *Little Sparrow*.

The staff left at different times, depending on their duties, and so I knew my observation would extend for at least another hour or so. Murmuring to myself that this was a waste of time, and probably an unnecessary exercise, I settled down with a hat pulled down over my eyes and summoning up the best I could by way of patience. I may have fallen into a light sleep, but a noise brought me to full attention. The car clock told me I had been there about thirty minutes and I now saw what had disturbed my slumber. A young woman was standing at an open door in the building opposite to my kitchen where she was arguing and gesticulating at the bright light shining from within. A loud voice came from within. As it rose in pitch she suddenly pulled from the pocket of her raincoat some sort of handgun and fired twice into the well-lit interior. She was very still. The scene was now quiet. The weapon was returned to the pocket and she turned towards my car but before she had taken any steps a figure appeared from the porch of the next house. It was a short man wearing a raincoat of similar colour to the gun-carrier. I was too far away, in the cocoon of my car, to determine whether anything was said as he ranged himself alongside the young woman and walked her briskly around the corner and out of my sight. A minute later I heard a car start up and drive away.

I had not intended being an unseen witness to this action but it all happened so quickly that by the time I recovered my senses the actors were gone. I left my car and walked over to the beam of light. A man's body lay in a crumpled heap in the elegant hallway. What was revealed, as my eyes flashed over the scene, was a floor of attractive black-and-white tiles that were already being stained by the blood leaking from his abdomen. He was naked.

Before I had a chance to move forward to ascertain whether he was dead — it clearly looked as though it was so — I heard a car approaching. It was emitting the sound of a siren being operated at a low pitch, most unlike the strident shriek usually to be heard in Paris. The police car it proved to be came to an abrupt stop within two feet of me and before I could draw a breath I was being firmly, but without excess force, held by my arms with a gendarme at each shoulder. They ignored the body and said nothing to me as I was gently inserted into the rear seat of their car just as an ambulance appeared on the scene. The paramedics moved into the hallway and shut the door. Quite suddenly the alleyway was plunged into darkness and as the police car departed, with me in the back, I saw Robert and Claude leaving the kitchen.

I was taken to the police station close to the Odéon and ushered into a room lit by a single pendant light and containing a worn table, a few chairs and nothing else. There was no window, nothing on the walls and the floor of rough concrete was uncarpeted. I was brought a cup of tepid coffee which arrived at the same time as the man I had last seen escorting the young woman out of my sight. He no longer wore a raincoat.

"*Monsieur*, I am Inspector Truffaut, What is your name?"

I told him.

"What were you doing in the alley off the Rue de Sevres tonight and what did you see?"

"Inspector, I am the proprietor and *Chef de Cuisine* of the Concorde restaurant and I will tell you frankly I was in my car at the rear entrance to my premises to see if I could discover who is stealing my tablecloths."

As I said this I realised how unlikely a story this must appear.

"As to what I observed, I saw a young lady shoot into a doorway and you appear instantaneously and take her away. It was as if you were expecting this crime to be committed, and even allowed it to take place."

This resulted in a sharp intake of breath on the part of the policeman.

"What an extraordinary thing to say. Do you want to call your counsel?"

"Why should I? I am not involved. You asked me to tell you what I saw, and I have."

"Just so, but it is your remark that perhaps the police were complicit in a crime that concerns me. Why do you make such an allegation?"

"It is not an allegation. It was how it appeared to me."

"Well, *Monsieur*. Let me put it to you that shots were fired and I was on the scene to apprehend a suspect."

"Inspector, that is so."

"The timing of the arrest is irrelevant."

"Truly. Very expeditious. I am very impressed."

"So you should be. I will get someone to take you back to the Concorde."

"I am grateful. Goodnight Inspector."

I had decided not to pursue my line of enquiry because it appeared to trouble the policeman, and I was tired. The restaurant had been fully booked for lunch and dinner and it had therefore been a busy day. I needed to be in bed and not concerning myself with how the Inspector just happened to be so close to the scene of the shooting I had witnessed;

and even if I had continued with that topic, I sensed I was not going to get a satisfactory answer that evening — or morning. It was now well past midnight.

When I arrived at the restaurant the next day I entered the alley through the kitchen. There was no evidence of last night's happenings. There were no policemen on duty at the doorway or any yellow tape restricting entrance to a crime scene. I had a feeling that if I were to gain access to the hallway of the house across from me there would be no traces of blood on that tiled floor. It was as if some greater authority had decided to eradicate what had happened; to remove a page from a factual journal and reintroduce it into a book of fairy stories. But, of course, this could not be achieved. I had seen a naked man, who I presumed was now on a slab in the mortuary, and a woman who, again I presumed, was in custody.

The kitchen staff had not yet arrived. For some reason Patrice, my *sommelier,* was on the premises early but he was in the cellar. My only companion was Connie who came in for two hours every day, seven days a week, to clean and polish throughout the restaurant. I had acquired her when I bought the business three years ago. She appeared to be as much a fixture as the cold room, or the cellar.

"Connie, how long have you worked here?"

"Must be three years since Chef came."

"No. Before then."

"Oh. I cannot recall. I was cleaning here when my husband was alive and he, God rest his soul, departed fifteen years ago next month."

"Do you know who has the house across the alley? Number 59."

"Very strange place. I see him often. When taking out the rubbish. Always smiles at me and lifts his hat, but never speaks."

"What age?"

"Well sir, a bit younger than you I would say. Handsome. Fair hair."

"Why do you say it is a strange place?"

"My friend is the concierge at the apartment block next door and she tells me there are many visitors, often policeman."

"In uniform?"

"No Sir."

"Well, how does she know they are policemen?"

"You can always tell. Cheap raincoats and dirty black boots."

"Any other visitors besides those with the dirty boots?"

"Charmaine says many. He lives alone but most evenings there are visitors. Mostly men on their own and young women — innocent looking types."

Connie picked up her bucket and mop and moved into the restaurant.

As both proprietor and chef I make a point each evening to walk through the restaurant to observe for myself if the diners appear to be happy, or otherwise. I do this in a low-key manner. I do not stop at each table and ask if they are enjoying the meal — rather I can, from experience, detect in the atmosphere whether my staff and I have, on that day, got it right. A few days after the shooting incident I was astonished to find the lady at the centre of that affair seated at a corner table — alone. I would have noticed her anyway because you rarely see women dining by themselves in the best restaurants in Paris, but I recognised her instantly. I stood at the table and asked if the *Noisettes d'Agneau Fines Herbes* was to her liking. She did not reply but asked if I was the proprietor and if so, could she speak to me. I sat down. She said nothing more and so I came to the point without delay.

"*Mademoiselle*. I am surprised to see you here. I assumed you were still in custody. I should explain. I was behind my restaurant on the night I saw the police arrest you."

"They told me about you. The police said I had shot someone but when they investigated they found the bullets that had been fired were not from my gun, and so they had to let me go."

"So, whose gun was it?"

"I don't know. That's why I came here to see if you might know."

"Who was the victim?"

"I would rather not tell you that. Did you see anyone else with a gun?"

"No, but now I am intrigued. I feel as though I am involved. A mystery I would like to solve."

"Do you know Victor? His *nom de guerre* is 'the hunchback'."

"No. Never heard of him."

"Good. *Monsieur*, I think it would be better if you forgot all about it. If you saw nothing else but Inspector Truffaut and me, please do not get involved. I have enjoyed the meal. Could I have the bill, please?"

"*Mademoiselle*. It is on the house, but please give me your name and address."

There was some hesitation before she replied.

"I am Catherine Record and live at 517 Avenue Foch. Goodnight. You are very generous, but keep away from Truffaut, I beg."

For the next seven days I was particularly busy. The restaurant was offering a week of North African cooking in the evenings, with some live music from the region, and the mystery of the unknown gunman — or woman — was not on my list of priorities. However, on the last day of our programme of specialist dinners, Patrice came to see me about a problem he had observed in the cellar. This was an important accessory to the Concorde where our wine list won much praise. This valuable stock needed to be kept in ideal conditions and our cellar provided these. At the rear it stretched to the centre of the now infamous alley where there was evidence of an access point where coal would have been delivered in the distant past. Patrice pointed out that the brickwork of the rear wall was in danger of collapse. The lime mortar had already severely disintegrated and many of the bricks were loose enough to be removed by hand. I did exactly that and saw the wall of the adjoining cellar was in a similar fragile condition — and then realised that the adjoining cellar belonged to number 59. I told Patrice I would call a building contractor immediately but that evening, after all the diners and staff had departed, I began my criminal career — breaking and entering.

I found an old pair of overalls in the kitchen store which I wore while undertaking the relatively simple operation of removing sufficient bricks to enable me to gain access into the adjoining property. I intended to tell Patrice that the bricks had collapsed of their own account as a result of the removal of one or two during our inspection of the morning.

The next-door cellar was dark and felt damp. I had a torch. It was clear that for number 59 these premises were not as well utilised as was mine as they appeared to contain nothing but old cardboard boxes and a few items of broken furniture. However, closest to the stairs to the ground floor was a door that appeared to be of a fairly recent origin. It was not locked, so I looked inside. The large room revealed was very different from the rather neglected cellar. The walls were of a pristine white and there was a considerable quantity of lighting equipment in evidence, together with two high beds without any bed linen. It seemed, at first glance, to be a photographic studio. It was not occupied but there was evidence of frequent use. In the corner of the room were two alcoves curtained off from the main room. Each contained a large, comfortable bed and one of these boudoirs had a mirrored ceiling.

At this point I hesitated. I had registered that the unkempt cellar and its modernised annexe contained no human presence but was I so sure that this would be the case upstairs? I had embarked on this adventure without too much forethought. What was I doing? Did my interest in the matter of the girl and the gun justify the risk I was taking? I thought about curiosity and the cat. Did I see myself as a cat burglar, or was it the admonition of Catherine Record to forget all about it that had really aroused my interest? The latter, I felt. I was challenged, and I hate not being in possession of the facts. If a rival of mine produces a new dish, I cannot rest until I have discovered the ingredients and cooking method. But this was not a matter of cuisine. One man was dead and I might be moving into dangerous waters.

The stairs from the cellar were, somewhat surprisingly, covered with a bright red carpet of a deep pile. I therefore made no noise as I ascended and gingerly opened the door at the top of the stairs. The house was silent, but then it was nearly midnight and, if occupied, it was well after most people's bedtime. On the other hand, I said to myself, I had been told that the only permanent occupant was that fair haired man — about my age — so perhaps I was safe. Although visitors came and went, it appeared that no one stayed overnight. If that was correct, the permanent tenant was now dead and since his demise there had been no more sign of police interest, or evidence of anyone else moving in. This proved to be correct. I moved silently through each room of the house — all were unoccupied. My torch was a powerful one.

It was a narrow property. On the ground floor was a drawing room, elegantly furnished with some good pictures on the walls, mainly of the eighteenth and early nineteenth centuries as far as I could tell. The dining-room at the rear and the kitchen were of similar quality. No clues here. The two upper floors were arranged to provide a comfortable bedroom and bathroom, evidence of the property's single occupancy, and no other sleeping accommodation. The rear of the first floor was utilised as an artist workshop and the second floor an artist's storeroom. There were a lot of paintings on show in both rooms, all of them recognisable. Amongst others I counted three copies of Manet's *Luncheon on the Grass,* several examples of Cezanne landscapes, a quartet of *The Dance Class* of Degas and two or three versions of the *Water Lilies.*

I was so astonished at this discovery I had failed to observe another room at the rear of the studio. When I investigated this I found not copies of paintings but the real thing, except that the artists on display in this room were not ersatz French impressionists but photographers: skilled ones as far as I could tell. The depiction of their subjects, naked men and women in close contact with each other, were of the highest quality. Now I knew what the cellar studio was used for but how did any of this help in the mystery of the blood on the tiled floor.

Both before and after the celebrated Mona Lisa incident, art forgery has been a constant dinner party subject. In 1911 this iconic work was stolen from the Louvre by an Italian employee at the museum who thought that da Vinci's masterpiece belonged in Italy. At least, that was one theory. What was clear is that a number of good copies of the painting were sold to greedy collectors who thought they were buying the real thing — even if it could never be openly displayed and only viewed by the man who had been duped.

Later in this saga I consulted a friend of mine in the art world — without being specific. He told me there was a ready market for quality copies of major works of art. The owner of a genuine piece might be concerned for safety and so hangs a fake on the wall and locks the original away in a safe. Next, the art lover who appreciates a good copy, rather than a print or reproduction of some kind, and welcomes the forgery on his wall and acknowledges it as such; or another buyer who pretends to all and sundry that the painting is genuine. Then there is the outright criminal who finds someone gullible enough to believe it is the real thing, a 'lost' work of Rubens, Degas or Tintoretto. I asked him if the market for pornographic photographs of some artistic merit was also brisk. Not his field, was the response, but he knew there were people who appreciated such objects and would pay well for them, particularly if they were so brazen as to be illegal. I checked the law. Confusing. Difficult to prosecute unless children were involved.

Was this the secret? Art forgery and pornography. Were these activities enough to warrant a murder?

Alan Shelley

Presumably so, I said to myself, and as a result of a perfunctory inspection of the crime scene, I was now ready to solve the case. Catherine was the bait. The hunchback Victor was the master criminal behind the forgery and the dirty pictures. Truffaut was the bent copper who was well paid to see that the authorities allowed these activities to continue without harassment — and the murdered man was the front of gentility that hid this criminal activity from the general public. He was also the artist and chief photographer.

At this point I brought my conjectures to a halt. Criminal activities! The art forgery needed to be offered for sale as the genuine thing before any law has been broken and who is to say that my fair- haired neighbour was not just a keen amateur artist who revelled in copying the Impressionist masters? After dealing with that, were the photographs obscene or only similar to those available in certain bookshops all across the city? And why murder? What had the part-time oil painter or photographer done to deserve the fate that befell him?

Of course, I nearly said out loud, I am no nearer a solution to this puzzle than I was before my act of trespass. At that moment I heard what sounded suspiciously like the opening of the front door. Before I had time to panic I instinctively moved behind the long curtains that shielded the studio, at that time, from the outside world. After turning on the light, the visitor did not tarry but, I conceived, went directly to the room at the rear. As he departed I peered around the edge of the curtain. He was carrying a small white box which I presumed contained photographs. He wore a long brown overcoat and as he exited the room and extinguished the light I could see his silhouette framed in the doorway. There was a decided roundness to the line of his back. This intrusion made me very uneasy. This was considerably worse than the fear that the jelly would not set when I cooked *Aspic de Queues d'Ecrevisses ā la Moderne.* I began to shiver.

517 Avenue Foch was a car showroom — offering the Daimler-Benz for sale. There was no living accommodation

within the premises and no one of Catherine Record's description — if that was indeed her name — worked there. My remaining contact was therefore Inspector Truffaut. I wrote to him. In view of the incident that brought about our last meeting, I was becoming concerned as to whether my restaurant was as secure as it might be and although I appreciated this was not really his field, would he come to lunch with me, at his convenience, to give some advice in this area. He must surely have seen through this device but coppers are simply incapable of refusing something that is free. At least that is my experience, and he did not dent my theory.

"Will you have a dessert?"

"Chef, no thank you. That was delicious. Now, as I was saying, my advice is to call Raymond Brint of Paris Alarms and get him to give your place the once over. To my knowledge, he is the best in the business."

"Many thanks, I will. No one seems to have moved in opposite. Haven't seen anything in the press either."

"No. It was reported. The investigating magistrate decided suicide. It wasn't the girl. We found a gun near the cellar steps. He obviously struggled to the front door. Trail of blood left. Seems her gun was not fired, and she had a permit for it."

"Well, that must be a relief for you — and her. Case solved. Is she a friend of yours?"

"*Mon dieu.* Never seen her before in my life before that night."

"Coffee?"

"No thanks, duty calls."

Another blank wall. Forget about it I said, but then Victor appeared. I was in the kitchen. He came in the rear door, unannounced. I said nothing. He told me, in guttural tones, not to contact Inspector Truffaut again and to stick to my kitchen and to stop being a nosy parker. My interest was re-activated.

I asked my artist friend at the Lampard Galleries to let it be known in the market that he had a client interested in a first class copy of Manet's *Luncheon on the Grass*. Some story about wanting to interest his girlfriend, or his wife, who might believe it was the real thing — or that it could add some zest to the bedroom if such a painting was hung there. All very dubious, but to make a good sale people will believe anything. The fish took the bait. A young lady, Sylvia Regent, contacted my friend and gave her contact details. I was back on the scent.

Leaving Claude in charge of the Concorde, I carefully watched her address over two evenings which seemed to indicate she lived alone, and went to bed early. I waited until someone left the block so I could enter without registering my presence. At this point, I got lucky. I rather assumed there would be a chain on her door but before I could ascertain if this was so, she left her apartment to deposit garbage into the rubbish chute — and we came face to face. She looked very startled which enabled me to follow her as she retreated into her flat.

She quickly regained her composure and asked if I would like a glass of wine. I said yes and then apologised for not bringing her a bottle from my cellar — as if I was calling by invitation to eat the dinner she had specially prepared from me. It was a rather poor white burgundy, but then I am probably spoilt for choice.

"May I ask if I am addressing a Catherine?"

"Of course not. Would you have given your true name in the circumstances?"

"And what circumstances are those, pray?"

"Where you have got yourself involved in things that are not your concern. I told you to keep away from Victor. He found some loose bricks in the cellar."

"Funnily enough, I had the same problem in mine."

"What is it you want?"

"I'm not sure. An explanation, I suppose. Perhaps I see myself as acting for the dead man. If you are going to commit suicide, why take off all your clothes?"

This seemed to take the wind out of her sails.

"I think you had better leave."

"Of course. I am sorry to upset you but you must admit it is puzzling."

I did not know where to find Victor but I had a feeling that unless I suspended my curiosity, he would find me. The other two participants were now accessible. If I was going to pursue this, who was likely to be the most vulnerable? Presumably the girl. How wrong that proved to be.

One of my oldest friends is Roland Joffre, a freelance journalist who, in addition to writing food reviews for a number of newspapers, also reports on whatever takes his fancy. He was very experienced; what he wrote tended to be featured in the daily or weekly press and so I wondered if I could use him to provoke some action from the ill-matched trio of players in this affair.

Roland was nearly as intrigued with the mystery as I was. His first piece concentrated on art forgeries, always a good topic for the Paris press, hinting that of recent times some very good copies were appearing under the counter, particularly of the works of Degas and Manet. Two days later he changed tack and wrote about a talented photographer who was producing rather better than normal nude studies of the female form — but the source of supply had apparently dried up as if the photographer had lost his camera — or left town. His next piece, only two paragraphs, was about an elderly lady living close to the Concorde restaurant who had heard some shooting a week or two ago but was glad to find that the well-known chef was not the target.

Inspector Truffaut rang to ask if I had dealt with my security problem. I told him it was in hand. He then mentioned a short article in a newspaper about me not being involved in an alleged gun battle and then hoped that the next time bullets were reported in my area, I would be equally lucky. I asked him if he was threatening me and he put down the telephone.

Was it now time to tell someone in the police department, senior to the Inspector, what was happening? But what would I say. I had seen a man shot — or thought I had. I had entered adjoining premises illegally and found fake paintings and pornographic pictures. A girl had given me an assumed name and address. So what! A hunchback man had threatened me — as perhaps had a police officer — but did I have any real evidence of possible misdemeanours?

Victor waylaid me as I walked to my car at the end of a busy day. He stood in front of me and grasped my throat with his huge right hand. I kicked him in the groin and then knocked him to the ground with a swing of the briefcase I was carrying that contained several tins of corned beef; I was intending using my domestic kitchen that evening to try out a new recipe for hash sent from the USA. I stamped firmly on Victor's hands, both of them, while shouting at the top of my voice. Several people were soon on the scene including, a minute or two later, a member of the local *gendarmerie* who knew me. He often drank in my bar. I explained that I had been assaulted by this stranger, who was still prone on the pavement. Seemed as though he was trying to steal my briefcase. Handcuffs were produced and Victor was removed to the police station in double quick time.

I visited him the next day with my lawyer. We were allowed to interview the prisoner alone.

"I intend to press charges. If, as I suspect, you have been in trouble with the law in the past, my solicitor thinks you will be parted from your friends and family for at least five years."

"*Bâtard*. It was you who assaulted me. Look at my hands."

"Five years, at least."

"What do you want with me?"

"Two things. Keep away from me in the future and tell me how and why the owner of the house opposite to my restaurant was killed."

"You're mad. I'll get you for this."

"Yes, no doubt. In five years time."

Victor screwed up his face. He was silent for a minute or two, as if in deep thought.

"You think you are so clever. Look beneath the surface. It's not the oil paintings, or even the photographs, it's them that's in the photographs."

My mind raced ahead. The girls in the pictures were all young and curvaceous, but what about the men? Had some of them seemed somewhat familiar? Did that studio double as a venue for low key orgies with blackmail as the end result? The contents of the white box Victor had taken was presumably on its way to being used for more extortion. I ignored this line of thought for a moment.

"Very interesting, but why was that man killed?"

"Not too difficult is it. Got cold feet, and was going to split."

"So, Inspector Truffaut arranged the killing."

"No, idiot. He tried to stop it. It was she. She's the brains behind the operation."

I thought afterwards that Victor had told me this much partly because he did not relish more time behind bars, but also because he probably realised that the blackmail racket, if that is what it was, was about to be exposed and if he could get a quick release from his present predicament, he could desert his colleagues and move on to evil pastures new. The better option. I told him I would not be pressing charges.

I believed I could now put into place most of the pieces of this jigsaw. The ringleader targeted the victims while the murdered man was the lure moving in a wealthy circle where men of a certain age would be attracted to sexual adventures not to be found in the standard brothel. Was he also the photographer? Perhaps not. She no doubt brought in experts in this field who, for a generous fee, would believe that the pictures being developed were for pornographic purposes only. The paintings! Another expert, and possibly a profitable sideline. Victor was obviously the heavy who delivered the incriminating photographs and collected the money. Inspector Truffaut? At first I thought he was simply taking bribes but, perhaps more likely, he was being blackmailed as well. Sylvia had gone to the house that night, with the Inspector close by as a bodyguard, intending to stiffen the backbone of her compatriot. Either he had refused to keep quiet or there have been a tragic accident but, whatever, blood had been spilt. Amazingly, the Inspector was by now so involved he had been able to substitute an innocent gun into Sylvia's possession and persuade his superiors that the murder weapon had been found near the door to the cellar — and therefore it was suicide and not homicide. Of course, my story still did not explain why the man who lost the blood was naked.

My version of the story seemed to hang together, but where was I to find the evidence to prove it. I was not likely to obtain this from Inspector Truffaut. He was too deep in the mire to quit now and it was clear that Sylvia was a very hard lady, who belied her youthful and attractive appearance. Nevertheless, I decided she had to be my target. If this had been a movie the next step would have been another visit to her apartment — and this time I would have taken a bottle of my 1924 *Haut-Brion* — with some form of recording instrument hidden under my waistcoat. I would then have taunted her into making a full confession before the Chief of Police, played by Gary Cooper, bursts in and arrest her just as she spits in my face and pummels my head with her dainty clenched fists. But I am not Douglas Fairbanks. I do not have a recording device and in any case, could I provoke her enough for the whole story to be revealed? Unlikely. There had to be another way. However, as I stood in the street and pressed the entry bell to her apartment, with the precious bottle of wine in my hand, I was no nearer deciding what that way would be.

She buzzed me in and we met as I got out of the lift. She was dressed more elegantly than at any of our previous meetings and around her forehead was an attractive blue band that kept her long blonde hair under control. She did not smile at me, neither did she snarl. The wine was gratefully received and at her request I opened it immediately. It should have been decanted, but the circumstances determined this was not to be. We drank in silence and then, since she asked me to, I recounted what I thought was the background to the event I had so innocently witnessed some four or five weeks ago.

"*Monsieur.* May I call you Herbert?"

"Certainly."

"You have some of the pieces but not necessarily in the right order, or with the correct emphasis. The dead man was Alain Petain. The first thing you need to know is that he was a superb artist. The paintings you saw were all by him. Not only talented, but he reproduced those masters at great speed — and all for his own pleasure. There was no attempt made to pass them off as the real thing. He used new canvas and modern oil paints; and the stretchers and frames were of current design and manufacture. He did not need to sell them. He was a wealthy man. The house he lived in was not the only one he owned in Paris. If he did sell a painting it was made clear that it was a copy. If the buyer wanted to suggest to his friends otherwise, then so be it, but you would have to be surrounded by some very gullible people to pretend you had one or two original Cézannes on your wall."

"Why did you contact Lampard Galleries? That's what lead me here."

"Oh, I had one or two of Alain's paintings and I could not resist making a profit out of him. The art was the nice side, the good side, of Alain but when he was not painting in oils he was a monster. Never needed to work; became a millionaire in his early twenties when his grandmother died. His wealth was secure but his sexual orientation was not. It seemed to depend on the phases of the moon. Sometimes he bought the favours of young girls and other times even younger boys, and occasionally all at once. The photographs were part of this mania. Sex in all its forms was an obsession, particularly when taking place in groups."

"My family were very poor. I had little education. I drifted from one thankless job to another. I was working in a bar when I met Alain. We became friends until he invited me to his house where he allowed me to be assaulted in a most degrading way. I vowed to keep well away from him after that but he was so arrogant and insensitive that when some months later we met by accident, he insisted on showing me his latest photographs, disgusting as they were. They titillated him but I recognised one or two of the men shown in them. In a flash it occurred to me that I could get myself out of the depths of poverty and misery that was my life at that time, and also exact some kind of revenge for what I had been subjected to in that evil house."

"I'd grown up with Victor. Rough neighbourhood, 13th Arrondissement. I recruited him to do the dirty work while I researched the victims. I pretended to Alain that I was just as turned on by his pictures as he was and as a result he was delighted to make extra copies for me. And if he kept back any of the more salacious examples, I sent Victor into the house to steal what was needed. I never went back to number 59 at night- time, but visited regularly during daylight hours to pore over the latest product with Alain and feign laughter at some of the antics those sad people got up to. He gave me a front door key, which Victor copied."

"But you did visit one night, when you shot him."

"Yes. I wondered when we would get round to that."

At this point she asked me to pour some more wine and, after doing so and resuming my seat, I saw she now had a gun in her right hand. It was pointed at my head. Like a drowning man my life flashed before me. Stolen tablecloths. Edith Piaf. Inspector Truffaut. She had killed once — would she hesitate to remove this troublesome chef but what happened next was to provide another twist in this extraordinary affair. With some force she flung the revolver at my chest, knocking over the bottle of *Haut Brion* in the process. It was, fortunately, empty. For a moment this projectile knocked the wind out of me but as I recovered my senses I picked up the weapon that had slipped down my chest and landed in my lap. The shock had made me close my legs together; an instinctive reaction. The gun, now in my hand, felt unusually light, and no wonder; it was an authentic looking replica. Sylvia explained.

"When I told Victor I was going to see Alain that night he gave me this pistol. Useless really, but a lot of women carry them to frighten off predators."

"So you did not kill that man."

"No. But let me go back a little. I put into operation the blackmail business. Very selective. I only chose the cream of society — but satisfyingly lucrative. One of my victims with more balls than the others must have told the police — but am I the lucky one — the case went to our friend, Inspector Truffaut, who was a regular at number 59 and he came to see me to make sure he was not revealed. As a second stroke of good fortune I had in my possession a picture of the good Inspector in a position that required him to be suspended by the ankles. I gave him a copy."

"What happened next?"

"Alain is not very bright. Extraordinary with a paintbrush in his hand, but I think what little brain he had is now addled by the sex thing. Even so, he found out what I was doing and called me to his presence. It was that night. I was nervous. He was not always rational and had recently begun drinking too much. Drugs as well, I think. So I thought it best to have some protection, other than Victor's toy gun, and I chose the Inspector. He was as interested as I was to make sure Alain did not go berserk — and perhaps put his own reputation in jeopardy."

"So, he was nearby."

"Yes. As soon as he saw the body he thought the best thing was to take me into custody."

"Did Alain kill himself?"

"When I got there he was very drunk, slapped my face twice and shouted at the top of his voice. He looked ill. Obviously had not shaved for days. Then all of a sudden he changed. Became sensual and leered at me. His body began to twist and writhe about like a snake. If I let him fuck me he would forget all about my naughtiness. Began to tear off his clothes and shook his penis at me. I told him in no uncertain terms, no. He pleaded. I told him I was leaving. He then became consumed with fury. His eyes were like pinpoints. He let go of his prick and dragged a revolver out of a drawer in the hall table. He was shaking. Either I undress immediately or he will shoot me — between my tits he says. I am really scared. I backed out of the front door to see if I my replica gun will frighten him. By this time he is foaming at the mouth but then he turned his weapon towards his groin and pulled the trigger, twice. The gun fell from his hand and skidded across the tiled floor as he himself sank onto those tiles, blood already beginning to flow."

"And Inspector Truffaut arrived as soon as he heard the shots."

"Yes."

"Presumably he called a squad car to make the arrest look as legitimate as possible?"

"I suppose so."

I told her I was going home as I had had enough excitement for one night but suggested we lunched together on the morrow. She was a criminal, but my conscience told me that her victims probably got what they deserved, so why should I intervene. I told her this over a rather splendid, if I do say so myself, *Tournedos Rossini* and when she left she kissed me on the lips. There were tears in her eyes as she squeezed my hand and said thank you and goodbye. I never saw her again.

For some reason, after this little escapade, the linen inventory remained constant. Perhaps the more serious criminal activity on our doorstep had persuaded the petty thief to mend his, or her ways.

All right, not much in the way of detection, but my Herbert is primarily a chef and not a Sherlock Holmes. Angela Warren, who eventually became my agent, had the same view about my first effort. She said it was not a detective story at all but a rather feeble attempt to imagine another mixed-up female like Simóne, albeit with criminal tendencies. She also began to talk about veracity, but by then I had stopped listening.

*Alan Shelley*

Conan Doyle he is not, but he writes in a rather quirky way and having a chef as the hero is moderately original. I told him he should write about his experiences in Paris. He is actually a better talker than he is author and so I knew all about the sad affair with that girl. When I got to know him better I could fully appreciate how distressing it was, but he is an ebullient character and seems to have recovered somewhat, although he did not want to write about Paris — too painful he said. He suggested a story about the General Strike but I was not encouraging. Not that he will take any notice of my suggestions. Very independent and sure of himself — too self-willed for my liking. Says if the reading public does not like his writing, the eating public will lap up his French cooking. He is probably right. We had a marvellous dinner at his flat last week.

On the other hand, none of us like the French. Stories are still going the rounds about their peasants charging our Tommies rent for the trenches but more seriously, it is already becoming evident that their relentless hostility towards the Germans, and the punitive reparations imposed at Versailles, are going to lead to trouble in the future. Many of the ex-soldiers I meet thought we fought the war on the wrong side.

I did find outlets for him eventually, after he had begun to take my advice rather than treat it like a blow to his person. I cannot see where the humour in his writing comes from. He is so serious about himself — and his literary career as he terms it. One rarely sees the lighter side. I cannot decide whether he is nice — or insignificant — but if I can continue to sell the stuff, we are good friends.

Angela Warren October 1925

## Chapter Seven

## London

*Salmorejo*

*Ingredients. One pound tomatoes: two cloves garlic: two ounces white bread: two tablespoons vinegar: olive oil: sea salt:*

*To Garnish. Diced Serrano ham: hard-boiled egg.*

*Method. Skin the tomatoes and remove their cores. Using a blender, liquefy the tomatoes and garlic and add the vinegar and seasoning, Soak the bread in water until tender, then wring it out. Now add half of the bread and blend until smooth. Continue adding bread and a little olive oil and blending until the soup has a smooth, creamy consistency. Chill the soup and then serve in a shallow bowl, garnished with ham and egg and accompanied by fresh bread.*

## 1926

The cuisine at the Great Western Hotel was, to say the least, somewhat different to what I was used to in Paris. Even writing fiction with some reference to French cooking could not compensate for the interminable Brown Windsor soup and over-cooked lamb cutlets; and my temporary abode in Paddington did not help. My two rooms were tawdry enough but they were as a palace compared to the hallway and stairs that had to be passed through to reach them. It appeared that the walls had not been decorated since the demise of Queen Victoria although the electric light provided by the landlord was of such a low wattage that a close observation was difficult, if not impossible. The treads of the stone staircase were so worn away that when a tenant of an upper floor left a tap running, a frequent occurrence, the escaping water gathered as puddles that, in my worst moments, reminded me of the damaged street in the village near Arras. I wondered if Clarice and her sister were still in business — a thought appropriate to where I lived now. I think I was the only tenant in that appalling block of flats off Praed Street that was not involved in the sale of their bodies for pecuniary reward — and I am not referring to Burke and Hare. I tried to keep my own space clean and tidy but could do nothing to prevent the atmosphere in those passage-ways filtering into my rooms so that I slept, night after night, with a perfume of pungent urine, like that of a horse I thought, and very old boiled cabbage.

All of this exacerbated the feeling of deep depression I had about Simóne — and about leaving Paris. I needed to move on; redirect my life.

Before doing this I felt it crucial to try and understand, or justify, or even accept, why I had left Paris. I had lived there for more than five years at a particularly formative period of my life and I had had some successes, and some failures. Well, one spectacular failure; Simóne. When I was first attracted to her, when we lived together and now we are apart, at none of those times could I explain to myself why I was captivated. But I was. It was as if my love for her was totally unavoidable; outside my control. On occasions I saw myself as the victim in a doomed love affair — the sort of situation that thrives most strongly in France; consider the death of Dumas's Marguerite Gautier and the tragedy of Emma Bovary. If these people are to be found in London or Birmingham, I do not know of them. Simóne had a psychological problem and nothing I could do, no amount of love, could alter that fact, but I still ached for her. Sometimes it seemed to be a physical pain that ran through my body as though I had been immersed from head to toe in ice-cold water. All I can do is to pray that the gods will be kind to me again and send her to the Notre Dame on one of the anniversaries of our first meeting. I miss her so.

That was my emotional state, at least for part of the time, but in practical terms, what was I to do with myself now? Where I had failed with Simone, I appeared to have succeeded with the Trois Perroquets. The sale of the business gave me the capital to move out of Paddington, but what was to be my career path? Cooking was my first love, but somehow I felt it would be more difficult to satisfy this in London than in Paris. I treated myself to lunch at Rules in Maiden Lane but when the chef there heard I had never cooked a steak and kidney pudding in my life, his advice was to look for some other kind of work. I wanted to respond to his advice in the sort of tones I used to that gardener at Versailles, so many years ago, but I did not. That chef was probably right and I was in any case coming to the conclusion that perhaps I might, in the future, make a living with the pen rather than the frying pan.

I will recount shortly the details of my expanding friendship with Peter Southern, but at this point I should tell you that he introduced me to his literary agent, Angela Warren. At first I thought she was more enemy than guide. To someone as sensitive as me her criticism of my early work was so unrelenting that I went back to the professional kitchen. I tore up the story I was writing at the time and found work as an assistant chef at a local restaurant called Chez Peter. French, I thought, in name only as there was little evidence of any of the influence of Escoffier in that modest establishment. Indeed, it had plenty to be modest about.

But, in my spare time, I persevered with the writing and as I did I found that I came to imbue my chef-detective, Herbert Montcalm, with more authenticity and more convoluted plots. This reduced the acidic Miss Warren's criticism a little and as she had obviously noted the change of direction, she finally made a positive suggestion. While Montcalm is being brought to the boil — a phrase typical of her so-called wit — why not write food articles with an icing of humour, her again, and she would try and place them in magazines. She could not promise me *Punch* but at that time a new breed of periodicals began to proliferate, mainly directed at women. They did not instruct the ladies how to secure an ideal husband, there was still a shortage of these, perfect or otherwise, but gave advice on how to beautify the home, how to deal with unruly children and how to use the ingredients found in the usual middle-class kitchen to concoct dishes of a new and daring variety. My recipes might fit in to this concept — but keep them simple, she said. I did as I was bid and as a result was able to say farewell to Chez Peter as I began to make a tolerable living with the articles — and eventually with Herbert Montcalm when my clever Angela began to sell them to mystery magazines, particularly in America, where they are rather fonder of the French than we are — and of detective stories.

The completion of the sale of my interest in the Trois Perroquets enabled me to get away from Paddington and find some more salubrious accommodation — in Maida Vale. I purchased a forty year lease over a mansion flat at 37 Wymering Road and this was to serve as my home until the lease expired and I retired to the county of my birth. Very handy for Lords. Would I ever become a member of the MCC? Who would I get to propose me?

Simóne and I had been very comfortable with Hubert and at the Trois Perroquets but this habitat was on a much grander scale. The rooms were spacious and elegant, had high ceilings and there was a uniformed hall porter. The drawing room overlooked the tree-lined street, the dining-room comfortably accommodated ten and there were three bedrooms sharing two bathrooms. There was also a box room that became my study — my writing parlour. The flat was in good condition but I found enough money to convert the kitchen to my taste.

I moved in a month after the General Strike had collapsed and my first guests were my mother and Francois.

## I Never Met Ernest Hemingway

Unfortunately, that visit was the scene of another collapse — or partial one — in my relationship with her. Our difference of opinion did not cause any permanent fracture but it was a serious break. The cause was the General Strike itself.

Before we came to be at loggerheads over the political situation, my mother had some news for me about my old school friend, Bob Patch. He had, like me, also left Gloucester, but in his case to work on the stage — to tread the boards. He seemed to be making some progress as, after the usual apprenticeship of scene shifting and props assistant in repertory at Bristol, he now had a small part in Edgar Wallace's, *The Ringer,* currently performing at the Wyndhams Theatre in London. I thought back. We were certainly in the same cricket eleven but was he ever the thespian I was? Come to think of it, he was in *The Importance of being Earnest* but rather missed out. He had the minor part of Lane, but if I remember correctly the next year he was cast as Macbeth and gave a good performance, although I did not see it. Not my favourite play. As I recall we were into an active period of outside catering at the time — I think it was some council bigwig's farewell party.

Strangely enough, during the General Strike theatres in London were attracting capacity houses. Perhaps people were staying in town during the emergency and not retreating to the suburbs of Pinner or Epsom. There was certainly a varied fare on offer. The first London showing of Sean O" Casey's, *The Plough and the Stars,* was at the Fortune and an old favourite, *The Ghost Train,* was at the Prince of Wales.

There had been some political differences with my mother at this time but they only emerged in their full glory during the General Strike. I shall tell you in due course of my part in this event, countered by what my mother did, but I will not bore you with too much detail of the 'why and wherefores' of the affair that dominated Britain in 1926; this is already the stuff of legend and there is no need for me to add to this. It continues to capture the public imagination, but is this attention deserved?

*Alan Shelley*

It began at midnight on the 3rd of May and was over nine days later. In addition to the country's miners there were between one and a half and two million workers on strike, depending on whether you accept the figures of the Ministry of Labour or the Trade Union Council, but little was actually achieved.

The abiding memory is of the way university students and white collar workers worked in the docks, drove the trams or took on the duties of special constables, but the reality is that it was only a handful so engaged out of the many that signed on as volunteers. There was a fervour to join the party and give up, for a while, a boring job as a clerk at Lloyds Bank and drive a bus, but there were over one hundred thousand volunteers in London alone of whom only ten per cent were ever used. Legends are often built on the flimsiest of evidence; a newspaper image of the patriotic citizen standing up to the threat of revolution and keeping the country going, never mind the real hardship in the mining industry.

I was one who was taken on. For ten mornings I got up early and worked in the bakehouse of J. Lyons and Co. Not very glamorous but at that time I had never driven any form of motor transport, never mind a double-decker bus — or a tram — although I did think that in view of my detective fiction, a special constable would have been more fitting. However, to be fair, I probably made more of a contribution at Cadby Hall than patrolling the beat — and I tried to see myself as being true to my roots; a view to be vehemently contested by my mother.

Why did I volunteer? I suppose I now instinctively saw myself as middle-class — even if strictly speaking I was not — and of course I had no direct experience of the suffering of the miners and other manual workers. For most of the years since 1917 I had been absent from the country of my birth and I had no knowledge of the economics at macro or micro level that required the Government to support, however vapidly, the mine owners in their fight to reduce colliers' wages. I had never visited South Wales, or the Midlands, or the North. At one time

I saw a report that said unemployment was only three per cent in High Wycombe compared with sixty seven per cent in Jarrow, but did the General Strike change any of that? By the end of 1926 the miners were working longer hours than they had for sixty years and only earning three pounds a week.

At that time my mother was still only forty four. She and Francois had run their little empire in Gloucester very efficiently and, despite the economic climate, had bought the freehold of the Westgate Street shop and still had money in the bank. However, none of this had changed the political views that she held, and practised. She still conjured up the tasty delicacies that were the main source of their fortune but in recent times the proceeds from her iced bonbons were needed to subsidise the losses being incurred on the bread. Obviously she could only reach a small proportion of the unemployed and destitute in her city but at all three shops, Whitwells bread was sold for less than the cost of its manufacture and if the need appeared to be particularly dire, it was free.

My actions during the General Strike were, to my mother, nothing less than treachery; I had deserted my working class origins.

"Percy, your cooking has certainly improved. The soufflé was splendid but I was shocked to hear you talk about baking bread during the strike. While your family was giving it away to the strikers, you were acting as a scab. Your grandad would have been as disgusted as I am. Who have you become?"

"Steady on Mum. Is it really that bad?"

"Yes, it is. Who do you think you are? Just because you have been living it up in Paris that is no excuse for you to become a turncoat."

"The strike was not going to achieve anything. The miners were going to be ground-down anyway. So why should ordinary citizens be deprived of their loaf."

"Ordinary citizens. Who do you think the miners are? Have you ever seen anyone so weak from starvation they can hardly lift their heads? Have you ever seen barefoot children crying because they're hungry? Seen mothers so suffering from malnutrition their milk dries up."

"Well, have you?"

"Of course I have. Do you ever venture from this middle-class Maida whatsit and go down to the East End of London? You go to Hoxton or Bermondsey. You'll see them. The people involved in the violence in the London docks were 'ordinary citizens'. And never mind London. Have you ever been to a mining village? Do you have any idea how they have suffered since the war?"

"Well, in view of your liking for miners, your sympathy is understandable."

"How dare you. That's a wicked thing to say. I could equally turn that jibe back on you. What sort of a miner's son are you?"

By this time her speech was becoming incoherent. The more she spluttered, the more red became her complexion. I had never seen her like this before. Francois tried to calm her down, but she was having none of it. She cleared her throat. I thought she was going to spit at me.

"The fact that the miners are now worse off than before makes your action even more shameful."

"Mother, I am no longer a little boy. I make my own decisions."

"Well, it's a pity you made this decision without doing some research first. You think you are clever because you can write nonsense stories but let me tell you my boy you will never amount to anything if you are false to your roots. No one will read what you write if it is full of lies. And that's what it was. Lies. That Churchill, with his *British Gazette*. Called the strikers, 'the enemy'. Who won the bloody war for him and his like? Those 'enemies' who work eight hours a day in the dark for less than a living wage to keep Blenheim Palace well-stocked with coal. I'd like to burn the bleeding lot down — with him in it."

Was this really Violet Glossop; she of the dainty pastries and exotic hats?

"We're going. Come on Francois. Let us leave this defector and much good it will do him. I hope from now on you burn all your cakes."

That seemed to be the final insult. There could be no more devastating a curse to direct at a cook. I made no attempt to persuade them to stay and it was six months or more before I saw, or spoke to my mother again.

I was shocked. What hurt the most was not the allegations about treachery and roots but the suggestion that I was ignorant of the facts. I knew about the mining industry. I knew there was plenty of poverty in our country. I knew Churchill was a bit of a bastard at times but then I thought to myself, what direct experience did I have to substantiate this professed knowledge? As already said, I had never been north of a line drawn from Gloucester to London. Many years before I thought about visiting the Rhondda Valley hoping to find traces of my father, but that notion came to naught. I had not even been to the coalfields closer to home in the Forest of Dean so my real experience was very limited indeed.

My mother would have been fully aware of the importance of coal-mining in the British economy. She may not have been familiar with the detailed statistics but when I made enquiries about mining accidents, to try and explain my father's absence, I was surprised to find that in the last decades of the nineteenth century, Britain brought to the surface nearly half of the world's production of coal. Much of this was exported, very profitably I assume, because of the proximity of some of the mines, particularly in South Wales, to the nation's ports. At its peak, the Rhondda supplied one third of the world's coal.

At the start of the war there were more workers in the mines, one million colliers in three thousand pits, than employed in agriculture and textiles put together. However, much of the precious coal was brought to the surface as a result of hard manual labour. Mine owners were slow to mechanise — not the case in the USA which country was soon to outstrip the UK in coal production — but this resulted in the British miner becoming endowed with a particular muscularity, both in mind and body. They were at the forefront of the burgeoning trade union movement and all seemed blessed with an independent spirit far removed from the relationship between such as Sir Luke Makepeace Thatcher and Alice's father.

The quarrel with my mother disturbed me more than I expected. Initially I took it to be the unreasonable ramblings of a middle-aged woman, but it was not of course. She had been a member of the Independent Labour Party, and then the Labour Party, since their inception and to the best of my knowledge she has lived her adult life within the socialist precepts of a fair deal for all. I found my writing labours were being distracted. I fell out with Angela Warren even more fiercely than normal and I began to be surly to Bert the doorman. Action was needed. I went to the local library and consulted a railway timetable. I had two trips in mind to significant destinations; South Wales in honour of my father and Eastwood in Nottinghamshire, birthplace of DH Lawrence. I took *The White Peacock* and *Sons and Lovers* with me.

I found Nottingham to be a most pleasant city. There is no cathedral to equal that of my hometown but, because of the lace industry, the girls are said to be more pretty, and more plentiful, than in other equivalent cities. I was not there long enough to find out by personal experience whether this was true or not but Nottingham is also home to Boots the Chemists and when I visited their branch No 1 in Goose Gate, the girls behind the counter seemed particularly comely. In addition to Boots, the city has major factories where Players cigarettes and the Raleigh bicycles are made.

There is a major pit at Gedling, about five miles east of the city centre, where parts of the adjoining village are really quite attractive but the collieries in the Eastwood area less so; the miners live in tiny depressing houses that stretch away from the Nottingham Road like ranks of badly painted, but identical, toy soldiers. But, as we read in Lawrence, the countryside is within walking distance, if the miners ever had the time, or energy, to make the journey. Miners are very independent and proud and those at Eastwood were no exception. Passionate about the local football teams and the local brewery — Eastwood drinkers had their own establishment at nearby Kimberley — and their own accents. Not obvious ones like the people of Liverpool or Birmingham or Newcastle, but distinctive all the same. I tried to write down the phonetics of a phrase or two. 'Aya gorra wee ya' means 'Is your wife accompanying you' or 'Ah they gorron' is a request to know what the score was at the latest Nottingham Forest game.

I enjoyed my visit. It was a useful first experience; the poverty was there to be seen but it was not until I got to South Wales that I began to fully endorse my mother's view. Whether this was because of my genes, or because the hardships were greater, I do not know but there is little doubt that as I was becoming a born-again socialist, what I observed in the Rhondda Valley acted as a most efficient midwife. Incidentally, when in Nottingham I made no attempt to find that Trevor Perkins, my erstwhile companion at the Hôtel Majestic. I avoided the Victoria Hotel where he worked and the Flying Horse where he drank, although I did take the opportunity of my visit to down a pint of Shipstone's ale at the Trip to Jerusalem that is built within the Nottingham Castle walls and reputed to be the oldest public house in Britain.

I then moved to Wales and stayed for ten days at a mining village in the Rhondda Valley in one of the three rooms available at the local pub, the Kings Arms. I did not sleep very well there. There was a certain amount of noise from the bar, plus the late-night protracted goodbyes outside the premises after closing time, but the main culprit was the bed. It was narrow, it was high and the mattress was misshapen. This deformity ensured that the sleeper, when asleep, would be relentlessly tilted to the starboard resulting in a fall to the floor that was most painful — it was a very high bed. The frame was of painted ironwork but at the head and foot were large brass balls at each corner. Every night, as I picked myself up from the floor, the half-light that entered the room through the uncurtained window gave them a glint of their own as they seemed, like malignant heads, to be grinning at my misfortune.

But why do I tell you of my discomforts when surrounded by the living conditions of those who had occupied this sad urbanisation all of their lives. The geography of the place was simple. The pit winding gear and ancillary buildings were sited in the valley. Above this were three rows of houses on each of the opposite hillsides that stood out incongruously against the lightly wooded slopes behind. They were all identically coloured; grey turning to brown plus patches of a dirty white, like rows of nicotine stained teeth. Totally uniform — no individuality whatsoever. No doubt some interiors were cleaner than others, as were a number of front doorsteps, but none of these houses had gardens, front or back, where some variation might have been discernible between the amateur horticulturalists who favoured daffodils to those who preferred the cabbage.

These were the notorious back-to-back houses. Light and air is only permitted passage through one elevation. There were thirty two teeth in each row facing the valley, backed by another thirty two looking up the hill. The arithmetic is not too difficult. Including both sides of the valley there were three hundred and eighty four dwellings for three hundred and eighty four miners and their families. Each front door entered directly into a living room with a kitchen of sorts alongside it. In each kitchen was a copper under which a small coal fire was lit every Monday morning for the miner's wife to boil the family wash. Always on a Monday. It was a shibboleth of the working-class that Monday was wash day. The children chanted:

Rain, rain, go away.
Come again on washing day.

Each of these two rooms had a window at the front, that to the kitchen being little more than eighteen inches wide. The living room had a cast-iron grate where a coal fire burned for most of the year. The one luxury the miners had was a generous allowance of free coal. Built into the side of the grate was an oven where all of the family's cooking was done, except for the boiling of water; a kettle hung above the fire from a strategically placed hook. Occasionally, the two shelves in the oven were removed, wrapped in an old blanket, and used to warm the beds on particularly cold nights. The staircase to the one upper floor was built alongside the rear wall giving access to the two bedrooms, each of the same size as the downstairs rooms. There were gaps in these rows of teeth. At every fourth house was a narrow entry that gave onto a courtyard where were two lavatories and a series of clothes lines stretched from wall to wall where the meagre apparel of the adjoining four families was hung to dry. I thought of the luxury of our privy at Westgate Street.

At the end of the valley was a small terrace of further housing, each with its own lavatory and washhouse in an enclosed yard where vegetables were grown with differing levels of success. There were no roses. These houses enjoyed windows in both front and rear elevations and were occupied by the various under-managers at the mine. There were not many of them. There were also one or two even more superior dwellings for even more superior managers, together with the village shop, the Kings Arms, the chapel and a small elementary school.

If the late night drinkers and the bed disturbed my sleep at the beginning of the night — although to be fair to the bed, it was equally deadly at any hour — my early-morning slumbers were interrupted by another factor. I look out of the window. It is not yet seven o'clock. The boots of three hundred men resound on the cobbled streets like a colony of sleepy woodpeckers. There is no other noise. I believe in happier times the walk to the pit was an opportunity to swap pleasantries with your fellow walker and join in the singing, but not today. No man talks to his neighbour. No one is singing — the morning walk to the pit is not used for choir practice. Amazingly, they all look the same. Surely some are tall and some are short; some are old and some are young; but they all seem to present the same image. Drab clothing of dark colours, flat cap and muffler. Most are smoking, the last fag until they re-emerge into the light eight hours from now. They all have the same droop of the shoulders. Many of them must be weak. They have spent most of the year on strike, and food will have been scarce. Many, particularly the older men, are sick with anthrocosis, the scourge of the miner — lung disease caused by years of inhaling coal dust.

I meet some of their wives in the shop, or when they are leaving the chapel where they have been washing the floor or dusting the pews. Some bring their children to school, but most of the infants make their own way. Not all have shoes. Otherwise my day is dull. I write until evening when the few miners that can scrape together a coin or two drink in the Kings Arms. Jack Owen is one of the younger ones. His wife earns a little extra with her needle, she is evidently a very competent seamstress. After twice meeting him in the bar, he invites me to his house to meet her. Clearly devoted to each other, but as they have no children, he has rather more spare pennies than most and therefore, during my stay, I see more of him with a pint in his hand than I do of any of the other inhabitants. He is a well built fellow with an open face, although even with his relatively short tenure as a miner, his hands show the scars of the job and reveal the ingrained coal dust that cannot be erased, however hard the scrubbing brush.

"We don't see too many strangers round these parts. What you're doing here?"

"I write detective stories and I had this mad idea to base my next one in a mining community."

"Not much crime here. Nobody has got nothing worth stealing, and we're mostly too tired for rape and pillage."

## I Never Met Ernest Hemingway

This rather amused me. Clearly a bright fellow. For a moment I was tempted to tell him about my father, but resisted.

"You're probably right. Anyway, I went for a walk out of the valley today. Very pretty and peaceful."

"Yes. I love this place. Pity about the colliery."

"How did you fare during the lay off?"

"Bloody hard. Don't really want to recall it."

"General Strike didn't help you much."

"You can say that again. Mine bosses and Whitehall bosses are sure-bet winners, but when your own working mates let you down, what chance did we have. Makes me sick to the stomach. I'd like to get some of them down pit. D'you know what it's like. My shift is eight hours. It doesn't start until I get to the coalface. That takes twenty minutes from the bottom of the lift. By time I gets to me working spot I'm covered in sweat. Most time I work naked. You should see the coal dust at the bottom of our tin bath where I washes each night. The missus scrubs me back, just like everybody else. Today I was at a seam only three foot head high. I had to swing the pick from a lying down position. Bloody murder — and for less than I was paid last year for a shorter shift. So much for, 'Not a penny off the pay, not a second on the day.' Did the TUC support us? No. I shit on the unions."

"But there's more competition in the coal industry now. It's cheaper in the States and from Europe. The only way we can be competitive is to cut costs."

"Yes. Our wages, not their profits. They've made millions out of us. Ever seen a poor mine owner?"

"Perhaps communism is the answer. Nationalise everything."

"Do you know mate, you're wrong. Few of us at this mine will join the Communist Party. We support the Labour Party, even if they haven't done much for us yet. But it will come. There'll be no revolution like with the Frenchies. But we've got the vote now, and eventually it will be better for the working man. And we pray each Sunday."

*Alan Shelley*

At this point an older man, who had been listening to our conversation, poked me in the ribs and suggested I might buy him a pint. I did so, and one for the articulate Mr Owens. Our neighbour then joined in, and Jack responded.

"You do talk such rubbish, young Owen. The only way we'll get out of this shithole is to fight. A bit of arson around the pit head. Some arsenic in their sherry."

"Bill, if you blow up the pit, we're out of work again. Use some sense man."

"I tell you, drastic action is needed. We're never going to win if we're too tired to raise a hand. I'm all in favour of revolution. Chop off their heads I say. The pithead shaft could easily be converted into a guillotine."

"You don't really mean that Bill, but as you know, it was talk of revolution and the 'Red Menace' that meant the government was well organised to snuff out the strike. Talk about the red flag flying over Buckingham Palace scared them."

"Sure, we would be idiots to blow up the pit, but the strike did nothing for us. They subsidised our wages for nine months while they got their defence ready. Okay, but as far as I know, the TUC did not get themselves sorted out. They were trying to avoid t'strike until the last minute."

"You're right there. That Daily Mail thing was a turning point."

The printers at the Daily Mail refused to produce the newspaper when it contained a report condemning the strike because it was in fact a revolutionary move with the object of destroying the government. As a result of this, Prime Minister Baldwin called off negotiations with the TUC. Jack continued.

"What happened proves my point. The general public supported the government because they were afraid of communism and the TUC were in a similar funk. Believing that the union movement would be taken over by revolutionaries. We didn't stand a chance. We were never going to win. Is it true, Mr Glossop, that Germany was allowed to flood the

market by exporting their coal to France and Italy as part of the reparations?"
I told them I thought this was the case. There had been some talk about it before I left Paris. This exchange continued into some further pints. I did not see Bill as an ardent anarchist — and I do not think he did either. The man at the other end of the bar did not join in; everyone seemed to ignore him. I soon discovered why. He was Richards, the shopkeeper, and nobody's friend.

Next day I visited the shop. It had none of the attractions of the establishment where I grew up. Like Westgate Street, the village shop had a low ceiling which added to the dismal scene it presented to the customer. It was also smaller, a factor exaggerated by the quantity of stock carried. At the rear wall was a door leading, I assumed, to some living quarters — or possibly a store, and on either side of the door were shelves from floor-to-ceiling. Deposited on them were household wares of every description; tinned vegetables with discoloured labels; custard powder; jars of jam — no two of the same variety or make; blocks of soda; a grubby selection of tea towels; scrubbing brushes and incongruously, two bottles of Empire sherry. Items most in demand were housed on the wide counter; loaves of bread; loose sugar ready to be packed in blue bags; rashers of anaemic looking bacon; a slab of pale yellow butter; bars of rough soap; a jar of loose tea and a set of scales that, when I came to know the shopkeeper better, I venture did not give an accurate measurement.

Richards presided over this emporium from behind the counter and when stationary, he stood on a conveniently placed wooden box. He was, I suppose, in a position to feed himself well but in his person there was no evidence of this. His face was so narrow, and his ears so small, it was only the bulbous and red mottled nose that kept his steel framed spectacles in place — or relatively so. When he became angry and ordered me from the shop, his agitation sent his eye-glasses skidding down that proboscis and bedding themselves into the mound of butter on his counter. The box was required because of his stunted growth but there was nothing stunted in his manner. He held the welfare of these hundreds of miners, and their families, in his hands and he revelled in this power. As I entered the shop he rubbed together those hands like a Uriah Heep of the valleys; here was a customer with cash in his pockets compared to his normal clientele who could only afford the barest of necessities.

"Good morning Sir. What can I do for you? Some nice apples — came in this morning with the bread van."

"Bread. That interests me. I've been a baker in my time."

"Only one type I'm afraid. How many loaves would you like?"

"Is that really the price? At the Co-op in Gloucester I could get two of those for what you are charging."

"Well, you see, it's the transport cost."

"Where do they come from?"

"Pontypridd."

"But that's not far. Is there anywhere else in the village where the miners can buy their bread?"

"No, only here."

"Oh dear."

"They are lucky to have me."

"Well, Mr Richards. It seems to me you are exploiting these people. They are very poor. The strike is only just over and I presume bread is a staple part of their diet, but you are using this to make excessive profits."

"Excessive profits. What is it to you? It is no business of yours. If you are not going to buy anything, you can get out of my shop."

"I would not buy from you, under any circumstances. I cannot believe you can be so heartless. Good day."

This is when the spectacles landed in the butter.

Unusually, the shop at this colliery was not the property of the mine owners. When this was the case, so I was told, the exploitation of the miners down the pit was extended to the shop. The miners' families were locked into a vicious spiral. The company shop was the only one available and so the customers had to accept the high prices because of this, and because credit was made available to add a further shackle. Richards followed this pattern. On Friday evenings the miners' wives paid off the outstanding debt and then immediately took the credit he offered by purchasing a loaf of bread at a price that would only have added fuel to the fire of my mother's anger. She would not have just walked away from those premises. She would have used her handbag to make sure the spectacles joined the butter.

My encounter with Richards fired me into action. If baking bread during the General Strike was, in effect, the starting point for my current odyssey, it would now figure in a reversal of roles to the benefit of those who had been defeated by that strike. With the agreement of the minister, who lived in the next village, I got Jack and Bill to call a meeting of the miners at the chapel. It was well attended. I told them about my mother and suggested they boycott the shop until the exploitative shopkeeper reduced his profit and sold the bread at a fair price. Many of the men, and their wives, were naturally nervous about this. He was the only source of groceries in the village, and they could imagine how vindictive he might be. I told them I could see that but I hazarded a guess that the loaf was the product most in demand, and no doubt the reason he was able to charge such a price, but I had a solution. Over the next few weeks the housewives should try and stock up with jam and margarine and the like, even if on more credit, and then ignore the shop altogether. I would then start, in a month's time, importing my mother's bread to the village, twice every week, to be sold at a proper price until the greedy Richards charged the same price for his. The chapel could be used as a temporary shop. The motion was carried and soon afterwards my mother and I became friends again.

As can be imagined, Richards was furious at this turn of events. He threatened me with the law. He promised his

*Alan Shelley*

cousins in Bridgend would break my legs after they had wreaked havoc at all three Whitwell shops. He then tried a bribe. He then told me to go to hell. His threats came to naught but I have tried ever since to avoid finding myself overnight in Bridgend.

I paid for the transport costs and my mother was pleased to receive for the bread the fair price paid by the miners. The problem of course was that the bread customers became rather fond of the superior Whitwell loaf and complained when they had to revert to the inferior product purveyed by Richards — but the expense of the special import from Gloucester could not be continued indefinitely. Nevertheless, this adventure did cause Francois to consider whether they should increase the capacity of the bakehouse and begin a wholesale business, supplying grocer's shops in the Gloucester area. My mother particularly liked the idea of her bread — that had been Alice Smith's bread — being sold in Newnham and making its way into the kitchen at Stockton Hall.

The bread convoy lasted four weeks before Richards capitulated. When that happened I wrote to him saying that if I heard he was reverting to his earlier pricing policy, my mother would proceed with the plan, already prepared, to supply her bread on a permanent basis to selected villages in the Rhondda Valley using a bakers van delivering door-to-door, two or three days every week. To reinforce this threat I told him of my father and the emotional connection my mother had with miners — particularly Welsh ones. It was not until I was back in London that I realised how appropriate my little action had been when we hear the words of the Welsh anthem, Cwm Rhondda:

Guide me, O Thou great Jehovah,
Pilgrim through this barren land.
I am weak, but Thou art mighty;
Hold me with Thy powerful hand.
Bread of heaven, bread of heaven,

Feed me now and evermore,
Feed me now and evermore.

    Jack and I corresponded regularly thereafter. He told me he would let me know if Richards went back to his wicked ways. A minor victory I thought but in addition I had gained myself a new friend.

    With just those brief forays into mining communities it was impossible for me to fully appreciate the hardships suffered by the working class at this time, but I had at least started the learning process and my friendship with Jack Owen provided me with a continuing course of education. He acted like a religious leader teaching the necessary catechism in the process of a conversion to socialism. We did not assume the role of instructor and instructed; it just seemed to happen naturally, but for the rest of my life, where politics were concerned, I always found myself measuring my beliefs and actions using Jack Owen as the yardstick.

    From the time of the Richard's incident he always addressed me as 'Percy, the bread'. Here is a letter from him of the 3rd of June 1929.

My dear Percy the bread.

I hope you are keeping well — and selling some of your stories. Please extend my kindest regards to your mother.

 We are told that unemployment has fallen to 1.1 million, which is around 10% of the working population, but if there is an improvement in employment prospects, we colliers are not likely to be taking part, certainly not at our wretched pit. The seams get shallower and some of the men now walk nearly three miles to the face to hew out the coal that the bosses can import from Europe for a price less than our cost of production. All of us are in work at present — but for how long.

Richards has sold the shop. Hooray. Even better, the new owner is a miner's widow, Bronwen Meredith. Her husband was killed a few years ago in a colliery in the next valley. I remember hearing about it at the time. Not an infrequent occurrence. Shoring at the pit bottom, not properly in place, leading to a collapse that cut him off from his fellow workers. The fall was so major they couldn't get to him before he died. Lack of oxygen. Awful end for any man. But it can happen to us at any time. His wife moved in with a married daughter and then last year she heard that her brother, who had left the Valleys many years ago to seek his fortune in Australia, had also died and left her a tidy sum of money. And so she bought the shop. Instead of the misery formerly associated with those premises it has now been transformed into a happy meeting place for all the women who treat it like we do the Kings Arms. She does not need to make a big profit, thanks to her brother, but that's not the only blessing. She is such a cheerful soul after that curmudgeon Richards, and she understands the miners' lot. So, that some good news.

Beth is very well and sends you her best wishes.

Most sincerely

Jack Owen

Cardiff City made their way to the final of the FA Cup in 1927. Although not a fan, I could not resist sending Jack and his wife rail tickets and stadium tickets for the final. And what did they do in exchange? They took the cup out of England for the first, and I believe, only time — but it was a wonderful weekend. I was back in the valley later that year for the christening of their firstborn — and was honoured to be asked to be a godfather.

Perhaps the quality of my authorship was improving because Angela finally invited me to dinner. I had cooked for her and the husband two, or was it three times, before my hospitality was reciprocated. Of course, she may have been nervous that she could not match the quality of my cuisine but even so, if she was prepared to accept my invitations, she should have asked me back. When I was the host the guest list was small but when I arrived at Angela's smart house in Kensington it was a rather large party. I never really got to know her husband well. A civil servant, but in what ministry I cannot recall. There was, I believe, some family money, but on her side. He was a nice enough man; reminded me of some of the minor staff officers I had served drinks to in the Divisional mess during the World War. His manners were immaculate, but conversation pedestrian.

I was seated next to a lady, about my age or probably a little older, whose name I failed to register when first introduced. She soon let me know she was a freelance journalist, favoured by the *Daily Telegraph*. She was perfectly charming towards me but I was quickly informed that she did not read fiction of any kind, particularly detective stories, although she did enjoy Ernest Hemingway — had I heard of him? Additionally, she was of the opinion that the quality of French cuisine was highly overrated so, in other words, we found ourselves to be soul mates from the start. When I ascertained that she thought cricket was the most boring pursuit ever devised by man, I concentrated thereafter on the pretty girl on my left, who was one of Angela's colleagues. I did not inform my neighbour with the bizarre tastes that Ernest Hemingway and I had drunk in the same bars in Paris because I might have needed to confess that this was not necessarily at the same time.

When we were leaving, the non-cricket lover made a point of saying goodbye to me, thanking me most warmly for my company and hoping we might meet again soon. This so astonished me that the next time I met Angela I asked who she was. Jennifer Lomax. Married young. Husband killed during the last months of the war; one son, now at boarding school. Good writer, respected for her down-to-earth style, and firmly held opinions. Just like me, I thought.

I have already mentioned that I was at the Oval for the Fifth Test. On the last day I took Bob Patch with me. He was performing in some play or other in the West End. Imagine my surprise when I noticed, some rows in front of us, Mrs Jennifer Lomax, together with a small boy. She was reading a book but he was following the action with the same rapt attention as Bob and I. She did not join the throng that congregated at the

Pavilion to congratulate our team, and neither did we. I caught up with her as we exited the ground into Vauxhall Street and I introduced her to Bob. Rather irritatingly she needed no introduction. She recognised him immediately having seen him on stage; she occasionally wrote theatre reviews. While they discussed the latest work by Noel Coward the boy and I swapped ideas as to how we would have played Wilf if we had been Australian batsmen.

## Jennifer

After the chance meeting at the Oval, this lady did not feature in my life, or my thoughts, until Angela mentioned that such was not the case with Bob Patch. She had evidently been to see him perform on stage, followed by a late supper. I had not seen the play my old school chum graced but when I was given the news about he and Jennifer, I decided I should repair that omission. I thought it a very slight piece indeed but I did negotiate entry to his dressing-room afterwards. Not an easy achievement. From where do they acquire those men who guard stage doors and who delight in being as difficult as possible? I thought the French concierge was the premier exponent in this market, but not so — at least not at this theatre. I explained that Mr Patch and I went to school together but the sentinel just continued biting his fingernails. Eventually he condescended to inform me that he had no one of my name on his list.

"If you're not on me list, you can't come in."
I told him it was a surprise visit.
"We don't like surprises at back door. Those are for on stage, not here."
I tried a different tack. This up-and-coming writer of detective stories was thinking about setting his next one in a theatre, tentative title *Murder in the Wings*, and this could easily be fashioned so that a certain doorman would have a major role

to play in solving the crime. I do not think he understood what I was talking about. I then tried a more dubious, but more aggressive approach.

"Look here, my man. Noel Coward and I share the same publisher and he will be furious if I tell him of the way I am being treated."

"That Coward don't pay me wages. Buzz off."

I told Bob of this little exchange while he was removing his make-up and suggested that the five pound note that had just changed hands should be reimbursed by him. Bob disagreed. We went to the nearest pub where I had by then sufficiently recovered from the stage door fracas to buy him a pint.

"I hear you made your mark with the lady we met at the Oval."

"Well, I don't know about that, but she seems to be attracted. But then, we stage people get a lot of that. Just a crush by an adoring fan."

"Bob, what nonsense you talk sometimes. She's hardly a lovesick teenager and, come to think of it, you're no matinee idol. She's too strait-laced for that."

"To be honest, I agree. Not my type at all, but she stood me a good meal and a decent bottle of plonk."

"Why?"

"She has a particular professional interest in the author of our minor epic. I think she's researching for a book about him — or at least an article — and wanted to look at the man's work through the eyes of someone who has to deliver the lines."

"And what did you say to that?"

"Well, as politely as I could, I told her that the dialogue this guy had produced was crap, and very hard to deliver convincingly. George Bernard Shaw he ain't."

"So, no holding hands before the bangers and mash arrived?"

"It was lamb cutlets actually, but no, she thanked me for my views and departed in a taxi, leaving me to tip the cloakroom attendant."

"You always were a cheap skate Patch. By the way, your turn to buy the drinks."

Why had I bothered? I had no interest in this woman and did not even admire her writing style, although I must admit she seemed to have convinced someone because I was always coming across her articles. Rather more successful than me; the Yanks had rejected my last Montcalm story. I therefore wondered if she might introduce me to some of the editors with whom she found favour in the hope that I could get a few more of my foodie articles published — and paid for. I would soon need to start drawing on my ten per cent Whitwells' account. I suggested this to Angela. She said, nothing ventured, nothing gained and then, sweet girl that she is, arranged for the three of us to lunch together. I found that despite her tastes she was lively company and seemed to enjoy my jokes — of which I have a fund. For some reason I told them both about my performance as Lloyd George those many years ago but not about how the phrase, 'Lloyd George knew my father', could have a particular connotation for me.

When she laughed she became quite good-looking. The eyebrows were not so raised and the lips became softer; in fact, now I observe more closely, she resembled Liza Rosen but with a rather smaller front. Her hair, which was bobbed in the fashion of the time, was auburn with an attractive sheen that reflected the restaurant's lights. It was a foggy day. She was smartly dressed, but not overly so, and I guessed that clothes did not really matter to her. It seemed to me that the colours of the non-matching skirt and jacket rather clashed. You would never have seen Angela so attired — in fact I sometimes thought the immaculate Mrs Warren only persevered with me as a client because she believed, mistakenly, that I could give expert advice on the subject of Parisian chic.

Jennifer asked me to send her some samples of my writing on food and cookery but before I could discover whether her efforts would bear fruit, the Americans changed their mind and Herbert was back in the mystery magazines and my finances became rather healthier. This event determined me to arrange a small dinner party to celebrate the success I was having in the development of an English version of Nero Wolf. It was a small group, only eight, including Jennifer Lomax and Peter Southern, with whom I was now in regular contact. She definitely improved with time, particularly when she turns on the charm.

Angela told me something of this lady's history and when I got to know her better I was inclined to think of her as a typical 'Home Counties girl'. She was born in Oxted in Surrey to a father who was a local solicitor and a mother who died at the outbreak of the war. There was an older sister. Jennifer left school when eighteen but before she had decided what career to follow, and there was no doubt that she was destined to be a career girl, she met Lieutenant Byron Lomax at a Christmas party. He was on leave from his regiment, which was at Ypres, and by the following June they were married; hasty romances were a feature of this time. Besides the final push by the German army, May 1918 was very significant in Jennifer's life. Her son was born, and his father was killed during that campaign. Her mother's unmarried sister had been running the household in Oxted since the death of Mrs Simmons and she now rose to the task of sharing the care of the fatherless boy with the grieving mother. The older sister, Ruth, also helped.

Jennifer did not mourn for long. She was determined not to marry again but to pursue the career path she had envisaged before that Christmas party. She was going to write — and by the time I met her, she had succeeded. Edward's care, previously shared between mother and aunt, was now in the hands of his boarding school, but the holidays were spent with his mother in the small house she had bought at Barnes.

*Alan Shelley*

Although I had only met the boy once, I was impressed with the way Jennifer had brought him up. It goes without saying that his interest in cricket endeared him to me — despite his mother's ignorance — and he seemed to be a polite, bright lad.

After my dinner party, Jennifer asked me to go with her to the Maddox Gallery which was showing some of the controversial work of Fernand Lêger, about whom she had been commissioned to write an article. She knew of my involvement with the Boutet Nudes but not, in detail, of the relationship between myself and the model. Not that I was hiding anything. It was, at this stage in my life and our friendship, difficult to explain Simóne. As a result of my Parisian experiences, Jennifer seemed to welcome my views on the paintings we saw but I noticed, when reading her review later, she had either forgotten what I said, or had had a differing view all the time. I was not too upset about this. I recalled how often Simóne's instinctive impression was seen by most others as superior to mine.

After the disappearance of Simóne, Paul Nerval and I saw more of each other than hitherto, and we became quite friendly. Not exactly close, his circle was not mine, but shortly after the visit to the Maddox exhibition, I made a surprising discovery. I was aware that he was a cultured man with a good command of the English language but what had never been revealed was the aberrant interest he had in crime fiction — at least, not revealed until he confessed it in a letter to me.

My dear Percy.
I received a final report from the other agency that I promised to engage to say they had come to a cul-de-sac in their search for information about Simóne. I was not altogether surprised, and I assume you did not have unreasonable hopes, so it does seem as though that unhappy girl has vanished into the Parisian masses. I am so sorry to write this, my friend, but I suspect that unless she contacts you, there is nothing more

we can do. As you know, I was strangely drawn to her and frankly, if it was not for this, I wonder if the Boutet Nudes, and Richardson's later work, would ever have been seen by the general public. Although, having made that point, I am contradicting my own maxim that true talent will always be revealed eventually. Do you hear from the man? Is he still painting?

I will not directly enquire of your fortune because I can to some extent assess this for myself. I have a confession to make — something I keep well hidden from my intellectual peers and acquaintances. I am very fond of detective stories and subscribe to a number of the American magazines devoted to such. I find they are in the forefront in this field — perhaps the French writers are too subtle for the genre. I like Herbert Montcalm. He is different, and I congratulate you on your creation. I had rather assumed you would still be engaged in some kitchen somewhere in London, but no doubt writing gives you the luxury of more convenient working hours. Are the magazines going to take more of your work? I hope so.

I know it is not really your — how do you English say — 'cup of tea', but I have arranged a small exhibition of the latest works of Raoul Dufy. It opens next month, and so if you feel like a return to Paris for a few days, we might compare notes on a new chef they have at the Ritz. The Baroness d'Breslau tells me he is quite superb and that a new culinary star is born.

Most sincerely yours
Paul Nerval


I replied and thanked him for his invitation, which I regretfully declined, and for his interest in my writing. I did not tell him how amazed I was to learn of his guilty deviation from the world of Guy de Maupassant and Marcel Proust. I was not yet strong enough emotionally to return to the city that had swallowed up Simóne and perhaps this was the reason I asked Jennifer if she would like to visit Gloucester and write an article about the lardy cake.

This intrigued her. I booked a hotel room — I stayed with mother and Francois — and we had a jolly time. She and my mother are similar in character. Jennifer admired the success made of the Whitwell empire and was fascinated with the story of Alice Smith and its origins. For her part, my mother approved of the independent career woman I had brought into their midst, and the way she had dealt, at a young age, with bringing up a son. Jennifer was no more interested in rugby football than she was in cricket, and so the comparison between the father of her son and my father was not exposed, but another difference between us was revealed; she did not really like my mother's lardy cakes. Incredible; but this contradictory creature was at least honest in her opinions, even if I thought most of them perverse. On the train back to London we quarrelled.

"They are starchy and have an unsophisticated taste."

"Unsophisticated? What nonsense."

"But I think my editor would be interested in an article, or perhaps a series of pieces, on regional food and their origins. The haggis and so on. Thanks for the lead, my dear Percy."

"That's all very well, but you will write more convincingly if you have tasted and enjoyed the product."

"No. Not necessarily. In any case, can there be anyone with any taste who would admit to liking that lump of fat and flour."

"Are you saying I am without taste? Trouble with you, Mrs Lomax, is that you don't mix with the real people. I can tell you of some Welsh miners that are worth ten of you with your nose pointed to the sky."

"Oh, really. And so you are a typical man of the people. Mr Average Englishman who runs away to Paris, mixes with artists and Bohemians and all sorts of loose women, and you criticise me."

"What do you know about loose women? You're a product of the middle-class suburbs — Acacia Avenue is your habitat. You probably admire Winston Churchill."

"I certainly do not. In any case, your mother told me that until recently, you were a bit inclined towards the right. My socialist principles are fully intact."

When we got to Paddington we went our separate ways but by the time I arrived home I began to wonder if defending the merits of the lardy cake was a worthwhile campaign and did I want to lose contact with this interesting woman over such an issue. And she was interesting. Perhaps a little overconfident; too sure of herself, but she and my mother were cut out of the same piece of cloth and did I really favour the compliant female — or those with some backbone? She must also have had some regrets about our acrimonious parting, because the following day I received a letter thanking me for arranging the visit to my hometown and would I like to join her when visiting her son at his school the next weekend for their cricket festival. She was not over keen at the prospect of watching that ridiculous game for two days but felt duty-bound to attend, particularly as Edward was captaining the most junior team on display. As you can imagine, I accepted with alacrity, particularly as I liked the boy and we seemed to get on well together.

There was a crucial moment that weekend, crucial that is in the future of Jennifer Lomax and Percy Glossop. Edward was at a stage where cricket was a religion to him. He had some success with both bat and ball in the two games he was involved in but during lunch on the second day he told his mother how much he regretted that he did not have a father playing in the highlight of the weekend — the annual parents versus pupils match that the school took very seriously. Jennifer agreed with her son but could offer little by way of comfort. I said nothing but took in what the boy was saying. Was this incident really so fundamental? Perhaps it is the romance in my nature that leads me to even mention it — and truthfully we did not eventually choose each other so that Edward would have a surrogate father, ready, willing and able to don his white flannels once a year — but was the cricket match a turning point? Or at least, the first rung on the ladder?

However, before a move to a second rung was even considered, I met Ruth.

Jennifer was close to her sister who was an unmarried teacher at a private girl's school in Sussex. Jennifer introduced me over a convivial lunch at The George in Crawley. We journeyed there in Jennifer's Austin 7 motorcar that she had bought when Angela had been able to negotiate a lucrative contract for her in the USA for a weekly column on the idiosyncrasies of English life. It was valuable to have such transportation, particularly when visiting Edward, but it did become a major problem locating a different idiosyncrasy, week in and week out. I helped of course — seeing myself as a member of the league of the idiosyncratic. After lunch we drove over the South Downs and visited Brighton. I had never been there before, not even to visit Ida Scrutton, but was attracted to the place immediately — and if my affair with Jennifer was to progress in a traditional pattern, a weekend there might be an essential ingredient. But that of course was Percy being fanciful. There were plenty of opportunities for illicit weekends to be spent at Barnes, or Maida Vale, without the necessity of a trip to the seaside.

At this time I was becoming very fond of Jennifer Lomax but with her sister, it was love at first sight. It does happen. I believe Abigail was a victim of this phenomenon and we can probably enrol Francois into those ranks. It was not the affection I had for Jennifer that drew me into this state; it was not a case of more of the same, but only better — because Ruth was another creature altogether.

She was one of the most contented women I have ever met; blessed with a sunny disposition that never failed to shine. I wondered why she was not married. After the war there was certainly a shortage of male suitors — the Somme and other places of an equal evil had taken their toll — but she was a handsome woman, and that supreme contentment added another dimension to this. Her sister was very different. More interesting perhaps, but equanimity, no. We did not seriously quarrel over major issues but were out of touch with each other for three weeks because I criticised the grammar in one of her articles. That would not have happened with Ruth. She was totally at ease within her world; she never lost her temper and was a devoted Christian who saw the good in everyone. However, this characteristic was about to be subjected to its severest test — because of me.

I truly could not help it. I was helpless: could not take my eyes away from her and was glad when the day's excursion was over and I was able, in the solitude of my study, to ponder over this dilemma with the aid of a large glass of whisky. Was this to be a farce or a tragedy? One sister was no doubt acutely aware of the interest in her by a man who already had a warm relationship with her fatherless son and was displaying all the signs of a desire to expand that relationship to the mother — while the other sister was hardly conscious of my existence. Was I to ignore my heart — or was it wiser to show my feelings to Ruth while keeping her sister in ignorance until I had ascertained whether my attentions would be at all welcome?

I love Jennifer. We have the same interests in common. With my guidance I could see her becoming one of the foremost female journalists of her generation. Edward was already like my own son and there was the parents/pupils match to come. My mother liked her. Peter Southern had told me that I was a lucky blighter to have found such a gem — and when we were together I was beginning to rid myself, in part, of the guilt I still carried over Simone, however undeserving that might be. I made her laugh and she enjoyed my cooking, although in recent times we have avoided the subject of the lardy cake.

I knew nothing of Ruth, other than occasional references by her sister. Except for Miss Rosen, and possibly that English teacher — my befuddled brain cannot recall his name — I was not over-fond of teachers. None of those at Edward's school seemed capable of dealing with the googly and off the field they tended to give an impression of 'holier than thou' even though we, I mean Jennifer, was paying their salaries. They all dressed alike. At least Ruth was wearing a pretty cotton dress; if she had arrived at The George in a tweed suit with leather patches at the elbow perhaps cupid would have had no place at that luncheon table.

I switched to brandy — always seemed more romantic than the Scottish water. Or should I have been using absinthe? Do you know this? It stirred the romantic juices of Baudelaire and Verlaine but was now illegal in France — since 1915. The 'Green Fairy' as it is called. Would it sooth my fevered brow?

This was hysteria. For goodness sake, you are a man of the world. You have conquered the fortress of French cuisine. You have aroused a passion in a tiny French girl such that takes your breath away. I count intellectuals, both French and British, within my circle of friends. I mix with miners and up-and-coming stage actors. I have created the world's first cooking detective and the Americans cannot get enough of my stories. I fought heroically in France, critically participated in the Paris peace process and put onto the pathway of fame one of the most talented American painters since John Singer Sargeant. I have drunk in the same bars as Ernest Hemingway. What did I want with a middle-aged country school maam, not married because she is probably sexually frigid — or of the Sylvia/Margaret fraternity? As you can perceive, the brandy was adding some telling touches to my assessment of the dilemma I faced. When I got myself to bed it was still there. It stood in a corner of the room like Marley's ghost — and I was not going to solve the problem, as did Scrooge, by a trip on the morrow to the local butcher to purchase the largest turkey on display.

On my awakening the following morning I became rather more rational. There were two priorities. I should arrange to spend more time with Ruth as soon as possible to see if my feverish ramblings of the previous night had some justification and then, if the answer was positive, find someone who might be able to give advice on a way out of this dreadful situation. First things first. I was devious. I asked both sisters if they would like to come and see the latest example of Bob Patch on stage, as a spear carrier — or that one who walks through the French windows and says 'Anyone for tennis'. Despite Bob, the play was mildly successful and tickets hard to come by. I had by chance overheard a conversation with Jennifer's contact at the *Daily Telegraph* that they wished her to spend two days in Liverpool and report, in her inimitable style, on the running of the Grand National. I ascertained the date of this years Aintree event and bought three tickets for that very day. Jennifer had an interest in the work of Mr Patch that was difficult to fathom, but the *Telegraph* fee was a generous one and so she had to curb this extraordinary passion and exhorted me not to miss the chance to see the latest creation of such an exciting new talent — and go with Ruth while she tried to console herself ensconced in the Adelphi Hotel in the north-west of England.

"I don't think Ruth gets much chance to go to the theatre, and she'll love Bob, so please do not return the tickets on my account. You must take her. I know the play. It is very funny and Ruth will enjoy it and you can go to the Cafe Royal afterwards, you old skinflint, and treat her to a good dinner. She can stay in Barnes and make sure the taxi driver you send her home with is respectable."

"How can you tell? In any case, is she not your older sister? She can surely look after herself?"

As I said that I wondered how effective she was in dealing with snakes in the grass.

"You just give her a good time. She works very hard and deserves a break. And try not to tell her any of those weird jokes of yours. I want you and her to be friends. And buy her some chocolates."

I felt as though I was being lectured by a mother anxious that her son made a good impression on a first date with the local capitalist's only daughter, considered by all and sundry to be a good catch. Was Jennifer going to tell me next to wear a clean shirt? To shave carefully. Have a haircut. She could not know she was, in effect, acting as a procuress.

Of course, that was nonsense. Ruth made her own way into the West End. We had a drink at the Ritz. She laughed at the play and thought Patch was as good as her sister had told her. She had a glass of sherry with dinner, but said no to the champagne I offered. I commented on the standard of cooking and she agreed with me. We did not hold hands at any time during the evening but she kissed my cheek as I handed her into a taxi. To me the driver looked like Jack the Ripper, but by that time I was past caring. Shipping Jennifer off to Liverpool had provided sparse and inconclusive results. Ruth was still an angel, but joining my firmament was no nearer a solution.

Jennifer, insatiable theatre-lover that she was, determined that I should accompany her to the end of term play at school where Edward was cast as the student, Peter Trofimov, in *The Cherry Orchard*. She invited Ruth as well. In the school hall I sat between them. I dare not move. The impulse to snake my left arm around Ruth's elegant white neck was unbearable. I heard and saw nothing of the play. These sisters thought Edward was destined for great things on the stage, but I wondered if Chekhov was too subtle for boys of that age. I shivered. It could easily have been a production of *Three Sisters*. What if there had been three as fair as Jennifer and Ruth? I thought of Ruth in the Bible. How aptly named she was. I was hallucinating. Go back to Paris and see if Julietta's sister is free.

I could not go on like this. Ruth had clearly warmed to me after three meetings. She seemed to listen more carefully to what I had to say and during that school play I had the feeling that during the dull parts she was looking at me out of the corner of her eye. Or was this a question of wish fulfilment? I was her sister's beau and she was not interested in men. I needed help. I turned, surprisingly enough, to Peter Southern.

I have given you some sketchy particulars of Peter's life since Etaples, including visiting me in Paris, but I will now provide some detail. He had recovered his composure since those awful times in France. His left-wing views were no less sincere and his pacifism unflinching. He lived modestly in a cottage in Madingley, on the outskirts of Cambridge, and dined regularly at Clare where he told me he enjoyed talking to young men who had not been through the war — people who believe that it had been a war to end all wars and were fully optimistic of a permanent peace in Europe. I did not share this view and neither did he. He kept himself busy. Outside of poetry, he was a member of the parish council, involved in his local church and in addition had become interested in foreign travel, particularly to Africa. One of the dons at his college ran a course in African history, unusual for the time, and Peter acted as an informal Emeritus Professor and gave a lecture from time to time. He was principally interested in the history of Nigerian Ife and Benin art and of the people who produced this. Peter had never married.

I invited myself down to his cottage for the last weekend in January. The year was 1928 and I had become the owner of a motorcar, a Morris Oxford. I soon became a skilful driver which is more than I could say for most of the other motorists on the King's highway. I think there should be some sort of driving test. Perhaps we should have the same in the kitchen requiring cooks to serve a period of apprenticeship and prepare one of the classic dishes, under test conditions, before being allowed to call themselves a chef.

He had some of his neighbours at dinner on the Saturday evening. I had come prepared and cooked for them a rather splendid *Caneton Molière*. This was not unusual. Whenever I visited Jennifer — and my mother and Francois — I carried the ingredients that allowed me to continue exhibiting my culinary genius, but the problem was I needed to travel with appropriate utensils. I deplored what most kitchens in Britain contained and so, over time, I had developed a travelling set of my own. I could do nothing about the stove available, but I refused to allow my creations to be subjected to the average casserole dish or grill pan. I did suggest to Angela that when she had a small party I might come as guest and travelling chef, but when I told her I would insist on bringing my own cookware, she rejected my offer with a rather nasty bite of sarcasm.

The visitors enjoyed the duck and after they had left Peter opened the bottle of 1902 Armagnac that I had brought for him. As you can see, I still kept alive some of my Paris contacts; very necessary as I found a number of my friends were somewhat parsimonious where good alcohol is concerned. Peter was the most generous of men but the sort of near-university life he had drifted into meant that on a number of occasions I have found that a sweet sherry — albeit of a superior quality — was all he was able to offer. He and his guests enjoyed the food and now we both enjoyed the golden liqueur. The time was ripe for Peter to reciprocate by concentrating his considerable intellect, bringing into play the wisdom of the poetic mind, into solving my problem of the heart. I threw two more logs on to the fire in his small sitting room, stroked the head of his recumbent, if not soporific labrador and lit a cigar. Peter declined to join me. I was tempted to quote Kipling: 'And a woman is only a woman, but a good cigar is a Smoke', but decided in the circumstances this would be inappropriate.

"You have set yourself up very nicely Peter. I enjoyed Sybil but George was a bit stiff. Local doctor did you say?"

"Yes."

"Were the other two ladies both academics?"

"Yes, but Jean is the clever one. Classics at Newnham."

"Just what you need. A clever woman to keep your bed warm and stimulate the old brain box."

"Well, what about you? When are you and Jennifer going to get hitched?"

"Peter, I am distraught. I need your help urgently. I am so, so fond of Jennifer but I think I've fallen in love with her sister."

"What. You are a disgrace. What is the matter with you? It started with that Ida in Etaples, and I never did understand what you could have done to that Parisian angel that made her want to leave you. I tell you, you rogue, if I could find Simóne, I'd marry her tomorrow."

"Peter, that's painful. It's not always my fault — in fact very rarely my fault."

"Oh no. What about that sister of Bob Patch who you abandoned?"

"That was not serious. This is. I adore Ruth Simmons."

"Who is she?"

"Jennifer's sister you dope. She has never married. Wedded to her job as a school teacher — and utterly delicious."

"You sound as though you're describing one of your celebrated dishes — *Steak tartare a la Glossop*."

"Seriously, Peter. You see the dilemma. Jennifer and I are not engaged and I can see she expects I will soon be playing in that parent versus pupils match at Edward's school as his foster dad — up until he leaves. What am I to do?"

"Marry her you idiot. She's a wonderful girl. Much too good for you."

"But I cannot. I love her sister."

"Are either of these two ladies aware of this?"

"No. Of course not."

I told Peter I had arranged for Jennifer's absence so I could take Ruth to the theatre on her own. He did not approve.

"And, that is as far as it has got."

"So, you hardly know her?"

"I don't need to. My heart tells me everything I need to know."

"Percy. That sort of reasoning would sound banal and false in the poorest examples of romantic poetry, but in your case, it is a complete and utter fraud."

"Fraud!"

"Yes, fraud. Even Freud would not take you seriously."

"Peter, flippancy is not going to help. How do I solve this?"

We talked on for another hour. I knew Peter could see I was serious, as well as we both knew that this was not a problem that could be solved like one might with a complex recipe — add more lime juice — but what I did recall the following morning, as my head cleared itself of the effects of the claret and armagnac, was one word: 'honesty'. He insisted on it. I needed to be honest to myself, and to the sisters.

All very well, but how was this to be achieved. I could not measure my own integrity without more knowledge and I could not gain that intelligence without having more contact with Ruth. As far as I knew her only love was teaching. I must therefore observe her at her most zealous — in her own habitat, the school. Her subject was history. Would the pupils welcome a visiting lecturer able to speak with authority about action on the Western front? I rejected this idea very quickly. If her charges were as smart as she, they would soon see through that guise. The Peace Treaty? More plausible, but would I have to reveal my true role as a bag carrier and interpreter — with some embroidery about the gathering of information using a lesbian informer. At a nice all-girls school in Sussex? I think not. There was only one avenue. Domestic science. I thought it wise for Jennifer to be involved so I asked her to mention to her sister that the generous-hearted Percy would be happy to visit the school to talk of his career as a French master chef and to pass on some recipes that might, in the future, prove to be the key that gives these young ladies access to the man of their dreams. Jennifer refused to pass this on verbatim to Ruth, but whatever she said, I was invited. There had been an addendum to my offer. Great chef he might be, but this personable young man was nervous about standing before a class of brilliant young ladies and it would be more appropriate if someone he knew, Miss Ruth Simmons for instance, could act as his assistant — weighing the sugar and beating the eggs. And this is how it turned out.

The visit to the school was both a triumph and disaster. The girls hung on my every word and Ruth was the most perfect of kitchen angels, but at the end of the day, I was even more in love. Our hands touched as she passed me the basin of stock, our eyes met as the onions caramelised and at the end of the display she was so grateful she hugged me to her breast. I could not say a word. I drove back to London in a trance. The only thing to be done, the only thing to do, was to turn up the heat. When making Hollandaise sauce the opposite is the favoured option, but I was not dealing with butter and eggs and vinegar. My whole future was at stake.

But how to turn up the heat? Write to her? As you know I have some skill with words but I soon rejected that avenue. Get her alone and then make love to her? Suicide! Tell Jennifer? Double suicide. Use an intermediary? Was this a possibility and if so, whom? Peter Southern: gentle, clever, articulate and understanding — and the only one appraised of my agony. But, to start with, how to get them together?

Love either sharpens the mind or deadens the senses. Mine was like a razor. During our last meeting I told Ruth I had recently visited Cambridge and she talked about the difficulty schools like hers had in gaining entrance for girls into the senior universities. Surely Peter could act as an adviser in this area and introduce her to people involved in entrance qualifications. So I did write to her. I thanked her for the visit to the school and then mentioned that I recalled the conversation about university entrance and would she like to meet my old friend, Peter Southern, who I thought could be of assistance. I told her all about him. Despite her upbringing, I guessed she was inclined politically to the left and no doubt had the same views about the tragedy of the war as did her sister — and of course Peter.

In the meantime I briefed my special agent. Despite the hidden motive, he was happy to do what he could regarding university entrance. He was a great feminist and I suppose we were all glad when, later in the year, women over twenty one were able to vote like the men, but he could also see that a meeting with Ruth would enable him to observe at first hand the qualities in the woman that had turned my life upside down. And, at a future time, let it slip that his quirky friend Percy admired her more than somewhat — but was embarrassed to express this in any way because of the sister.

The next time I visited Peter I was aware, courtesy of Jennifer, that my friend and Ruth had already met three or four times and that the teacher and the school were delighted with the progress made as a result of my introduction. Indeed, so Jennifer told me, her sister had been given the role of university entrance adviser to the whole school with an increase in salary and time and expenses available to visit the great institutions. It was, according to Jennifer, the outbreak of a feminine revolution in scholastic circles for which the instigator deserved an 'extra special hug'. For the moment I eschewed what usually went with 'extra special hugs' but was delighted at Ruth's success — and hopefully Peter's.

There were no guests that evening. I had brought a Glossop pork pie with me and Peter tried to make a salad. Fortunately the pie was accompanied by some rather special sweet-sour pickles — a new recipe of mine. On the drinks front, Peter's tastes were improving. The claret he had ordered from Corney and Barrow was very passable and before we had got to our second glass he began his speech. I need to describe it as such because until it was over I never said a word. Speech? No, perhaps declaration is a better description.

"Percy. You and I are very different people but I saw at Etaples that you are blessed with a certain sense of compassion that not everyone possesses. In parts of Africa it is known as 'ubuntu'. I know you have not had the benefit of the classical education that I had, or my upbringing, but you have made your own way and I admire you for that. A lot of credit is of course due to your mother — a most splendid creature. You were especially humane and sensitive when it came to dealing with Simóne and Hubert always thought you were the catalyst that formed his career. I cannot say I am a fan of Herbert Montcalm, but I know you get great pleasure from devising those ridiculous and far-fetched plots and they do pay you extraordinary well. My advice, don't try and live off the publishing of poetry."

He had a serious look on his face while delivering this unnecessary eulogy, but his mien prompted me not to respond — other than with a grimace.

"You came to me some months ago for advice on what I now dub, 'The affair of the two sisters'. If you wrote romantic stories instead of those of the detective genre, this might be a rather intriguing title, but this is not a fiction but a real drama in which you are the principal player. At least you thought you were but I thought then — and am now convinced — that you failed to understand the position, the feelings, even the futures, of the two ladies involved."

He raised his hand indicating I should not interrupt.

"I agreed to visit the school and acquaint myself with Ruth Simmons. My mission was to see if I could get close enough to her and, at best, let her know of your feelings for her or, at least, for me to form an opinion of the lady so as to advise you how best to forward a future relationship. As it happened, and I view this result with some satisfaction, the ploy used to introduce me into her circle has advanced the cause of university education for women and given Ruth another interest in her academia, about which she is immensely pleased. And so am I."

He did seem pleased; even self-satisfied. I looked at him more closely. He was different. The frown he usually wore seemed to have disappeared.

"But onto your concerns. It is a tribute to the qualities of Ruth that after two meetings I was able to observe and appreciate the special attributes that had attracted you. She is so open: there are no hidden demons — she is the antithesis

of Simóne of course. You described her as contented, at ease with her world and I concur. It is a surprising state for any human being to be as blessed as she appears to be. Not that she is dull. Very different from Jennifer, but Ruth has her own brand of vivacity, particularly when the subject is education, and this adds a further dimension to her charms."
I was delighted to hear this. I was not the only one who saw what a special person she is — but if there are two of us, why was she still unmarried?

"Like you, I could not understand why this attractive and intelligent mortal had not been wooed and wed years before and as I got to know her better, I raised this with her. She was not modest. She did not explain away her single situation by referring to the imbalance of men and women in her age group due to the war. She told me, with a frank candour and in some detail, of four men she had been fond of, but in all cases she had sent them packing because none was fully prepared to accept that she would insist on continuing her teaching career as a married woman — and as a mother if that should occur. The one she felt most for agreed with such conditions but he was an ambitious architect who had just set up his own practice and at the last, Ruth doubted whether he was genuinely committed to having two equal careers within the family. She was simply not prepared to take the chance."
I did not see this as a problem in my case. As her biblical namesake said: 'Whither thou goest, I will go.' I work from home anyway and would be delighted to look after the children. A picture formed in my mind of the proud father walking down Wymering Road taking his attractive twins, a boy and a girl, to school. He could even hear the chatter about best friends and cricket practice.

"She accepted that Rod, the architect, might wish to practise away from the London area — or the south-east in general — and this did not worry her. She could teach anywhere in the country but however much in love they both were, she was intuitive enough to see that his work would dominate. All the men she knew, even those in the teaching profession, could not help but think like that. It was bred in them. How many members of Parliament were women? How many were dons at Cambridge? Did Cazenove or Cox and Kings have any female directors? It would need to be a special man, so she told me, to think and act out of this role — this position that seemed to be ordained by God. There were not any women priests either, she added. She wants to do her bit in changing this and facilitating the bright girls she teaches towards a place at the major universities and this gives her the opportunity. I thoroughly agree with her. What you may not have known is that her enthusiasm was such that she made several unscheduled visits to see me in Cambridge and on two occasions stayed at Tumbleweed Cottage. I found this very enlightening; to see her in a domestic setting. She makes excellent coffee and even complimented me on my sherry."

I thought, lucky you. Oh that I could have been a guest at the same time. Why was I not invited? Oh, yes; only two bedrooms.

"I can also tell you she impressed the admissions tutor at Clare even though there are of course no women there. Are you familiar with the current situation of girls at Cambridge? I shall tell you. You may know that although women can take examinations here they are not awarded degrees and in any case they are only admitted to the two all-female colleges, Girton and Newnham. Ruth wants to increase the chances of her girls getting into these places but I believe she has a fanciful notion that women will one day be admitted to other colleges. Not in my lifetime, I'll be bound, but that is the sort of lady she is."

"I have given you as much detail as I can about my intervention on your behalf with the delightful Miss Simmons but if you have been paying close attention, you will have noticed that your role in any of this has become lost in the bigger issues of girls education and universities — but at the personal level, your suit has also been submerged by a most unexpected development. I have been so long-winded in an attempt to prepare you for this, but realise I will have failed." What on earth was the dear fellow rambling on about? Before I found out, he poured me another glass of wine, a large one.

"I know this will come as a great surprise and shock to you. I can hardly believe it myself. This was not the outcome I expected — or foresaw — or planned — but I cannot keep from you any longer an astonishing revelation. Ruth and I love each other and propose to be married in the Spring. Once this had become clear to us — simultaneously it seemed — I told her that you had become very fond of her but had been reluctant to express this because of Jennifer. She told me this was not news to her. She had seen it from the first meeting and so had Jennifer. Both of them had decided to let this typical piece of Percy impetuosity — their words — run its course and no harm would be done."

I do not think I heard that last part. To say I was amazed would be to understate the case — like comparing the Whitwell loaf with that sold by that man Richards. Staid, old-fashioned Peter. Much older than she — and me. Not even handsome. Losing his hair. Complains of arthritis in his knees. How had he got down on those distressed joints to propose? Only one fully effective arm: no carrying a bride over the threshold for him, or her. Was she mad? Was she hypnotised by poetry and images of the romantic versifier? Were Shelley and Byron to blame? I found it difficult to breathe.

"My dear friend. I can see how shocked you are. I told Ruth I was going to reveal this to you today. She wanted to be here, but then realised how inappropriate that would be. She told Jennifer of course. No one else knows. My friends will be as incredulous as you obviously are. This has never happened to me before. I saw myself as a permanent bachelor — we both saw only an unwedded future — but you are a romantic person and you, perhaps more than anyone, can know how the best laid plans fly out of the window when the heart takes over. Having to tell you this is the only dark cloud on my horizon. I'm so glad it is over and that you have not thrown the claret jug at my head — at least not yet — or stood up and walked away."

I had thought of both options but this was Peter Southern, a man I had admired, respected and even loved since our first encounter. If Ruth was the epitome of contented *Homo sapiens*, he was Mr Genuine. It had happened. Nothing could change that. As you know I am a quick-witted sort of chap. I absorbed what I had just been told and stood up. Not with any violent intent — or to make my escape — but as I rose I dragged my friend from a sitting position and embraced him with tears in my eyes.

Jennifer and Ruth decided it should be a double wedding — and so it was.

## Hester

I am obliged to confess that I have not been altogether truthful, or have deliberately given the wrong impression, about my earliest sexual experiences and also about Bob Patch and his sister. With him, perhaps it was jealousy. I found it difficult to accept that of the two boys of similar humble Gloucester origins, he should turn out to be the more successful of the two. I will deal with that later, but at this juncture I must admit, with some shame, that I only reveal these facts now because of the appearance of Hester.

Let me return you to the winter of 1917. My first sexual encounter with the gargantuan Clarice was not as unsatisfactory as I have suggested. I was drunk. I did fall off, but next day I began to savour the experience and looked forward to more of the same. Unfortunately, a bullet in the elbow stood in the way of further excursions but when back at the officer's mess in 1918, I found Clarice's sister more negotiable. Not often. Cash was short and I was kept busy. So, you ask, why was this not revealed before? Why are we given a single incident described in a partly humorous way so as to show the chronicler as the typical innocent abroad? Perhaps I was exactly that, but why the reticence thereafter? Was I ashamed to admit to being a brothel visitor, if those two rooms behind that café can be so designated? You will notice that when describing the district where the Trois Perroquets was located, I was scornful of such. I think that was a genuine sentiment at the time, but I was still duplicitous about my earlier involvement. Did I omit to mention the sister of Clarice because my readers would have no interest in hearing of this? The truth is I wished to paint the most flattering portrait possible of Percy Glossop as a young man — and since then, you might retort — but now, an honest account will need to follow, however, sordid, because of what happened between Brenda Patch and this newly revealed libertine.

1919 and back in Gloucester. I was in the market for female company and Bob's sister provided this. As I have said, I have disparaged Bob in these writings of mine and by implication I may have done the same with his sister, but she was an attractive girl and before I went to Paris we spent time together, including one or two visits to the store room at the bakery where I was conceived. I later heard from my mother that Brenda had married with a baby being born six or seven months after the wedding day. That store room. What was in the air? Are sacks of flour an acknowledged aphrodisiac? It was my child. I did not know. In 1927, Brenda and her husband were killed by lightning while resting under a tree on Robinswood Hill during a storm. After that, the girl, Hester, was brought up by Brenda's mother who, immediately before she died a week or so ago, had told Bob that his niece was the son of that reprobate, Percy Glossop, whereupon the uncle came to see me with the news.

I had therefore sired two daughters. Jennifer was also fertile, Edward was the evidence, but together, nothing happened. We took advice. We consulted the calendar, and we persevered, but still no progeny. And then came the news about Hester. Were we both destined to be step-parents, me to Edward and she to Hester? In the event, that is how it turned out.

I have stated these facts in this blunt fashion to emphasise my previous deceit. True, I did not know of Hester's parentage until the visit by Bob, but I have kept from you, and Jennifer, the story of Brenda and me. Jennifer was angry but then, I think to cheer me up, confessed that before we met she had been intimately involved with a newspaper photographer, a man I had met and did not like, and so perhaps we were equally devious. Forgive and forget. Whether you the reader will feel the same is, I suspect, more problematical, but the crucial relationship to be affected by these revelations was that with Bob — and then my daughter.

And that leads to the other item of embarrassment. I have, I know, presented my school friend, in his acting persona, as something of a failure. This is not correct. Let me give you an accurate picture.

By the late 1920s, Bob Patch was a rising star within British theatre. He was seen as versatile and reliable, rarely out of work and had transferred one of his most famous parts to Broadway, so he could already be deemed to have made a considerable success within his chosen profession. He was equally at home in farce and tragedy. When he went on tour with RC Sheriff's *Journey's End*, the eminent critic, James Agate, told him that the actor's experience of the trenches shone through in the play like the light from a Verey pistol. Not only have I failed to reveal this, I have been misleading about his earlier acting career. In *The Importance of Being Ernest*, I was to play Lane, the manservant, with Bob as Algernon Moncrieff. However, the casting was reversed because Bob had quarrelled with one of our classmates engaged in making the set and threatened to pour a tin of red paint over the unfortunate boy's head. I did play Mrs Malaprop — I think Bob was suspended from the school at that time — and Puck, but in that same production, the clever, but wayward Mr Patch, had the parents in stitches of laughter with his performance

*Alan Shelley*

as Nick Bottom, the weaver. He had also been a brave soldier. You will notice I made no mention of the Military Medal he won at the third Battle of Ypres.

Regardless of what I have recorded to date, in real life Bob and I have always been the greatest of friends. Like Jennifer, I admire his work on the stage and have not been slow in letting him know this. In later years, when I attempted to write for the theatre we became even closer, but for now let me record accurately the conversation that took place when he came to Maida Vale to tell me about Hester. He was between plays and had just returned from the funeral of his mother. His father had died some years before.

"Bob, by God, you look serious. What's all this about? You are normally too busy to come and see me. Have they found you out at last for the ham you are?"

"I think we had better have a drink. Any whisky in the house?"

"Sure. My sideboard is groaning. Soda, tap water or neat?"

"Neat please, but more importantly, pour yourself a large one."

"You really are serious'.

"Yes, my friend. I have some extraordinary news for you. I suppose you heard of the terrible tragedy a year or two ago when Brenda and Tony were killed in that freak thunderstorm."

"Yes. My mother told me. I was so sorry, and then I heard last week that your mother had died. You have had the most awful bad luck of it. What did your mam die from?"

"She had a stroke. Very unexpected. Always been so full of life and energy. She was only fifty seven. They got her to hospital, but she only survived three days. Thank goodness I was able to get to see her before she died. I loved her dearly. She was so proud of my stage success and this gave her some comfort after the tragedy of Brenda and her husband."

"They had a daughter, did they not?"

"Yes, and it's about her that I needed to see you so urgently. She's yours!"

"What."

"I know you and Brenda had a bit of a fling before you went to Paris and she married Tony, but only mum and she knew that it was your child and not his. He never knew. They were married in the February. I was still in France. The girl was born on the 3 September but the first time they slept together was not on their wedding night, and it was naturally assumed he was the father. Did you ever meet him? Bricklayer. Got out of the army some months before me. I think they met at a dance at Ma Kings. Remember that place? Brenda was always one for the boys and Tony had been without female company for some time."

"Now you raise the matter, I think I remember seeing them together in the Lower George. Redheaded chap."

"Yes. Well, seems he took over from where you left off."

"Bob, I've never talked about this to anyone. I kept it secret from you and my mother and it seems Brenda did the same with you and with her husband. We were intimate a few times. I was really sweet on her for a week or two and then, quite suddenly, it was all over. No regrets, I thought, on either side. I went to Paris and she found a husband — but it's not over is it. You say their daughter, your niece, is my child. I never knew. God's truth, I never knew. Why did she do that to me? Why didn't she tell me?"

"Well, pretty obvious ain't it. You hot-foot it for Paris, she misses a period and Tony is now in the picture. It was the preferred option."

"It's all so banal — so sordid. Oh, sorry. Didn't mean that. Poor Brenda. I'm a bastard. What can I say?"

"Well, Perc, its no good crying over spilt milk. There's the girl to think of. Mam has looked after her until now — but what next? Me or you?"

"What's her name?"

"Hester."

"But you can't look after a young girl. You're on tour most of the year. And you're not married. I'll take her. We'll take her. I'm sure Jennifer will agree, although I will have some explaining to do. She knows nothing about Brenda. She is your greatest fan, as you know, but I don't suppose she's ever asked about whether you had a sister?"

"No."

"What a situation. I'm a stepfather to Edward, and now we are to have a stepmother in the family. It's bizarre. But steady on. Will Hester come here? Is she a nice girl and pliable? Well-behaved?"

"From what I understand, no. However, I think this is the right decision for her. She needs a stable home. Not that I thought I would ever describe you as stable, but thank goodness for Jennifer."

"Where is she now?"

"You mean Hester?"

"Yes."

"With Auntie Elsie. My mother's youngest sister. But she's got seven of her own and lives in a tiny terraced house. Her husband is out of work. Stevedore. They can't keep her."

"I can see that. And in any case, if she's mine, she should be with me. But steady on. How do we know she's mine? Just your mother's word for it."

"Percy. I have known her since her birth. Now I have been told the truth, and I look at her, she's yours all right. No question."

"What do we do next?"

"Well, obviously you have to talk to Jennifer, but I think the best thing is for me to try and explain the situation to her and then bring her here. That would be less painful than you charging down to Gloucester and kidnapping her away from Elsie's mob. It will be hard, but I think we should tell her the truth."

"I agree."

And that is what happened. Bob let us know in advance. Both Jennifer and I were together as she came into our drawing room. She was carrying a small suitcase; her possessions were obviously few. Bob came in behind her. For what seemed an age no one spoke, and then Jennifer smiled at the girl and attempted to take the suitcase from her. There was some reluctance; it was as if she felt that by giving up her belongings she was committing herself. Jennifer persisted and motioned Hester to sit down. She shook her head at Jennifer and me and stood in front of us, feet firmly anchored to the Axminster. Her lips were clenched. I could hardly see her eyes because the hat, firmly attached to her head by a band of white elastic under the chin, was pulled down very low.

"Would you like to take your hat off, Hester?"

"No."

"Please. We want to look at you. Uncle Bob has explained to you that this is your father."

"He's not. My dad is dead. Got struck by lightning. Came from Jesus."

This stopped everyone in their tracks except for Jennifer who gently removed the girl's hat. However much I might have wished otherwise, she looked like me. From what I can recall, the brown straight hair came from Brenda, but this little girl now stared at us with eyes that were mine, her pursed lips were mine, as were the puffed out cheeks. I wanted to crush her to my breast, but resisted. She moved first. She stamped her right foot, and then began to cry. When Jennifer took her hand, she did not demur, neither did she object when my brilliant and sensitive wife led her from the room, presumably to the bedroom we had prepared for her. To begin with, Bob and I were silent. I made him a gin and tonic. He then said:

"The reference to Jesus. That was a show-stopping line if you like. I don't think she's particularly religious. From what I know of her, she's a smart child, and I can only think she said that to register how uneasy she is."

"Sure took the wind out of my sails."

"Looks like you, don't you agree, although she is actually quite handsome, so perhaps she's not yours."

"I've got a snap of my mother at that age. Spitting image."

"That's the first time I have ever seen her cry. I suspect she's pretty tough, but, for goodness sake, this is a traumatic moment for the poor kid."

Bob thought it best he should leave before Hester re-emerged, and I agreed. Jennifer and she returned to the drawing room shortly afterwards. Jennifer gave her some milk and we looked at each other. She was still scowling at me, but this could not hide the fact that she was an attractive youngster. Small, I thought, for her age. Slim, but not frail. Neatly dressed, but clearly cheap clothing. Was I going to get the opportunity to be involved in buying her lots of pretty dresses — and ribbons — and hats? Show her the sights of London? Take her to Paris? The pouting of her lips made me wonder if these things were likely in the very near future. When she looked at Jennifer, the frown seemed to relax a little.

Jennifer and I had been married for nearly three years. We were very happy together, except for the absence of children born to us both. The aberration over Ruth was in the past and the sisters were planning a trip to the French Riviera to celebrate our next joint wedding anniversary. Jennifer now had a full-time position with the *Daily Telegraph* as a sub-editor in the foreign section of the paper, which she thoroughly enjoyed. For the moment this had not meant too much travelling; she put into shape reports from the paper's full-time overseas reporters — and some stringers — and on most days she left Wymering Road just after nine each morning leaving me to ponder on Herbert Montcalm's next adventure, or to try and add some sparkle to a report on the declining quality of England's fish and chip shops. By tea time I was in the kitchen cooking our dinner for that evening — unless we had determined to sample the food at a new local restaurant or were spending the evening with friends. It suited me very well. My cuisine invariably found favour and most nights we made love and then lay in each other's arms as she regaled me with the latest *Daily Telegraph* gossip.

Her salary covered our living expenses and my royalties paid for the luxuries. Fortunately, the depression in the USA had not affected the sale of their many mystery magazines. In fact, as the number of unemployed grew and Wall Street had become America's Dolorosa, people looked for an escape from the appalling reality around them to the trashy periodicals that featured my stories, and so I was doing quite well. This was reflected in the quality of the Riviera hotel that had been decided upon. I wondered if we might encounter Paul Nerval. Did he really dine with a different Duchess every night? I then recalled his time there was August.

We four were great friends. We were at Tumbleweed Cottage for the weekend at least once a month, and it made me feel warm inside to see how my old friend had taken to married life. Ruth taught at the Perse School in the town and Peter dined less frequently at Clare.

I did sometimes ponder whether spending most of every day on my own in Maida Vale would begin to pall. It did not, but I was sustained by the thought that if in due course Jennifer had to be more involved in travel — reporting on the spot — I would carry her typewriter and check on the local cooking. She endorsed this vision but now it looked as though my idyllic and solitary daytime existence was to change. I was about to have to learn some new tricks; not just as a house-husband but as the father to a stranger.

More than tricks were needed. It was certainly a new role, and I welcomed it, but I did not foresee how difficult it was to be. She was a little monster. If I had at times been perplexed about the dark side of Simóne's nature, this little girl kept me disturbed all of the time.

During the first year Jennifer and I wondered if we had done the right thing by her. Was it fair to tell this child, at the age of eleven, that the man she had called 'Daddy' was not her father and was it right for us to move her from her friends and relations in Gloucester to London to live with two strangers? Of course it was not right; but what was the alternative? Uncle Bob was an itinerant; we could give her more opportunities than Auntie Elsie who, from what Bob told us, did not want the girl anyway even if she could have found room for her. As I got to know Hester better, I could understand why.

Then there was the question of truth. I suppose Bob could have kept to himself what his mother had told him and found foster parents for his niece, but we all decided that she should be told the facts now, at an age — so we hoped — when she would be able to best absorb and accept this revelation. Whatever, the deed was done. She was now my responsibility and I was determined to make it work.

But it was not easy. Ruth helped us to enrol Hester in the best school in the area and so my working day was disturbed as I walked her to classes each morning and brought her back to the flat each evening. She liked the school, tolerated Jennifer, but hated me. I use the word with some justification. She saw me as the enemy and she proved to be a most formidable opponent.

Her most effective weapon was to subject me to the 'silent treatment'. I had sometimes endured this with Simóne but my daughter was a past master, a superb practitioner in this special art. I love conversation. I have always been considered something of a raconteur and so I began to dread the walks to and from school, and the period at the end of the day before Jennifer returned home. I tried. I tried very hard. All questions about her day at the school were answered in monosyllables. Invitations to talk about Georgina, who Jennifer told me had the pleasure of being Hester's new best friend, were answered in a similar fashion. She always seemed to have an inordinate amount of homework to deal with that required her to retreat to her bedroom as soon as we reached number 37. She was not to be tempted by my cakes. I think she was the only female of my acquaintance whom I have not been able to win over with my chocolate éclairs.

## I Never Met Ernest Hemingway

    This situation made me very unhappy; but it had the opposite effect on Hester. She was at her most contented when I squirmed; when I struggled to keep my temper in face of her cold scorn, and she was winning because, in her new life, she was actually happy. Not immediately of course. It took time but, like me, she had an equable and easy-going nature that soon led her to appreciate her new circumstances. In the past she had always enjoyed Uncle Bob's visits, but she was lonely as an only child, whether living with her parents or her grandmother, and two of Elsie's oldest boys liked poking her with sticks and had told her that at the next bonfire night, she was going to be the guy. Brenda and Tony were not affluent. From the time Hester could be left with Grandma or Elsie, both parents worked, Brenda at the Moorlands match factory, and they were too tired at night to discover that their only child was being bullied at the rough school she attended.

    It was not like that now. She loved the uniform. The teachers were more able than she was used to, and she adored the ballet lessons Jennifer took her to every Saturday morning. The Gloucester accent was becoming less obvious, and the headmistress had told me that already they could see signs of scholastic prowess.

    But, to make it worse, she soon became a firm favourite with Ruth and Peter. Inwardly, I was furious. Was she going to ignore me forever? I felt as though overnight I was no longer a member of our quartet. We took her to Cannes. She deigned to allow me to teach her to swim, but still only spoke to me through other people. She was a little fiend. One example. The other three had gone on some excursion or other. We sat by the pool after she had just swum a length unaided for the first time. We were protected by a colourful umbrella, but it was very hot. We were approached by a young waiter whereupon the haughty Hester said: 'Would you ask him', inclining a hand towards me, 'to order me a *Citron presse avec Perrier*'. As you can see, signs of a linguistic ability already.

*Alan Shelley*

I kept my temper. By now it had become a game — but I was tired of playing it. She needs a spanking, I said to myself. Let's throw her back into Auntie Elsie's maelstrom. Lock her in her room. No more chocolates. But then I thought, these tactics would be useless. Something more subtle was needed.

The others, particularly Jennifer, were aware of the relationship between Hester and me and, in unison, they told me it would soon change — but how soon was soon. A germ of an idea entered my brain and when we got back to England, and before Hester went back to school, I tried it out. I was going to write a story; a fiction about an unhappy father and a daughter he loved, but who did not love him.

It worked. Perhaps she had decided the campaign had gone on long enough, and my writings gave her the excuse she was looking for to declare a truce. Perhaps; but then again, after she had read it, I thought I saw a hint of a tear in her eye. Another explanation, one of my fancies, was that she was naturally of a literary bent and my words tripped a switch in that complex brain of hers. I hoped so. She hated cooking. Nothing I could do would persuade her to help me in the kitchen — Alice Smith would have been so disappointed, never mind my mother — but at last we were friends.

But, I hear you say, what did Edward think of this surprising turn of events. It seemed that Bob, the bachelor, had handled the delicate question of how someone becomes a father with some panache. I did not enquire too deeply. He had evidently told Hester that before her mother met her husband she had been very friendly with a Percy Glossop and, after the first shock had been absorbed, Hester seemed to understand what was implied. She may have understood, but that did not mean she was prepared, at least initially, to accept me as her father. Fortunately, the angst was now over, but what about Edward?

Jennifer and I had talked about this as soon as Hester moved in. Half term was approaching. We could not allow Edward to turn up and find he had been moved into a smaller bedroom in favour of some strange girl. But what do we tell him? Was he as advanced in the knowledge of the process of reproduction as Hester appeared to be? She was a girl, more advanced than boys at that age, but was I now to tell him that before I went to Paris I had made a baby with the sister of Uncle Bob, as he was called, and that this fact had only just come to light? Did he know how babies were made? Jennifer thought probably so, but there had been no discussion on the subject, to date, between mother and son. That was not unusual. Sex education was more or less unheard of at the time. Masters at the school were no doubt more concerned to pass on, by hints and innuendo, the dangers of becoming too friendly with another schoolboy than discussing matters relating to the opposite sex.

I was very cowardly. Jennifer wrote and told her son about the revised sleeping arrangements in the flat but when he arrived for his half term holiday, I found I needed to go and see Angela Warren urgently. I need not have worried. Jennifer was able to explain the position with a minimum of embarrassment and when I returned home I found the two young people arguing about cricket. Hester thought it was a stupid pastime, and she was letting Edward know this in no uncertain terms. She had just told him how asinine any game was that could take five days before a winner was determined — and not always then — and that anyone who took part in such a nonsense was an idiot. I was about to join in when Jennifer entered the room and suggested that the four of us should go for a stroll in Regents Park, have an ice cream and perhaps visit the zoo.

While Hester and I were doing battle at Cannes, our war was in direct contrast to the sense of peace enjoyed by Ruth and Peter. Twins were born to them in January 1931, twelve months after Hester had appeared on the scene and entered the world of Jennifer and me. We were all delighted about the Southern's good news. Jennifer and I both figured amongst the godparents, as did Bob Patch, but the new babies meant that we did not see quite so much of the parents as hitherto. A nanny had been engaged but, as was to be expected, Ruth became very much involved with the offspring and Peter, at the age of forty five, was besotted. To see that staid don-like figure cradling a child in each arm, to the best of his ability, and reciting to them lines from his latest poetry was a sight to behold. I wished Hubert had been nearby to paint a picture of this remarkable scene, although I did manage some passable photographs with my Box Brownie. We, the youngsters of the quartet, also had two children, but by now, Edward was nearly thirteen and Hester twelve. They were not very interested in babies — and not very interested in each other.

We left Ruth, Peter and family to their own devices and rented a cottage near Abersoch in North Wales for three weeks in August. En-route we stayed for two nights near Snowdon. All members of the party climbed the mountain and felt fairly self-satisfied as a result, although I must admit I only succeeded because of the theoretical slipstream produced by the others. I was out of breath by the time the summit was reached, but I made it. The youngsters carried the rucksacks. None of us had ever been to North Wales before.

The weather was very kind to us, but not the young ones, although the blame was wholly Hester's. Jennifer and I saw nothing in her behaviour to suggest that the first ten years of her life had affected her in any way, but when it came to dealing with Edward, we were not so sure. Whether she was blaming all boys for the bullying by Auntie Elsie's lads, who can tell, but she was invariably very horrid to poor Edward.

That those early years gave her some resources not available to him can be debated, but what was not in question was the fact that she was brighter and smarter than he. More savvy. Harder — and more cruel. Although he was doing well at school, she was in advance of him scholastically, but this was an irrelevancy. She seemed to have at her disposal weapons that this young man, nearly twice her size, could not combat. She was incredible. If I had not felt for Edward, both as stepfather and another male, I would have looked on with admiration and wonderment at her gifts. She was sweet and sour at the same time. Coquetry was mixed with bitter sarcasm; charm with insult. She had my way with words but deflected my criticism of the way she used them in connection with Edward like a professional boxer slipping the left jab of an amateur. Unless we locked her in her room, we were helpless. She could not have been jealous of Edward; we treated them both the same and if anything rather spoiled her because she was with us all the time while Edward was away at boarding school.

She was not unhappy with us in the family. She seemed perfectly well-balanced and rational, but not with boys, and particularly not with poor Edward. We were a long way from Padua, but she was developing into a junior Katherine and up to now we had been unable to tame her. Jennifer was less worried than me. Her view was that girls like Hester change overnight and soon become, as she described it, 'boy-mad'. I would have preferred that. I no longer accompanied her to school but I did sometimes wonder if one day there would be a knock at the door to reveal the mother of Jonathan or Mark or Sebastian, intent on blacking my eye because of my wayward daughter's treatment of their sons. The weaker sex! Not a hope, I thought.

Back to our August holiday. Although it was midsummer we found a small cove a few miles away — we used the car — which we often had to ourselves. It was hot. Jennifer was asleep and I was reading a proof of *The Beef Wellington Case*. I am getting better, I thought. The children were bathing. Both youngsters were strong swimmers; Edward had more stamina but over fifty yards Hester would be in front. Suddenly I saw Edward thrashing the water around him and shouting but I could not hear what he was saying. There was no sign of Hester. He was about one hundred yards from the shore, close to a rocky headland. As I reached the water's edge, he was already staggering towards me. His face was red, and his breath sounded like a rusty hinge.

"I've drowned her", he said. "She was teasing me, like usual. Said I was getting fat. Said my penis was tiny. I could not help it. I pushed her under. Held her down for ages. She disappeared. I dived down, many many times, but she'd gone. She must be on the bottom. I've killed her."

All of this came out as one unpunctuated shriek but as it did I had turned him back seawards and instantly he dived through the waves in my wake as we swam out to where I had seen him thrashing the water — or at least as close to that spot as could be guessed. We searched under water for about fifteen minutes. During that time Jennifer joined us. After a quick explanation, she also dived. Nothing. I felt so powerless. The sea was calm, but merciless. At this point the beach shelved quickly, and none of us had been able to reach the sea-bed. Would she float to the top? Which way was that tide running? Would she be swept out to sea? I had no expertise in these matters. I was distraught and all of us were exhausted but I was able to say to Jennifer, as we dragged ourselves up the beach to the picnic spot, that we must contact the Coastguard Service as soon as possible.

But, when we reached our stretched-out towels, who was there but Hester, drinking orange squash. I did not ask for any explanation. The relief at seeing her was not sufficient to stay my hand as I slapped her face, more than once. Very hard, then kicked sand at her and knocked the glass from her hand.

She was shocked. Corporal punishment was still administered in schools, but not often to girls of her age, and in our household, not at all. When she was frustrating me with her silences, I never smacked her once. When she pushed Robin Edwards off the school wall, and he had broken his arm, my hands were not used. But today, this was diabolical.

The story was as follows. She soon escaped from Edward's downward thrust and deliberately swam underwater to the nearby rocks. From there she had seen Edward's distress, his attempts to find her and the joining of all the family in the search. As we dived and spluttered, she clambered over the rocks and returned to the beach, unscathed — except for the bruise that was already starting to show on her left cheek. She was crying. Edward had his mouth open, and Jennifer did know what to do. Eventually she cradled both male members of her family to her chest and told Hester what a wicked girl she was.

I did not discuss Hester's comment about his penis with Edward, but I did with the girl. She admitted that she had never seen that of the boy, but her remarks had been prompted by 'some pictures that Charlotte had'. I decided to enquire no further.

As can be imagined, this incident rather spoiled the holiday, but one good thing did emerge. Her treatment of Edward in this way must have been a salutary lesson for Hester. She never stopped teasing him but it became less intense, more something he could dismiss with a smile and a wave of the arm, and this resulted, over time, in a warm and happy relationship developing between them.

As Hester entered her teens, I began to find her an interesting companion. She still avoided the kitchen as a place of work but was happy to sit on a stool there drinking ginger beer and regaling me with details of her day as I cleaned the wild mushrooms. I was making risotto. She eventually called me 'Daddy', but this had now been replaced with 'PG' since discovering such is the new brand name for a tea. I did not object. I thought it rather quaint.

"PG. What's for supper?"

"Wait and see. It's a surprise."

"I would tell you what they gave us for lunch at school but I cannot find enough awful words to describe it. We call it pink puke."

"Not in front of your teachers, I hope."

"I want to ask you something."

"Fire away."

"How do you think up those stories you write?"

"Well, that's the job of a writer. Imagination. Would you like to be a writer?"

"Miss Robertson says I'm good at English, but it's too quiet for me. I want to fly aeroplanes."

"Good heavens. What put that idea into your head?"

"Amy Johnson of course. Have you ever been in an aeroplane?"

"No. I like my feet on the ground."

"Did you have fighter planes in the war?"

"Yes. Later on."

"Did you win any medals?"

"No. But Uncle Bob did. He was very brave."

"If I can't be a pilot, I'm going to be in Parliament. So as to make sure girls can have any job that a boy can."

"Did you hear that from Jennifer?"

"No. Why can't I play cricket for England?"

"It's a man's sport. Girls don't play cricket."

"Why not?"

"Because you're different from boys."

"I can run faster than Eddie."

"Still. Why not go into Parliament. I think you would be a good debater."

"Why?"

"Because you always answer a question with another question. That's what they do."

"Can I have more pocket money? I'm the poorest girl in my class."

"Another attribute. An astute negotiator. No. I do not believe other girls have more generous parents."

"Amy's got a new bike. With three gears. And why don't we live in the country so I can have a horse?"

"Haven't you homework to do?"

"Yes. Boring chemistry."

The following year, we all went to Paris where I delighted in acting as a tourist guide. It was a first for the children but Jennifer had visited once or twice before. She knew all about Simóne of course but on the boat-train I gave Edward and Hester a précis of the story. I went alone to see Marguerite, but we all visited the Notre Dame on the 21st of June. Paul Nerval entertained us at La Tour d'Argent. Even my daughter was impressed. We also dined at the Trois Perroquets but I am afraid to report it is not what it used to be.

Marguerite had no news for me.

*Alan Shelley*

*I regretted our falling out over the General Strike, but he soon made amends, and I shall keep him on the true socialist path from now on. You cannot fault him for ingenuity. Frankie and I could hardly believe it when he hired that van and transported our bread over the border, but it worked. I went with it once or twice. Sentimental journey. I never visited the shop but came to like the Owens as much as Percy does.*

*I never did get to the bottom of the business with Ruth. Jennifer dropped some hints but it seemed to me she was best suited to Peter. He told me that at his darkest hour in the hospital in France, my son's brashness and love of life had cheered him up no end. I have always had a soft spot for 'the professor', as I call him. I cannot say his poetry does much for me, but his manners are so sweet and when he wrinkles his eyes at me, I could eat him up. Imogen and Adam. Not names I would have chosen, but they're a bonny pair. They all called in to see us on their way to Worcester. Wonderful to see Peter pushing them around the Gloucester Park in that funny double perambulator they have.*

*What a wedding it was. They do spend money that lot. Whitwells turn in a tidy profit every year, but I know what it's like to be poor, so we're more careful. Percy ought to know better, but there's no telling him. But what about me. I have a new granddaughter. What a surprise. I knew more about Percy and that Brenda Patch — God rest her soul — than I have let on. And about the flour store, but as it goes, 'less said, soonest mended'. She's certainly a spirited little thing. I can't see her serving in a shop when she grows up like the other young uns.*

*Abigail writes regularly. They now have two children and Hubert is selling his paintings despite the depression. Evidently his grandmother's trust was not affected by the crash on Wall Street, but the family bank is going bust so justice has been done. I hope they finish up living on the 'wrong side of the tracks'.*

*I"m getting a bit plump, but can still make Francois jealous. As usual, I had Peter hanging on my every word — and it wasn't my new hat he was admiring. Harmless fun, I always say. Can't teach an old dog new tricks.*
　　Violet Chambord May 1929

# Chapter Eight

# Europe

*Sauerbraten*

*3lb. fillet of beef. 1 lemon. 2 bay leaves. 6 cloves. 4 peppercorns. Salt. ½ pint vinegar. 2oz. butter. 3 rashers of fat bacon. 1 onion. 1 tablespoon flour. 1 oz.lump sugar. ¼ pint sour cream or sour milk. Juice of 1/2 a lemon.*

*Skewer beef to a good shape; place in a bowl. Into a saucepan put enough water to cover the beef in the bowl. Slice the lemon. Add to the water the lemon slices, bay leaves, cloves, peppercorns and salt and bring to the boil. Add the vinegar and allow to cool. When cold, pour the liquid over the beef and leave to stand for several hours — all night if convenient. Remove the meat and dry it — retain the liquid. Put the butter in a large heavy saucepan and heat. Put in the bacon, onion (sliced) and meat and fry, turning the meat on all sides until it is a rich brown. Add the flour and fry until brown. From the liquid in which the meat was standing, take a ½ pint, also the bay leaves and cloves, and add it to the meat in the saucepan and bring to the boil. Remove the pan to a moderate oven, see that it is tightly covered, and cook gently for one and a half hours. Put the sugar with a few drops of water in a saucepan and cook slowly until a deep brown colour. Add the sour cream to the sugar and stir. Take up the meat and keep hot. Strain the liquid formed in cooking and add it to the sugar and cream. Add the lemon juice, bring to the boil, and serve with the beef.*

# Germany

I did play in the parents versus pupils match. Twice. One year it was rained off but when I did get a bowl, Edward was delighted. At one of the games we were told in advance that the father who usually kept wicket had fallen off a ladder and the school was happy to bend the rules to allow Bob Patch, that star of West End and Broadway, to take over the gloves and try and deal with my chinaman. Because of Hester, we saw more of Bob than hitherto. When I referred to him as 'Uncle Bob' he would invariably call me 'Father Percy' and cross himself. About this time it occurred to me that in addition to Hester and cricket, we had one more important thing in common — words. He made his living speaking them; I mine with the written ones.

However, and not for the first time, he was having rather more success than me. My detective fiction kept me occupied, most of the time, but it was 'more of the same' and I began to derive greater pleasure from the articles I wrote for magazines. These were on varied subjects, although mostly with a culinary slant, and there was a possibility of a series of cookery talks for the BBC but this came to naught. The BBC thought, somewhat surprisingly, that my voice was not what they called 'radio friendly'. One of the people involved in this curious decision suggested I ask my friend Bob Patch to speak my words. You can imagine my response to that.

Par for the course, Jennifer evinced little interest in the cricket match even though graced by her husband, her son and her favourite actor, but by now Edward was in the first eleven and scoring runs on a regular basis so she was honour bound to be there. Sad to say, that boy found no terrors in my off-breaks, but we certainly had much delight in analysing the game afterwards. On that occasion, Ruth and the family came so Jennifer had someone around the tea table to talk about matters other than a turning wicket and this gave her a chance to move on to European politics — a subject of some concern to her at that time. Bob was interested in the discussion because he knew of the American film that had been made of *All Quiet on the Western Front*; I believe he was acquainted with one of the actors. Jennifer was telling us about a report from their correspondent in Berlin on the reaction in that city to the movie.

"It's that awful man Goebbels again. He looks like an emaciated toad, but he is smart. He knows how to stir things up."

Talk of politics in Germany always made Peter hunch his shoulders. This time was no exception. Jennifer went on.

"I haven't seen the film yet, but I believe it is very good. One of the most realistic depictions of the horrors of war there has been."

"If it follows the book, it will be." I said.

"It did not suit the Nazis. They are trying to get people to believe that it was the Generals who lost them the war but a major theme of Remarque's book, and presumably the film, is that by mid-1918 the average German soldier in the trenches knew the war was lost. They wanted the Generals to sue for peace. And so, Goebbels organized objections to the film to reinforce their policy. Storm troopers in the cinema shouted out things like 'filthy film' and 'throw the Jews out'. They flung stink bombs and even let loose some white mice in the auditorium. Our man was there. Pandemonium. Then the film was banned as injurious to the reputation of the German people. In other words, the Nazis got their way."

"I don't like it one bit." said Peter. "Did all those millions die for nothing? We should do something."

We all subscribed to such a view, but what could be done. I suspected I had been on the periphery in Paris at the birth of the problem. We should have got it right in 1919. The anti-German sentiment was very strong, particularly with the French, and as a result the Allies damaged the German economy so ruthlessly that some form of revolution was inevitable. I tried, unsuccessfully, to move the mood away from politics by directing the conversation back to a closer examination of the cricket match but Bob did rather better when he told us about Paul Robeson's success with *Othello* and the passion he was said to be arousing in Flora Robson's breast.

Since leaving Paris, the centre of my life has been Jennifer, but I am conscious of the fact that other people, and other incidents, have intruded into my account so as to seem to cast her in the role of an understudy rather than a star. This was not the case. While I was reconciling myself to my mother and delivering bread to the Valleys; while I was playing the fool over Ruth and coming to terms with having a daughter; Jennifer was at the heart of my existence.

You may already agree with the notion that I enjoy the company of women and by the time I was establishing myself in London there were a sufficient number within my acquaintance to satisfy that inclination. However, after Simóne, and the tragedy of the miscarriage, I was not looking for a long-term relationship; and as for children, I gave such matter little thought. I was not looking for a mother for my future offspring. In addition, I was more than occupied with not only a change of locale but also with a change of career. In the last decade, cooking had been uppermost in my life — even if practised in the kitchens at Whitwells the Bakers or the officer's mess at Arras — but now it became a part-time activity. I was to earn my bread by writing, not baking.

But it was, of course, the word that led me to Jennifer, and however I might have resisted a commitment, I was powerless. I fell in love with Simóne, and I have attempted to explain what a strange creature she was and how this happened, but I have not accorded to Jennifer the same prominence and I propose, therefore, to remedy that omission now.

What do you already know? Married during the war: husband killed before he saw his son. Career women — journalist with bobbed auburn hair, fond of the theatre, but not of cricket or lardy cakes; tower of strength during the difficult times with Hester. A perfunctory character study, to say the least.

She rarely talked about Byron Lomax; her tragedy was shared with millions of other women who lost husbands and boyfriends. I tried my best to understand how she must have felt. I could compare it to my loss of Simone, but it was not the same. Jennifer's life was turned upside down by an event that took place many miles away during a conflict that, to an intelligent girl in 1918, appeared to have no meaning. She had a fatherless baby in her arms. She told me she wept for days. She wept for the child, she wept for her husband who would never see his son, and she wept for herself.

First of all, Jennifer Glossop née Lomax née Simmons was a strong woman. Until we married she had been one of the estimated two million single women who, after the war, survived without men. A number of them survived very successfully. Jennifer never aspired to write fiction but in the 1920s there was a raft of unmarried women who found fame in this area; Phyllis Bentley, Ivy Compton-Burnett, Elizabeth Goudge and Winifred Holtby to mention but a few and, as Bob reminded me, there were examples in the theatrical world as well, notably Gwen Ffrangcon-Davies and Flora Robson.

Virginia Woolf famously said that women, particular writers, need a room of their own but in Jennifer's case she was, most of the time, sharing hers with Edward until he went away to school at the age of eight. Despite that, from the time the boy could be left with his great-aunt, Jennifer worked in the newspaper industry; initially with local papers but by the time her son was at the village school, she commuted to London daily where she was a junior reporter with the *Daily Herald*. By the time I met her she was sufficiently skilled to have become a freelance operator — until she was persuaded to join the

*Daily Telegraph* full-time. Her sympathies and politics were represented by the *Herald*, but her current employer offered a more generous level of remuneration and so, if she wished to support the Labour Party or the suffragettes or the feminist movement, she did so outside of writing hours.

This gives you a taste of her as the career woman, but in the past I had fallen in love with someone who had no career whatsoever and I was certainly not looking — if indeed I was looking at all — for a replica of my mother. Violet, I love dearly, but she was inclined to boss me around. If a wife is what I wanted I thought someone soft and pliant like Norma Shearer would best suit me, not a Gloria Swanson or a Greta Garbo. But, as we all know, you do not always get what you want, or think you want, in this life.

This debate could be reversed; indeed, it should be. If Jennifer was looking for a husband and a cricket enthusiast as father to her son, what specification did she have? Was Percy Glossop likely to measure up? Probably not — but all of this constitutes a fruitless diversion from the facts of the case. I fell in love, and so did she.

And why, in my case? Let me tell you something more about her. She held herself very erect. Not in a formal aristocratic and ladylike way, but with grace and a national athleticism. She stood tall, you might say. Even when seated she never slouched. Do I give a picture of someone stiff, and even forbidding? If so, my words are failing me. In bed, she was far removed from being stiff. Sex to her was as natural as breathing — and she had not been taking lessons from my mother.

She was interested in people; a useful attribute for a reporter, and this was reflected in her hazel eyes that seemed to flick around the room like a swift skimming the rooftops. Her cheekbones were rather pronounced, but her most distinctive feature was the mouth. It was inviting, not just as an object to be kissed, but as an indication of a friendly nature. It was also the outlet for her speech. Her voice was soft — in later years when I began to go deaf I needed to keep close to her to hear what she was saying — and her accent was neutral. At least that is how I heard it.

Jennifer bought little at Whiteley's cosmetic counter. Her perfume was a combination of cleanliness and earthy vigour. Her teeth did not match those of Abigail but they were sharp, as the occasional lesions on my neck confirmed. Except for the aberration over lardy cakes, her appetite was liberal — perhaps a little too much. Before we went to Berlin she was beginning to thicken-up around the hips.

She had some well defined causes. Before the vote was won she did not have the leisure to go to the races, or chain herself to railings, but when the franchise was obtained, she believed passionately in using the prize of the vote. She loyally supported the Labour Party, in one form or another, all her life. I was sometimes ambivalent but at one stage she even considered standing for Parliament. She deplored what happened over the General Strike and her opinion on the subject of Mr Churchill was no less vitriolic than that of my mother. Her most earnest campaign was to secure equality for women in the workplace, and in the professions.

When Edward decided on medicine as a career, I introduced her to Liza Rosen, who had moved from St Mary's to the Royal Infirmary in Glasgow. She was Jennifer's sort of woman and tales of the early discrimination that Liza suffered only rendered my wife more assiduous in this campaign. Ruth had the same views, but was less active than her sister. I think that is why Jennifer coped so well with Hester. She identified with the girl's free spirit, even if not always put to its best use. She was not a member of a trade union, rather difficult working for the paper she did, but during her freelance days she became something of a specialist in the stories of women in work and of the obstructions and prejudices many of them faced. I suppose she simply believe in freedom for all — as in later years she demonstrated by her actions. She was certainly the first person within our circle to support what Gandhi was trying to do in India.

I rather gloss over her career as a newspaper woman. Except for those working for the specialist women's magazines, there were few engaged in the daily, or even Sunday, newspaper trade. Jennifer encountered a wall of prejudice. You could not have a woman picking up leads to stories in the smoke-filled bars of Fleet Street; or any other bar for that matter? Could the gentler sex survive the sight of blood, whether spilt by accident or design? Would a woman be able to insert a size ten boot into the door of a reluctant interviewee? And they were just unsuited to the garb of grubby mackintosh and felt hat, either pulled well done over the eyes or perched cheekily on the back of the head. I did think Mae West would have been marvellous as Walter Burns in the Hecht/ Marshall 1928 hit, *The Front Page*, but of course the play revolves around hard-bitten journalists with the woman's role reduced to the fiancée who might seduce the ace reporter away from the newspaper.

In her role as one of the sub-editors at the foreign desk she tended to only deal with the human interest stories. Political events and the doings of the Mafia in the USA were not directed at her desk. Her usual fare included the plight of the 'okie' families fleeing from the dustbowls of Oklahoma, the rescue of a mother and baby from earthquake ruins in Japan or this year's skirt length in Paris. However, at the time of the most serious political event of the 1930s, she visited Berlin in a private capacity and I went with her. We left London on the 27th of January 1933.

Bob, naturally enough, had friends who had moved from the stage into the burgeoning cinema industry and when he learned that we proposed visiting Berlin, he gave us introductions to German film makers. The German film industry was a very active one. In 1930, Sternberg's, *The Blue Angel*, began the spectacular cinematic career of cabaret artist, Marlene Dietrich. Another notable achievement was Fritz Lang's first talking film, *M,* starring Peter Lorre, but the coming to power of the Nazis in 1933 had seen a mass exodus of people connected with the cinema, particularly the Jews. Fritz Lang and Max Ophuls went to France and others who left, mainly for America, were Peter Lorre, Conrad Veidt, Robert Siodmak and Billy Wilder.

When we got to Berlin we found that most of the people Bob had contacts with had left, except for Joanna Stein. She had been born in Whitechapel, was Jewish and had run away from home at the age of seventeen to work as a dancer throughout Europe, reaching Berlin in 1930. She had married the manager of one of the nightclubs where she performed. Carl Stein was also a Jew. Bob was unforthcoming about where he had met this girl but they had kept in touch over the years and he told me he had sent them some Spode pottery as a wedding present.

We met her in the shabby apartment she occupied close to the Müllerstrasse.

"Fraulien Stein, thank you for inviting us here. Bob Patch is a very old friend of mine. We went to school together."

"Please call me Joanna. Do you know, I can't for the life of me remember where I met Bob, but we have kept in touch."

"I hope we can meet your husband."

"Not likely. He's scarpered. To tell the truth, I'm not sorry. We weren't having a lot of fun together."

"Oh dear. Where's he gone?"

"Dunno. All I know he's got out of Berlin. Scared he was."

"Scared. Of what?"

"Well, to start with, he's Jewish."

"We hear and read so many stories. Are all Jews at risk?"

"I keep out of politics. As long as the punters come to the show — and I get bought the occasional bottle of champagne — that's all I need. Come and see me. Great fun. The Kit Kat Club."

"Yes. But if your husband has left, wouldn't it be wise for you to leave?"

"I've been here since 1930. Those Hitlerites are as fond of pretty girls as all men are."

As we walked back to the hotel, Jennifer echoed my thoughts. She often did.

"I want to find out the truth about what's happening to the German people, but I'm afraid that naïve silly girl is not going to help much — and we are certainly not going to that club of hers."

"If she really is a good friend of Bob's we should wrap her up in brown paper and take her back to England with us."

"Be serious."

"She is quite pretty, in a coarse sort of way. Nice ginger hair. I think we should check on her before we leave."

"Pretty. You think so?"

"For Bob's sake."

The long walk to and from her apartment gave Jennifer and I the first opportunity to form an opinion of the Berlin of 1933 — or at least that part we traversed. The war had been over for fifteen years but as I recalled how swiftly Paris had recovered by the mid-1920s, it was self-evident that it was a very different story for this city. Buildings were poorly maintained, roads and footpaths neglected, and it seemed that the famous sense of order had deserted the German people. There was rubbish in their streets, rags on their backs and gloom on their faces. A slight exaggeration. Only the beggars were in rags but the general air of neglect and despondency could not be avoided. Jennifer commented on this but we both knew that the folk we passed on the streets had suffered much hardship since November 1918. Their government had at times lost control of the populace and certainly of the economy. Food and coal was scarce. There had been violence on the streets and a large proportion of the population were unemployed.

When we reached the hotel we were told that President Hindenburg had just appointed Hitler as the Chancellor of Germany. Most of the guests at the hotel, and evidently all of the staff, were pleased at this outcome but I found some handful of drinkers in the bar with long faces. I had left Jennifer to rest before dinner and decided a glass of lager would lighten the shining hour. The man standing next to me, and sharing a small saucer of salted biscuits, looked very grim. He had the bearing of a soldier and I asked him if I was correct. I did not explain my illustrious military career in detail but told him I was stationed near Arras. He knew the town and I wondered if he had met Clarice and the sister, but did not enquire. He spoke passably good English.

"Like you, I can say what a waste of human life. My wife lost her father and two brothers. It has made me bitter. I joined thinking our cause was just. It was not. I went to see that American film of Remarque's book. That told the truth, but those crazed idiots who are now in charge of my country do not believe in truth. We were a great nation. I despair."

"Hadn't you better be careful what you say. I'm told those brownshirts will crack your head open for remarks like that."

"Precisely. Violence. Brother against brother. What am I to teach my students from now on. Hitler's lies — or the truth."

"My sister-in-law is a teacher. What is your subject?"

"I'm at the university. Humanities faculty. I could not tolerate the celebrations on the streets. Retreated into here; and if I drink enough schnapps, I might forget. This is a sad day for Germany."

I excused myself and went to rouse Jennifer so that we might have dinner. On our way we passed the bar and I saw the university man was still there, sitting on the same stool. I thought he had probably kept to his promise and drunk more schnapps, as threatened, but if so it had neither rendered him intoxicated or any more cheerful. I introduced him to Jennifer and on the spur of the moment asked if he would like to dine with us. He said he would, and for the first time in our short acquaintance the frown on his face faded a little.

As I have said, he had a soldiers bearing. He was several inches taller than either Jennifer or I and probably two or three years older. His hair was grey and cut short and he had a neat little goatee beard of the same colour. He was soberly dressed; dark suit, stiff collar and a striped tie that, I conjectured, signified membership of a club of sorts — of the military or academia. He was very thin. In contrast, the lines etched along the forehead were wide and deep, almost like duelling scars.

We had intended to eat in the hotel restaurant but my drinking companion, Kurt Valler, cautioned against this and offered to show us a small restaurant behind the hotel where the cuisine was better and cheaper — and more authentic. As we strolled to the Restaurant Zimmer I told him of my interest in cooking and he promised me a dish of sauerbraten, the Rhineland recipe with raisins, that he believed I would want to add to my repertoire.

However, this interesting subject matter soon vanished into thin air as we passed a flight of narrow steps leading down to a basement. Two young men emerged at street level and both collided with me. There was no apology. They appeared mildly excited and looked rather pleased with themselves. I could detect the smell of beer on their breath but when they saw the three of us, one of them reached forward to stroke Jennifer's hair while making a comment that brought a shriek of laughter from his companion. I kicked the ankle of the amused one and Jennifer swung her handbag at the other, but there was no reaction and they left the scene as quickly as they had appeared.

I remembered Liza Rosen very well; but not any of the language she had attempted to impart. I asked Kurt what the man had said.

"I hardly need to interpret for you. It was a mindless obscenity directed at your wife, as I suspect you both guessed. These monsters wear heavy boots and have thick skins so they hardly noticed your joint efforts at retaliation. I'm sorry you have become involved, but I regret to say that ruffians like these have become a common feature on our streets."

We then looked down into the stairwell. It was dark but at the bottom of the steps we could distinguish the shape of two inert bodies. As I moved to descend, one of the shapes stood up and attempted to raise the other one but such efforts were not successful until Kurt and I joined in. It was an elderly man and a younger woman; father and daughter I presumed. The man's face was bruised and bleeding and his right leg appeared to be set at an unusual angle to his body; clearly the reason he could not stand. The woman was not wounded but her dress was torn and she was sobbing. The noise she made was low and guttural as though she was trying to vomit at the same time as expressing her grief. At that moment a band of artificial light was introduced into the darkness; a door was opened a few yards away from which emerged a boy, about ten years of age. He said nothing but helped the girl to drag the old man towards the prism of light and then over the threshold, followed by a bang as the door was abruptly closed. No one said a word. I moved towards the door but Kurt indicated, by a loud sigh and a shrug of the shoulders, that we leave well alone and move on to the restaurant.

We ate our dinner in sober mood, as was reflected in the premises and the other customers. It was off the beaten track, but the food was good although not matched by the furnishings and table linen that were, to say the least, rather humble. The tables were occupied by people built in the same mould as Kurt Valler; and no more animated than he. He explained that he knew several of the other diners as it was an establishment favoured by men and women who worked at the University, or were middle ranking civil servants.

"Those two louts. I'm afraid the Berlin of today nurtures such as if it was a greenhouse used to force out-of-season strawberries."

"Why the assault?"

"Well, you've probably guessed. The old man and the family were Jewish. I know it seemed heartless to leave them like that but I have tried in the past and become desperate because there is so little I can do. Or anyone else who thinks like me. The anti-semitic fever has reached pandemic proportions in Germany. I'm not sure whether it is yet formally declared, but the policy of the Nazis is to get rid of all of the Jews in the country and I think this is more likely to happen using foul means than fair. And with Hitler, it is not a religious matter. It is racist. It won't do if you've converted from Judaism. For him, you are still a Jew and must not be allowed to interfere with the belief that the Germans are the master race. This is not only the work of the Nazis. Our schools teach that Germans are racially superior and therefore destined to rule Europe. Have you read Nietzsche? He saw men as warriors and warriors must fight. However, to be a fighter, you need an opponent. Hitler has found one for the German people — the Jews. And it's not only them. Gypsies, the mentally ill, or more or less anyone without good German blood in their veins."

Jennifer was bursting to join in the conversation.

"But, how has this come to pass? Why does that family not report that atrocity to the police? Why have you voted Hitler into power?"

"Well, Mrs Glossop, as you can probably guess he did not get my vote, but he is a clever man — and as for the police, they will not intervene where the 'Master Plan' is involved."

"How awful. Hitler. Seems difficult to believe when you look at him — and those interminable speeches."

"Yes. I agree, but you have to understand the background."

I explained to Valler about my minor involvement in the Versailles Treaty and how, even in 1919, there were some people in Paris who foresaw disaster in the future, particularly as a result of the reparations.

"That, plus the world-wide economic depression. Germany has been through very hard times, and we still are, but Hitler has used these conditions, and the threat of the menace of the Communists, to persuade the people that his party will put food into their bellies and make Germany great again. He has also promised to improve conditions in the army and to re-equip it. He tries to show he wants a strong military — and he does — but eventually it will be under his personal control."

"But why the violence?"

"That, I think, can partly be attributed to the general corruption of the spirit of our people, brought on by the hardships they have borne — but, more crucially, it seems to be a precept of the Nazi party. Militarism, uniforms, a charismatic leader. All the ingredients of Fascism. Look at Mussolini."

"There have been hard times in our country. Percy will tell you about the hungry miners he knows in South Wales — and of the General Strike. The entire workforce of the country joined in, but there was very little violence. There is of course anti-semitism in some areas but we have lived alongside the Jewish people for centuries without problems."

"But, my dear lady, perhaps the difference is that you won the war."

When back at the hotel, we both agreed that this was too simplistic an explanation but we did elicit a different view when, over the next few days, we spent some time with a young Berliner. Although Jennifer was in Berlin in a private capacity, the *Telegraph* correspondent was very helpful. We did not ask for his views on the situation in the country; for one thing he had only been in Berlin for nine months and, as Jennifer said, she could read his reports. However, we grasped the opportunity to quiz his secretary, Lisl Gunter, who had been responsible for arranging hotel and transportation for our visit. Working for the *Telegraph,* her English was good. She was rather squat and wore steel rimmed spectacles. Clearly intelligent. Inevitably, the main topic of conversation was the appointment of Hitler as Chancellor.

"I can already guess that people in your country, and in the West generally, will see him as part monster, part buffoon. In other circumstances I might agree, but you have to understand the background and the circumstances. My country has been on the brink of disaster — off and on — for most of the years since the war and people of my age, of my thinking, believe he might be able to move us forward. Away from the disaster scenario."

To my shame, I did not participate in this discussion because I was concentrating on her eyes. One was blue, the other brown. Jennifer spoke for both of us.

"I concede that, but are you sure he is the man?"

"No. Who can tell? But what is the alternative. The Communist Party, unlike your country, is strong here but do the Germans want to be ruled from Moscow; by Stalin. There is a lot of gossip in newspaper circles about the atrocities he is perpetrating. We are a proud people. The Reds are not the answer. In the opposite corner, the Junker aristocracy. You may well have heard the saying: 'Prussia rules Germany, and the Junkers rule Prussia.' Well, the youth of the country think it is their failures that have brought us to this. My father was killed at the Somme. My mother had four children. She worked and scraped and begged, firstly to keep us from starving, and then to get us some education. It killed her. Do you think I want to see those times again? There has to be a turning point, and my friends and I believe that, with all his faults, Adolph Hitler is our best chance."

"But can you accept his Jewish policy?"

"I was waiting for that one. No, not altogether. You must understand. Many Germans believe the Jews made money out of the war — and the peace — and need to be curbed if the country is to recover."

"How will such curbing be achieved?"

"The National Socialist party will give Germany back to the Germans and if that means exiling the Jews, so be it."

"But where will they go? They are Germans."

At this point Lisl shrugged her shoulders and suggested we visited the Pergamon Museum that has one of the finest collections of Middle-Eastern artefacts in the world.

The incident at the basement steps considerably depressed Jennifer and I must admit I took advantage of her low spirits to persuade her that we owed it to her friend Bob to visit Joanna at her work. She was initially very reluctant, but I prevailed.

The room was small and the air laden with smoke; lighting very subdued. At one end a raised platform, less than two feet off the floor, was used to accommodate eight girls who appeared to be on duty continuously. The music was supplied by a trio of clarinet, double bass and piano and when they took a rest, the girls remained on the stage and only began their gyrations again when the band resumed playing. They were off-key, I thought. All of the girls were similarly garbed. Above the waist the only items of apparel were two pieces of red shiny material, about the size of a half-crown, attached to their nipples. I did contemplate asking Jennifer how she thought they were attached — glue or invisible elastic — but thought better of it. I did not want her to think I was over interested in female mammaries. Below the waist the girls wore skirts that fell to the ankles. Very demure, you might have thought, except that these garments comprised of a multitude of strips of cloth fastened at the waist so that if the dance became even mildly energetic, the girl's posteriors were exposed, as would have been their pubic hair if that area had not been carefully shaved. However, in Joanna's case, I thought I could see some ginger traces. When the dancer's movements were really vigorous the strips spread out, as well as the limited stage would allow, at right angles to the girls so as to resemble nothing less than human maypoles. A bizarre sight.

Most of the paying customers at the Kit Kat club were male who were more interested in the scantily clad girls who sat at their tables, or on their knees, than watching the antics of the maypoles. If George Grosz had not already left the country, this scene would have been an inspiration for him. Or would it. I presumed what was on view to Jennifer and I was available at many other locations in this sad and decadent city.

Jennifer felt very out of place. She dealt rather severely with a short fat man, wearing the heaviest pair of horn-rimmed spectacles I had ever seen, when he attempted to place his hand on her bottom. Her vigorous slap, more like a short-arm jab, knocked the wind out of him and before he could recover she returned him to his seat with such force that the chair collapsed under him and he fell across the table shattering two glasses of champagne in the process. She then gathered together the few words of German she had and told him he was a capitalist pig. Or did she say 'fascist'? His strangled response, as far as I could gather, suggested that my wife was more than likely to be a member of the House of David.

The place was very crowded; I do not think Joanna knew we were there. Our visit was a short one.

Before leaving Berlin, we did go to her apartment to see if she was all right. It was some minutes before the door was opened. When it was we first saw a man without trousers, but still wearing his shirt. It was brown. Over his shoulder I caught a glimpse of Joanna wearing a vivid green negligee patterned with dull yellow flowers. We turned on our heels and went to catch the train for our departure from Berlin.

The *Telegraph* correspondent bade us farewell at the Zoo Station and told us that the Reichstag was burning. I later learnt that Bertolt Brecht left the following day. I never met him either.

After our visit we tended to read the news coming out of Germany with a keener interest.

It transpired that Bob met Joanna in Nottingham. He had been in a touring company performing *Private Lives* at the Theatre Royal while she was a chorus girl in the variety show next-door at the Empire and they had met twice in the pub most convenient to both centres of entertainment. Evidently Joanna had followed Bob's career after that, sending him best wishes on each opening night. They had never met again and he had not responded to her letter telling him she was going to try her luck in Berlin but, generous fellow that he is, he did send that wedding present.

I told Bob about our visit. He was not very interested. Jennifer was. Not about the girl, but the country. As I have said, her political credo began with the word 'freedom' and our visit had only reinforced this, and her anti-fascist stand. Hitler wasted no time in enforcing the Nazi party's policies. The book burning scandal in May incensed us both. I read that Hemingway was included but even I did not think he deserved that fate. Mind you, he was in good company; Proust, Gide, Zola, HG Wells and Upton Sinclair, to mention but a few. Jennifer showed me a cutting from the *New York Times* on a speech by Goebbels at the Berlin conflagration.

Jewish intellectualism is dead. National Socialism has shown the way. The German folk soul can again express itself. These flames do not only illuminate the final end of the old era, they also light up the new... The old goes up in flames, the new shall be fashioned from the flame in our hearts.

Reports such as these exercised Jennifer more than somewhat and so, a few months after our return, and with the approval of the *Daily Telegraph*, she persuaded one of the serious weeklies to publish a modest satirical piece she had written, based on her observations. I helped. There was little reaction when the magazine came out — there were plenty of local issues to occupy the minds of the thinking classes — but the very act of writing, however feeble a scrap it was, helped her. As she said, I have nailed my colours to the mast. They did not edit her work. It follows.

## The False Prophet

In recent times in the Kingdom of Reichweimar, the people were unhappy. Indeed, more than just miserable; many were hungry, many were cold, and many were short of an arm or a leg because of a terrible war. The war had been with their neighbours to the West. They were not good friends. When they fought each other fifty years before, they won, but at the last conflict, they lost.

This Kingdom was not an ancient one but an amalgam of former Princely States, joined together in a loose confederation. As a result, now the country was under one leader there were still many divisions between the people.

The war had been a disaster. Many citizens of the Kingdom were killed or wounded and the victors ordered the defeated to pay huge sums of money to those who won as a penalty for starting the war — or so it was alleged — and for losing it. These payments were so large that there was little money left in the country, and it became bankrupt. The King tried to help by printing more banknotes — the days of the gold and silver coin were well past — but this did not help. The only section of the economy that prospered was in woodworking. Wheelbarrows were in great demand. They were needed to transport the new banknotes to the baker's shop to pay for a loaf of bread.

To the East of their country, the neighbour was a vast land that had been ruled for centuries by wicked leaders who kept the working people in virtual slavery. Some two decades earlier, the workers had revolted, murdered the senior wicked one and all his family, and set up to rule themselves. The new leaders were proud of what they had done and promised to export their kind of freedom to workers throughout the world.

The people of Reichweimar were very interested in this promise. Their rulers were not feeding them very well, or providing jobs, and therefore any change of leadership would be preferable. But there came into the land a Prophet who vowed to deliver the starving and the jobless into a land of milk and honey; or at least for some of them. He told them to be careful of the Eastern promise.

The Prophet did not look like a prophet. He was small and bad-tempered. He was exceedingly fond of cream cakes. He did not have a beard but a rather small bristly moustache, arranged on his top lip like a toothbrush that had been used to clean the silver, or someone's boots. He was however a good talker and a good schemer. Not at the beginning. One of his plans in the town of Munchen failed and he was sent to prison for five years. While there he wrote a boring book about his life and setting out what he intended to do in the future.

Amongst those intentions was one of particular wickedness. Although he had not been born in the Kingdom of Reichweimar, he believed that the only people worthy to be the citizens of that nation were those of one of the former Princely States, where everyone had blue eyes and blonde hair and stood two metres tall; the men that is. Women were not catered for. He called these beautiful heroes the Master Race. Strange. He was only one and a half metres high and when he did become the leader, one of his most important lieutenants was even shorter. Everyone else living in the country, who did not conform to this specification, was to be disposed of. At first it was assumed this meant they would be sent away on a permanent holiday but the Prophet's intention was much more sinister. They were to be killed and their possessions, including their spectacles and gold teeth, confiscated.

Before that the man with the black moustache had to depose the King's present leader and become leader himself. It was to be shown that despite his own incongruous appearance he was very clever. To the fittest of the blue-eyed paragons he gave uniforms in exchange for their tattered shirts and encouraged them to break the noses, particularly hooked ones, of anyone they met on the street who did not qualify as members of the Master Race.

He knew that, unlike his neighbour to the East, he could not persuade the workers to rise up and shoot the King but he did manoeuvre so they would cast their vote for him at the elections. These were frequent. At first the Prophet and his followers did not do very well but he bided his time during which he told the voters of two evils, one from the East and the other from the old enemy to the West. The first would take away their businesses — if they had any — their property and even their wives. All of them would have to be the same and no one would be able to make a profit. The members of the Master Race did not care for that prospect.

The next spectre was over the Western frontier. They were still collecting the dues exacted after the war. They would not allow Reichweimar to make guns and battleships, so if there was another war, there would be no doubt as to the identity of the winner. The Prophet promised no more payments would be made to those awful neighbours and the army and navy and air force would be expanded and re-equipped with new tanks, new warships and new aeroplanes.

Finally, he kept the unemployed amused for hours. He arranged massive candlelit parties where he entertained the guests with splendid displays of marching by the blonde giants and long witty speeches by himself, accompanied by an imitation of a windmill using his flailing arms. And, as the *piece de resistance*, he gave everyone a new salute. This entailed making a rude gesture with the right arm while clicking one's heels together.

It worked. More people voted for his party than any other so the King put him in charge of the country. The new leader did many things, quickly. He set up a convenient camp where those who were not members of the Master Race could be sent, and he told his people he would not allow anyone to criticise the party or produce anything that did not, in his opinion, accord to their policies. Books, plays, paintings and music that did not respect this maxim were not allowed and those cultural items in the past that were opposed to his dreams were to be destroyed. The people much enjoyed the warmth generated as bonfires around the country burned all copies of unlawful literature, particularly that written by authors who were citizens of the victors in the last war.

The Kingdom became strong again. The populace — at least the favoured — became happy again. Members of the Master Race became healthier — and taller. More people were at work. Wheelbarrows were only used by gardeners. The quality of the bread and the sausage and the beer improved remarkably. No one asked what the new guns and aeroplanes and submarines were for, except to defend their native land against their foe. Or was there a more ambitious plan?

After this was published, Jennifer paid close attention to what was happening in Germany; in the papers she always looked at the European news before any reference to British politics, the hats at Ascot ladies day and certainly before the cricket scores. I naturally looked at these but I acquired another view of that benighted country through a startling piece of literature, Alfred Döblin's *Berlin Alexanderplatz*. It was first published in Germany in 1929 and then in English by Martin Secker in 1931. It did for Berlin what *Ulysses* did for Dublin. I found this novel helped me to understand the underbelly, as it were, of the city rather better than a visit to the Kit Kat club or talking to that conservative University professor or to Lisl or reading the leading articles in *The Times* and the *Daily Telegraph*. Did André Malraux's 1938 novel, *Days of Hope,* similarly help me, retrospectively, to make sense of the Spanish conflict?

The hostility towards the Jews, where we had witnessed a minor incident, was brought back to mind when over a sequence of breakfast-times Jennifer exploded as she read the newspapers reporting on the so-called Nuremberg Laws.

"Incredibly, he seems unstoppable. Jews have now lost their German citizenship. They are to be 'state subjects', whatever that means. You imagine if in Britain everyone who was born in Gloucestershire would no longer be English. Called 'yokels' for instance."

"I don't think such flippancy is warranted. Wonder what happened to those sorry people we saw at that basement?"

"Sorry. Just trying to provide a local context. See what's next. If the Gloucester precedent can be continued, you and I would not have been allowed to marry. Or have sex. Marriage and sexual intercourse between Aryans and Jews is now forbidden."

"That makes me recall Joanna. Does that mean she can no longer have a truly German boyfriend?"

"Suppose so. And listen to this. They cannot hoist the German flag."

"Shouldn't think many of them would want to, but the sex thing is horrible. The State decrees who you can fall in love with. If it was not so awful, I might get my Herbert Montcalm taking up this theme in *The Mystery of the Suspicious Sauerkraut*."

When the twins first arrived Ruth and Peter moved to a larger property, but still in Madingley, and so we were more likely to see them on their ground rather than ours. Peter was not yet fifty but he was immersed in academia and his wife and children. His poetry was becoming more lyrical, but he still got it published. We were with them just after Jennifer's piece, *The False Prophet*, went into print. Ruth complimented her sister but Peter's reaction was different. Memories of the last time Germany had taken up arms could not be erased and although he understood Jennifer's intention, he simply thought the subject too painful to be treated in this way. I think, above all of us, even including Jennifer, it was Peter who felt, at gale force, the chill wind of another conflagration while to us it was still an irritating breeze. He knew what was happening in Germany, and Italy, but he could not talk about it and so he retreated into his verse and into his African studies. I, for one, did not blame him. On the question of sex between the Jews and other Germans, he pointed out that there had been a similar prohibition in South Africa relating to black and white since the 1920s. Another defeat for the cause of love.

## Spain

The position in Germany continued to cause concern. Peter refused to talk about it but Edward, sportsman that he is,

*Alan Shelley*

wanted to go to Berlin for the Olympics in 1936. Jennifer would not entertain the idea. Hester told him he was now eighteen and could do what he liked, but he knew better than to cross his mother on that particular subject. I supported her stand on this; we must not show any support for the Nazis, in whatever form. I regretted this. I saw sport as the great leveller. Many of the working class in Britain pulled themselves up out of the gutter because they were better than the next man with boxing gloves on their hands of football boots on their feet. Not quite the same on the cricket field; I was not happy about the class concept of 'Gentlemen' and 'Players'.

At the 1932 Olympics in Los Angeles, the Germans won few medals and the National Socialists opposed participation because all ethnicities were included. However, when they were in power they sought, particularly through the cinematographic lens of Leni Riefenstahl, to use the 1936 event in Berlin to extol the virtues of the Third Reich. The film she made, intended as a propaganda weapon, was also extraordinarily beautiful in parts but Hitler was furious when the star of the show turned out to be a black man.

But then, another story stole the headlines: war in Spain. If anything this worried Jennifer more than the rise and rise of the Third Reich. Fascist control of Germany and Italy was an established fact but she became really agitated at the possibility of Spain joining the club. It also worried Jack Owen.

Jennifer was always more political than me. So were my mother and my Welsh friend. They were true socialists and, like George Orwell, opposed to totalitarianism and supported democratic socialism. Violet and Jack brought to the table an inherent affinity with the working class but it seemed that Jennifer's political philosophy was more a mixture of the emotional and the intellectual.

Why should that be? She was middle class. Her son was at a public school and she was well-educated herself. She spoke what was known as 'proper English'. She had never been hungry or without shoes. Jack and she were as far removed from each other, materially that is, as I was culturally from that moron Perkins with whom I first shared a room at the Hôtel Majestic. At the age of thirteen Jack was running errands to and from the coal-face — bringing forward extra pit props or empty coal wagons at the same time as my wife was playing hockey — or 'Postman's knock' at the sort of birthday party where an entertainer was hired; a ventriloquist or a magician. Jack's politics were fully understandable. And probably so with my mother. She had worked long hours in the bakery from an early age; she had become acquainted with the working-class families in Gloucester who came to the shop every day, even if they could not afford her cakes; and she had seen conditions worsened for such families in the depression of the 1920s and the early 1930s.

For all of that, Jennifer's socialist values were no less secure, no less genuine, and I supported her and my mother, and Jack, in their beliefs; but politics was not at the top of my agenda. I paid rather more attention to good food and wine and the latest offering by George Bernard Shaw than I did to the antics of Oswald Mosley and, frankly, the Jarrow marchers. There, that's a confession for you. I suppose I was simply more selfish than the two ladies and the coalminer. I admired Ellen Wilkinson and I visited the Owens in the Rhondda Valley when I could, but current politics was not at the centre of my world and in all honesty, as Jennifer became more concerned, I suppose I became more inclined to be apolitical.

This did not create any divisions between us. Jennifer understood my position. When all was said and done, I was only acting in a similar fashion to the majority of the people of Britain; *laissez-faire*, 'up the Arsenal' and 'let's have another pint'. However, a conflict did arise because of Spain. Not between us but between Jennifer's pacifism and her implacable hatred of Fascism. We had both witnessed its strengthening in Germany and Italy and the spread to Spain equally concerned both the ardent and the lukewarm. Peter of course felt the same, but he and Jennifer could not accept combating this by

*Alan Shelley*

employing war as a weapon. The cause of democracy must be supported by other means than firing bullets and dropping bombs. But for this I could have seen Jennifer volunteering to drive ambulances for the International Brigade — and no doubt taking me along with her as navigator or general dogsbody. But this did not happen. She supported the Republican cause, as did I, in as many ways as possible short of joining up but this did not deter Jack Owen. He believed that if a call to arms was necessary to combat the fascists and totalitarianism, he would fight. And he did.

Until the failed *coup d'etat* in Spain of July 1936 we were living comfortably in Maida Vale and enjoying life. After our visit to Berlin, Jennifer reverted to a freelance status — it suited her temperament better — and the Americans were still buying my silly stories. There were no signs of a baby but Jennifer was now thirty eight years of age and I think we both realised that we would need to be content for Edward and Hester to provide us with comfort in our old age. There was however one pleasant change to our ordered and uneventful existence; I had renewed my friendship with Fred Kimball, my Colonel Kim. After he married I visited them occasionally but when they moved to North Yorkshire, there never seemed an appropriate time to get together. We lunched in London once or twice but then his father died and he and his wife moved into the family baronial pile in Berkshire. It was not a very big pile, but rather more handsome than I understood Stockton Hall to be. They had no need for the extra rooms, but they moved for sentimental reasons; my old friend and mentor had been very fond of his father.

Soon after they took over Flintoff Manor, we went to stay for the weekend. There were horses, so Hester and Edward were included in the invitation. My daughter was now as infatuated with horses as she was with members of the *Ballet Russes*. She rode most days in Hyde Park and was delighted at the prospect of a proper run in the Berkshire countryside. Edward was thinking about the possibility of the army as a career and was looking forward to talking about this with the Colonel. Neither Jennifer nor I thought Edward would ever take up soldiering, but it was a good excuse for all of us to be together, and in pleasant surroundings with interesting company.

On the Saturday night there were no other guests, just the four of us and our hosts. As was my habit I attempted to invade the kitchen and contribute to the cuisine on offer but at Flintoff Manor I was thwarted. Rebuffed even. Mrs Gertrude Pugh, no one called her Gertrude or, heaven forbid, Gertie, had been cook and housekeeper on the premises for the last thirty years. Her husband had served with the Royal Hampshires at Gallipoli, and he, like Byron Lomax, had never lived to see his son, who, for reasons never determined, was given the name Antonio by his mother. No one liked to ask the lady whether the father had any Italian blood and in view of her nature, I thought it unlikely she was inspired by the music hall song about a young man and his ice-cream cart.

We did not realise how eventful that weekend was to be. The blood of my mother must take some of the blame.

It happened so quickly. Before concerns for Jack Owen predominated, we had Hester to deal with. School had not yet ended for the Easter holidays and Jennifer was in Cambridge helping her sister who had sprained her ankle. When I looked at the clock in the kitchen, as I was preparing supper, I realised that my daughter was well overdue. She had not told me she had a play rehearsal or might visit Rosemary, her closest friend, to speak Italian together. I was not too concerned; a spur of the moment thing I assumed. When I was ready to eat at eight o'clock and there was still no sign of her, I rang Rosemary. Hester was not there and had not been at school at all that day. I went to her room. It was very tidy; she was orderly by nature. Her school hat was not there, but why should it be; she had left that morning wearing her uniform. Was anything missing? I sat down on the bed as it came over me. The last time I had been involved in a similar operation was when Simóne disappeared. But is Hester missing? Was

*Alan Shelley*

I in a panic over nothing? Her diary was on the desk. There were no entries for yesterday, or today and so I looked in the wardrobe again. I thought she had an overnight case — used on our last holiday — but it was not there now. I started to sweat. Then I heard the telephone. I ran.

"Percy. Fred Kimball here. I've got your daughter. Confined to barracks."

"What do you mean, confined to barracks?"

"She's locked in the Rosebud room."

"She's what."

"Locked in. She's a spirited thing. Reminds me of a horse I had in South Africa."

"What is she doing at Flintoff Manor?"

"Thought she was going to bite me. She certainly kicked me. Yes, that colt was like her."

"For goodness sake Fred, explain."

"Percy. I think you and Jennifer should get down here pronto. Bring your toothbrush and stay the night. Better explanations are face-to-face. I think I used to say that in Paris, did I not. She's safe. Not harmed, but dangerous."

As he laughed at that attempt at humour I said I was on my way and put the phone down. As long as I now knew where she was I thought I deserved a drink. After two swallows, I rang Jennifer and told her that, for reasons not yet understood, Hester was with the Kimball's and I would meet her there. She had the car and so I went by train and taxi and arrived just before she did, but only by a few minutes.

It must be remembered that Colonel Kim had married late in life and he was not as experienced in the extraordinary workings of the female mind as I was. For this reason, most of the following was related by Helen. Mrs Pugh was also present. We sat in a circle in the drawing room as though Miss Marples was about to tell us who was the murderer.

"Even Mrs Pugh was not in the picture. You met her son, Tony. Nice lad. Keeps the garden in wonderful heart. Bright too. Freddie thinks that with some help he can get himself to university, but there's plenty of time. He's not eighteen yet."

For the life of me I could not see how any of this concerned Hester. We had still not seen her but Mrs Pugh told us when we arrived that the girl was now a little calmer and had eaten a large plate of her sausage and mash. I wondered if she did onion gravy.

"Hester and he met when you've been here, but it appears that at first they did not hit it off. I discovered he and Edward sneaked out to the Plough in the village and refused to take her with them."

I could imagine the fracas that caused.

"However, it now seems that Hester is somewhat smitten with our Tony. He is quite handsome, I suppose, but anyway she began to write to him regularly and he was flattered. She may not have been a suitable companion for a clandestine trip to the pub but she is a lively pretty thing and he rather liked the idea of a girlfriend, even if their only contact was by the pen."

Now I thought about it, there had been some letters arriving at the flat addressed to her.

"From all accounts, his prose became more and more extravagant and she responded likewise. After about three months, they began to think they were Elizabeth Barrett and Robert Browning."

I had not realised Helen was interested in literature and love and poetry; but then I do tend to get rather superior within this province.

"I really don't think Tony knew what effect this was having on Hester. I suspect she's good at keeping things to herself. Anyway, this morning he got a letter from her saying she had made all the arrangements and he was to meet her at King's Cross to catch the 3 p.m. train to Scotland so they could get married at Gretna Green."

Jennifer stood up. Paced the carpet. She glowered at me as though I was to blame.

"Poor lad. He did not know what to do. Said nothing to anyone. Tried to persuade himself it was a joke. As it happens, I thought something was the matter. He forgot to bring in the flowers I had asked for. As you can see, those on the bureau are rather past it."

"For goodness sake, Helen", said Colonel Kim, "get on with it. This is not a Shakespeare epic. Just a girl being naughty. Deserves a long period of detention in my view."

"But we are not in your army, my dear. Let me go on. He should of course have spoken to his mother, who knew nothing of the affair, but he thought it would all blow over and next day he would get a letter from Hester berating him for being unfaithful and telling him she never wanted to see him again — ever."

She obviously did not know my daughter very well.

"But, what happened. Just after tea a taxi draws up at the front door. Tony was at the flowerbeds but before any of us could do anything, Hester was chasing the boy across the lawn armed with a garden fork. Fortunately he can run faster than she and when she collided with a wheelbarrow, Freddie was on hand to take her into custody. She screamed abuse at all of us and was shaking with rage so we thought it best to let her lie down for a while."

"And I locked the door", said the old soldier.

We did not stay the night. We took her home. Jennifer and I had decided to leave the post-mortem until the following day but in any case she sat in the back seat and did not utter one word for the whole journey — and refused cocoa by a shake of the head. We met at breakfast. I do not know why but I thought the occasion called for kedgeree. Jennifer and I had decided what our joint approach was to be.

"You have my blood running through your veins. If you were more like Jennifer, you would not have acted as you have done."

"Correct, but do not let your father give you the wrong impression. I fell deeply in love with Byron, and I think it happened when we first met at that Christmas party, and then I fell again. What other reason could there be for me to agree to marry PG."

"The point is, my life to-date has not run on conventional lines. I have told you how I was so attracted to Simóne and she was far from being pretty. Not like you at all. So I know about things irrational, but you are only sixteen."

"I hope you're not going to tell me all about how when you were my age you left your bed at four in the morning to work sixteen hours a day in the bakehouse — or about going barefoot to school. In the snow."

"No, I'm not. You will go to university. You don't really know this boy. Did you really want to get married?"

"Not now. He's horrid. Fancy me thinking I could rely on him. He's a toad."

"Hester. You have to think before you act, particularly where emotions are concerned. I have not wanted to tell you this before, but you grandmother was very like you at your age, so I think you have to guard very carefully against over-reacting when you think love has struck you down."

I told her about a prop forward, Frank Sinatra, and how her wayward ancestor had been rescued by a hat blown away in a strong wind. As I finished, she stood up and kissed us both. She had not eaten any of the kedgeree on her plate.

Half terms for Edward and Hester did not always coincide and on one occasion, when this was the case, I decided to take the young rebel for a few days to the Owens. I suppose I thought the view from a bedroom at the Kings Arms would do her good; she might appreciate how privileged she is. My supposition was wrong. She may be wayward, but she is not stupid, and not without sensitivity. The excursion was a great success, even if she did get cross when told she could not go down the mine.

I saw a new face to the girl. She was just at home with the Owens as she was at Flintoff Manor or with the Flowers, parents of a girl in her class who lived in a house in Regent's

Park with an indoor swimming pool. The Owens now had three children; my godson who was nine and twin sisters of six years of age. All three went to the village school and when we were there Hester went with them and, by arrangement with the head teacher, was allowed to help. Thomas told his mother that his new friend Hest — as he called her — told the class some wonderful stories of a horse that was a ghost and about a poor flower girl who lived in Paris. You can imagine my reaction to this news

There had been some other changes with the Owens, in addition to the twins. Jack had become a full-time union official with the South Wales Miners Federation and the family had moved out of the back-to-back house on the hillside and now occupied the residential space above the shop. Bronwen Meredith still owned this, and was behind the counter on most days, but she had moved back to live with her daughter, who was now also a widow; her husband had died in middle age with lung disease. Before that sadness, Beth Owen, when all three children were at school, worked in the shop for a few hours a day but as Bronwen moved back to live with her daughter, Beth became more or less full-time, and when Jack discarded his pit boots, the kind lady offered them the rooms over the shop. Altogether a very satisfactory outcome for the Owens and the small wage Beth had for shop-keeping helped to bridge the difference between the stipend of an under-manager at the pit and the smaller pay packet the union could afford.

In my view, Jack was very fortunate to have Beth. Whenever we met she always pulled my leg about how it was her cheering for Cardiff City that brought the FA Cup to Wales — not that they kept it very long. She could be light-hearted about things in general, but there was much more to her than that. She had lived all her life in this valley. Her father, and his, had been miners and the poverty they endured was just as pronounced, if not more so, in her own generation. But, from this background had arisen a woman who deeply cared for people and had an intuitive intelligence that not everyone saw. Hester did. She asked me to explain how a woman who left school at the age of thirteen was so wise. I replied; I do not have an answer, but what I do know is that like attracts like and that Jack and Beth were clearly destined for each other. I forbore to say that such was not the case with Hest and Antonio.

Jack was still the optimist I had first met in the bar at the Kings Arms nearly ten years ago. Conditions for miners in South Wales were deteriorating and unemployment levels continued to rise but he was still confident of the merit of the commission set up in 1934 to see what could be done to improve conditions in four distressed areas of the kingdom, South Wales being one. I was not so sure. If new employment opportunities were to be introduced, these would take time to come to fruition and in the meantime, I could see the poverty in this valley as clearly as everyone.

He did not avoid his responsibilities by escaping to Spain. It was simply fundamental; he considered he had to join with other workers to fight against Fascism. I could not understand this. As I have said, if it was not for Jennifer's pacifist principles, she would have joined him, but not me. Surely Jack's fight was against capitalism? Why should he care about the political changes taking place in Germany and Italy and now Spain? He had never travelled out of Britain. He rarely left South Wales. No holidays on the Riviera or at Abersoch for him — so why would he risk the possibility of Beth becoming a widow, and his children fatherless, in a battle to defend Madrid.

Perhaps it is impossible to explain his motivation. Like many of our generation — he was only seven years younger than me — we were directly aware of the losses incurred in the World War. Jack could list seven members of the extended Owen family who had been killed and so all I can offer is that he saw Fascism as an international threat and that it was his duty to oppose this to avoid a repeat of the last war. At the outset it was as simple as that. Beth tried to persuade him not to go, but retreated when she saw how determined he was — and I suppose she understood his reasoning better than me. I also told him not to go, but in my case I was not diverted and continued my opposition until the day of his departure. He did hesitate for a while; it was January 1937 before he left Wales.

As a result of Jack's involvement, Jennifer and I followed the events in Spain in even closer detail.

Some arrangements had obviously been made within the International Brigade so that its members could send and receive letters. The last one Beth had from Jack was in March telling her he was still at the training depot but was likely to be moved to a front-line position shortly. She read the newspapers, as we did, and as news came in of fierce fighting, and no further letters, she became very concerned. There was now a telephone installed at the Kings Arms and in May she made use of it. She was distraught. Unusually, her speech was hurried and partly incoherent. I did not seem to be able to interrupt her flow to say anything and then, we said the same thing — together.

"I will go and see what the position is."

"Will you go and find out what has happened?"

With a coincidence like that, how could I do other than what I did? Jennifer agreed, and so I found myself once again following in the footsteps of Mr Hemingway. He had gone to Spain to report on the conflict for the North American Newspaper Alliance but he also used this opportunity to provide the background to his novel, *For Whom the Bell Tolls,* one of his works I do admire, particularly as I could empathise with Richard Jordan. Not that I was subjected to the same sort of action as he, but we came to share the same cup of pessimism that this conflict eventually brewed.

The stand of the British press on Spain varied. The *Daily Mail* favoured Franco while the *News Chronicle* supported the Republicans. The *Daily Herald* printed only Republican news but the *Daily Express* and the *Daily Mirror,* although having similar sympathies, believed nothing should be done to provoke Germany and Italy. The *Daily Telegraph* and *The Times* attempted to be impartial.

It was some years since Jennifer had been on the staff at the *Daily Herald* but the current Foreign Editor was her most particular friend. I asked if this had begun at the newspaper's Christmas party, or during a joint visit to Jarrow, but I did not get what I thought was a satisfactory answer. However, what I did get was a press pass and a letter accrediting me as a temporary war correspondent commissioned to write a series of articles on whether the British members of the International Brigade were being properly fed and watered and whether any of them had been won over to the delights of gazpacho or paella. Of course, the letter did not exactly say that, rather less detail: 'To observe the impact of the International Brigade on this conflict...' — or something like that. It was genuine enough, and it worked. No one in Spain questioned my credentials; they were used to having writers and reporters sharing their Rioja.

I must not be frivolous. This was a very serious war and I was on a serious mission. Politics in Spain were confusing and these were exacerbated by the involvement of the church and the army in the very fabric of that country's governance. So different in Britain. Where in Spain the church has a stronger role than in my country, the same could also be said of the communists. Governments were difficult to form. Neither left-wing nor right could obtain a clear majority but in 1936 the Popular Front gained 34% of the votes and the coalition then formed was more to the left than the right. Tensions in the country were rising and two tit-for-tat political assassinations in Madrid in July led to a rising by the army. This *coup d'etat* failed and the war began, Republicans versus Nationalists. Amongst the Republicans were some who favoured a capitalist liberal democracy in contrast to revolutionary anarchists and communists with strong links to Russia. The left-wing faction was mainly secular and urban, but it did include some landless peasants. The Nationalists were easier to define. They were anti-communists and in this they received spiritual support from the Catholic Church and material support from Nazi Germany and Fascist Italy.

I went to my battleground scenario via Paris; the usual route taken by volunteers joining the International Brigade. I was held up there for two days and so used this opportunity to visit Marguerite. When she came to the door and saw me, she lifted her chin to show me a beaming face. She hugged me to her chest and in excited tones told me she had heard from Simóne. No actual appearance, but a long letter.

"You can read it. Came last week. She is fine."

"Where has she been? Why did she not contact us?"

"When she ran away, she could not stay in Paris. She knew very few other places outside the city, but then remembered the holiday you had together. At le Treport. Somehow she managed to get there. Train, I suppose. Went to the same hotel and found work in the bar. Stayed there for some years. Then met an artist. In that bar. Irishman. They married and have two children. Have moved to Boulogne. She says she was too ashamed to write before. Reading between the lines I think she needed to be totally easy within herself before she came out into the open. Here, read exactly what she writes — but in the envelope was a sealed message that she asked me to send to you. As you will see, she tells me that she has written to try and explain her actions. An *Épilogue du Coeur*, as she calls it."

I read Simóne's letter as Marguerite and I drank together the bottle of champagne I had brought with me. Simóne's other missive I took back to the hotel and opened in the solitude of my room.

My dear Percy
I pray to God you are reading what I have written.

I have spent ten years composing these lines in my head, but even now as I put them down on this paper, I realise how inadequate they are. How difficult explain.
Difficult. Impossible to explain myself. So much hard to make you understand. Even if you do not, I beg that I can be forgiven. I cannot forgive myself until you do the same.
I am happy. I have kind husband and little boy and girl. But why not with you?
Can you understand my guilt? I acted very badly and killed our daughter. You were so nice but I had found myself guilty. I had to be punished. You should have hated me. That would be good punishment. But you did not. You still loved me so I decided I needed to deny that love. Throw it away. Was only way I could pay for my sin.
After all these years, I think that is why. But you know how my mind plays strange tricks sometimes so am I really sure I found that right answer. I hope so. Cannot think of another reason. I had to say sorry, but words were not enough. I know what I did hurt you, just as much as it made me so unhappy, but I could not help it. It was like those people of God who beat themselves with whips.
I know I should have written this down and got it to you somehow many years ago, but I was so worry this would make you hate me even more. I am a coward and full of shame.
My dear love. I hope you are happy now like me. I have explained everything to my husband, and he helped me write this letter.
I sorry for the grief I cause Marguerite as well. I shall write to her from now on, very often. She has my address but I am sure it would be better for you and for me if we do not meet.
I remember you so well. Are you still trying to cook like French man?
I will never, never forget you. I think you saved my life. Perhaps I should go back to Notre Dame to thank Holy Mary.
Simóne

*Alan Shelley*

I read this testimony again. Was testimony the right word? Why was it written in English? The letter to Marguerite had of course been in French. I found it difficult to decide how I felt. Old wounds re-opened. My immediate reaction was one of anger. I suppose I had in my mind consigned Simóne to a cell of oblivion; all alone and unhappy. How dare she be a conventional married woman with two children, and half Irish at that? She deserted me. She does not deserve what she now has; but then I realised how mean-spirited these thoughts were. I did a *volte face*. Pleased that she is happy — like me. Glad I can visualise her life, rather than the limbo of before. Should we meet? For the moment I returned her letter to its envelope, determined to concentrate on Jack Owen and his family until I could talk to Jennifer about this surprising turn of events.

I decided I must first go to Albacete which, from the outset, had been chosen as the headquarters for the International Brigade. This brigade was an extraordinary phenomenon. It came into existence, mostly because of the influence of Russia, but people from many other countries, Jack Owen included, joined. There were a variety of motivations for this but the most satisfying reason for the majority was to prevent the Fascist barricade, which now stretched from Hamburg to the toe of Italy, from being extended into Spain. The International Brigade is perhaps better known than it deserves because of the anti-fascist writers and intellectuals, who rallied to the cause, but the facts are that 80% of those that came from Britain were manual workers. Many of them were unemployed or trade union members or communists. In total there were over thirty thousand volunteers from fifty three countries which led some observers to refer to this action as a 'World War in miniature'.

The brigade headquarters at Albacete had been set up in what were formerly the barracks of the Nationalist Civil Guard. I could not have been prepared for what I found. The only comparison I had was the regimental depot in Gloucester and the officer's mess near Arras, but these places were as far removed from those in Spain as could be imagined. I hardly dared think what Colonel Kim's reaction would have been. At the training depot there was a joke, with some truth to it, that if it moved, salute it; if it did not move, whitewash it. At Albacete I saw few salutes and no whitewash. I was later informed that when the first volunteers arrived they crowded into the upper quarters because the rooms on the ground floor were still stained with the blood of the Civil Guard, killed at the beginning of the uprising. I did not see any blood stains, but they could have been hidden under the dirt.

My press pass got me past the guard room without comment and a disreputable looking pale-faced young man was detailed to take me to the Commandant's office. I guessed he came from somewhere in Eastern Europe. I realised that most of the men were at the front line, wherever that was at the moment, but I was depressed at the general overall impression of neglect — and lassitude. There were a few personnel on view either slouched against walls or lying prone within the shadow those walls provided. It was difficult to tell whether they were soldiers or just camp followers; not one wore identical clothing with his fellow. There was an obnoxious smell. If there was a sanitation system it was not working, and had clearly not worked for some considerable time. I assumed there had been a party the night before because in the corner of one of the courtyards we passed through was a pile of empty, and mostly broken wine bottles from which emanated a sweet and sickly odour that made an unsatisfactory partner to Messrs. Shit and Urine.

I never did discover the name of the officer left in charge of that shambolic place, but he had sufficient wit to know what a press pass was and he knew enough words of French to understand my questions about Jack Owen. As I presented these he barked at a man, I assumed to be a clerk, whose head was resting on a desk that had only three legs; a pile of books kept it from collapsing. This man appeared to be fast asleep but stirred himself when he heard his master's voice and fetched from a cupboard a box of bedraggled index cards and dropped them in front of the officer like a coal merchant delivering a hundredweight of coal.

I was informed: 'Training completed. Appointed Lance Corporal. Posted to the 35th Division under General Walter in Madrid.' Nothing more was said. I could not get out of the place quick enough; and I then went to the Spanish capital.

Those newspaper correspondents with a generous expense allowance were quartered at the Ritz. I found more modest accommodation but was delighted to encounter in the bar at that grand hotel, one Gerald Bloomer, the *Daily Telegraph* reporter I had met in Berlin the year before. Obviously the Berry family thought one of their senior foreign correspondents would be better employed, for the moment, in Madrid rather than the German capital. I bought him a drink and asked what he knew about the International Brigade, and in particular, the 35th Division. He appeared to be very well informed.

He told me it was fairly common knowledge that the Republicans were planning a major campaign to take Brunette, fifteen miles west of Madrid. This town occupied a strategic position on the Extremadura road and if taken by the Republicans could hinder the Nationalists sending reinforcements to their soldiers besieging the capital. Bloomer also asserted that the Republicans thought a major offensive of this kind might persuade the French they were a serious and potent force and that consequently the border with France should be opened for the supply of armaments.

Useful information, or was it? I was not too interested in military tactics or any political overtones to such military activities. I needed to find Jack and see if he was safe. I may not have shown much interest then in what I had been told by Bloomer, but I needed to be more concerned when I found myself dodging bullets.

*I Never Met Ernest Hemingway*

Bloomer was content to report the situation to his masters from the bar at the Ritz but he arranged for me to be taken to the front by a young and more adventurous reporter who worked for *Le Figaro*. He was only slightly more knowledgeable than me on affairs military, but he did manage to find the headquarters of the 35th Division where I was fortunate to quickly become acquainted with another Welshman, called Rogers. He was happy to tell me what was happening when he discovered my father was one of his countrymen and became even more cooperative when I presented him with two small cigars that I had brought for him. Well, not specifically for him. Bloomer had told me that tobacco, in any form, was a useful currency at the front, and so it proved. I had a box of twenty five.

On the subject of the Welsh, I did not think this the time or place to repeat to Rogers the story about the bigot who goes into a bar and after a few drinks says in a loud voice that the Welsh are all either rugby players or whores. At this, a very large man standing next to him says: 'Watch it mate, my wife is Welsh'. Quick as a flash our man replies and asks what position does she play?

It was impossible to tell from this Welshman's garb whether he was a harlot or a scrum-half or a private or a general. I supposed the bottom half of his uniform had, at some stage in the past, been a pair of riding breeches of a rather extravagant cut but now, somewhat surprisingly, one leg of the garment was a shade of blue and the other, apple green. I do not think the boots matched either. The shirt would have done well on the beaches at Biarritz but it was only partly visible because my latest Welsh acquaintance wore, despite the heat, a khaki coloured woollen scarf of such a length that it was able to circumnavigate his neck and trunk at least a dozen times.

If his uniform did not identify him, he soon banished my ignorance. He was, so he proudly informed me, a member of the British Communist Party, but now enjoyed the title of Lieutenant Hugh Rogers with an important role in the 'Q' section at headquarters responsible for keeping the fighting troops supplied with bullets and rations, particularly the wine. I told him of my professional interest in all matters concerned with food — and drink — and asked him what he had eaten for breakfast. This opened the conversational floodgates. By the time he had explained, in excruciating detail, about horsemeat, rotten potatoes, sour wine and how he pined, like Ben Gun, for a piece of cheese, we were firm friends. I then asked if he knew Jack Owen. He did, and as he was about to deliver some porridge oats and a box of grenades to the front line, I could accompany his detail and see Lance Corporal Owen in the flesh. Was he wounded? Not as far as Rogers could recall.

And that is when I found the bullets. I thought back to Arras. The machine gun we eventually silenced — no thanks to me — was expertly fired but at this site of conflict there appeared to be no evidence of soldierly professionalism. It was July; the sun was hot and our route uneven and hazardous. Shell craters were in prominent evidence. They had clearly been utilised as rubbish dumps; ammunition boxes, shell casings, torn sandbags, a variety of broken digging tools and several battered bicycles. In addition they were home for a specie of rats, the like of which I had never seen before in my life. Not that I am an expert on such rodents, but some of these I met on my way were nearly as big as Jack Russell terriers, and twice as fierce. They seem to be attracted to my footwear — a fresh leather, new to their menus. They were not disturbed by the bullets, but I was.

As we reached the front line where the Republican troops were dug in and the Nationalists counter-attacking, or so I was told, a grenade, presumably one of the enemies, flew over my head and exploded in one of the shell craters I had recently avoided. It disturbed the debris somewhat but worst of all fragments of rat were included in the shower that fell around us. By now I could hear the exchange of rifle fire. Bullets were criss-crossing the area; some straight up to the sky while others were bedded in the earth or skewed away at an acute angle — just like my Arras projectile. The noise was deafening and yet no one paid any attention. It seemed to be assumed that none of the missiles would actually find a man as a target although, to be fair, as far as I could see most of the forces on both sides were well below ground level. Rifles were discharged at the enemy by pointing them over the parapet and firing at random. Targets were not identified — too dangerous. Snipers they were not.

While Rogers was meeting with the officer in charge I decided, on the spur of the moment, to try the direct approach. I cried out, as loud as I could above the noise of battle: 'Corporal Jack Owen. To the rear. At once.' It worked. I could hardly recognize him, but as the creature staggered towards me and referred to me as, 'Percy the bread', I assumed I had found my quarry. He was thin, he was unshaven and he was very dirty. He smelled of cordite and sweat. Although, as he told me later, he had only been in combat for five days, it had been continuous with no chance to bathe, or sleep for that matter.

"Fancy seeing you here. Have you joined the Brigade?"

"Not on your life. I've come to find out why you have not been writing to Beth, although the powers-that-be think I am a newspaper reporter."

"You what. You come all this way to see me. My CO and my mates will think I have a mad man for a friend. In any case, I write every week."

"So you say, but do you post them?"

For a moment both of us looked at each other and grinned and then simultaneously had the same thought. What were we doing discussing a postal service in the middle of a battle?

"Let's get you under cover."

I was dragged into a trench that led to a deep hole, partly covered over, where Lt Rogers and the officer in charge were drinking some colourless liquid that smelt putrid. Before introductions could be made I brought out my box of cigars, whereupon Rogers, the CO and Jack took it in turns to clap me on the back. Another explosion seemed close at hand but this did not deter any of the trio from lighting up and puffing away like members of the Travellers Club calling for a glass of port to go with their smoke. I thought it best not to discuss with the two officers any complaint about the local postman.

I stayed with Jack and his section for lunch, their next meal. It was truly horrible; a stew of distinctly dubious provenance. I hoped it did not include the flesh of the rat. As we ate the shells and bullets provided us with background music for our repast but shortly thereafter Jack's troop was replaced and we all retreated to some farm buildings at the rear taken over for use by reserve forces. I say all, but Jack could not help himself but tell me of his comrades who were now dead; men from all over Europe. Madness, I said to myself.

When away from the noise of conflict, Jack and I indulged in another foray into the cigar box.

"Has it been worthwhile, Jack?"

"Percy. I'm going to come home soon. Tell Beth I am unharmed, at least in the body. I must tell you. In Spain the men I have met are as wide a mixture of saints and sinners that you can imagine. Perhaps it was to be expected. Were we all clear as to our motives? My letters. I can now see they have been deliberately destroyed. That man in the Company office was worse than Richards the Shop. He was taking money from the men to make sure they were excused guard duty. I told him he was a disgrace. He did not like that. Took his revenge. Destroyed my letters. You wait until I catch up with the bastard. I'll stuff his guard duty roster down his throat."

"Beth should be there to help you, but back to my first question. As you know, I was always unsure whether the cause was worth fighting for."

"If I was to now agree with you I would be angry and disillusioned. But I do not. Well, not altogether. In principle I would fight again to prevent Fascism taking hold, but the problem is we're all human with all our human failings and frankly, I've seen too many failings."

"I suppose I saw that in the last war."

"I accept the situation. I am not naive, but the rules have changed. This is not a case of the workers of the world joining together to defeat tyranny — if it ever was. No. The influence of the Communists, particularly the influence of Russia, has distorted things."

"I heard a similar view from some of the journalists I met in Madrid."

"Just so, but I am giving you the view from the front line, as it were, from the ordinary man, the foot-soldier. The Russians are not interested in the Spaniards. They want to spread their doctrine all over the world — and are their politics really any better than the Fascists? I believe in self-help. I believe that I can better myself and help my fellow colliers without bringing everyone down to the lowest common denominator. The Spanish peasant has been downtrodden for centuries by the landlords and the church and I am willing to shed my blood for them, but not for Mr Stalin. Percy. I don't think the war in Spain is going to curb Hitler and Mussolini. I don't want my boy fighting Germany again, but I think it might happen. Oh God. We've heard all this before. I'm tired, and I'm hungry."

I gave him another cigar

The Republicans did reach Brunette, but it was soon recaptured by the Nationalists. Like in my war, losses were heavy on both sides, just to gain a few yards of ground but of course, in this case, the land gained or lost, was Spanish soil. They were both fighting over their own land. The Republicans also lost a lot of equipment in the campaign and were never able to obtain control of the Extremadura road. Jack told me later that some sections of the International Brigade refused to continue to fight because of failures of leadership, a not unusual complaint.

The war dragged on until 1939. In February of that year the UK and France recognized Franco and the Nationalists and the Republican forces surrendered two months later.

Alan Shelley

There was a frightful aftermath. Republican supporters were imprisoned and many thousands executed.

Somehow Jack and I instinctively came to the decision not to hold any post mortems. What was the use? Jack had seen the horrors — and the eventual futility of it all — at first hand. The pacifist Jennifer did not want to say: 'I told you so', and I remembered the stories of the men killed by Jack's side. I simply thanked God for his safe return but many years later I visited the *Valle de los Caidos* — the Valley of the Fallen — built by Franco between 1940 and 1958 to commemorate those who died in the Civil War. It is a massive basilica, carved into the Guadarrama Mountains. Very impressive. Above it stands the tallest memorial cross in the world, over one hundred and fifty metres high, but to what memory? When its construction is taken into account, it seemed to me that this edifice was more a monument to the folly of the Spanish Civil war than a memorial to those who died: as ostensibly it is, but mainly for the Nationalists, and Franco, his last resting place. It was built using forced labour from the Republican ranks, twenty thousand of them.

Before I returned to England, I made enquiries about the conditions of service for the volunteers who had joined the International Brigade and as far as I was able to ascertain there were no formal contracts in place. Whatever, before the end of the year Jack had negotiated his release, whether above the board or by subterfuge I do not know, but he was home to spend Christmas with his family. Jennifer and I sent them a large hamper to assist Beth in her campaign to add some pounds to the weight of the somewhat emaciated husband who had been returned to her. She was delighted to have him back but in the future, whenever she became angry with him, she always questioned the story about the company clerk and accused Jack of not writing to her.

Once Jennifer and I were satisfied that, but for some last-minute changes, Jack would soon be back home, we talked about Simóne. My dear wife understood my ambivalence;

anger or relief; action or leave well alone. I think her most telling argument included the words 'sleeping dogs' and I could only agree with her. A meeting would achieve nothing. It was not as if we were just old friends who had drifted apart. The loss of our daughter and the mother's vanishing act were too traumatic to treat like an old boy's reunion. I replied to Simóne's letter. I spent some time on its composition. I wanted to be sincere, but I wanted her to agree with me, as I think she had already done, that we should say goodbye as tenderly, but as finally, as possible.

There was no further contact but many years later I dreamt about her, most vividly, and thereafter the dream was repeated every six months or so. Do you recall the heavenly scenes in the 1946 film: *A Matter of Life and Death*? David Niven and Kim Hunter. Simóne and I occupy a similar landscape. She is dressed from head to toe in a sparkling white dress and she is young, no more than twenty. We do not speak. We hold hands and walk through the white mist until we reach a beach, but it is not at le Treport, it is at Abersoch.

But back to the real world. Angela suggested I should try writing for radio. Francis Durbridge had come up with a detective called Paul Temple and listeners seemed to like these stories. I told her I thought them rather crass, particular the man's wife, Steve, who sounded too precious for words. I can hear her voice still; full of enthusiasm and excitement: made one immediately feel tired. As usual, Angela poured scorn on my views — talked about money — and so I gave it a go but the BBC thought Herbert Montcalm was too sophisticated, being 'French and all' as they described him. Well, of course he is French. He's a chef, for goodness sake. Nevertheless, I conceived of an English detective who was also a doctor and wrote a few radio plays in what I liked to think was the style of Dashiell Hammett. None were broadcast, but I was paid and it gave me a foot in the door, so to speak. I then wrote two romantic pieces about Paris and a courtroom drama about a confidence trickster and Reith's successors seemed to prefer these to my detective stories. So, the listening public heard of Glossop for the first time and I bought Jennifer a string of pearls with some of the proceeds. Actually, that is not quite accurate. They were ignorant of the very existence of PG; at Angela's suggestion I entered into the world of radio as Curt Jameson. Glossop would put people off, she said.

They did however like the sound of the name Bob Patch. When he was acting in London he found a second string to his bow with radio. I would often hear his voice while in my kitchen engaged in the delicate operation of perfect mayonnaise manufacture, or when introducing the cloves to a firm knuckle of ham. He performed in radio plays, or narrated books, but I always knew it was him even before the cast list or reader was announced. I had, after all, been listening to him from the time he moaned at me for bowling down the leg side but, at this time, there was another development in his career; the cinema. The British movie industry in the late 1930s had its ups and downs, but Bob found a niche for himself as, later on, so did I. Well, to some extent.

Enough about the arts. In the real world, even if I wanted to reverse the decision made more than two years ago about visiting Simóne, it would now be difficult to do so; she is behind enemy lines. Ever since Jennifer and I went to Berlin, and Chamberlain returned from Munich, we had been apprehensive and now our worst fears have come to pass. We are again at war with Germany. Jennifer's disgust at this, as well as her immense sorrow and regret, was distilled into a series of vehement articles written for publication in the American press. These deplored the path leaders had taken, going back to 1919, and after Pearl Harbour they were published in book form in the USA under the title of: *The Monstrous Tragedy of Europe.*

And, should my grandchildren one day say to me: 'What did you do in the war, Grandaddy', I shall be forced to admit that, at least initially, I wore a tin hat and tried to monitor Hitler's air raids on London; specifically, the areas of Maida

Vale, Swiss Cottage and St John's Wood. I was a member of the ARP — an air raid warden. I had hoped the authorities might have billeted us at Lords, but no such luck. We used the hall attached to a Methodist Church, just off the Finchley Road.

*Alan Shelley*

*When we were young we always spent Christmas with Auntie Cis. We were poor, as we still is, but they were happy times, mainly because of Uncle George. He had every one in fits of laughter. Not funny jokes, or funny faces. He just seemed to be a bundle of happiness within himself. Some people are made that way. Percy is more complex. He tries to give the impression that he is a bit of a 'dilettante'. The minister used that word last week and I looked it up in Thomas's dictionary. It means 'not serious'. This is what he wants to present to most people, but he is not really like that. When you see him and Jennifer together, she seems to be the forceful one, the one who cares about the workers and the threat of another war, but I see beyond that. They suit each other perfectly, but under the 'gay' exterior of PG — as they call him now — there is one of the most caring people you could ever want to know. Not just because he went to Spain when I was so worried about Jack — went at the drop of hat, as they say — but for all the little things. He always makes me feel like a Duchess. He certainly has a way with the women, but he is always so kind. Never hurtful. Perhaps it comes from loving the kitchen so much. That daughter of his — she is so like him. Thomas adores her.*

Beth Owen May 1939

# Chapter Nine

## London

*Fried Pilchards on Fried Bread*

*1 tin pilchards, 15-oz size; 4 slices of bread; fat for frying if necessary.*

*Fry the pilchards till brown on both sides. They should be sufficiently oily to fry without extra fat. Remove from the pan and keep hot. Add a little extra fat, if necessary, to fry the slices of bread till golden brown on both sides. Divide the pilchards on to the 4 slices of fried bread and serve hot.*

## Film

I could just about remember 1914 and the start of that war but 1939 was very different, at least those of my circle thought so. All the world had seen Hitler in action; reoccupying the Rhineland, invading Czechoslovakia and now Poland, but Jennifer and I considered that our short experience of Berlin in 1933 had given us an insight into the ambitions of the Third Reich that were not necessarily apparent to others. I was still only forty one and so I assumed I would soon be in uniform again but until then I was content to contribute with a role as an ARP warden. At least there was no bayonet included in the equipment and uniform issued for that duty, but like many, particularly Londoners, we were not spared the horrors. The opening scene and sounds are familiar to most of you:

the siren, the searchlights, the black-out, the rationing, the evacuees and the square brown cardboard box containing the gas mask that we never used. And the words: 'Careless talk costs lives.' 'Is your journey really necessary?' 'Dig for victory.' — and, later on, '...we shall fight them on the beaches, we shall fight on the landing grounds, we shall fight in the fields and in the streets, we shall fight in the hills; we shall never surrender....' There were no beaches for me — it was the destruction on the streets that I was about to experience.

While wearing my ARP helmet — they were painted black — I was to witness the beginning of the attack on London by the Luftwaffe but it was not until I visited the East End that I saw the full extent of the tragedy. Just after forty people had died in one air raid shelter, I went to Plaistow with Bert, the doorman at Wymering. We were both off duty and he asked if I would go with him to check on his father, an ex-docker, who lived on his own. Mother had died before the outbreak of the war. We walked there. It was a long way but I was not sure what the public transport situation was and I had no petrol for the car. In any case, we welcomed the exercise.

It was a clear autumnal day but the smoke and dust rising from the ruined buildings we passed was thick enough to inhibit the rays of the sun as they gallantly attempted to bring some cheer to the sorry scene. It was an extraordinary sight. Some areas were untouched and others so damaged you could not tell whether the original structures had been of three storeys or ten. Volunteers were clearing up the debris, or searching for survivors, but most of the populace were busy with their everyday tasks. The milkman was late, as was the paperboy, but shops were open, and trading, and the queue at the butchers' establishment seemed no longer, or shorter, than normal.

There was inevitably an air of gloom and doom. We saw no cadavers but many people had died, or were seriously injured. The raid on London of the 7th of September caused a thousand fires, over four hundred deaths and one thousand six hundred were seriously injured. And that was just the start. From 1940 until May 1941, the period that became known as the 'Blitz', the RAF blunted the attacks on Britain by the Luftwaffe but at times many people wondered if we would be able to carry on. It is pointless to speculate whether we would have survived if Hitler had invaded this 'demi-paradise' instead of turning his attentions towards Russia, but what I saw during my ARP days did make me believe we were close to the brink.

Bert's father had been lucky: his little house was intact. Good fortune was the only sure defence any of us had. Our fighter aircraft gave Jerry hell but we could not fully protect ourselves once the bombs had been jettisoned. The Government had done their best. Brick and concrete air raid shelters had been built and it was reported that over a million Anderson ones had been issued throughout the country. There was also the Morrison type used inside the house; a bit like a reinforced table. For Londoners, the Underground stations were widely used but Bert's Dad had stayed in the house during last night's raid.

"The Boche didn't get me in the last lot — and they're not this time. Two fingers to 'em."

"You and Mrs Temple next door seem to have been the only house in one piece on this street. Next time they come, you must go to the shelter."

"All right, Bert. I might be able to get Edie Temple in a dark corner."

"You behave yourself. I've brought you some Guinness."

"Well done, lad. How you doing up West? Maida Vale still there?"

"Yes. We've had our share, but our blocks not been touched. Mr Glossop lives in number three."

"Pleased to meet you I'm sure. You in the last lot?"

"Sort of. Now you do as Bert says and go to the shelter."

"Do you?"

"Well, not every night, I must confess."

Inconsequential chat, but whomever I met during that visit had the same attitude. Considering the devastation, the spirit was extraordinary. The King had been to see the damage in the East End; great morale booster and Winnie of course had risen to the occasion brilliantly. We were all now finding it necessary to begin a revision of our former opinions on Mr Churchill.

The courage of those East Enders was beyond anything I had witnessed before, or could even comprehend. My experience of intense warfare was extremely limited, but I had seen men in Spain who volunteered to face danger so what they saw as an evil force could be thwarted, but these Londoners had no choice. They were unwilling participants in this one-sided conflict against an enemy they could not even see. There was ingenuity as well. Bert told me that even before the war the Home Office had, through the relevant union, asked London taxi drivers not to volunteer for the armed forces as their knowledge of the streets of the capital would be valuable if the city was bombed. How foresighted. Many of these cockney cabbies performed superbly as they drove fire engines, ambulances and other vehicles bringing assistance to the areas of devastation caused by Hitler's bombs.

Bert's father was killed the next time bombs were dropped on Plaistow. I did not have the heart to ask Bert whether his father had gone to the shelter or not.

Angela Warren's office was in Connaught Square, convenient for Kensington where she lived. I was a frequent visitor, the coffee was very good, but on this occasion I met her close by in answer to a telephoned summons.

"Percy. When are you next off duty? I have something very interesting to discuss with you."

"What is it?"

"Can't talk about it on the phone."

"Top secret?"

"Yes, or nearly so."

"I get a twenty four hour break this Thursday."

## I Never Met Ernest Hemingway

"Busy all that day. What about the evening? Why don't you take me to supper at the Bayswater Hotel. About seven."

"I bet the cooking will be lousy, but I am prepared to risk that. You've got me intrigued. What a mystery. Should I come in disguise?"

"Stop playing the fool. This is serious."

I had first been introduced to Angela nearly fifteen years ago when our earliest encounters had been rather fraught. She was often over-critical of my writing and I thought she was inclined to be somewhat snobbish — pretensions of grandeur — but as time went by our relationship improved. Still haughty sometimes, but she was smart. There were no children and so her considerable energies were concentrated on the business. She had kept this small. In her opinion the strength of the literary agent is the personal contact with the writers and those who brought our wares and I suppose I was lucky to have her. She rated Peter's poetry very highly and I often felt, at least initially, that she only tolerated me because of him. As my output became more varied, tolerance became an agreeable acceptance. After all, she earned considerably higher fees from my rubbish than she did from Peter. As her reputation had blossomed, her husband, Charles Warren CMG, had progressed through the ranks of the civil service and the last time I enquired I was told he was something senior in the Ministry of Information.

The meal was execrable but the topic discussed over the fishcakes was an exciting one.

"I'm here under false pretences."

"I always knew it. You're a spy. Are you one of ours?"

"I'll ignore that. What I mean, I have been asked to approach you by Charlie."

"Chaplin?"

"No, be serious. By my husband, or more accurately, by His Majesty's Government."

"You want me to be a spy."

"Charlie is involved, within the War Office and the Ministry of Information, in propaganda and they are recruiting outsiders to help them, specifically with propaganda films. Writers, artists, filmmakers. We are taking a leaf out of Goebbels' book."

"And I'm chosen?"

"No. Not exactly. I believe Churchill himself will be involved, but because of my connections, Charlie asked if I would approach you. You will need to be vetted, security-wise, and in the end they might not think you are quite suitable, but I've been asked to ascertain whether you would agree for your name to go forward."

"But how did they get my name in the first place? I'm not exactly JB Priestley."

"Well, it was my idea. I have never told you this before but I admired the way you went to Spain to rescue your mining friend and, mainly thanks to Jennifer, I think your political philosophy would fit in well with what Charlie's unit wants to do. If they take you on you'll need to learn some new tricks, but under that light-hearted facade I think there lurks a serious, if not committed, writer. And, you and Jennifer didn't much like what Goebbels was doing when Adolf first came to power, so here's a chance, perhaps, for you to give him a dose of his own medicine."

"Hang on. Are you suggesting I become a civil servant? Paid by the Crown. For goodness sake, I couldn't get away from all that quick enough in 1919. Join up again?"

"Well, think about it. This is going to be a long war. You may not have any choice. You will not be able to hide in your ARP overalls much longer. I can see you in the Catering Corps. You'd love that."

"You win. Okay."

"Let's see if they'll have you first. I'll be in touch."

We left the hotel just as the sirens began. Neither of us took too much notice; we were becoming accustomed. Angela said she would walk home and I did the same. It was mild and the night was clear. There was a full moon.

After my visit with Bert, the East End had continued as the major target but the bombers soon moved on to Central London. In mid-September a bomb hit the Marble Arch Underground station killing seventeen and the following day the John Lewis store in Oxford Street was destroyed. By October around a quarter of a million people in London had been made homeless. This continued throughout November and December and in January this year over a hundred people were killed at the Bank Underground station when it took a direct hit. The raid on the 16th of April was even worse, over a thousand people died and then earlier this month seven hundred tons of bombs were dropped and one thousand five hundred Londoners killed. Since then there seemed to have been a halt, but I did wonder if tonight's siren signalled a resumption of normal service.

As I reached Paddington station I heard the familiar whine in the air followed by a flash and an explosion on the other side of the Harrow Road. This seemed to indicate a rogue bomb; the last message of the night by a Luftwaffe pilot on his way home; his final calling card after a fruitful excursion over the London docks. The streets were not exactly busy. The siren had sounded and many people in the area would have gone to the shelters, whatever their choice: the cupboard under the stairs, the Anderson shelter in the garden or the Warwick Avenue Underground station, but I was not totally alone as I saw debris from the blast rising in the air.

When not on duty, Jennifer and I had given up leaving our bed at the siren's behest. Some sense of fatalism perhaps, or had we become immune to the threat and succumbed to a lassitude that allowed us to just pull the blankets up a little higher. Some others did the same. The Bakers Arms that I had just passed had a knot of people outside, some of whom followed in my wake as I hurried towards the site of the explosion. Because there had been a sequence of bombless nights, when I arrived on the scene there was only a single ARP volunteer there: he was wearing the same tin hat I had sitting at that moment on my hall table. He tried to shepherd me away but when I told him we were brothers in arms, we looked together at the damage.

It had clearly been a single device, and not one of Germany's heaviest. The smoke and dust were already settling and by the light of the moon we could see that the bomb had landed in the street; we stood on the edge of a crater as big as a double-decker bus. The explosion had torn off the front elevation of a pair of three-storey semi-detached houses. The properties on either side appeared to be undamaged, structurally at least, although all of their windows, and of the houses opposite, had been shattered. We went round the crater towards a pile of rubble that had presumably been the front half of the two houses. This pile of debris was higher than me and was still emitting vapours of dust and cordite smelling smoke. The usual problem; what was underneath? Was anyone trapped under the masonry and the flooring timbers and roof rafters? If so, still alive? Instinctively we both began to scrabble and pull aside bricks and timber to see if any cavities were evident but as we did so two more ARP personnel appeared and a policeman. I then looked up at the two houses whose interiors had been laid bare by the blast. At the second floor level I could see a double bed, one end of which was perched precariously over the broken floor and looking as though it would fall over at any moment. I could now see what prevented this happening. Four bodies were bunched together at the far end of the bed providing the counterweight that ensured the seesaw would remain close to the horizontal. For the moment. As I looked again, I saw the occupants of the bed were all children.

I thought of Buster Keaton, or was it Chaplin. The covered wagon, or the bus, or the caravan, halfway over a precipice. We see it threatening to fall as the occupants move towards the cliff, only to be brought back to relative equilibrium as the actors retreat.

I tried to shout for the children to keep still but my mouth was dry with fear. I waved, but then realised that any return of such a gesture could be fatal. I just acted. As I raced up the dark staircase at the rear of the house, it still appeared to be stable, I recalled Arras. Then I had not thought in advance of how I was going to attack that machine-gun post any more than I knew now what I was going to do if I reached the room before the bed fell.

It seemed to take an eternity to climb that stair. My head was spinning. Was this referred to by their parents as: 'The little wooden hill to Bedfordshire?' Where were the parents?

The room had no door but the bed was still there: the moon lit the scene. The children were quiet, except for a community of sobbing. Now what do I do? Grab them one by one and the bed disappears before all are safe. Clearly someone in the quartet had already worked out that any reduction in the counterweight, however minimal, could send the bed on its destined course. I clung to the bed head, anchored my legs to the floor, and strained.

"Well done you kids. Keep still for the moment. Now, carefully, the two on the outside of the bed gently roll out and slide onto the floor, and then stay there."

This was done. Although only a few stone of weight had been lost, I felt the bed pull against my arms.

"Right. I've still got it. You two on the floor, crawl very gently to the back of the room."

They did. Both were crying.

"Now. The two on the bed. Get out as fast as you can and move to the back wall. Ready, steady, go."

As they flung themselves clear the pain in my upper arms became unbearable. I shouted out: 'Watch out below' and then that bloody bed disappeared. Although it was a full double size, the frame and base were of wood, fairly lightweight, and as it crashed to the ground the noise of impact was relatively muted; silenced, perhaps, by the thin mattress. Bought from the Co-op, I wondered. It did not seem to have hit anyone.

I turned and looked at the quartet. They were all wearing identical winceyette pyjamas. Their ages ranged from about six years old to early teens. All were girls, and considering the austerity of the times, well built. Incipient obesity had probably saved their skins. They were huddled together draped around the eldest girl. They were all sobbing, except for her. The relief on her face was clear to see as was the gentle rise and fall of her juvenile breasts under the faded pyjama jacket.

I did not know how safe the house was so I ushered them carefully down the staircase as rapidly as I could and when we reached the bottom I asked who else was in the house. As I did so, a tall woman in a faded nightdress appeared and threw her long arms around the four children. She was not crying quietly, she was shrieking.

I withdrew to join the others searching the rubble. One body had already been found, an old lady. From the disposition of the rubble no one thought it now contained anything other than bricks and timber. The mother came over to me.

"Thank God. You are a saviour Mister. I thought they were going to die."

"Who else was in the house?"

"My mother was in the front bedroom, the girls above. I slept at the back. The other back bedroom is for the lodger, but he's on duty. Hospital porter."

"Lucky man. I'm sorry about your mother."

"Poor love. She refused to go to the shelter, and the kids followed her lead. Little devils. As for me, I was just too tired. It's hard work looking after Mum. She was more or less bedridden — and the mad four are a real handful. Dad's still in hospital. He was at Dunkirk. Due to be released next week."

"How about next door?"

"It's a miracle. They've done a bunk. Midnight flit. Owed bags of rent. Went yesterday."

By this time a senior policeman was there and as he had heard all of this conversation, I thought it was time I went to see if there had been any action a few streets north, at Wymering, and, assuming not, joining my wife in our bed. I bade farewell and the mother grabbed hold of me and kissed me passionately. I got the feeling she was missing her husband. The four girls said nothing, but the youngest waved at me as I left and gave me a very sweet smile. I felt tired but as I wandered home I thought of our children.

At school Edward had been an enthusiastic member of the corp. His soldierly activities had been suspended when he was at Edinburgh University in his first year studying medicine but these studies had also come to an end as he had joined the Army at the outbreak of war. We had not seen him for some time. He was, last we knew, in Cairo. Hester still wanted to be a latter-day Amy Johnson and Jennifer had finally persuaded me to pay for flying lessons. Before she went up to Cambridge, she had been accepted at Girton, there had been insufficient of these to have given her a licence and so, by the early months of 1940, she was in the WAAF and during the Battle of Britain was a member of the ground staff moving models around a gigantic map of the area of conflict.

Angela did not keep me in suspense for long. A short telephone call required me to call and see Charles Warren at a specific time the next day. The address was close to Horse Guards Parade.

On the day before my interview, Bob Patch came for lunch. Interview. Had there been any previous interviews in my life? The recruiting office in Gloucester in 1917; the chat in Colonel Kim's room at the mess; the invitation from Madame Ricard; hardly the best suit and 'sit there please' type of affair. I did have a best suit. Several in fact. Now I could afford Savile Row, I did like to dress well when the occasion demanded. Tomorrow I would be ushered into a large office and faced by at least a tribunal of the 'great and good' who would confirm that I was just the man they were looking for. Over lunch Jennifer and Bob very quickly punctured that balloon. They were a pretty good double act.

"It will be in a cellar dug under the Foreign Office."

"Charlie will get some clerk, an Under-under-Secretary Grade 3 to see you."

"You'll get lost on the way out."

"And don't drink too much before you go in."

"Yes. This is important. Otherwise they'll push you into the Catering Corps in charge of potato peeling."

"You should have had your hair cut."

"And don't come out with any of your supposedly funny jokes."

I just grinned. They were enjoying themselves and I was complimenting myself on the Beef Stroganoff I had cooked. With the almond tart, Jennifer became more serious.

"This could be important work. We're not yet strong enough to batter the Hitler bodies on the ground, but we can attack their minds. You have always had a fertile imagination, PG. How many different crimes has Herbert Montcalm solved? This awful bombing is sapping our strength. It will help if it can be shown in the cinema that we are coping, we are laughing, we are carrying on as usual, and that the enemy is failing. Portraits of the brave few. The Land Girls. Those making munitions."

"I'm not sure Herbert can do that."

"No. But you can. Write a story about Bert's father canoodling with the widow next door, or about the ARP."

"Quite. But there must be lots of more experienced writers out there who would be a better bet."

"PG. I think propaganda films — and stunts — are going to be bigger than you imagine, and they're going to need lots of help."

Bob broke in:

"I think you're right, Jen. I hear Noel is involved, but let me tell you both, I'm off on another tack before they get me back in the trenches. You know Basil Dean? I've been in a few of the plays where he has been the producer; well, he has set up ENSA to provide entertainment for the troops, and I'm joining. See the world without being shot at."

"What will you do? Sing comic songs?"

"No. I expect I shall do extracts from plays — or sketches. Not all of our soldiers are boneheaded you know."

I thought privately that Bob would be a valuable asset — as proved to be the case.

At this juncture in my tale, I realise that I have not told you about Pamela. I suppose, inevitably, Bob married an actress. We liked her and thought they made a good couple but their profession did not provide the stable background to be found in the union of a journalist and a stay-at-home cook. If she and Bob had parts in London, or even in the same play, all was well but so often when Pamela was in Plymouth, he was in Dundee. That, plus the fact that from the outset she decided there would be no children, rather presaged a failure. Bob took it very well. The divorce is through and he simply works harder. And now he is off to bring art and culture to the troops, alongside George Formby and Gracie Fields, who became members of ENSA at the same time as he did. It stands for, rather grandly, Entertainments National Service Association, although some wag substituted: 'Every Night Something Awful'.

I was taken on.

When I presented myself, Angela's husband was not a member of the panel that had the difficult job of passing me in — and then deciding what I should do. Presumably he had bigger fish to fry? Not that I ever saw him in the kitchen but I did meet Jack Beddington who was the Director of the Film division at the Ministry of Information. An important man; not much older than me. Before the war he had been in charge of publicity at Shell. He was a great fan and friend of John Betjeman, and also admired Peter Southern. He was well briefed about me — not that my literary career would take too long to absorb — but we seemed to hit it off from the start. Told me to quit the ARP and report next Monday.

I had to sign a piece of paper based on the regulations to be found in the Official Secrets Act. I did not bother to read before appending my signature but I told Jennifer I had used the name

Herbert Montcalm for this piece of official gobbledygook. She failed to rise to the bait.

At that time the Film unit was busy helping with *Next of Kin* and *Went the Day Well,* being made at Ealing Studios. The first of these had originated within the War Office and dealt with the subject of careless talk. After its release we heard around the office that Lord Alanbrooke had told the director, Thorold Dickinson, that he believed the film would save fifty thousand lives. That was what we were all aiming for.

*Went the Day Well* was concerned with a platoon of soldiers, Royal Engineers, billeted in a typical English village where they are entertained at the vicarage, the manor house and elsewhere, but in due course they prove to be a troop of Germans who had been parachuted in by night. The villagers ignore signs that there are things about this unit that are not quite right, but in the end they defeat the enemy; the moral being — do not be deceived by the church bells and the quiet conservative Britishers — they can be ruthless when necessary.

Of course, I had no experience of filmmaking but as Beddington said at our first meeting: 'Your job is to think'. I was given a tiny office, a battered desk and a share in a secretary and I sat down, and I thought. Plots; themes; ideas; stunts; anything that might be converted into a propaganda weapon.

Do writers only use their own experiences for inspiration? Yes and no. I was an expert when Herbert Montcalm was acting as a chef but when he was solving crimes I had no direct know-how. Should I consider a series about a chef who is a master spy? Gets taken on to the strength of Hitler's entourage and poisons him with lethal fungi? A non-starter, I thought. I then moved on to think of cooperation between our underground movement and that in Paris? Simóne as Mata Hari? Again, not very inspiring, but I was at least thinking.

You will not be surprised that my first serious project was on the subject of food. I thought it might be valuable if the newsreels, Pathe, British Movietone News and Gaumont-

British News had a slot each week showing the housewife a different way of using the family's sparse allocation of butter, lard, eggs, meat, etc. I did not pursue this too assiduously. Like my masters, I thought this would be better suited to radio; as proved to be the case.

My next project came from thoughts of Hester who was certain to be attracting boy friends from amongst our boys in blue. In these hard times, I argued, we needed romance — or even sex, if we could get away with it. The sex angle I soon abandoned. You are allowed to ogle Betty Grable's legs but even at the Windmill the naked flesh on view must not be seen to move — and I was involved with the movies. Romance was the answer; *Target for Tonight* with some love interest. This film was wholly documentary, following a Bomber Command crew and a raid over Germany, but would it have had more propaganda value with a girl in the background?

In the end it was Jennifer who was the inspiration for my first serious piece of work and not Hester. At about this time Jennifer went to New York in connection with the publication of her book, *The Monstrous Tragedy of Europe.* When she returned we inevitably talked about when, if ever, the Americans would enter the war.

"Trouble is, of course, most of the Mid-Westerners don't even know where Europe is. Paris is sex crazy, London is foggy and Birmingham is in Alabama. As for Hitler — no concern of theirs."

"But what does Roosevelt think?"

"He's a politician. Votes. But I would suppose he instinctively wants to help, and I think he and Churchill get on well together. But as you know, the issue is more serious than that. We need them. At best we will be isolated. Hitler will take over Russia and rule Europe from Calais to Vladivostok. And we'll be excluded."

"Gloomy thought."

"We need the Yanks. PG, I know you want to make another *Target for Tonight*, but with a romantic interest. Why not make the girl an American? A young and demure Alice Faye type. That might help. The flower of Yankee womanhood, instilling some courage into our flagging airmen."

"Whitehall will never buy it. We don't get budgets that will stretch to Alice Faye."

"I know. But some young starlet. Blonde, blue eyes and long legs."

"But what is she doing in England?"

"Well, my little genius, that's what you're paid to think out."

Before I give you any details of my effort I must record that using Ministry of Information films to influence opinion in the USA was at the top of the agenda long before I joined. The most important example was a short piece entitled: *London Can Take It.* When viewed today it seems over-sentimental, even naive, as it pictures London during the Blitz with scenes taken from Movietone newsreels, but the most telling feature was that the voice-over was spoken by an American, the veteran correspondent Quentin Reynolds of *Collier's Weekly.*

The film begins at the end of the working day; Londoners queuing for the bus to take them home where they change their city suits for the uniform of the fireman or the air raid warden or ready themselves to spend another night in the shelters. They are referred to, more than once, as 'London's army'. As night falls the commentator says, 'Here they come'. There are then shots of the searchlights, the guns, the bombs falling and the fires started etc. Daylight comes; the city worker goes to his labours and the housewife collects the milk from the doorstep at the same time as she pushes away with her shoe the broken glass that arrived there before the milkman. I discovered later that here was an example of art not reflecting reality when I read the allegation that Quentin Reynolds kept well away from the Blitz, sheltering in the basement at the Savoy.

But, back to my contribution. I spent the next two weeks on an outline screenplay without as yet a suitable title, having already rejected *Soft drinks and hard bombs* or *An American on a bicycle.*

Scene 1
Bombers leaving and returning to a typical RAF base. Shots of tired air crew walking slowly across the tarmac.
Scene 2
Affluent office. American commercial company.
The CEO at his desk interviewing a middle-aged man who sits opposite him. Both have crew cuts and are wearing light coloured formal suits.
CEO
"I know, it sounds mad. Bombs falling all around and we're thinking about building a goddam factory. But the Brits are going to win. They aint been invaded for a million years. And in any case, the Germans like Coke."
Broughton
"What exactly do you want me to do?"
CEO
"The full works. Local tastes. Property law. Construction costs. Labour market."
Broughton
"How long?"
CEO
"Simpson, long as it takes."
Broughton
"There's a problem. Dawn's due to go to Brown next fall. And she doesn't get on with Mabel. The divorce is through, by the way."
CEO
"Good. With all due respects Simp, you should have got rid of her years ago."
Broughton
"I agree. But what do I do with Dawn?"
CEO

"Take her with you. She'll have a ball. All those young men. We can show her in the books as a food parcel sent to our gallant brothers."

Scene 3

Porch. Typical middle-class home in the USA. Simpson Broughton and his daughter are together on the swing seat. She is nineteen, blonde, pretty and self-assured.

*Dawn*

"But I'll be killed. So will you."

*Broughton*

"We shall not be in London. Our man there has rented a cottage close to Newmarket. Roses round the door."

*Dawn*

"To hell with the roses. What about Jake?"

*Broughton*

"He'll be around when you get back. Won't be long. Six months to a year. I can't leave you on your own that long."

*Dawn*

"Why not? Don't you trust to me?"

*Broughton*

"It's not that. I want you with me."

She turns to one side and gives him a hug.

Scene 4

Officers' mess, RAF Mildenhall. About seven or eight tired looking men on view. Someone is playing the piano. A mournful tune. No one is listening. Mostly staring into their pint tankards.

*William Strawson*

"God. That was bloody murder. Don't know how many more of those I can take."

*Rodney James*

"You'll feel better after a few pints. Or a whisky or two."

*Strawson*

"Glad we're off tomorrow. What shall we do?"

*James*

"I'm planning a foray into Newmarket."

*Strawson*
"Got any petrol?"
*James*
"Just about enough. We'll go and see if the landlord's daughter at the Feathers is any more friendly."
*Strawson*
"You'll be lucky. She's already promised me a night of a thousand thrills."
*James*
"Good. You're sounding better. Have another."
Scene 5
The Feathers. The saloon bar is crowded.
*Strawson*
"Are we going to meet after you've finished?"
*Maureen*
"No, me duck. I've got to wash my hair."
*Strawson*
"Oh come on. You promised."
*Maureen*
"No can do. Want another pint before the beer runs out?"
Scene 6
Outside the Feathers. Moonlit night. William Strawson stands in the middle of the road looking up at what he thinks is Maureen's bedroom. No sign of any light. The blackout is effective. He probably has his eyes closed so he does not see the bicycle that comes round the corner and collides with him. The cyclist is a young girl. She finishes up in a heap on top of Strawson. Neither are hurt.
*Dawn* (for it is she)
"You idiot."
*Strawson*
"Mind my bike."
*Dawn*
"It's not you bike."
*Strawson*
"That's what Jack Warner says."

Alan Shelley

*Dawn*
"Who's Jack Warner?"
*Strawson*
"Of course. I can tell. You're a Yank. Every one knows Jack Warner."
*Dawn*
"Well, I don't. And look at my stockings. You've ruined them."
*Strawson*
"Well, you should look where you're going."
*Dawn*
"And you should keep to the sidewalk".
*Strawson*
"Sidewalk. Lambeth walk. They're all the same to me."
*Dawn*
"Are you hurt?"
*Strawson*
"No. Are you okay?. Is the bike all right.?"
*Dawn*
"Yes. Seems to be in one piece."
Pause.
*Dawn*
"I'm Dawn Broughton."
*Strawson*
"I'm Bill Strawson."
Scene 7
Typical High Street tea shop.
*Strawson*
"Did you come on your bike?"
*Dawn*
"No. I walked. It's not far."
*Strawson*
"What are you doing in England?"
*Dawn*
"My Dad is looking into building a factory here."
*Strawson*
"What, so Jerry can knock it down."

*Dawn*
"No, silly. When the war is over."
*Strawson*
"You have pretty eyes."
*Dawn*
"Thank you kind Sir. You flying to night?"
*Strawson*
"Careless talk. Not a word. You're probably a German spy. Where do you keep your radio? Oh, I know, in the saddle bag of your bike."
*Dawn*
"Don't be ridiculous. Do I look like a spy?"
*Strawson*
"Yes, and I do hope I shall be your target for tonight."
*Dawn*
"Rubbish. Come and have lunch on Sunday and meet my father. He admires the RAF, but you might disillusion him. But let's take a chance, shall we."
*Strawson*
"Suits me. Roast beef and Yorkshire pudding, I hope."
*Dawn.*
"Wait and see."
Scene 8
Airforce base. More bombers leaving and returning. Shots of bombers over Germany. Attacks by Messerschmitt fighters. A bomber plunges to the earth in flames.
Scene 9
Dining-room at Pear Tree Cottage.
*Strawson*
"Wonderful. Pumpkin pie. First time for me. Can I help with the dishes?"
*Dawn*
"You stay here and see how much smoke you and Daddy can make with your pipe and his cigar."
Exit Dawn
*Strawson*

Alan Shelley

"Mr Broughton. Kind of you and Dawn to invite me. A real treat for me."
*Broughton*
"Pleasure. Call me Simp. It's not for 'simple'. My dear old Mum called me Simpson after her grandfather. Bit of a mouthful. Grand job you chaps are doing. I don't think it will be too long before our people are helping you out."

I will not bore you with the whole thing. Tedious, is it not, and rather stereotyped. You can imagine the rest for yourself. Walks in the countryside, hand-in-hand, with Newmarket racecourse in the background. Goodnight kisses. Introductions to Rodney James, and even Maureen. A bedroom scene where the atmosphere is one of pure and innocent love with the act of passion being decorous, and somewhat underscored. Bill Strawson in the cockpit as his plane is hit. Tense moment at the station watching the aircraft return. Charlie Foxtrot 30, Strawson's plane, does not make it. Rodney tells Dawn. She does not cry. She is expecting it, but then becomes violent and attacks Rodney and blames him, and all the British, for fighting in this stupid war. Comforted by her father.

But then comes my *coup de théâtre.* Before Pearl Harbour, Dawn gets permission to join the WAAF and saves an airman trapped in a burning plane. Awarded an Honorary George Cross — or something like that. And then has a lesbian affair with my daughter. No. Scrub the last sentence.

I suppose there could have been a final scene; the war is over and Dawn and her father are present at the opening of the new factory for Coca Cola (East Anglia) Ltd, but I will not write that. Hate the stuff; not allowed on my premises.

My Head of Department liked it, even *sans* coca cola. He thought the American involvement just right — and what was needed. The synopsis was discussed at the highest level and even a couple of outside film makers were approached, but in the end it was decided that we should concentrate on the plucky civilians rather than the regular armed forces. There had been too many aircraft lost in reality, without repeating it on film. And so we became involved in Humphrey Jennings' documentary: *Fires Were Started* and I did some preliminary research and background writing for the factory-girl story: *Millions like Us.*

I found the work fascinating and had some certainty, within my own breast, that what I was doing represented the best use of my limited talents in the crusade to defeat the Fascists. Jennifer agreed with my view, as did Jack Owen. I saw little of him at that time; he was back working as an under-manager at the pit; a reserved occupation. I suspect he would not have wished to face any more bullets after his Spanish adventure but he was very interested in what I was doing, particularly when I tried to interest our unit in a new version of *How Green was my Valley*, without success.

On the periphery, the Ministry of Information was involved in the affair of Churchill and his objections to the film being made by Michael Powell and Emeric Pressburger, *The Life and Death of Colonel Blimp*. These two had worked on *49th Parallel,* which had been partly financed by our ministry, but now we, at the instigation of the War Office — and the Prime Minister — were trying to prevent the Blimp film being made. I am glad we did not succeed. It was one of the first films made in technicolour and is based on a character created by the cartoonist, David Low, and shows the life a British soldier, Clive Wynne Candy, from the Boer War to service in the Home Guard in 1943 — and his progress from Lieutenant to Major General. The authorities considered the film to be critical of the British Army at a time when it was involved in the most monstrous war the world had ever known but, in the end, they stopped short of a total ban. All they appeared to be able to do was to restrict the supply of technicolour film stock and refuse to release Laurence Olivier from the Fleet Air Arm. He was the first choice for the central role but as we now look of the finished product it is hard to see that he would have outshone Roger Livesey.

In retrospect it makes me wonder about Churchill's view of this film. Did he object to the compassion? The action of the young officer who begins the war before midnight is eventually accepted by Blimp. Was the objection that he, in true British style, then invites the officer to dinner? To me, it was just a piece of cinema, over sentimental even, but the device of using Deborah Kerr in a variety of roles was attractive. In my view, the objections were a storm in a teacup. Fred Kimball thought it was great fun.

Gloucester was bombed. Jerry would have known of the Gloster Aircraft Company where they were making Hurricane fighters, but the Whitwells, people and property, were unharmed and undamaged. At the start of the war my mother had offered to take evacuees but at the age of sixty she was thought to be too old. Jennifer and I went to see her and the family as often as we could and, when Edward was on leave after involvement in the desert war and the invasion of Italy, he came with us. Hester was now commissioned and had been transferred to the new airfield at Fairford making Gloucester a convenient rendezvous for her. They were very busy during the D-Day landings; Fairford was a principal base for troop carriers and gliders. Hester had no doubt left a few broken hearts in Suffolk, but my mother met her future husband before we did. The wheel had come full circle. He was a Welshman.

Jennifer and I were not frequenters of nightclubs. Not just because of our experience in Berlin; she did not like the music and I always complained about the food. In addition, since those days at the Hôtel Majestic, my dancing feet seemed to have atrophied and Jennifer said she could not afford any more visits to the chiropodist. She usually came back from such consultations muttering that if she had known what they charge, she would have trained as a toe mechanic instead of a journalist. Our evenings out were therefore confined to the cinema, the theatre or those restaurants that came up to my exacting standards.

Nevertheless, Jennifer had just received an overdue cheque from her American publisher that had brightened the face of our joint account at Barclays and so she took the initiative and booked for us to see a lauded review at a nightclub, new to the London scene, close to Piccadilly Circus.

I had determined that we should dine elsewhere, which we did, but when we arrived at the venue we were told champagne was available and so we indulged ourselves. However, before the show began, a flying bomb hit the building next door. The lights in the club went out and I was conscious that the ceiling was moving, inexorably, towards Jennifer and I. Amazingly, the candle on our table was still alight. I dived towards her but she had risen to her feet in panic and, at my next conscious moment, I was looking at another ceiling; this one was painted white and Hester was holding my hand. She told me Jennifer had been killed instantly. Shards of metal had entered her heart and cut her throat. I had been in a coma in hospital for five days, but the only damage was a broken leg and a deep gash to my forehead.

The first VI bomb fell on London on 12 June 1944, six days after the landings in Normandy. More than eight thousand of these dreadful weapons landed in London killing five thousand and injuring eight times that number.

Both the Daily Telegraph and The Times asked me to help with an obituary. My first reaction was one of abhorrence; but then I changed my mind and contributed. It was the most painful writing task I ever had.

I never really recovered, psychologically that is. We had been married for seventeen years. The gash to my head hid the deepest sorrow of my life. Why me? I had effectively lost Simóne and now Jennifer. I could not think of the other thousands who had been killed. Why was it not me on the death roll? In the mortuary? She had striven all her life, since the death of Edward's father, to oppose the forces that killed him and were still killing so many others. At the end of the

Second World War the casualty list showed that forty six million soldiers and civilians had been killed. Including Jennifer.

After her death, I left the Ministry. As we advanced through Europe our unit was less busy and, in the circumstances, I was not put under any pressure to stay. I spent a lot of time with Peter and Ruth and it was she who suggested a project to occupy my time, even if it did nothing towards easing the pain. A cookbook. She also came up with the title: *The Cambridge Cookbook*. While comfortably at my rest in their spare room I wept: from the diamond quality of my love for Jennifer to the dross of a cookbook. Angela had no problem in finding a publisher. Perhaps the book-buying public at the end of the war, and at the end of rationing, could see there might soon be an abundance of cream, saffron, venison and red currants to fit my recipes. 'Yes, we have plenty of bananas.'

I paid little attention to any of this. The years immediately after the war were drab for most of the British population. For me, they were dire. I had Hester and Edward as a diversion and the Kimball's and Ruth and Peter were very kind, but otherwise I spent my lonely days at the flat sending Herbert Montcalm into more and more bizarre scenarios and producing the occasional article on the renaissance of the British cuisine. Ha ha. What a hope. The glossy magazines took my work more readily than in the past, due to the success of the Cambridge thing, but as my bank balance grew, I got little satisfaction from this improved state of affairs. I needed something new.

I had enjoyed working on the periphery of the film world but I was really more interested in the theatre and therefore decided that the next West End hit should come from my pen, even if my qualifications for this task were not too impressive. A series of repetitive detective stories, a few pieces for radio — long forgotten — and a putative film script gathering dust in the Ministry of Information archive. And, to top it all, a best-selling cookbook. Bob was back on stage in London and I showed him my first attempt, a slight piece about a couple of corsetieres plying their trade in Chelmsford. He thought it a bit too slapstick and perhaps a little risqué for the current Lord Chancellor, but tolerably funny.

Nevertheless, there was an enormous vacuum in my life and I was minded to see if the theatre could fill it; but was this just an idle and unattainable dream? And, even if I managed to achieve some success, the stage, however grand, would not warm my bed at night; it could not provide the wise counsel my personality required nor act as a guide and mother to our children. I miss her more than words can tell, whether written by me — or a latter-day Keats.

Years later I used a local taxi firm where the owner had been a prisoner of war in Germany for four years. He refused to countenance German or Japanese cars in his fleet. I felt the same; bratwurst and sauerkraut were not to be found in my kitchen.

## Stage

I found it difficult to celebrate VE day and I know many of my friends felt ambivalent about crying 'hosanna' at a victory over Japan that entailed so many deaths by that new horror of war, the atomic bomb. What did give me joy was to see that Edward and Hester had emerged intact.

Hester spent the whole of the war in the UK. She had not been involved in rescues from burning aeroplanes like my fictional heroine but she had been engaged in vital work within the RAF. She was not as changed as Edward, but she was different. No doubt inevitable, after six years of war. Perhaps it had happened to all of us, but for me there was additionally the physical deprivation I had over Jennifer — and it was physical. The pain and the ache seemed to move day by day from one part of the body to another. At one time my shorter left arm twitched, then it was in my stomach, but mostly across the front of my head as if my brain was in overdrive. I had the feeling of being diminished. I was diminished.

Alan Shelley

On one of my trips to Fairford, before Hester was demobilised, I went to the city of my birth and without quite realising what I was doing I found myself on my knees in the church where my mother had been married and where I was baptised; St Mary de Lode. It was a weekday. I had found a side door that was open but there was no sign of any other worshippers, or clergy — or cleaners.

Did I want to visit a house of God to communicate my anger over the loss of Jennifer? This would have been a not unfamiliar approach. I had been of that frame of mind on the few occasions that I had kept my promise and visited the Notre Dame on the 21st of June and cursed him for not returning Simóne to me. I had wanted to shout out. I had wanted to cause a riot.

But now, I quietly went on to my knees. I had only one prayer. I did not ask for Jennifer's return; I did not bewail her passing; I did not even pray for her — for the 'repose of her soul'. No, all I required of the Lord was an audience where I could use my hesitant whisper to impel a demonic cry into the stillness of the church; a simple message.

Dear Lord.
If there is a you. If you hear me. If I can believe in you. I beg you to recognize and accept that without Jennifer I am less than the fifty per cent that might have been my share of the partnership. Without her, I am less than the half. It was she that made up the whole. My contribution was insignificant. Give me the strength to carry on by agreeing with me. I need this truth to be acknowledged. I am not nothing. I am still here. But without her, I have become stunted and insignificant.

I can hardly write this down. Have I made any sense? What I do record is what I tried to say in that possibly false kneeling position in the church. What a selfish act. It is all about me, no thought for the children. I could not help it. My agony was all encompassing but, as I left, I did feel slightly better. I had taken some action to bring this matter out into the open, even if only to myself. I did not raise any of this with my mother, or the children, or Ruth and Peter. Strangely enough the only person who seemed to read my thoughts was Beth Owen. Now I think about it, she had many of those mysterious instinctive weapons of deep insight that Simóne had. Some years after Jennifer's death she added a note to her Christmas card:

Percy. Time heals many sorrows and Jack thinks you have recovered well, but I see a broken mirror that does not reflect the true self; it is not complete. When Jennifer was alive, you looked at your image and saw the whole person. But now, even if it was not cracked, the picture would not be as true, as full as it was.

But, like people all over the world, I lived with my wartime tragedy and got on with my life.

Edward returned to his medical studies at Edinburgh, but I was worried as to his state of mind. Countless servicemen and women had been away from home for so long that many of them must have found it as difficult to resume life away from the war as it was for Edward. We had seen him for a few days when his regiment was fighting in Italy — he had been sent back to the UK for some briefing or other — but other than that he served overseas from 1940 until 1945. He had been unable to attend his mother's funeral and I think this had affected him more than anyone realised. He had adored her. She was his model. Until now he had used her as the yardstick by which he measured his own conduct, his own path through life. We were close, but the blood line was clearly paramount.

He was back in Scotland by early 1946 but it seemed as though he let himself be directed back into medicine without giving the matter any thought. This was what was expected of him, so he acquiesced. There was no enthusiasm. I told him there were lots of other things he could do and he appeared to listen, but did not respond. Why was Jennifer not here to help him — and me?

On the 4th of April I was telephoned by the Dean of Studies and told that Edward had not been to lectures over the last three weeks, and when enquiries were made, his landlady also reported him missing. I immediately went to Edinburgh. His teachers and his colleagues said he had been acting strangely since his arrival; detached was the word used. I was told that his closest friend was a girl called Louise Brooks. She had not served in the war; she was only twenty two and had met Edward for the first time at the beginning of the year. She was only too willing to talk to me.

"Mr Glossop. I am very fond of Edward. I do not understand why he is attracted to me. He is so much older. So much more experienced. He has already finished nearly a year at medical school."

I did not say so but I could see why Edward was drawn to this girl. She was pretty, and she was lively, but crucially she bore an uncanny resemblance to Jennifer.

"He was not easy to befriend. He seemed so lost, so not with us. Somehow I was drawn. I could not resist it. I already had a boyfriend in Edinburgh. He works at Lloyds Bank. We were sweethearts from school days, but compared to Edward, he was a child. I was honest, Mr Glossop. I told Jimmy. Edward and I became lovers. It seemed to relax him, but there was still that distancing. I know he was sad about his mother. I know he had awful memories about the war. He told me a story about some Italian peasants who were executed by the Germans for not supporting them. Or something like that. But he never cried. When I saw the memories haunted him the most, he said nothing but looked down at his glass of whisky."

"You seem very perceptive. But you have known him for such a short time?"

"I know. But it was love. I don't know how you feel on the subject, but when you're in love, you get special insights."

"I'm inclined to agree with you."

"However much I felt for him, and I hope he for me, it did not prevent him from drinking. The whisky. There was more and more. He missed days at school because he could not get from his bed. His landlady did not seem to notice — or the people at the University. But I was becoming desperate. If he had not disappeared, I was going to call you."

"But where has he gone? And why?"

"I have no idea where. As to why, I think the drink so disturbed him that he needed to get away from the establishment here. I don't think he wants to be a doctor. The war has killed that in him."

"Has anyone been to the police?"

"I presume not. It's early days. He's only been missing for about a fortnight."

"And I assume you've heard nothing from him?"

"No."

I had told Hester I was going to Edinburgh and the next day she tracked me down at the Royal Caledonian. She had some news about Edward; he was in a hospital at Inverness. He had been on his own walking in the Highlands, trying to decide what he was going to do with the rest of his life, and had collapsed. A mountain rescue team had found him and taken him to the hospital suffering from exposure. He had clearly been drinking. When admitted he was in a sorry state. The hospital authorities could not decide whether he was a tramp, or someone of simple mind or a potential suicide. It was days before he spoke. When he did they tried to ring my number, but then made contact with Hester. Evidently he was now on the road to recovery and would be discharged the following week. I told Louise what had happened and then went back to London and waited for Edward to emerge.

He did, and Louise took a break from her studies and came to London with him. I was unsure as to the etiquette involved. Jennifer would have known, I thought, but they occupied the one bedroom anyway. Edward told me he had made three decisions. Firstly, they were to be married. Secondly, he was giving up medicine and thirdly, he was going back into the army. I was speechless. I do not think I have been so surprised at anything since the time Simóne had charmed Paul Nerval into taking on Hubert Richardson.

"I know, you would have thought that after all these years I would not even want to use a khaki-coloured handkerchief — even to clean my shoes with — but I was a good soldier and I do not think I would have been a good doctor. The war has inevitably hardened me — taken away a layer of sensitivity — and losing Mum has of course made it worse. I was drinking to avoid making a decision. And, remember, my father was a soldier."

"I still cannot believe it. A career soldier. Voluntarily. Your father was a soldier because he had no choice. And, Louise. You've known her such a short time. What does she think? A life in barracks?"

"I know you believe in love at first sight. It was so with us, more or less. If she was not prepared to be a soldier's wife, I would not have entertained the idea. I would have become a writer. Or a cook."

I wrinkled my forehead at this.

"But she is fully prepared to be a camp follower. She is on the course at Edinburgh because both her mother and father are doctors. She is not committed to medicine, but she says she is committed to me."

What could I say? I gave them my blessing. So did Fred Kimball although he added myriad pieces of advice; from a life-time soldier, he said, forgetting that his protégé had just returned from six years of intense warfare that stretched from the deserts of North Africa to the banks of the Rhine via Monte Cassino. Jennifer the pacifist would not have approved, but then I am sure that if she had been there Edward would have acted very differently anyway.

The wedding was a quiet affair. I made the cake, and then continued to try and arrange my entry into the London theatre scene.

My apprenticeship proved to be a long one which meant I needed to resort, at regular intervals, to Herbert Montcalm to avoid becoming impecunious. My first action was to look at the opposition. Firstly, JB Priestley. I was already a fan. His output was prodigious: as well as the theatre there were novels, essays and journalism in addition to his career as a professional Yorkshireman. Jennifer and I saw Basil Dean's production of *When We Are Married* at St Martin's Theatre in London in the autumn of 1938, just after Chamberlain returned from Munich. We both enjoyed it: very amusing but it was the provincial snobbery it portrayed that really took our fancy. Priestley wrote carefully constructed plays but, in light of his socialist leanings, they were sometimes more political than most of his contemporaries. I admired his 1945 work, *An Inspector Calls,* but just after the war the best writing, in my opinion, was coming from America; in particular, Arthur Miller. I did not like Tennessee Williams' portraits of women in *A Streetcar Named Desire*, but I was swept away by *The Rose Tattoo.*

The following year, Terence Rattigan gave us *The Winslow Boy*, but we had to wait until 1952 for the one of his I admired the most, *The Deep Blue Sea.* This appeared in London at the same time as *Waiting for Godot*. For me, there was no contest. Perhaps because of my limited connection with the theatre, and perhaps because I was nearly fifty five years of age, I had no difficulty in deciding which was the better play. And I said the same thing four years later when *Look Back in Anger* erupted at the Royal Court. I like the well-made play. I like romance — or perhaps you already know that — and I thought I knew something about tragic heroines. Rattigan was a superb craftsman and *The Deep Blue Sea* is, in my opinion, his finest achievement. It is said that Peggy Ashcroft, who first played Hester Collyer, hated the part because Rattigan's skill made her feel she was walking around the stage naked. I agreed with her. This woman is stripped of all dignity, because of love. If only I could write like that. Strangely, at least for me, it is said that Rattigan would have liked the anguish and shame of Hester to have taken place in a homosexual relationship, but of course at that time the censor would not allow.

I made some comparisons, but only to myself, between Henry James and Somerset Maugham. The former, perhaps the greatest of modern novelists, loved the theatre and craved success for his plays, but it did not happen. On the other hand, after Somerset Maugham's first novel, *Liza of Lambeth,* had been well received he could find no one interested in his next efforts but his plays were accepted; at one time he had four of them running in London at the same time. At that point he decided to give up novels for the rest of his life and concentrate on the theatre, but did not keep to that promise and five years later produced *Of Human Bondage.* I found the fates of these two interesting because clearly Maugham had no difficulty, eventually, in moving from the page to the stage, and back again, while the infinitely superior writer could not perform this trick. I was a long way from being a writer of their quality, even though I had made a reasonable living with my pen for many years, but it seemed as though I was more likely than not to suffer the same fate as James.

Despite my association with the film world while with the Ministry of Information, my involvement with the theatre was limited to buying a ticket and, of course, my friendship with Bob. But he was an actor and not a wordsmith and as I was to discover, writing for the stage is a special art. I had not even been involved in amateur dramatics and had not needed to understand how theatrical words work since my thespian efforts at school.

Both Angela and Bob helped as far as they could. She found an agent, Walter Frew, who dealt with play scripts and my old school friend gave advice on staging and read aloud most of my feeble attempts. After a while I did think of an outline that Walter thought might work, and that Bob said he would not mind acting in. I called it *The Two Sisters*. Walter did not care for the title, but as it was unlikely to ever be staged, this was a minor matter. If he did get someone interested, it could be called *A New Play* for all I cared, but perhaps it was good practice.

The action takes place in three different acting areas: Stage Left; a ladies boudoir: Stage Right; a masculine meeting place; a pub, the bar at the golf club, a room with a billiard table, a cricket pavilion, a river bank favoured by coarse fisherman — it did not matter, any will do. The centre of the stage is where the male and female members of the cast meet. There are two of each; Sister One and Sister Two and the Suitor and the Friend.

I hardly need to go on. You already know the story but what I wrote for the stage included, I thought, a number of different twists compared to the real life happening. The synopsis, scene by scene, that I finally came up with was as follows.

Scene One. Centre Stage.
As the curtain rises Sister One and the Suitor are shown in a passionate embrace. They break apart and begin conversing. Initially their exchanges are warm and loving in nature but a subject arises they do not agree upon and they begin to bicker. This develops into a serious quarrel and they exit, stage left and right, both in high dudgeon.

Scene Two. Centre Stage.
The same couple. They have evidently made up their differences and the dialogue that follows indicates they have just left a bed where a satisfactory act of love has taken place.

Scene Three. Stage Left.
The two Sisters in earnest conversation. Sister One tells Sister Two she is in love and going to be married.

Scene Four. Centre Stage.
Sister One introduces her sister to the Suitor. Light-hearted conversation arranging a trip to the seaside for the threesome. The Suitor appears to be attracted to Sister Two.

Scene Five. Centre Stage

*Alan Shelley*

The three on their excursion. The Suitor's interest in Sister Two becomes more noticeable.

Scene Six. Stage Right.

Suitor tells Friend he has fallen in love with the sister of his fiancée. Friend dismisses this possibility. The Suitor confirms he is serious.

Scene Seven. Stage Left.

Sisters discuss the Suitor. Both acknowledge that he appears to be somewhat attracted to Sister Two. Treat matter as a huge joke.

Scene Eight. Stage Right.

Suitor asks Friend what he should do. He thinks he loves both sisters, but cannot get Sister Two out of his mind. Suggests Friend should meet Sister Two and assess whether she might also be attracted to Suitor.

Scene Nine. Centre Stage.

Friend and Sister Two meet and have a lively and humourous conversation. When they part, Friend kisses the hand of Sister Two. He is rather flamboyant: an actor.

Scene Ten. Stage Left.

The two Sisters show they fully understand what game is afoot and that Friend is being introduced into this embryonic *ménage a trois* to assist Suitor in finding a solution to his dilemma.

Scene Eleven. Stage Right.

Friend reports to Suitor. Says he needs further meetings with Sister Two before he can advise.

Scene Twelve. Centre Stage.

Friend and Sister Two meet again, and by the end of the scene it is conveyed to the audience that they have fallen in love.

Scene Thirteen. Stage Left.

Sister Two tells Sister One of this turn of events. They laugh together, uproariously.

Scene Fourteen. Stage Right.

## *I Never Met Ernest Hemingway*

Friend breaks the news to the Suitor. And then tells him both sisters have decided on a joint wedding. Suitor is dumbfounded.

Scene Fifteen. Centre Stage.

Couples walk slowly forward as if proceeding down the aisle.

Walter encouraged me to complete the dialogue but Bob was now not so keen. The story was new to Walter, but well-known to the actor. Nevertheless, I finished about half of the scenes but by that time all three of us decided it did not add up to a piece of dramatic writing that was ever likely to grace the London stage. I showed my masterpiece, as far as it went, to Ruth. She did not like it either. I was of course disappointed at this setback: was I to fall at the first hurdle? The trouble was, I thought, I have no history in this field.

Take the case of John Osborne. I did not like his plays and I did not like him; we met twice with Bob, but I could not deny his apprenticeship in the theatre, a background I sorely lacked. He had been a stage manager and actor in touring companies performing West End successes, and also in repertory companies stretching from Ilfracombe to Derby; while I was writing a cookbook.

I tried again. My next serious attempt had some reference to my limited experience of both of the World Wars of this century. Audiences did not want to be reminded of these tragedies but I still thought they provided a rich seam of human interest that ought not to be ignored; particularly within the working class. Those wonderful writers of prose and poetry that emerged from the first conflict were mostly of the middle-class but I wanted to give voice to the under-privileged. The other inspiration was Jennifer. When I wondered what I might write about at the Ministry of information, she had suggested Bert's father. So, that is exactly what I planned to do; a family and the impact of war.

*Alan Shelley*

I did not want to duplicate Coward's, *This Happy Breed*. My characters were all of the East End labouring class; the folk who were least cared for after the war and suffered most during the slump of the mid-war years. However, as the plot developed in my unpractised theatrical brain, a very different story emerged; involuntarily I was set on a path to write a sort of twentieth century morality play. A miracle in an ex-docker's kitchen: good overcoming evil.

When I reached this stage the title was, *The Stepney Saint* — but in the end I choose, *The Rescue of the Lambs*.

The Lamb family. Arthur Lamb worked in the London docks in a reserved occupation. In 1915 he marries a local girl, Gladys Fairchild, and their son William is born the next year. They are very happy but before William's first birthday, Arthur is impelled to give up his protected position and join the Army. After he has left, Gladys's father dies and her mother, Emily, comes to live with her daughter. At the third Battle of Ypres Arthur looses a leg. He is discharged after an artificial replacement has been fitted but he is a changed man. He is bitter and angry. Feels impotent. No longer whole. He cannot go back to work in the docks. He blames everyone and manifests this in the cruelty he metes out to his wife, her mother and his son. Not an unfamiliar picture. Thousands of returning soldiers were so affected. It gets worse.

In 1921, Gladys dies during the influenza epidemic. Two years later Arthur marries again, Florence, a narrow-minded spinster just as embittered as her new husband and equally as harsh and cruel to William and Emily, who is still living in the house: she has nowhere else to go. In particular, Florence wages a campaign of hatred against her and so, on one fateful day in the summer of 1927, she commits suicide. It is William who finds his grandmother lying on the kitchen floor with her head in the gas oven. He is eleven years old. The early scenes show quite clearly how truly malevolent Arthur and Florence are. We see William, by Scene Six, as a tall and well made boy for his age but his disposition is one of a quiet sadness mixed with a hint of rebellion.

All of the action takes place in the kitchen at the Lamb's modest house in Stepney. The poverty is self evident. A Belfast sink in one corner. Gas stove at the rear wall, centre stage. Kitchen cupboards in need of a coat of paint. Rough wooden table and four chairs.

Scene One. 1916
Happy meal in the kitchen when Gladys tells her husband they are going to have a child.

Scene Two. 1916
Tearful farewells as Arthur leaves for France. Introduction of Emily.

Scene Three. 1918
Arthur, in his new personality and with his artificial leg, returns home. Signs of deterioration in relations between him and his family begin to show.

Scene Four. 1921
Ill-tempered wake in the kitchen after Gladys's funeral.

Scene Five. 1923
Ill-tempered wedding breakfast after marriage to Florence.

Scene Six. 1927
Arthur has gone to work. He has a tedious job in a factory warehouse. Florence, in a particularly vicious mood with Gladys and William. He goes to school. Florence goes to visit a neighbour. Gladys can take no more. Kills herself. William returns from school and finds her.

A sordid tale, but there is some hope. See how I finished the play. If this last scene did not grip the audience, and made sense of what had gone before, the play did not work. What do you think?

I hoped that the character of Arthur and Florence would have been well established in the previous scenes; abrasive, insensitive, coarse and loud. William, inevitably, reflects some of the personality of his father: not saying much but when he does his speech is guttural and his behaviour rude and uncooperative.

When Scene Seven opens we see Arthur and Florence in the personas already established but the actor playing William needs to show, early in the scene, that he has changed. He is still quiet, but it is quietude of peace rather than resentment. The change in the other two, brought about by William's vision, needs to be shown in a very gradual manner. It needs to be hesitant and suspicious, but believable. All speak in strong cockney accents. They wear their Sunday best.

At the start of Scene Seven, we see the kitchen as it has been shown in the earlier scenes, except for the minor changes that would have taken place between 1916 and 1927. At the outset the curtains at the window are of a bright clean chintz but by the end of the play they are dirty and torn. The kitchen cupboards still have not been repainted. However, during the last scene there should be a subtle and imperceptible change in the lighting; brighter, as if a strong sun has risen and directed its rays into that squalid room.

William mentions a séance. In the 1920s in Britain many working class people were drawn to spiritualism. My mother had some fun at the expense of one of her customers suggesting that a spirit session be arranged because she was anxious to contact Alice Smith, urgently, on a problem she had with a chocolate sponge.

Scene Seven 1927
Arthur, Florence and William in the kitchen, having just returned from Gladys's funeral.

Arthur  Stupid cow. Why did she want to go and do that and show us up with the neighbours?

Florence  Well, you drove her to it.

Arthur  And I suppose you were all sweetness and light. I'll be glad when you follow her example, and that's a fact.

## I Never Met Ernest Hemingway

Florence  You bastard. Just because your leg is giving you gyp, no reason to take it out on me. You killed her as sure as putting the shilling in the meter.

Arthur  Oh shut up. What do know about it? Make the tea.

Florence  Do it yourself. I"m not your skivvy. You could order your mother-in-law about, but not me.

Arthur  Are you looking for a good hiding?

Florence  You dare lay your hands on me. I'll have the police round in a jiffy.

They square up to each other.

William  Please stop quarrelling.

Arthur  And you can shut your mouth. You make the tea.

William  I will. (*Long pause*) But Florence, your face has suddenly become beautiful.

At this both adults stare unbelievingly at the boy. Florence has not changed.

William  You seem to have a special light. There seems to be a special light coming out of you.

Florence  For God's sake. What are you talking about?

William  It's true. Can you see it Dad?

Arthur  I bloody well can't. Make the fucking tea.

William  I will do. But I can't get over this. Florence, look in the mirror. Even your hair is glowing.

Florence  Well I did wash it last week.

William  You look taller.

Arthur  What?

Florence  Is it these new shoes?

William  No. You just seem to be standing more upright. Your shoulders are not hunched up, as they mostly are. Like a sapling. A young tree. Not a twisted and gnarled old branch, like usual.

Arthur  What crap is the boy talking about? Tree? Yes. One of those that dogs lift their legs to. Is it running down your stockings? What a sight, gal. You should see your face. Not very beautiful now, old thing.

Florence looks as though she is about to spit at her husband.

>William  I don't think anyone has noticed before, Florence, but you have an elegant neck.
>Arthur  What do you know about necks? What's your game?
>William  Certainly her eyes are shinier.
>Arthur  He's gone mad. Get him to the loony bin.

Florence looks quizzically at William. She cannot understand, and this frightens her, but even so she runs her hands over her cheeks (or whatever other actions seem appropriate as long as they are not too dramatic.)

>Florence  Get away with you boy. Perhaps my eyes are brighter, because of the tears.
>Arthur  Tears. You damned hypocrite. You would never cry for Emily. You made her cry plenty of times, but I can't see you shedding any tears for her, alive or dead.
>Florence  She had a sad life — since Gladys died.
>Arthur  What do you care?
>William  Yes she did, but she is at peace now. With me mam.
>Arthur  When did you become religious all of a sudden. You keep away from them vicars.
>William  Dad, don't you believe in anything?
>Arthur  Let me tell you son, no one believes in me or gives me anything and I say to hell with all of them. I fought for the bleeders …
>Florence  …..For God's sake, we're not about to have the sad story about leaving your leg in Flanders field.
>Arthur  You can shut your mouth.
>William  Dad, you have to believe in something. If you do not, you're not a human being.

Arthur  What I believe in is enough money for a pint. For more than one. How do you think I've managed to exist in this life? If it wasn't for me mates at the Cobblers, I'd have gone mad years ago.

William  Yes dad, I know, but there has to be something more than that? I know that false leg hurts you sometimes but otherwise you're alive, and look over there, you have a beautiful wife.

Silence. Arthur is about to explode, either in rage or laughter, but he looks across the room at Florence. He screws up his eyes. He then closes them. When they are open again he abruptly looks away. Florence says nothing, but there is a hint of a smile, even though she is as bewildered as is Arthur. The actor playing William should extend the silence for as long as the audience will tolerate.

William  It's so nice to see you smile. You've lost that anger. It makes you look even more pretty.

Arthur  I do not understand what the hell is going on here? Is this a joke? Are you making fun of me?

William  Well dad, I think perhaps grandma is making us open our eyes properly for the first time in many a long day.

Arthur  There's nowt wrong with my eyes. Any more of this nonsense and I'll black both of yours.

William  That's the other thing you believe in, isn't it dad. Violence. I would have thought you had seen enough of that in France.

Arthur  It's what I've bloody well seen that makes me violent. You should have been in the trenches. There was nothing beautiful there, I can tell you. And no God either.

William  What about that Angel who helped us at Mons, or wherever it was? I've read about it.

Arthur  All rubbish. Propaganda by the toffs to make us keep on fighting their war.

William  But you volunteered.

Arthur   More fool me. What did I get for it? Bugger all, except for this bit of plastic that still does not fit proper.

William   But more violence doesn't help, does it. Look, let me unclench your fist for you. Try not to be so tense.

William takes his father's hands into his. Arthur shudders, but makes no attempt to move away. This action needs to show that touching of this kind does not happen in this family.

William   Florence, why don't you hold his hand as well?
Florence   Not me, you don't know where he's been.
William   You look quieter dad. Are you thinking of grandma?

Again, Arthur seems unable to speak.

William   This is not a séance. I know about those. Mrs Jenkinson at number 54 does them. No. There's a change in this room.
Florence   What do you mean?
William   It is affecting all of us, mostly me. I should be sad. I loved grandma. She was the only person who was kind to me after mam died. But I wasn't good to her. And yet, strangely, her love seems stronger now she is dead.
Arthur   Christ. I'm getting out of here. This boy is going to have us on our knees soon. I've just told you, there's no God — at least not for the likes of us.
Florence   Arthur, I don't think you ought to leave. You do look steadier. Not so angry. That frown of yours seems to have disappeared.
William   I noticed that too.
Arthur   No. I'm not going to be caught up in this. It's nonsense.

Florence scratches her nose. She is still puzzled. But then the spell appears to be broken.

Florence  All right, I agree. She was good-for-nothing when she was alive. Totally buggered now she's dead. Let's go down the pub.

William  Florence. They won't recognize you there. What with your best dress on, and the glow on your cheeks, they won't recognize you.

Arthur  Tommy rot. I can't see no glow.

William  Dad, I think you should look more closely. I think you should also look more closely at me.

Florence  You know Arthur, the boy looks different.

Arthur  How long are we going to put up with this claptrap?

William  Do you feel any different inside?

Arthur  Can't say I do. Just thirsty. We never did get that tea.

William  Sorry dad. I'll put the kettle on.

Arthur  Good, but no more talk about change. We're a sorry lot as it is. We don't need any magic changing us here.

William  Dad. I don't think it is magic. I think it's just happened. And it's happening now because we have just come back from grandma's funeral.

This is too much for Arthur and Florence.

Florence  Look, she's dead. God rest her soul. Let's forget about it. It's bloody morbid.

Arthur  Right. To hell with the tea. I need a drink. Coming Flo?

Arthur and Florence exit. Quick blackout. When the lights go up all three are sitting around the kitchen table eating bread and cheese. Arthur and Florence are somewhat happier, but they are not intoxicated. No one seems to be enjoying their sparse repast.

Arthur  Seen any more lights, son?
William  No. Haven't seen any lights.
Arthur  Is Flo looking more lovely?

*Alan Shelley*

William turns to view her — but not very enthusiastically.

    William  No. Still miserable as ever.
    Arthur  Hey, you watch your mouth. That's your step-mam.
    William  I know.
    Arthur  Looked arter you.

Silence.

    William  Dad. Do you remember me mam?
    Arthur  Gladys?
    William  Yes.
    Arthur  Suppose so.
    William  Tell me about her. Wos you happy?
    Arthur  She was a pretty little thing. But that's the old days. They're gone. I had two good legs then. Good job down the docks. Good money. We bought this table before we wed.
    William  I've seen the snaps. Not very clear. Was she beautiful?
    Arthur  Sure. Just like you sez Florence is.
    Florence  Give over, Arthur. We've had enough for one night.

Silence.

    Florence  William. Do I still look pretty?

This time William looks at her closely. She feels embarrassed. Stands up and moves next to the gas cooker. Spot light on her increases, just perceptively.

    William  Yes. (*pause*) Grandma's back. There is a light around you.
    Arthur  Stop this nonsense, or its my belt you'll see, and not any light.

Florence stands very still.

    William  I can't help it. Look yourself.

Arthur  Not me. I see enough of her at night in her curlers. Has she become the bloody Mona Lisa? Or that Venus de whatsit. The beauty Queen of Stepney. I think not.

Florence still does not move except to straighten her arms at her sides.

Florence  There's a different smell in here.
Arthur  Hope it's not the bloody gas. We'd all be seeing Emily then.
Florence  No, it's not gas. It's sweet. No. Like lemons. Come over here Arthur. See if you can get a wiff.

Arthur reluctantly gets up. All the cheese has been eaten.

William  Dad. Hold her hand. Please.
Florence  Let's do as he says.
Arthur  If Bert looked through that window and saw we two idiots standing here like silly kids, he'd laugh his bleeding head off. And, all I can smell is the port and lemon she downed at the Cobblers.

But they do stand hand-in-hand, saying nothing. William smiles at them. There is a long silence.

Arthur  How you getting on at school?
William You see, there is a change. Something's happening. You never asked me anything about school before.
Arthur  Well. I am now. I want to know. You need education in this awful world.
Florence  Yes, William. You keep at it. Don't want to finish up like us.
William  Why not? What's wrong with you?
Arthur  Everything.
William  Is your leg hurting?
Arthur  No. Funnily enough it's not. Must have been something they put in the ale.

*Alan Shelley*

**William** Or is it this room. Tonight. Education. Yes. But, tonight, I want to be like you dad.

**Florence** I think I know what he means. It's not the drink. I can see you as you used to be. As you were when you first met Gladys. We wos friends until you got married. Then I hated her. Nobody wanted me. There were no men left. Bloody war ate em all up. Like sodding Goldilocks did to the porridge. That's when I needed to have some of the boy's magic. Make me into a good-locker. Perhaps you'd have had me then instead of Gladys? No, I became bitter. Angry. Still am. No kids for me. Who's going to look after me when he's dead and gone?

**William** I will

**Florence** Why?

**William** Because tonight you've become something special. I love you.

**Arthur** Christ.

**William** You too dad. You won't need to hit me any more. Or Florence. You are bigger than that. I hated what grandma did. I hated it when I comes into this kitchen. Her dress was up. I could see her knickers. I was disgusted.

Florence moves and puts her arm around William.

**William** But, perhaps it all had a purpose. None of us took a blind bit of notice of her while she was alive. She was a nuisance. For Flo, she reminded her of me mam. Dad was angry that mam died. I'm sure you must have said why wasn't it grandma. I always thought she smelled of piss. So, she couldn't do anything for us when she was alive. Now, she is trying to help.

**Florence** How?

**Arthur** Am I hearing right. Come back to make us better people?

**William** Yes.

**Arthur** Can't be.

**William** See for yourselves.

Florence and Arthur look at each other. Both look at William. Another gradual upgrade of the lighting.

Arthur   But what exactly is she doing? Where are the signs?
William   I don't know. I can't explain it. I aint Einstein. I just feel something.
Florence   So do I.

Florence moves and kisses William and then takes Arthur into her arms and kisses him passionately. They break and all smile at each other.

Arthur  Well, if it is the gas, must be that laughing stuff.

Blackout.

Both Walter and Bob were impressed, but not the people that mattered. Most said it was too improbable; they asked is it a piece of social realism, or is it a fairy story? One producer, so Walter told me, said it was an unsuccessful mix of *This un-Happy Breed* and *Blithe Spirit*. Bit unfair I thought. I had worked hard on this and had derived great satisfaction from doing so but the rejection was very painful. My first thought after all that effort was to assume I was not destined to be a playwright, but I persevered.

Were the inadequacies in *The Rescue of the Lambs* because I was writing dialogue about people I had never met; in a language unfamiliar to me? Well, not altogether. The Lamb's kitchen was superior to that of the Owens in their back-to-back house, but it would have been similar to the one in the 'two up, two down' cottage I moved into as a boy with my mother and Francois. The people I met in the shop did not speak with cockney accents but they were no more prosperous than the Lambs. When Bob came back from the war he had not lost a limb, and he went on to make a great success of his life, but there were many of his colleagues who did not; those who failed to make the transition from war to peace.

Alan Shelley

Trouble was I did not really know any of these failures. Peter Southern was affected psychologically, but he recovered. Simóne was more mixed up than anyone I have ever met, or that I ever saw on the stage, but, as far as I know, she survived. That was it. I had little or no experience of people who were bitter and twisted. Peter Lons was unpleasant, but I had limited contact with him and I did not think my experience of the Nottingham Perkins would establish me as the new scribe of the discontented working classes.

I therefore decided I would revert to something I am an expert in; romance. Once that decision had been made my pen travelled at lightening speed. I wrote two full-length dreamy plays; both about Paris and both light-hearted and uplifting but I will not bore you with plots and scenarios because they fell on ground just as stony as that which received, or did not receive, my Lamb saga. That particular piece of *terra firma* only grows thistles. After that, I gave up.

Edward and his new wife were in Germany, at Bad Oeynhausen in the British Army of the Rhine. Louise was pregnant but Hester had beaten them to it; she already had twins. Her husband became a lecturer at the University College of Wales Aberystwyth and while I was deciding what to do next, I accepted their long-standing invitation to have an extended stay with them and become acquainted with the art of babysitting.

And so, in time, I found a new career; grandfather.

I write this with some pleasure. I had been denied observing the growth of Edward and Hester, from suckling infant to the first day at school, but now my time had come — even if somewhat removed and, thankfully, without the responsibility. You generally give them back after a while. When not wheeling the pram, or arranging visits to the zoo, I had one other major activity. I am in the process of turning my life story into the great European novel. My tentative title is: *A Time of Grief* but I shall probably think of a better one. As you will have read, my life contained its full measure of grief, but also many joys. It will not be called, *I never met Ernest Hemingway.*

Hester told me that when I had finished my epic I should write what she called 'a proper story'. I knew what she meant. Not a hotchpotch of memories and facts, imaginings and reality, but a book that was not about me: of me, but not about me. A love story, she said. It did not need to be site-specific, or of our time, just about love.

I shall do as I am bid.

*Alan Shelley*

*We read his play about Stepney, wherever that is. I thought it was both sad and uplifting. I have never met people like that. Neither had Edward, even amongst the soldiery, but Percy has moved in so many different circles. When we were posted to Lagos — Defence Attaché staff — he seemed to know so much about Africa and in its history.*

*I know he was sad when no one would produce his plays. Although he kept it very quiet, after the* Rescue of the Lambs *he wrote two more, one about Americans in Paris; nothing to do with Gene Kelly. He let me read them. They were so wonderful, so romantic. But that's what he is. A romantic. That speech he made at our wedding about the power of love; it should have been as corny as hell — but somehow it was just right. Even mum and dad liked it.*

*He has had such an interesting life. Eddy sometimes said that he went into the army because he knew he could never do what his stepfather had. Fair enough, but Eddy has not done too badly. They say he could be one of the youngest Brigadiers in the entire force. He made the right choice. Gets on well with everybody. He says that comes from his mother. Wish I had met her.*

*Percy is a wonderful grandfather.*

Louise Lomax April 1961

## Envoi

*The Times* today informed us of Ernest's death where they suggested their readers would be surprised to learn he was only sixty-one. It was a revelation to me as well. I had always assumed he was my senior in age, as well as in writing skills. *The Times* piece began:

For many people, the main shock will come from learning that he was only sixty one. There was not merely the grizzled beard, the likeness to that other a wanderer, ODYSSEUS, which has been mentioned more than once. There is also the fact that his last masterpiece, *The Old Man and the Sea*, seemed to have that wise simplicity supposed to come with great age. He had been before the public, and something of a legendary character, for a long time. Views about him had changed from the early days; his reputation had settled. The youthful pioneer of a new style of American writing had long ceased to experiment. No one knew whether yet another fine work would not come. No one would have expected it to set a new course or break new ground.

The short report went on to suggest that his two best works. *A Farewell to Arms* and *For Whom the Bell Tolls* came from his direct experience of the war:

He wrote about it with pity and tenderness; these are the qualities that will keep his work alive long after the toughness is forgotten. They were the truest part of the man himself.

As I read reports of his life after we had failed to confront each other, either in Paris or Spain, I could see what a complex creature he was, right up to the end. He used one of his own guns; a double-barrelled one. Evidently he lent his forehead on the barrel and pulled both the triggers. He was said to have suffered from manic depression, like Simóne

During one of my visits to Paris I stayed at a small hotel in St Germain-des-Près, Hôtel d'Angleterre, where they proudly announce that Ernest stayed in Room 14 on 20 December

Alan Shelley

1921 and so it now seems as though he can be compared with our Queen Elizabeth I, who slept in many places.

My mother also died earlier this year; in her sleep. She was seventy nine. She had lived a happy and fulfilled life. Francois's death, two years before, prompted her to suggest that she was now free to look for another husband, but in reality she was very saddened. They had been married for fifty four years. In addition to stability, he also appeared to have imbued Violet with his faith. Before she died, she often spoke of joining him. He was also influential in directing me towards the Catholic Church. The instruction still left many questions unanswered, but I was received into the faith last Easter and this gives me a warm comfort. Am I now a true Christian? He must decide.

Bert has been running the Whitwell empire for some years — and doing it very well by all accounts. The main shop is still in Westgate Street, next to the Lower George. For a time it had a relatively famous landlord; a boxer, Hal Bagwell, who was a Gloucester man. He features in the Guinness Book of Records as the fighter with the most consecutive wins and I am sure that when visiting the pub, my mother would have told tales about her illustrious son meeting Georges Carpentier.

I watch a lot of cricket thanks, not for the first time, to Bob Patch. Many of his show business colleagues are members, like he is, of the Marylebone Cricket Club, and with his support, so am I; elected 1959. I might have thought the Hall of Mirrors at Versailles was rather splendid but, for me, it pales into insignificance compared to the pavilion at Lords. The Aussies are here this summer: last season for Ritchie Benaud as captain. They are lucky to have him. Superb leg break bowler. Reminds me of myself; in my prime. What a joke.

My grandfatherly duties are varied. Louise and Edward's three boys are all at boarding school so my contact with them is limited but if the parents are overseas the boys came to me for the short holidays, half terms and so on. I see more of the Welsh lot. The twins, both girls, go to school in

Aberystwyth as does their younger brother, whom they adore. In between children Hester completed a degree in English at the University but she did not move into teaching like Owen. Owen Thomas. He could be nothing other than Welsh. A little slow on the uptake I find. My jokes seem to pass straight over his head but he is a good husband and father and Hester is happy. Particularly so because last year she finally obtained her pilot's licence. The last time I visited them she insisted on taking me for a trip along the coast. I think we got as far as Abersoch. I did not enjoy it very much, but I will my next flight. I am planning a trip to New York to see Abigail and Hubert. A Boeing 707, so I am told.

I will let you know how they fare when I get back.

## Acknowledgements

Margaret Macmillan's *Paris 1919. Six months that changed the world* (Random House New York 2001) provided invaluable background for Chapter Three. Recipes were culled from a variety of sources but special mention should be made of *The Alice B Toklas Cookbook* (Penguin Harmondsworth 1961) and *Escoffier A Guide to Modern Cookery* (Heinemann London 1973).

Printed in the United Kingdom by
Lightning Source UK Ltd., Milton Keynes
138297UK00001B/11/P